RUBBER GLOVES
OR JIMMY CHOOS?

Faith Bleasdale grew up in Devon, did History at Bristol University and then moved to London. After sampling a huge variety of rubbish jobs, she decided that she would put her passion for writing to good use.

She now lives in London with her tropical fish and writes full time.

Also by Faith Bleasdale

Pinstripes
Peep Show
Deranged Marriage

FAITH BLEASDALE

RUBBER GLOVES OR JIMMY CHOOS?

FLAME

Hodder & Stoughton

Copyright © 2000 by Faith Bleasdale

First published in paperback in 2000 by Hodder and Stoughton
A division of Hodder Headline

This edition published 2003

The right of Faith Bleasdale to be identified as the Author of the Work has been
asserted by her in accordance with the Copyright, Designs and Patents Act 1988.

A Flame Paperback

5 7 9 10 8 6

A CIP catalogue record for this title is available from the British Library

ISBN 0 340 76815 0

Typeset in Centaur by Palimpsest Book Production Limited,
Polmont, Stirlingshire
Printed and bound in Great Britain by
Mackays of Chatham PLC, Chatham, Kent

Hodder and Stoughton
A division of Hodder Headline
338 Euston Road
London NW1 3BH

For Dad, Mum, Thom, Mary and Jonathan
with love

ACKNOWLEDGEMENTS

Special Thanks To:

To my mum for all her hard work on my behalf, for being
the first person to read the book and lavishing me with
loyal praise. To my father for being an ace photographer
as well as an ace dad. To my brother, Thom, for his
support, inspiration and wonderful creativity, and to my
sister, Mary, for being the best sister in the world.

To Jonathan, my constant supporter for putting up with my
moments of enthusiasm, madness and occasional despair.
Thank you for your love, and for not trying to have me
committed. You're a top fellow.

To all my friends, especially Vicky, Jo, Holly, Jac,
Tommy, for allowing me to test out story ideas on them,
for not complaining when I didn't allow them to read the
book, and for helping me to keep my sanity intact.

To Shelley Power, my agent for believing in me, teaching
me so much, and being a great person to work with.

To Sara Hulse and Carolyn Caughey for making this whole
experience as enjoyable and as painless as possible. It
has been a pleasure working with you.

Finally to Jimmy Choo. Thanks for the shoes.

He looked at me with his deep blue eyes. They sparkled like sapphires, and I melted inside. He stood so close to me, I could smell his sweet breath. I could hear my heart beating like a thousand drums. The air was potent with him, and I tingled with the anticipation of his touch. He was the most beautiful man in the world, tall, strong, powerful. His dark hair, glossy with sweat, curled and framed his angelic face. His nose, small, perfect, made me want to kiss the tip. His heart-shaped lips were full, red and moist. His taut body was defined by the T-shirt he was wearing; his muscles rippled beneath the thin fabric. My eyes wandered to his legs, long and lean; as though they had been made for the jeans he was wearing. He slowly leaned closer and closer to me. I could almost hear his heart beating. I could feel the intensity of his gaze and the electricity in the air. I was glued to where I stood, moist with anticipation. My breathing became louder. Our eyes locked in mutual understanding and I felt faint as he took me in his arms and lowered his full lips onto mine. I swayed back in his arms as if I was falling, as the kiss went deeper and deeper until I could feel it in my heart. Time stopped. I stopped.

After a while the kiss just wasn't enough. As he ripped at my clothes, his hands were searching my entire body, his strong hands, I felt safe in his hands. They moved expertly to my breasts, pulling me out of my blouse, my bra. Suddenly I was naked, vulnerable, wanting, hungry for more. As desire flooded me I pulled him out of his T-shirt, his jeans and he, too, was naked. I gasped at the beauty of him, standing in front of me in all his glory, hardly daring to look, hardly daring to look away. As we explored each other's bodies, touching, *teasing, probing, I felt I never wanted this moment to end. As lovers we were made for each other. Desire was all I could feel, love was all I wanted. He thrust himself deep inside me, and I was finally in heaven. Heaven. We made love as if it was the greatest of songs, and again and again I reached heights higher than I had ever thought possible. Moaning, arching, moving until we were one. As we reached the final crescendo, he moved his head closer to me until I could feel his every breath. Closer, closer, closer until he was almost touching my ear. Then he whispered the words I was longing to hear . . .*

'Beep, beep, beep, beep.' Oh, shit. One of life's greatest mysteries is why an alarm clock always goes off just when you're getting to the best part of your dream. Every single time. Then it seemed even more cruel, for my dreams were the only place where I could find happiness. The man in my dreams could offer me everything I wanted. He would tell me he loved me and he'd take care of me for ever. I in turn would take care of him. He could give me what I needed. Reality couldn't, or wouldn't. Reality had nothing to offer. I dragged myself reluctantly from my bed and said a fond farewell to my dream. A few moments ago I had been in heaven; now I was in hell.

I went to the mirror, not to see how awful I looked, or how great, but to see if I looked different. If I did, I couldn't see it: nothing seemed to have changed. My eyes looked terrified, but the rest of me showed no sign of the impending danger, my doom. I looked the same as I had one day before, but I felt completely different.

Today was significant to me. Not in a good way. Today my life would change, not a change I welcomed. I was moving to London. I was going to start my first ever job in a city I knew only from brief acquaintance. Life had finally taken me over and I had surrendered to it. I was constantly told by everyone that my life was about to start, at twenty-one years of age, with the world at my feet. The truth was that the only reason the world was at my feet was because somehow I had managed to fall off it. I had been ejected into space, rejected, cast out by the world I knew and loved. My world. Perhaps I had better explain.

Chapter One

I heard a gentle voice whispering outside my cave, 'Come out of the cave, come out.'

Tentatively I looked out, but it was so dark I couldn't see anything. 'No,' I shouted, and looked again.

The gentle beckoning voice kept trying to coax me; 'Come out, come out, come out,' over and over again. It wouldn't stop. I couldn't see anything, only the darkness outside and the walls of my cave, which was my home. The cave had everything I needed, familiarity. I knew it, I knew my way around. I looked outside again, yet still could see nothing. 'Take a chance, fool,' the voice said. 'There may be great things waiting for you out here.'

'Yes,' I said, 'or there could be many bad things.' I retreated as deep into my cave as I could.

I have had an ordinary life, not particularly exciting but wonderful. A wonderful, ordinary life. I grew up in Sussex, went to school, went to university. I finished university with a fondness for lager, a degree in politics, and true love. But then a bad thing happened. Education ended. Nothing had prepared me for that. I saw my university years as the best of my short life. Graduation was supposed to be a symbolic ceremony, a coming-of-age. It represented my success, it represented me.

Where previously I had seen this as positive, all of a sudden I realised I had been tricked, duped, had. Suddenly my graduation marked the end of my life: in one fell swoop all my security was cruelly snatched from me. My life crashed, and when my world crashed around me, it really crashed. It fell apart so violently I could hear it – I could feel the force of its impact. My life was great one day, then totally destroyed the next. And I had been taken completely and utterly by surprise.

Change is not always invited, sometimes it just gatecrashes your life.

I faced a number of problems when I was kicked out of the womb of education and into the unknown. The first was losing my security. At every stage in my formative years I had managed to keep a security blanket: my parents, school, university. But when education finishes you're on your own. Like any child, I didn't cope very well with being parted from my security blanket. The second, interconnected with the first, was the realisation that I didn't know what I was going to do with the rest of my life. All of a sudden Life had gone from being planned and fun, to something *I* had to fill. It seemed such a big thing to fill. And filling the rest of my life meant I had to finance it myself. So I needed to and was expected, to get a job. I had never had a job before and I didn't know what sort of job I wanted. In fact, my knowledge on the whole job thing was limited. One minute you're worrying about where your next pint is coming from, the next you're wondering what council-tax band you're living in. And I didn't even know what a council-tax band was.

One thing I haven't mentioned in the ingredients of my life falling apart, the worst thing, was my broken heart. Oh, yes, on top of everything else, I had a broken heart. My loving parents, who had supported me all my life (financially and spiritually), asked me when I was getting a job and moving out. My friends were acting like mad people in their enthusiasm to start their new careers. Then my boyfriend, Ben, whom I loved and adored, told me that he no longer loved and adored me. And I had been going to marry him. He had been going to save me from the real world, we were going to conquer it together, but now I was on my own with my conquering tools broken and blunt. I was filled with fear at leaving university, fear at losing Ben, and the horror that now my marriage prospects really didn't look good.

Ever since I read my first Jane Austen novel I had known what I wanted. Marriage. I wanted romance, courting, poetry, Mr Darcy. I had managed to find my Mr Darcy, although instead of poetry he had come with dirty laundry – but that was OK, you have to adapt a bit. My ambition was marriage, my life was love. Not very modern but there you go. So, suddenly I had found myself unwelcome at home, directionless, loveless. What did I do? I began to hate the future and would have given anything for the past.

I remember my first day at university so clearly: my parents drove me to my hall of residence, my new home. I was filled with excitement. This was freedom. I could do whatever I wanted (and, believe me, I wanted to do a lot). I came from a small village and my life had verged a little on the sheltered side so I was eager to embark on a life of sex, drugs and rock and roll, or something like that.

Driving with my parents to Wyatt Hall, my new home was exciting and scary. It was a huge modern building, ugly and uninviting. Seeing my new room for the first time was a bit of a shock. It wasn't like my pink princess room at home: it was bare, with only a wardrobe, a desk, a chair and a bed. Immediately it made me think of prison. My mother was horrified – I think she'd imagined somewhere posher. Then she cried. My father tried to lift our spirits by putting up my posters, which improved things a bit. After each one he glanced at me triumphantly, proud to be transforming the room into a palace for his little princess. I loved him. The initial oh-my-God-do-I-really-have-to-live-here? feeling left really quite quickly and my excitement came back. So the bed wasn't big enough for two, but where there's a will there's a way!

My parents tried to stay with me as long as possible, but

after a while I really wanted to be alone with my new life. So after some tears (my mother), and a speech about how proud they were of me (my father), they eventually left. I started unpacking, trying to feel confident but failing.

Being alone was scary and strange. Someone knocked on the door. I opened it to find a tall girl with long dark hair, great cheekbones, a huge chest and bright red lipstick. It was my new neighbour: Jess. She was really confident and insisted on us going to dinner together. That suited me fine: it was imperative to have that first friend and I don't think I would have cared if she'd had three heads. Before dinner we decided to have a look round, really only to be nosy and see what the other girls were like. Our block was all girls, the opposite block was where the men lay in wait. We found a kitchen, made some coffee and started talking about ourselves, our schools, A levels, homes, etc. It was a conversation I had about a million times in the next few weeks.

While making coffee, we met Sarah and Sophie. Sarah was small, with short blonde hair and glasses. I don't think I'd ever met anyone with eyebrows as thin as hers. She was almost as confident as Jess, but in a quieter way. Sophie was tall, slim, breathtaking. She looked like a china doll, with long curly dark blonde hair and pale blue eyes, which looked terrified. We did the conversation again by way of introduction, and Sophie started to relax a little. We all went to dinner together, sharing a bond that was really necessity. At that moment we needed each other as much as we ever would in the future. I had a feeling that we'd all stay friends and I thought the others felt it too. Jess, larger than life, Sarah, who organised us, Sophie, beautiful and nervous, and me, Ruth: who was beginning to feel more excited than I had first thought possible.

The first few weeks of university passed in a haze of parties and on the whole it was fun. At times I felt homesick, at times insecure, but I had my friends to reassure me. Many, many things changed in the three years of university, but the one thing that didn't was my best friends. University quickly became my home. By the end of the first year, it had become a home I loved. When it ended as quickly as it had begun I felt as if I had lost my structure.

Let me tell you about Ben, the one true love of my life. He was good-looking, in a floppy-haired little-boy way. He had such beautiful light brown hair, the sort you couldn't help but touch. Actually Ben always hated me touching his hair but, well, I just couldn't resist. His physique was that of a rugby player although he was a hockey player. He didn't smile much, but when he did I just melted: he had an amazing lazy smile, which spread slowly over his entire face. He could never be accused of talking too much — he was a man of few words — and, in fact, I spent most of our relationship talking at him. When he did talk, it was usually about hockey or law (his course). He never talked about us, but as we were perfect he didn't need to.

I was attracted to Ben the first time I saw him: he looked like he needed taking care of. I have always been the type of person who needs to take care of things — hurt animals, then Ben. I saw him first in our hall of residence and I knew I wanted him. It was love at first sight. To win him, or so I thought, I needed a plan. I told my friends I had found the man of my dreams and I pointed him out at dinner.

'Why?' Sarah asked, but I ignored her. Then, being the dramatic person I was, I sat in my room, cross-legged on the bed, for hours, with Jess fidgeting to find a comfortable position next to me, Sophie at my desk smoking, and Sarah on the floor hugging a cushion, plotting how I could get him to notice me.

'I just need a foolproof plan to get that man to fall in love with me.' I sighed. It sounded so simple but love was such a complicated process.

'How about asking him out?' Sophie suggested.

'God, no, I can't rely on that working.' I was appalled.

'What exactly are you going to do then?' Sarah asked.

I gave her a dirty look. 'Shush, I'm thinking.'

The first plan I came up with worked on the principle that if you save someone's life they belong to you. I think I saw it in a film, or maybe it was a book. Anyway, that was a good way of getting the commitment I was after. I explained this to my friends.

'You're mad,' Sarah said.

'How romantic,' Sophie said.

'Can you please explain how you think this is going to work?' Jess said.

'Well, it's simple. All we need to do is to get him in a life-threatening situation. For example, Sarah could get into her car and try to run him over and I could push him out of the way.' I smiled triumphantly.

'Ruth, I am not prepared to try to kill him or you or anyone in the name of love.' Sarah folded her arms defiantly. I tried to protest, but in vain.

'I know, we could follow him, find out his daily routine. Then when he leaves for lectures Jess could wait on top of a building with a large brick and when he walks past she could drop it and I could push him out of the way.' I smiled again. I was sure I'd seen that one in a film, and things like that always worked in films.

'Ruth, I'm not prepared to get arrested for throwing bricks. Anyway – God, what am I saying? That's the most stupid idea I've ever heard.'

I looked pleadingly at Sophie.

'No way.'

Back to square one. I came up with plan B, which cut out the saving-him stuff and concentrated on following him. If I found out his regular haunts and I was always there, he would definitely notice me. I could become his very own stalker (but a nice stalker, of course), I told my friends.

'Well, trailing him is a lot better than trying not to kill him,' Sarah said.

'Oh, yes, he'll notice you really quickly and then you can ask him out,' Sophie added.

'What if he realises you're stalking him and thinks you're mad?' Jess, ever-practical, asked.

'Um, yeah. OK, Jess, you can come with me. Then it won't be obvious.'

She rolled her eyes dramatically. 'All right, as long as I don't have to throw any bricks, I'll do it.'

Plan B was ready for operation.

I found out where his room was and I followed him to lectures, I followed him to the bar, I followed him everywhere. One day I had cleverly manoeuvred myself behind him in the dinner queue. I smiled at him, asked him if he was looking forward to the appalling stew we were about to sample, then somehow, as we were in a conversation, we sat together. A combination of my looks, my brilliant strategy and my jokes seemed to do the trick. So I congratulated myself on a successful campaign because that night we arranged to meet at the hall bar, got drunk on lager and had our first snog outside my room.

The following day I nursed my hangover with the hugest grin stuck to my face. Ben had lived up to all my expectations. Cute, oh, so cute, funny (well, his nun jokes were), cute – did I say that? And those lips, the kiss. It was the most wonderful kiss in the world. Actually, I think it was but it's all a bit fuzzy now. It definitely made my head spin. We fell into a relationship pretty quickly. And I took care of him pretty quickly. I did his laundry (in the launderette), I tided his room, I made sure he got fed, not quite cooking for him but getting him to dinner on time. I cheered him on when he played hockey, in the sun, the wind and the rain. I celebrated with him when he won and let him sulk for hours when he lost. And he loved me. He was affectionate, he held my hand in public (even in front of his hockey mates), which to me meant he loved me. He never actually told me he loved me, except in a Valentine card, which, come to think of it, was printed 'To the one I love.' But I knew.

I made him happy and he made me happy. It was a most perfect relationship.

Hockey was Ben's life, therefore it became mine. When the hockey team won we went to the student union bar to celebrate. I usually dragged my friends along, because it could be a bit scary. The boys would all get drunk, play drinking games, sing rude songs and show their bottoms to passing girls. Actually they were quite disgusting. Ben didn't show his bottom to anyone. Instead he would find me, kiss me, then go back to the singing. On the way home we would have curry or a kebab. If we had curry, my friends would feel they had done their friendship duty and refuse to come – the boys were a little badly behaved: they would steal the crockery, sing more rude songs and someone always fell asleep in their dinner. If we had a kebab, Ben filled it with chilli sauce (apparently it was a manhood test), then suffered all the way home while he ate it. It was horrid. But whenever we got home, whichever culinary delight we had experienced, he'd pass out fully clothed, stinking of beer and curry/kebab. That's when I first realised I loved him: when I woke up in the same bed as him and could smell the whole of the previous evening on him. The fact that I could look at him then and think him adorable proved it all, in my opinion. My friends all liked Ben, but thought I was slightly mad in my commitment to his life. They thought I should be more independent, like they were – but, then, they weren't in love.

We lived together in the second and third years. Ben, myself, Sarah, Jess, Sophie and Thomas, Ben's friend. All in a huge house like one happy family. We never spoke about it, but I made plans for Ben and me. After university he would take his law finals, I would work, he would qualify and get a good job. We'd get married and buy a big house in the country. I would spend my days taking care of Ben. That was the thing I did best, the only thing I wanted to do. I know it doesn't sound very modern, but I was smart, I was sassy and that was still my choice. I'd still do something interesting, I'd still *be* interesting but, most importantly, I would be interesting and with Ben.

As university drew to a close everybody had a plan. Apart from me and Ben. Well, I had plans for us, but we'd never discussed them. On entering the third year, I found everyone was planning, careers, post-graduate courses, where to live. They showed a new excitement, even before finals. By the start of exams, everyone knew what they were going to do. Apart from me and Ben.

Jess had secured a job with a PR consultancy, which was no surprise because from the word go she had known that was what she wanted to do. I remember in our first year she would tell me how wonderful PR was and she studied *Absolutely Fabulous* as if it was a fly-on-the-wall documentary, not quite but almost taking notes. She was born for PR, whatever it was. Sarah had got a job with a recruitment consultancy. She liked the sound of organising the workforce. I think she would really have liked a government post in employment – she'd have got everyone working, believe me. Sophie had been spotted by a model agency, ages ago and had been modelling in her spare time, which she was going to continue while securing herself an agent for her acting work. Thomas had got a place to do his law finals. They would all live in London.

I would live with Ben. Of course, I expected that Ben would be doing his law finals too, but as yet there was no sign of that. I wasn't worried: I knew that with Ben it would be all right. I often told him of my plans and he didn't object, so I guessed I didn't have to worry. My parents, on the other hand, were getting worried. They kept asking me what I was going to do. So did my friends. I told them I'd discuss it with them as soon as I'd finalised things.

But nothing was finalised. All of a sudden exams were drawing to a close and then we would be leaving university. I would no longer be studying politics and I would no longer live in Portsmouth. In my three years at Portsmouth University I had never thought about the end, but here it was. I was beginning to panic a little. So I asked him, 'Ben, we really should sort out what we're going to do after graduation.'

'Huh?' he replied.

'For God's sake, you know, where you're going to do your law finals and what job I'm going to get. We should start making plans.' It was like banging my head against a brick wall.

'Ruthie, why the hell do you always have to plan everything?' he shouted at me.

I was puzzled because I never made plans until absolutely necessary. Like now. 'I didn't mean anything, it's just that in four weeks finals are finished.' The subtle approach was called for.

'Don't be such a woman. We'll work it out, but not today, OK?' Ben's final word.

My lip quivered like it does when I'm about to be a woman and cry.

Ben softened a bit. 'I'm sorry, babe, it's just, you know, stress. We'll discuss it after finals, OK?' I nodded my agreement. I was still panicking, but trying not to. Ben said it would be fine so it would be fine. After all, I had Ben. What more did I need?

Finals finished. We survived them and we celebrated. It was a wild time of freedom, relief, achievement and fun. I wished it could last for ever, but it didn't. The results came in, we all got what we wanted. More celebrations, but this time I knew it would end. The lease on our house was up, and we had to move out. Everyone was going home until graduation. Then, after graduation, they would all be starting their new lives. Where was I going?

On the last night in our happy house, we had an Indian takeaway, just the six of us. We looked back at our university years. 'Do you remember when . . .' started most sentences, and we laughed at things we had laughed at a million times before, but which were still funny.

'I'm so glad I have these great memories to take with me,' Thomas said sentimentally, and, yes, we agreed. For a moment

I felt that I would never be lonely or sad again because I had memories of the most wonderful three years of my life. But then I did feel sad. I always hated letting go of anything I loved, and I loved this house and I loved my friends and I loved Ben. I wanted us all to stay together, but we couldn't. I cried that night in bed, silently, as Ben snored next to me.

The next day I started packing. I packed for Ben, not that he had much: clothes, a few books, his hockey stuff, that was it. I packed my things and wondered about our future. I had to ask him now: finals were over, we were leaving, it was my last chance.

'Ben, it's our last day. I know we're both going back to our parents', but what happens next?'

'Next when?'

I was experiencing *déjà vu*. 'In our lives, Ben. What are we going to do? Should we plan a holiday, or should I get a job? Where are we going to live? We need to sort things out.'

'Ruth, you worry too much. Look, I've just finished three years of a difficult degree and what I want to do is relax until graduation. Then we can sort things out, OK?' He smiled at me and, as usual, I melted.

I wanted to pursue things, say that we needed to sort things out now, not after graduation, but I couldn't. I guess I was a wimp. I kissed him. 'I'll miss you so much, Benjamin, but rest assured, we won't be apart for long, I won't allow it.'

He kissed me and we made love for the last time ever on the bed.

There are certain days in your life that become magic days: your wedding, certain birthdays, romantic occasions and special achievements, such as graduation. Graduation was supposed to be a special day, surrounded by family and friends: we would don the gowns and the mortar-boards and, looking stupid, celebrate the last three years and the passing of our degrees. It would be like a twenty-first birthday, a coming of age, a rite of passage into adulthood. The occasion would be marked by a ceremony, a nice lunch and a champagne reception. In the evening, the bit I was looking forward to most, we had our ball. The only thing required for perfection was the sun to shine.

The sun was shining. But when I woke up I didn't feel perfect. I felt, well, weird. I didn't feel excited any more and I didn't feel nervous, I felt horrible. My parents were excited enough for all of us. They had the camera out, my mother wore a huge hat, my father a new suit, and they were cooing and saying things like, 'My baby's really grown up now,' my mother, and 'My clever little princess,' my father. Which would have been lovely, had I not been feeling hugely depressed.

We got to the university, where I put on my gown, then found Jess. She was so excited she kept hugging me and squealing while her parents were filming us on their camcorder. I felt as if I was in a ridiculous movie. When we found Sarah and Sophie they were like Jess, although Sophie was a little nervous. They all kept saying this would be one of the best days of their lives. So why did I feel it was one of the worst of mine? I wanted Ben by my side, but every time I got near him, either he or I was whisked away – first to go into the hall, then when I found him after the ceremony, I had to go to lunch. It was a nightmare.

At the champagne reception I finally got to speak to him. I went up to him, kissed him and told him I loved him. He looked awkward, but I put it down to the fact that he looked really ridiculous in his gown, which didn't seem to fit him. I chatted to his parents, who were posh but nice. Then my parents came and spoke with his parents and it would have been a wonderful sight had Ben not snuck off to join his mates. I tried to tell the girls something was wrong, but no one wanted to hear anything bad on this day. As I told you, it was magical for everyone apart from me.

I tried my best not to worry about Ben – after all, we would be going to the ball together. Sophie was going with Johnny,

Ben's best friend, Jess was going with Jeremy, a hockey-team member, and Sarah was escorting Thomas, because they didn't have dates. It would be wonderful, all our friends together. But, no, however hard I tried I couldn't shake the feeling that something was horribly wrong – in fact, that everything was horribly wrong.

The day passed and I tried to be cheerful, mainly for my parents' sake. Trust them to have given birth to the most miserable graduate on earth. When it was time for them to leave, they drove me to the hall of residence where I would be staying, and it was just like the first day I arrived at university, only of course it was my last. We had a tearful farewell, and I really was tearful, then they left me again. My spirits lifted slightly as I found they had left me a bottle of champagne, and my friends came into my room so we could do the girly getting-ready bit. We all looked so lovely in our dresses with our hair and make-up done nicely. I was determined that when Ben saw me, I would knock him dead.

The guys came to collect us at seven and they looked wonderful. Beauty is a man in black tie. Ben seemed awkward, but he never had been one for dressing up. I thought perhaps he was feeling the same loss I was. Yes, that was it. As soon as we got a chance to talk, I would reassure him, and everything would be fine.

We had our photo taken as we walked into the dining hall, which had been transformed for the occasion, Thomas towering above us with his dark hair and glasses, Johnny, smaller than the others and as blond as Sarah, Jess in her purple velvet dress, Sophie in black silk, Sarah in a short black dress, me in my puffy ball dress, and Ben, with his fake bow-tie, which was already crooked. The hall was decorated in silver and blue, lit by candles and spotlights. Each table had silver flowers in the middle. It looked so lovely I was determined to have the best night of my life. It *was* fun and I finally managed to relax. We ate (loads), we drank (loads) and we danced until I thought my feet would fall off. I lost my shoes and I lost Ben.

Determined to have fun, I had ignored Ben's mood. I talked at him and, well, there were so many people to say goodbye to that we didn't spend that much time together. But at one point when I realised I needed to see him I couldn't find him anywhere. I got Sophie, who got Johnny, who got Jess, who got Sarah, who got Thomas, and we looked everywhere. He was nowhere to be found. I was still shoeless and hysterical. Sarah had the main job of calming me down, but the drink and the fact that I was feeling weird convinced me he was dead. This went on for what seemed ages, until Jess ran in and said that they'd found him. It was five in the morning and for the last two hours he'd been outside.

I was so relieved I ran straight up to him and hugged him. He pulled me off, looked at me and said, 'Ruth, we need to talk.' That was when I realised there had been a reason for my end-of-the-world mood today.

I felt my heart sink into my stockinged feet. That phrase 'we need to talk' heralded bad news, especially from Ben who generally only talked when absolutely necessary. I looked at him, all serious but gorgeous in his tuxedo, and I knew that no matter how hard I tried not to think so, he wouldn't have looked so solemn if it was to be anything but bad. I made a decision there and then that I would go to my impending doom guns blazing.

'Where the hell have you been? I've – well, me and your friends and my friends and just about everyone at this damn ball have been looking for you for hours.'

'I needed to think.'

That stumped me. I'd never thought of Ben as a thinker – in fact I couldn't remember the last time he'd had a single thought. Ben wasn't that type, he was more your dumb jock. I recovered a little from the shock. 'You? Think? Christ, Ben, this is our graduation ball. Why did you have to choose a moment like this to start thinking?' I realised that I was still very drunk and, perhaps, had chosen the wrong way to handle the situation, but I was in no state to control my mouth.

'Ruth, stop a minute. I really need to talk to you.'

Ben looked so serious – actually, the three Bens standing in front of me looked very serious. I closed one eye and reduced him to one and a half. I was making some progress although the conversation wasn't. 'So talk.' I know I sounded like a bitch but, well, that was how I felt.

'I think we should break up.'

He breathed a sigh of relief, and I became instantly sober. There was only one Ben in front of me and my heart fell out of my body. I know that I said I was expecting bad news, but this, well, this was devastating. Smart-crack Ruth was gone and panic rose through my whole body. Disbelief was all I could feel.

So Ben broke up with me and I was sick on his shoes. The perfect relationship was over and I was over. Jess found me sitting on the steps where Ben left me. I couldn't tell you how long I'd been there. For ever. It felt like for ever.

'Come here.' Jess grabbed me and hugged me tight. I felt her warmth and realised how cold I really was. 'I found your shoes.' She handed them to me but I didn't put them on.

'He's finished it,' I managed.

'Shit, Ru.' Jess looked as if she didn't have a clue what to say.

'He's going away with Johnny,' I sobbed.

'I had no idea.' Jess held me tighter.

'I know. Only Ben, Johnny and Thomas did.' The tears were falling more slowly. I think they were running out.

'He's a selfish bastard.'

'Yes, Jess, but at least he was my selfish bastard.' My reserve tears were now kicking in.

'He shouldn't have told you today of all days,' Jess said.

'They say you never forget your graduation, I certainly won't forget mine.'

'Ru, I know it doesn't help, and it doesn't feel like it, but it will be all right, somehow.'

Jess smiled weakly and, to my surprise, I managed to smile weakly back. 'You know I was sick on his shoes.'

'*No*, really?' Jess laughed, and I started crying again. I just cried and cried. I think I used up my whole bodyweight in tears that night. I was staying on my own in a room similar to my first room in the hall of residence. It was empty and bare and I didn't sleep: I sat up all night, chain-smoking, crying and feeling oddly as though I had regressed.

So there you have it. The best day of my life turned into the worst day of my life. The break-up was pretty crap. Ben turned red, I was sick, I didn't say half of what I wanted and he said more than he wanted. Which probably sums up our whole relationship. Now I'm in deep mourning because I didn't want him to go, I didn't want him to leave me and I miss him. They say love is blind; in my case it was also deaf and dumb.

I did a lot of thinking. Well, I tried to think. But all I could do was concentrate on the huge feeling of fear that was running though me. Fear of facing the world without Ben. Fear of tomorrow and the next day and the day after that. I couldn't let him go. I couldn't let the one thing that made me happy desert me. It hadn't occurred to me to plan my life without Ben. Why should it? We were a couple, we were together. I felt that if I'd made plans perhaps I could have handled the situation better. 'So what, Ben? I've got a great job, you just piss off,' but I knew that wasn't me, not the me I knew or not the me I'd let myself become.

I had based my future on him and although I still hold university responsible for ending, the real reason for my anger was that with it, the love I had had ended too.

At first I tried to make him stay. As all reason had left me, I managed to convince myself that I could do this. I called him and I cried and I told him I loved him and I asked him to reconsider, not to throw away the best thing in his life, me. Funnily enough it didn't work. He said he needed to go, to travel, to have fun. This was something he had wanted to do ever since he'd first started university. That was a recurring theme. It kept coming back to the fact that Ben was doing something he'd always wanted to do, something that excluded me to the point of my ignorance of it. It was like there was old Ben, whom I had been with for over two years, and there was new Ben, whom I didn't really know at all. Well, to hell with new Ben, I just wanted old Ben back.

A couple of days later I tried a different tack. A minute amount of reason had returned. I told him that he was right. Of course it was a wonderful opportunity and I was really happy for him. Of course he must go, but we shouldn't break up over it. We should see how it goes and keep an open mind, so when he came back we could start again. I know I had tried that tactic before when he first broke up with me, but now he'd had time to think I was sure he'd see sense. Well, I was the one who needed to see sense because he told me that wouldn't happen, that he'd meant what he'd said about us breaking up, that it just wouldn't work out. For a second after that conversation I thought about having 'Moron' tattooed across my head.

After that, reason left me again (bloody unreliable that reason thing). The next plan of action was to beg my parents for money. I would go too. We'd travel together, and he would see how much he needed me. After all, who else was going to wash his underwear? My parents refused. I told Ben anyway and he sounded so relieved I cried and shouted at him and called him names. I also told my parents that I hoped they could live with themselves, knowing that they had ruined the life of their only daughter.

By this stage reason was miles away and had been replaced by desperation. The last attempt I made was to tell Ben that

I understood everything, including us breaking up, but that I needed to see him one last time, just to say goodbye. He was reluctant, but I pulled every emotional-blackmail trick in the book and he finally agreed. He drove to my parents' house. He arrived looking as gorgeous as ever and we talked, or I talked. I asked him how he could just ignore everything we'd been through. He shrugged. I asked him if he had missed me at all. He shrugged. I asked him if he'd ever loved me. He shrugged. And so on. When it was time for him to leave, I did what any woman trying to hold on to her last bit of dignity would do. I threw myself on the floor and grabbed his ankles, refusing to let go. Ben went white, my father had to drag me off him and my mother told me to stop behaving like a lunatic. Then Ben walked out of my life. When he left I felt as if he was taking my life with him. It had been smashed beyond all recognition and now he was taking it to ensure that I could never put it back together. Reason and desperation had both left me, and they had been replaced by total desolation.

I was alone. I had nothing. I lay on my bed staring at the pink walls, listening to songs about lost love, I listened to the Smiths, I refused to eat (apart from in secret), I cried a lot and my parents despaired. God, I knew I was being a self-absorbed bitch, but then, for some reason I couldn't change. My parents, who had done nothing to deserve it, became the victims of my immature, brattish behaviour. They were worried about me. My father didn't know what to do, so my mother sat me down one night, poured me a glass of wine and had a career chat. She said that if she had been born when I was and had the opportunities that women had today, her life would have been very different. 'Ruthie, when I was young, women had limits put on them. We were expected to marry and have children and those were our priorities.'

'You were lucky.'

'No, not really. If I was you, I'd be really successful, I'd make something of my life, I would achieve things. The possibilities for you are endless, darling.'

This really upset me. 'But, Mum, you run a clothes shop, you and Dad have a great marriage, and you have me.'

'I know, darling, and I wouldn't give you and your father up for anything. And, yes, I do have a good life, but I have one shop and it's hardly Harrods.'

'You read too much Barbara Taylor Bradford. We have to do what's right for us, surely.'

'Of course, but the point is you can do whatever you want. You really can. I just wish you wanted things from life. I don't want you to look back and regret things.'

'Do you?'

'No, I don't really regret anything. I just wish there had been more choice when I was younger. Today marriage and children don't signify the end of a woman's career. They did in my day.'

'Mum, do you think they got us the wrong way round? I mean, I should have been you and you should have been me.' We laughed.

'Ruth, I just want you to be happy, you know that, and you're not. I want you to know that there's more to life than Ben. I know you're hurting, darling, and I hate to see you hurt. Just promise me one thing, that you'll remember you can do whatever you want.'

'OK.' I had no energy to fight. So, because I was an only child and my mother was a huge supporter of women's lib, I was educated and I went to university, I was expected to do things, or at least to want to do things, with my life. I couldn't help but wonder why the hell I didn't.

My mother and father still hadn't made any progress with my career, so they did what any loving parents would do: they called in Sarah. She arranged for me to visit her at her parents' house in Berkshire and told me that the reason I had gone to university was for this moment: this was freedom, opportunity. Now I'd start my career. That's what women did: they got careers, climbed ladders, wore suits, strove for designer handbags. Well, it all sounded perfectly appalling to me. I protested that I went to university to wear scruffy clothes (the ones my parents hated), to find men and drink cheap beer, but Sarah ignored me.

Actually the conversation went like this. We were sitting in her garden drinking orange juice and catching a bit of a tan. The flowers were in full bloom and the air was sweet with their smell, bees were buzzing, the children next door were shrieking with laughter and Sarah's dog, Monty, was sleeping peacefully in the shade. I was thinking how, as a housewife, I could do this all the time; Sarah was preparing herself to lecture me.

'Ru, I'm taking you to choose a career or, at least, to learn about the options.'

'Uh?'

'A career, Ruth. You know, the thing that I have and Jess has and even Sophie has, the thing all women have these days. It could even be said that, in this day and age, your career is as indispensable as your favourite lipstick.' Sarah smiled sarcastically.

'Never, never could a career be as necessary as my favourite lipstick.' I grinned back.

'Yes, even for you. Now the first step is to choose one, then we'll apply, then you can drag yourself from your melodramatic stupor and join the real world.'

'Bitch. How could you? I'm not melodramatic, I've—'

'Been dumped. I know. But how can you expect to get over the dumping without a job or at least a new challenge?'

'I could always buy a new lipstick.' Sarah hit me. 'OK, you win, just don't expect me to be happy about this.' Huh, I'd show her.

'Ru, we've all gone past the phase where we expect you to be happy about anything.' Sarah was quiet but indignant, and I was offended. But, then, I didn't really have a leg to stand on.

*　　*　　*

The careers office, according to Sarah, was the graduate's Mecca. This was where I'd find my enlightenment. This was where my new life would begin. Well, as a Mecca, the careers office was lacking in ambience and mystery. However, going there was certainly an experience. It was a vast expanse of files that held jobs: banking, marketing, computers, accountancy, consultancy, management, just about anything. None of it sounded like fun, and none of it sounded like me. I had to take one of those aptitude-test things, where you answer loads of questions and they tell you what you'd be good at. Sarah said I must have lied because my test said I'd make a good rocket scientist. Actually I did lie a bit, but I thought everyone did.

By this point I was having fun (really), but I was no nearer to finding my future. So, out of frustration, Sarah chose a career for me, got all the information and the application forms. My chosen-for-me career was in the creative world of advertising. At the time I was horrified, but later with hindsight I was glad for a number of reasons: it is fiercely competitive, you have to know a lot about it and people who recruit in advertising would not hire someone who thought most advertising was corrupt and an insult to people's intelligence. It was great. I applied for ten jobs. My parents were thrilled ('Our daughter is thinking of working in advertising'), my friends thought I had suddenly become sane, but best of all was when I got my first ten rejection letters and everyone was really nice to me. I got so much sympathy, much more than when Ben left, and I had avoided being employed.

I was tempted to make a career of applying for jobs that I didn't have a hope in hell of getting, but there were a few problems with that. I was living at home now. The only home I had once again was my parents', and since I'd gone to university it had felt less and less like mine. They insisted on trying to get me to find a job. Instead of realising that they were worried about me wasting my life, I got the feeling they didn't want me there. That was my because-Ben's-dumped-me-nobody-loves-me stage. I entertained the thought of having myself certified, on the basis that my emotions were so screwed up I was totally mad.

The trouble was that since I'd left home, instead of building their lives around me, they had started to build them without me. Which I suppose was good for them but not for me, and I felt a bit of a spare part. They played golf on Sundays, then had lunch at the golf club. On Monday, my mother and her friend Amelia went to their women's charity thing, and my father went back to the golf club. On Tuesday a group of four couples took it in turns to do dinner, on Wednesday they went to the theatre or to see a film, on Thursday they had a night in, on Friday they went out to dinner and on Saturday there was always a party. I found their social life quite exhausting. I was tired just thinking about it.

This produced a number of problems for someone like me, the first being that my parents had accepted that I was grown-up and were getting on with their lives far too easily. You would think that having me home they would spend all their time with me. They'd fuss around me, they'd do everything for me, but no. They expected me to get on with my life, the life I had without them. They said things like, 'I expect you'll be glad we're out of the way so you can get on with job hunting,' and I'd say, 'No, actually, I'm going to mope around and cry a lot because I've just been dumped and I would appreciate you staying around to give me sympathy,' to which they'd laugh then go out anyway. In response I would keep my promise and mope and cry a lot.

The truth was that by the time Ben left, just under two months after graduation and just under two months of my living with my parents, I wanted out. I was bored, I had no friends around and I had nothing to do. As a last resort I asked my mother to fix me up with some of her friends' sons, but she refused, telling me that I needed a job not a man. I had no choice but to leave.

*   *   *

The day of Ben's flight, I got up early and decided to have a Ben day. (I wasn't quite ready to stop acting like a drama queen, even if I was the only one to witness it.) I took out the shoe box in which I kept everything he'd given me; a couple of Valentine cards, some flavoured condoms, a hockey badge, a Kylie CD he gave me for my birthday, a Meatloaf CD don't ask me why, a pair of his socks (I asked for them), and, well, that was it. I read the cards, they said 'love, Ben', both of them. I wore the socks and the hockey badge. I played the CDs. I didn't know what to do with the flavoured condoms. I cried. At three in the afternoon his plane was leaving. I stared out of the window, wondering if I'd ever see him again. I had to face the fact that Ben was gone, but the thought of me and the rest of my life just kept sending me into despair.

No one else could understand the seriousness of it. They kept saying that I was young, too young, we weren't married and we weren't even engaged. 'You'll meet someone else,' they said. I could just go right out and replace Ben. Of course, I could just get up one day and find another man who would take the place of the man I utterly loved. The man God put on this earth to be with me, the man I was meant to be with. The man I loved (have I already said that?). Oh, I could replace him. I was young, lots of nice men out there, plenty more fish in the sea and all that crap. I hated people. Just because I wasn't older and dumped, it wasn't serious. People don't seem to understand that true love knows no age limits. And if I had been in my thirties and Ben had dumped me, I bet you I'd have got a whole lot more sympathy. People would expect me to fall apart: 'That was one of her last chances of walking down the aisle,' or 'That biological clock is going to have to stop now, isn't it?' But, no, just because I had nine years on the thirty-year-old, my heartbreak wasn't taken seriously. The over-thirties should not have the monopoly on heartbreak, you know.

By the time Ben was well on his way to wherever he was

started to calm down, partly because I had run
things to rant silently about and partly because I was
tired. Perhaps I could find someone else, if I had to. I mean,
I knew that I would never get over Ben, with his floppy hair
and beautiful smile, but I didn't want to be alone. I tried to
face facts. Ben was gone and I was alone. Those were the facts.
In the end after much brain-scraping, I realised that the only
sensible thing to do was get on with my life and wait for Ben
to see he'd made a terrible mistake and come back for me.

By the time my parents got home, I'd cried as much as I
could and I'd also made a decision. Although I still had a broken
heart, I would do as everyone wanted. I would move to London
and get a job thing. I gave Sarah a call.

Sophie had a very nice, very rich aunt who had bought a house in
Clapham and decided, when Sophie wanted to move to London,
she would let her and her friends have it for little rent to give
them a helping hand with the massive difficulties facing young
people today. Or something like that. The house had three
bedrooms, but in my honour one of the downstairs reception
rooms was turned into a fourth bedroom. Now, although not
ready to make the commitment to live there, I arranged to stay
while I attempted to find a job. Jess met me at the station.
She looked even more glamorous than usual, and next to her
I looked like a hick. We took the tube to Clapham Common
and all the way she filled me in on the life and times of a young
PR executive. She was so happy that I was happy too.

We arrived at the house and I was surprised that it was quite
pretty. Compared to our student house, with its ancient oven and
stained bath, it was a palace. It was painted white, inside and out,
and it had three floors, a fitted kitchen and a power-shower.
My room had been the dining room so it was off the lounge.
I nearly cried when I saw that Sophie had put in it a double
bed, a wardrobe and a dressing-table (all from Ikea).

It was quite a large house, and the lounge was huge so a dining table had been added to it. It had two vast yellow sofas and was light and cheerful. The kitchen was also big, with a pine table in the middle. As she gave me the tour, I knew she loved it here. She showed me the small patio garden she'd filled with pots of flowers, the first floor where Jess and Sarah had their rooms, and the bathroom. Her lovely attic room at the top of the house with skylights that meant she could hear every raindrop fall and feel the sun. I fell in love with it, it was a home.

I was so happy to see Jess, Sarah and Sophie that I smiled, really smiled, for the first time in ages. I also bought lots of wine as a thank-you to them for putting up with me, and I felt safe again. We gossiped, they filled me in with tales of London, what they had been doing, who they'd met, and I made them laugh with tales of how I hadn't been doing anything. Well, I managed to make it sound funny rather than sad. But we were together again, the four of us, and I knew that I was lucky because I wasn't even near to being on my own.

Sarah, who was working in recruitment, came up with my next plan of action. She had seen an advertisement in the *Guardian* for graduates and apparently there were loads of 'great opportunities'. The best thing was that you went to an agency and they found these jobs for you. Easy. So, again after lots of threats, I made an appointment.

At the agency a cheerful girl, Sally, with a red-lipstick smile, interviewed me. She asked me loads of questions. What's your greatest achievement? I felt I couldn't say being rejected by Saatchi & Saatchi, so I said it was passing my degree. The smile on her face froze into a joker-like grin, so I embellished it: it was such a struggle, I said, for someone who didn't have any parental support to go through university. I told her my parents thought I should have been working since I was sixteen. (I kept my fingers crossed and apologised silently to them.)

Where do you see yourself in five years' time? (Married to a rock star, five kids, a huge mansion, never working.) I said I saw myself wearing suits, carrying a designer handbag, and being a fair few rungs up the ladder I was about to start climbing. (Thanks, Sarah.) What is important to you? (God, this was beginning to sound cheesy.) The environment, world peace and getting a company car.

Describe yourself in ten words or less. Intelligent, loyal, organised, team player, funny. These were skills I thought might work. In reality, I am sometimes funny, perhaps intelligent – after all, I was good at education – but not very organised. I am loyal to the death but I don't remember being in any teams. What I failed to add was that I'm highly sensitive, emotional, dependent and attention-seeking. Oh, and prone to odd bouts of being boring, not funny at all and totally neurotic.

Anyway, I digress, that seemed to do it. Sally told me I'd be good in sales. This worried me: I had never sold anything in my life. It was media sales she was thinking of putting me forward for. (I didn't know what that meant.) She arranged for me to have another interview with the agency, but this time in a group. This was another bizarre idea: I was going to get a job selling media and to get it I had to be interviewed with other interviewees. At first I wondered if group interviewing was like group sex, but one look at Lipstick Sally made me realise I was letting my imagination run away. Or perhaps group interviewing was really like group therapy: you all sat around the table and the person doing the interviewing was just going to pick the least mad of the bunch. If that was the case I had no chance.

Sarah was encouraging. She explained that selling media meant selling space in magazines, newspapers or on TV. I still didn't understand but in my apathetic state I didn't care. Although when I told her how I'd impressed the interviewer with my answers she said they must have been desperate for candidates. With a lot of coaching from Sarah, I breezed through the group interview, and eventually I had a real interview to go to. Even though I was determined to dislike everything about the job process, I had a momentary lapse when donning my suit. I'd never admit it, but I was almost excited.

The interview turned out to be another group thing: me and three others in a plush publishing house. They were looking for a number of candidates for a number of publications, all of which remained nameless. By this time I had envisaged selling ad space in *Vogue*, *Cosmopolitan*, *Tatler* or any of the other glossy women's magazines. I thought about all the free products, male models, glam lunches – they'd probably promote me to journalist or even, in my wildest fantasy, fashion editor. I thought maybe I'd got the A word, 'ambition'.

The interview: me, another girl, two boys, one cute, one a geek. Sarah had put me through a gruelling rehearsal of answers, and I was hoping that a combination of that with my natural charm and wit would make me successful. It did. The cute boy gave me his phone number and I was called back for a second interview.

Three months after leaving university, when I was offered my first job I thought I might just become a career woman. Sarah, Jess, Sophie and my other girlfriends from university might just have been right: this was fun, this was the start of my new, exciting life. When I found out that the job I had been offered was for a trade publication called *Nuts and Bolts Monthly*, I felt differently. My salary was eleven thousand pounds plus commission, and I wanted university and Ben back more badly than ever. Before taking the drastic step of accepting, I spoke at length to a number of people.

Sarah: 'It's only the first step, take it.'

Jess: 'Well, we can't all work in PR.'

Sophie: 'It'll be lovely to have you living with us.'

My parents: 'We can always tell people you've got a great job in publishing.'

Thomas: 'Is it a porno title?'

I decided, in a last-ditch attempt to salvage my sanity, to

talk to Lipstick Sally the recruitment consultant. I asked her what my chances were with *Cosmo*.

Sally: 'Ha, ha, ha, ha.'

I took the glamorous job of sales executive on *Nuts and Bolts Monthly* (the leading publication in its field), and I felt that my life had ended. Although reason and the advice of friends and parents pointed to my having to start this sales job, I still explored on my own a number of options to get me out of having to work. The first involved Ben, on a white horse, arriving just in the nick of time to rescue me. Every time I heard a horse going by, which didn't happen often, I thought it was him. It never was.

Then real fantasy took over: I'd be a rock chick. Simple, find a rich, successful rock star, become his girlfriend, travel the world with him and never have to work again. Now, that idea appealed to me, apart from the fact that I didn't know any rock stars.

I also thought about becoming a new-age traveller. I could take to the road in a bus that doubled as my home and I'd only have to work when we protested about trees and stuff, and as I believe very heavily in preserving the environment I thought I'd fit in quite well. I could find my male companion and we'd live happily ever after in our bus (it had to be a bus: I couldn't possibly live in a caravan). I discussed the idea with Jess, because I really thought I had something, but she pointed out that I wouldn't be able to count on the mod cons I loved so much (hair-dryer, shower), I'd never be able to wear mules again and I'd be poor. She said other horrible things about parasites using the environment as an excuse not to get a job, but as that was the reason I was considering it I decided not to argue and I struck it off my list. I hadn't realised that buses don't come with central heating and power-showers.

Perhaps I could advertise for a husband. 'Young twenty-one-year-old, eager to learn to cook, quite intelligent, seeks young man for marriage, preferably with money.' Yes, I could just imagine the perverted responses I'd get. Again, I came back to the fact that dependency was something I'd always been good at; independence was what I feared. But now it seemed inevitable: with no Ben to hide behind and parents who were looking forward to me making them proud, I was left with no alternative. Of course, most people in my position would start a career with a smile on their faces and decide to make the most of their lives, but not me. If, for some reason, Ben didn't come back, I'd have to find someone else. Being independent is not all it's cracked up to be.

I considered not moving to London, but going to Scotland or Wales, somewhere remote where I'd work in a post office or be a goat-herder. Anything would be better than starting work on a magazine about nuts and bolts or whatever. I was told numerous times that this was a stepping stone. *Nuts and Bolts* was owned by a large publishing house and getting into a company like that might be advantageous to me, if I made my own opportunities. Sometimes I felt as if I was surrounded by people quoting from the same book: *How to succeed in* 1999. I did not see it as a great opportunity. I saw it as the thing I had to do to get to London to be with my unsympathetic and interfering friends. Perhaps goat-herding was the best option, after all. No, London was my only option, and the only hope I had was that London would be filled with men who would love to marry me and take care of me. And one of those men would be, if not quite Ben, my nearly Mr Right.

Chapter Two

A little man approached me. He was very fat and very red. He introduced himself as the Devil. He asked me if I would sell him my soul. I said OK. He asked how much money I wanted, but I said he'd have to make me an offer; I didn't know what the going rate for souls was. He said he'd give me two million pounds. It was a lot of money. We struck a deal. I can't tell you what life is like without my soul, because I can't remember what it was like with it.

I sat on the train having had a tearful farewell with my parents. I knew that somehow, albeit reluctantly, my life was moving on. I thought, I might replace Ben, but then I thought, Ben will come back for me. I thought, I might enjoy my job, but then I thought, I'll hate it. I couldn't think in a straight line, my mind was in knots. I don't know what I expected out of London, if I had any expectations at all. I was in such a state of confusion and contradiction that nothing was clear.

Once, people had been drawn to London in the belief that the streets were paved with gold. Even now it is seen as the city of opportunity, although the streets are paved with litter and homeless people. My impression of London when I first came here was somewhat confused. I was terrified by the idea of London and terrified by its enormity, but the tingle of excitement I felt when I first entered it was unmistakable and unexpected. I couldn't help but feel I had entered a whole new world and that in this world a number of treasures awaited me.

London looks as though it deserves its status as capital of our country. It commands respect; it has an arrogance and confidence about it that are both intimidating and comforting. It is a city of contradictions. It cries out to you yet defies you to understand it. I sometimes feel I never will, but it challenges you all the same. It's breathtaking one minute, ugly and cruel the next. Streets that house the rich and estates that house the poor sit next to each other, showing the contrast, the divide. Shops that are famous, intimidating, and streets so full that it takes hours to walk down them dominate the centre.

I live in a twenty-four-hour, seven-days-a-week city. It never stops, it doesn't relax, so you don't either. Its personality is complex, attractive and frightening. London is the man your father never wanted you to meet. You will be exposed to its evils, it won't protect you. But when you see its beauty it captivates you. It is beautiful when it shines its lights and sparkles like the most precious of crowns, but ugly when stripped of these jewels, its warmth and its love.

You could never live in London and not notice both the beauty and the ugliness, but in the grip of its ugliness you may be blind to its beauty. You find its soul in markets that have been around for years, but it is also soulless; it doesn't always smile. The city is always in a hurry, bustling you along, not always giving you time to look. And it gets cross. But if you catch it at that magical moment, it fills your heart. It is your best friend and your cruellest lover. It is the family that neglects you then tells you it loves you. It takes from you and it may not give anything back. Living in London, that's the chance you have to take.

The chance I had to take. London was my new home. I

wasn't sure what I was going to find there, or even what I was looking for. But I did know that I had entered the brave new world. I settled into the house, got used to being with my friends and tried to prepare for my new job. But I was still devastated about Ben. In fact, I was pretty much devastated by everything. My friends and family had long since given up their words of comfort (and who could blame them? There's only so much ranting from a mad person that anyone can take), apart from Sophie. Poor, sweet Sophie kept trying to help but I think she was running out of ideas. Because she was the only person who didn't tell me to pull myself together I used to trail after her when we were at home and talk about my broken heart. She would respond with cliché after cliché, which I didn't mind because at least she was showing me kindness. The day before I started my new job, I was lamenting my lost love and Sophie said, 'It's better to have loved and lost than never to have loved at all,' which summed up the dramatic sorrow I was looking for.

Until Sarah interfered. 'No, it's not.'

We both looked at her. 'It's not what?'

'It is not better to have loved and lost. You're a perfect example of that. I've never been in love and I'm happy and you're not.'

Sarah could be so heartless. Sophie didn't know what to say so she left the room. I looked at Sarah. 'You haven't had the joy I had with Ben, the unadulterated happiness. I may be sad now, but I was happy.'

'No, you weren't.'

'Yes, I was.'

'Ru, you spent most of the time you were with Ben crying, moaning about him, calling him a bastard. You stayed with him for ever, but I don't think he made you happy.'

Sarah was now trying to be reasonable, and I hated it. 'That is not true. I have lost the one true love of my life and he did make me happy.' I pulled my childish indignant face.

'Whatever. Anyway, Ru, there's more to life than men and

love. You should concentrate on yourself for a bit, I'm happy and I'm alone and I have no intention of being any other way.'

'But I'm not you. I need Ben or someone – No, I need Ben. He's gorgeous, I love him *sooo* much.'

At this Sarah shook her head and left the room. Which people seemed to be doing around me a lot. I knew that I should stop making people leave rooms. I knew I was putting my friends through hell. I knew that if I didn't stop they might even grow to hate me and I knew that they were wonderful friends because they didn't hate me already. I was becoming a monotonous bore, or I was already one.

But I didn't stop. I had to act out the drama and I had to milk my unhappiness for all it was worth. I was not in the situation I wanted to be in and because of that my progress was blocked. I've always been like that. You see, the main problem is that if I became happy again I would be betraying my pain and betraying the life I loved. In my heart of hearts, I knew that I loved Ben and I knew that he had made me happy. I knew he was my Mr Right and that I would never, ever get over him. You know how reason had left me? Well, it seems that it had forgotten to return.

I felt I was on the outside looking in. My friends had said goodbye to our old life so easily. I found it really hard. For three years all we had worried about was getting up in time for *Neighbours* and if we had enough clean knickers. Now all that was gone and had been replaced by structure: getting up, going to work, doing well, the future, we had to worry about all that and more. Oh, and if we had enough clean knickers. It was enough to give you a headache.

I started my sales job on the Monday. I didn't sleep much on Sunday night – I was so terrified. I got up on Monday and the house was a hive of activity. Jess and Sarah were running around getting ready for work, Sophie was drinking coffee and I was lost. I put my suit on, I did my make-up and I left the house. I felt as if I was in a daze. I didn't really know where

I was going, or what would happen to me when I got there, but I went anyway.

When I arrived, I recognised Steve, the unfortunate-looking sales manager who had interviewed me. He welcomed me, introduced me to everyone and showed me to my desk. For a moment I felt excited. Everyone was friendly, I had a desk and a computer and, well, it seemed quite nice. The office was open-plan, the desks arranged in twos, there was a water machine, plants dotted around and a big collage made out of nuts and bolts on the wall. It was quite funky. Someone gave me coffee and someone else explained a bit about the magazine, then Steve announced that I and a guy called John, who had started with me, were going to spend the first week training. That didn't sound too bad.

I recognised John as the geek from my interview. I also made a mental note to think about calling the cute guy. John looked so awkward and excited in his first suit and tie, which really didn't do a lot for him. The grey flannel, the ironed white shirt and the navy blue tie made him look boring and even more geek-like, so I decided I'd try to be nice to him. He and I went into a room and for the rest of the day were told about the magazine, the sales techniques used and the art of selling. John asked lots of boring questions, and by the time we left at five, my head hurt. But the point was that it was OK. I didn't have to do anything and the selling thing didn't sound too difficult. Steve the boss seemed nice, even though he was unfortunate-looking, and John the geek, well, he was my main competition and he was a geek. I went home feeling that it wasn't going to be as bad as I had first thought.

The rest of the week carried on in much the same vein. I didn't love getting out of bed in the morning, I hated wearing suits, but as the day was really quite easy I didn't mind it half as much as I'd thought I would. All in all it was OK. I had become a working woman and without even realising I was a modern woman, or almost a modern woman, a temporary modern woman. It still wasn't a long-term plan.

I knew what I wanted. The same as everyone. Happiness. But I had a vision of what would make me happy. I could see it, I could feel it, I longed to touch it. I was clear-minded enough to know that if I achieved my vision, it might not make me happy. That was a risk I was willing to take. But the reason for my life, and I believed very deeply that I needed to have a reason, was that I believed I'd achieve happiness. I wasn't unusual in that. I had a plan and my plan was that I'd never climb any ladders – I'd do something, but I'd never make my mark on the world. My children would not have a mother with a cool job and my husband would have a wife who cared for him, cooked for him and was at home. That view of my future was what I was striving for. I wanted it so badly that that was my career. That was my world. And I knew I was young and might not find anyone to take care of me for years and I was certainly not ready to have children and I couldn't even cook very well. But one day I'd have it. Until then I would work to pay the rent and buy my clothes and wine. I'd have as much fun as I could and be as unstressed as I could. It was simple, but it was my view of the world in which I lived.

My parents were so relieved. I had forgotten to spend my telephone conversations with them telling them I was miserable and it was all their fault. My friends were relieved – I had forgotten to moan at home. I was more like the old Ruth and everyone, including me, was pleased. On the first Friday of my first week as a working woman, Sarah had decided we would celebrate. I was the centre of attention again and I loved it. Sarah told Jess and Sophie that we were celebrating my first working week on Friday. Jess was enthusiastic but Sophie went a little bit quiet.

'What's wrong, Soph?' I asked.

'Um, I'm really pleased for you, and I really want to celebrate, but I've got a date.'

Wow, all of a sudden I was no longer the centre of attention. Questions flowed.

'Who is he?'

'Where did you meet him?'

'His name is James and I met him at the Atlantic bar last night after my modelling job. I was there with Lia — you know Lia? So we were in this amazing bar full of trendy people. It was a really scary place, the sort of place where no one smiles at you because they're too cool and you're not. Lia and I were nursing a glass of wine and moaning about the job we'd been doing and this amazing guy, or two guys but one was amazing, came up to us and asked if they could buy us champagne. Imagine, champagne!' Sophie was animated and pink, and I was impressed. I mean, the guys we were used to meeting would maybe stretch to buying us a bottle of Beck's if we were lucky, but champagne, no way. Sophie continued, 'Lia talked to Jonathan while I talked to James, who was amazing. He's tall, blond and so good-looking. And he was so smart and funny. Then they bought us dinner and afterwards James put me in a cab and asked for my number and, wow, he was such a gentleman.'

Now I was even more impressed. I thought it said in magazines that guys like this were extinct. Trust Sophie to have found one. 'Soph, that's great! You go. We'll celebrate some other time.' She hugged me and thanked me and I felt good again.

Until I started living in London, I hadn't thought about dating. At university we didn't date. You met someone in a college bar, got drunk, kissed them and either saw them again or decided to forget it. Simple. We didn't need to phone anyone, we all lived in close proximity. Relationships were easier to find, fall into or fall out of than in the real world. Dating therefore was an alien concept to me. As you know, I was a little slow off the starting-block in moving to London, so Sophie, Sarah and Jess seemed to understand it.

Sophie admitted she was a little uncool about the phone

business: she had driven herself mad waiting for this guy to call and she was also a little uncool about the actual date, wailing about having nothing to wear, worrying about her hair and make-up. I couldn't remember the last time I had seen her in such a state.

When she had gone, I asked Jess and Sarah why things had never been like this at university. Your favourite jeans and a bit of lipstick were the first-date uniform, and, as you knew so many people, it wasn't nerve-racking at all. I had never imagined it would be like this. I mean, the whole thing took so long and looked so painful. Was this really how grown-up dating would be?

'Ru, this isn't university, this is real life. Kind of like dating for grown-ups,' Jess explained. 'You'll understand when you get your first date, darling.'

I felt like a country hick again. This was unfamiliar and scary. This was where's-Ben-and-where's-university. I couldn't do this. How could I ever know someone as well as I knew Ben? How could I feel so comfortable yet excited at the same time? How could I wash anyone else's underwear? I felt as though I would never go on a date again. And once again my old friend Panic returned.

When Sophie went on her date, we stuffed ourselves with pizza and wine, and Jess and Sarah tried to explain things to me.

Jess's version: 'So, you go to a bar, or a club or just out, which is where you're likely to meet someone. I used to think I'd meet someone at work, but it's not a good idea to date someone you work with, Ru, take note of that. Anyway, you meet someone in a bar, they maybe buy you a drink, or you can make the first move, it's 1999, after all. At the end of the evening they'll do one of three things. Say it's nice to have met you then leave, ask you to go on to a club or another bar, or ask for your phone number. If it's the last, then you go home, like Sophie, and wait for him to call. If you go on somewhere else with him, one of three things happens. If he's lost interest he'll just leave, he'll try to get you to go home with him or he'll ask you for your number. If it's the second option and you sleep with him, he'll do one of two things in the morning. He'll say goodbye and thank you, or he'll ask for your number. In my opinion, if you sleep with a guy on the first night, you'll never see him again.'

I was confused. 'But what if you get his number?'

Sarah answered this time. 'It's good to take control of the situation. But once you have his number you have to wait at least four days before calling and more if you can. The point is that this way you're being cool. The cooler you are, the more interested he'll be.'

'It just doesn't sound as natural or painless as it was with Ben. You must see it was easier for us at university.' It still sounded awful to me.

'It may have been easier but it was so haphazard. It's far more organised this way. You go out once. If it goes well, one of you calls the other after a few "cool" days and you have another date. It progresses that way. It's much tidier than it was at university,' Sarah explained.

How could dating be tidy?

Jess took over. 'What Sarah means is that once we started seeing someone at university we saw them all the time but never really knew when we were going to see them. Look at you and Ben. Now we have responsibilities, we have careers to concentrate on, and we need time for ourselves so it takes longer to get to know someone and we have freedom for other things. Dating gives us more freedom than before. It means we can see men but at the same time concentrate on our careers.'

I felt tempted to ask them where they had got their information: neither of them had dated since moving to London, but I refrained.

'What happened to romance?' I asked. Jess and Sarah both looked at me.

'That *is* romance.'

I realised then that I would never date again.

We were still up when Sophie got back and she was full of how wonderful it had been. James was fantastic. He was good-looking, funny, had a well-paid job and he knew how to treat a lady. He took her to a very expensive restaurant, then brought her home. He behaved like a gentleman and said to her, 'There will be plenty of time to get to know each other.' She was so happy. James was something in the City, she thought he was a trader, but he might have been a stockbroker, she didn't know the difference, so she hadn't wanted to ask him. Jess knew the difference and explained it to all of us. We looked at her strangely, but she wasn't giving away where she gets her information from.

'He's so lovely. I'm seeing him on Monday, two days' time. He's taking me to the new Conran restaurant. I can't believe how lucky I am, I really can't. He's wonderful.' With that she swept off to bed.

Jess and Sarah were playing the cynical sisters as usual.

'There has to be a catch,' Jess said.

'Obviously too good to be true,' Sarah said.

'Men aren't like that any more,' they both said. How they got to be such experts on men was beyond me. I just told them not to say anything to Sophie and they promised they wouldn't.

My second week of work was not quite as great as my first. In fact, it was pretty awful. Apparently training was over and now it was time for us to earn our keep. I was given a list of people in the 'trade', whatever that meant, and I was supposed to sell them advertising space. When Steve explained this to me, I asked him how the hell I was supposed to do that and he asked me if I had paid attention to my training. 'Of course,' I replied, knowing full well that I had spent the whole of last week daydreaming about

Ben coming back for me. So I had a phone and I was supposed to use it. I remembered something about asking some sort of questions and some sort of facts about the magazine and just as I felt as if I was going to burst into tears, Brian, a nice man who wore a cardigan under his suit jacket, told me to listen to one of his calls. He telephoned a client and introduced himself, explained about the circulation of the magazine, asked if they'd seen it, then offered to send a media pack. That was a successful sales call apparently.

I took the bull by the horns and called the first person on my list. He was in a meeting so I left a message. The same happened with the next fifteen people I called. This was getting boring. Then I struck gold. One guy called Sam Peterson was in. He sounded interested in what I had to say and accepted a much-needed media pack. I was triumphant, until I realised that in my excitement I had forgotten to get his address and had to call him back. I then asked Brian what a media pack was. I made a mental note to pay attention in future.

The second week ended, and I'd spoken to some people, sent out some media packs and Steve said I'd done well. But, to be honest, it was so boring, having the same conversation over and over again. And I hadn't actually sold anything yet. I realised that this job was not half the fun I had thought in my first week. I left on Friday, not looking forward to when I would have to return. I explained my fears to Sarah, who brushed them off, saying that I would love it once I got more used to it. Jess laughed and said that in her office they hated salespeople, as if we were a subhuman life form. Even Sophie was devoid of her usual sympathy; she had yet another date with James.

She had been out with James on the Monday after her first date then again on Wednesday, Thursday and now tonight. She was having a night off tomorrow because she had to go away on a modelling job. I have to admit I was jealous: obviously, in my delicate state of mind, anyone else's happiness just highlighted my misery. I didn't begrudge her her happiness, of course I didn't, but I couldn't help the way I felt. Before she left for her date on Friday she filled us in on James. Dinner, the theatre, dinner, the cinema, dinner, he paid for everything, treated her like a queen. Even Jess and Sarah were beginning to think he must be all right after all.

Then Sophie made us all happy. 'I've invited him to dinner next Thursday, here, with you guys and Thomas. I told him you were my best friends and I needed you to approve of him.' She looked triumphant, we all looked happy. We were going to meet this fabulous man. I for one intended to ask him about his friends.

When my alarm clock announced to me that it was Monday morning again, it did so joyfully. I jumped out of bed and cursed it. My usual morning routine. I showered, dressed and slapped the minimum national requirement of make-up on. I was out of the flat within twenty minutes. One of the main skills I had developed since moving to London was getting ready for work in this short time and although I'd never be mistaken for a supermodel, I was presentable enough not to scare children.

You always hear about workers having Monday-morning blues, but until you experience them yourself you cannot understand the intensity of the feeling. One of my main objections about working was the culture of living for weekends, the week being just a pain in the arse for your social life. Well, after three weeks of working, I was doing that, even though I had no social life and my weekends were pretty awful too.

There were two significant events in my third week at work. John made his first sale on Monday, and the fuss made of him made me feel insignificant. So John had made a sale, big fucking deal. I'd make one soon, I was sure. Steve took me aside and did the don't-feel-bad-this-should-make-you-more-determined speech, but it didn't. I felt even more keenly that this job was a big mistake. I was still talking to people and sending out my media packs, but nothing more exciting than that. I felt disheartened and fed up, and I didn't want to be working any more. Desolation returned. It had left me only briefly. Life was as bleak now as when Ben had left — actually it was bleaker, because now I had a shit job.

The other event was Thursday night, when we got to meet Sophie's man. I had cheered up by then, because I was so excited about it. I couldn't wait to see if a guy this amazing really existed. If he did I thought about putting him in a museum. Sophie had been working really hard to make everything nicer, including us. We were all told to be on our best behaviour and I'm not sure if it was us or him up for approval — both, I think. She was wearing a lovely black dress, she was flushed from cooking, her hair was tied back but a couple of locks had escaped and framed her face. She looked like an advert for *Good Housekeeping*. Anyway, she'd cooked and we had wine, so we were certainly ready for him. Actually we weren't.

James turned up with two bottles of red wine. He handed then over and told us that it was such-and-such a year and very nice, but as we were hardened plonk drinkers we weren't very impressed. He also made the mistake of trying to be buddy-buddy with Thomas, who already hated him because he was in love with Sophie himself. He kissed each of us on both cheeks, as if we had known him for ever, which I thought was polite, Sarah made a face, which meant she thought he was slimy. He complimented the house, told us he had heard so much about us, laughed politely when we told him not to believe a word of it, and he seemed OK. He was nice-looking in a clean-cut, clean-shaven, laden-with-aftershave way. A bit too clean, if you know what I mean.

Sophie cooked us roast beef and Yorkshire pudding (actually that was the only thing Sophie could cook), and it was really good. Apparently it was the only thing her mother could cook too. She had put a white tablecloth, which I didn't even know we had, on the table, and a candelabra in the centre, lighting the room. It looked a bit like a restaurant, a posh one, of course. Sophie was very nervous around James, which I don't think is unusual in a new relationship. I noticed, when he first saw her, she held her breath until he said she looked nice. Love can do funny things to you.

We all sat down to dinner and started drinking James's wine. I drank slowly, thinking how horrible it was. I looked at Sarah sipping hers and I could see she agreed. Thomas grimaced every time he took a mouthful and Jess didn't even bother after the first mouthful. James did: he drank in huge gulps, with a noise that made me cringe. Sophie didn't drink at all: she was too busy smiling at James.

We started eating and James made overtures at conversation. He asked each of us in turn what we did for a living.

'I work in PR,' Jess said.

'Oh, really? That's where you suck up to people and all wander around saying "darling" and being superficial,' he said, and I couldn't figure out if he was joking or being rude. Jess obviously thought the latter.

'No,' she said, through gritted teeth.

James laughed. 'Yeah, nothing against it myself but, well, all this creative rubbish is rubbish, nothing like the reality of the City.'

I thought that Jess was going to hit him, but Sarah stepped in to change the subject. 'I'm a recruitment consultant,' she said.

James took another large swig of his wine. 'Huh, very nineties,' was his contemptuous reply. His cheeks had reddened and I guessed that perhaps he was just drunk, drunk and obnoxious. When it came to my turn, I said I didn't want to discuss it, I'd had a bad week, but I don't think he even listened.

'What do you do, Thomas?' he asked.

'My law finals,' Thomas mumbled. He was looking at his food intently.

'Oh, interesting. In the City you can earn a fortune as a lawyer. You should think about specialising in City law.' Off

James went. He spent the next half-hour extolling the virtues of the City while wiping gravy off his chin with his sleeve. He spoke of the money to be made, the challenge and the intellect. He made it sound like the most important workplace in the world, the most difficult and the most rewarding. I believed the money thing (I've seen Wall Street), but the rest, well, I doubted the intellect because James didn't have any.

The second bottle of wine was half empty and James was the only one drinking and burping now. In between talking, dribbling gravy and drinking, he was burping for England. To break the tension I went to put on some music; part of me thought that if I chose well I could drown out the irritating James. I chose Nirvana, which upset Sophie, who ran to the CD player and put on the Beautiful South.

James was not about to be drowned out. On and on he droned, belittling us all in the process. 'You and your creative fancies' and 'Recruitment is an unnecessary industry' – he wouldn't stop putting Jess and Sarah down. Thomas looked happy; he had been hoping that James was a jerk. But Sophie didn't seem to notice, just sat beaming at him the whole time. Sarah and Jess were having trouble meeting Sophie's eyes and the air was tense, full of hostility.

Jess evidently felt it was time to retaliate. 'So if you hate the creative world so much, why are you dating an actress?' She almost jumped across the table with this accusation.

'Oh, acting's a hobby for Sophie, she's really a model and no bloke would ever do anything but applaud the modelling world, eh, Thomas?' James chuckled, or sneered, I wasn't sure which. We were all too shocked to react. Jess looked defeated, and no one defeated Jess. Sophie was still smiling. Thomas was getting happier by the minute, and Sarah was concentrating on her dinner. I kept quiet. Luckily thick-skinned James carried on talking. Dessert was served, the CD was changed and still he talked. He was so flash. He talked about his flat in Kensington, his job, again, his holidays, 'I'm thinking of Barbados this year.'

At that he looked at Sophie and said, 'If you play your cards right I may take you.' Sophie just smiled. 'I'm buying a Porsche when I get my next bonus. At the moment I've only got a BMW.'

'Bad luck, mate.' James was ignorant of, or just ignored, the sarcasm in Thomas's voice.

'Well, a Porsche is a man's car, really sexy,' he continued. I looked at Sophie, who still seemed oblivious to James's effect on everyone.

'Well, I guess you need all the help you can get,' Jess said. James ignored her.

It was awful. Jess was sulking, Sarah was silent. Thomas just sat smiling to himself and I didn't have a clue what to say. The evening couldn't end soon enough.

The following evening Sophie asked us what we'd thought of him. We all went quiet. Jess was the first to break the silence, 'I thought he was bloody rude.'

Sophie looked shocked. 'What do you mean?'

'Well, you have to admit he was pretty rude about Jess and Sarah's jobs. He even said you weren't serious about acting.' I tried to be reasonable.

'No, he didn't.' Sophie was defiant.

'He bloody well did,' Jess stormed.

'Oh, he didn't mean anything, he's just more mature than us.'

We were all dumbfounded. I was furious, more about Sophie's defence of him than anything. 'Actually, Sophie, he wasn't mature, he was a prick. "The Porsche" is only concerned with status symbols and he sees you as one of them.' I knew that I was treading on dangerous ground, but she just had to see how awful he was.

'No, he doesn't, and who's the Porsche?'

'James. The name suits him, don't you think?'

Jess and Sarah giggled.

Sophie burst into tears. 'You bitches! He's my boyfriend, I'm happy and all you can do is be horrible.'

Oh dear.

'God, you all seem to have totally misunderstood him, he didn't mean to be rude, but, well, he has an important job and he's older than us. You just totally misunderstood him.' It was the weakest defence I'd ever heard, but it was the only defence she had.

We all apologised and she forgave us. I just couldn't understand what she saw in him. If it was his money I'd almost understand – I mean, if he really had a Porsche, I'd sleep with him – but Sophie wasn't interested in money. Their relationship became one of the great mysteries of the world. It was up there with Stonehenge.

If ever there was a bone of contention in my friendship with Sophie it was the Porsche. She begged me to stop calling him that. I begged her to stop seeing him.

'Sophie, he's horrible.' I pleaded for her to see it.

But Sophie became bitchy, which she never had before. 'Right, and Mr Wonderful Ben, who made you cry more times than I could count, was so nice.' She pointed out that every time Ben was horrible to me I wouldn't listen to her so I was not in the best position to give her advice. I said Ben was never a prat and Sophie got upset. I said sorry and it was forgotten until the next time.

She did make me think about Ben, though. I remembered once when he had won a hockey game and I had stood on the sidelines cheering him on in the pouring rain. At the end when his teammates were engaged in a bonding moment, I had made the mistake of running up to him, throwing my arms round him and kissing him in front of them. Ben peeled me off and said to his team, 'Christ, it's OK having sex every night, but putting up with the leech thing gets tiring.' Then as they all laughed he walked off leaving me dripping wet in the middle of a hockey-field. So, yeah, he was a prick sometimes, but then, as he explained later, I had interrupted a laddish moment and I really should have known better. No, my Ben wasn't like the Porsche, who wouldn't have apologised afterwards. I tried to keep quiet, but I hated to see someone as wonderful as Sophie wasting her time on such an idiot. I was trying to be a friend, but the truth was that I was not in any position to cast the first stone. As well as being a bore, I was a hypocrite now. How much worse a person could I become?

I needed some excitement in my life. But I didn't know how to find it. I had been in London a month now, and things weren't good. I hated my new job and still hadn't sold anything. Sophie was in love with the most obnoxious guy I'd ever met and, of course, it goes without saying that I was missing Ben like crazy. (Oops). It wasn't just my life that was dull, I was dull. Even my friends were getting bored with me. I had been a drama queen for long enough so Sympathy had got bored and left our house. I knew I should take control of my destiny, but I wanted Fate to do it for me. That way I had someone to blame: 'Fate dealt me a cruel hand,' I would say, and on the whole it had. I felt I was becoming more and more isolated from the real world; the world I had tried to shun was shunning me. By cutting myself off from the normalities of the world, the world was now cutting me off. I didn't belong and I wasn't wanted. I had to get out but I didn't know how. I was trapped. I had trapped myself. I didn't understand. I didn't want to understand.

I had had so many lectures about getting on with my life that I decided to do the decent thing: I would fool my friends into thinking I was doing just that and hopefully I might fool myself in the process. The first stage in my getting-on-with-life plan involved calling Simon, the guy I had met in the first interview I had for my job. I don't really know why I decided to call him. Perhaps it was just because I was in the grip of madness and therefore my actions could not be accounted for. I really was in the grip of madness: I heard voices and everything. Or perhaps it was just because it was the sensible thing to do.

The human heart is a fragile animal: once broken, it does not take kindly to attempts at repair. It's like a self-healing wound. It mends by itself so there is no point in pushing it. That was what I thought. My friends, of course, felt differently. Jess said that all I had to do was pull myself together, stop being a victim, stop living in a dream world. She said that if I did I would get over Ben in a flash. Sarah said I had to accept that Ben and I were over, accept that I had a life and take control of it. Sophie said that of course I needed time, but (and I hated her for the but) I should be trying to make new friends and build a social life in London. Thomas said that all I needed was a good seeing-to. Thomas was probably right.

So I did it. I arranged to see Simon. I think the voices told me to so I called him and asked him out. He seemed really pleased to hear from me and agreed readily to a date. We were meeting on Friday, at a bar. I might not have been very modern when it came to my career, but I was when it came to sexual liberation. I felt almost positive: perhaps people were right, perhaps meeting someone else was the best way to get over heartbreak. Although I was excited I was also a little nervous: I wasn't sure what to expect. After all, this was grown-up dating and I'd never done it before.

After work, Sarah was at home so, to calm my nerves, I persuaded her that a couple of glasses of wine before we both went out would be a good idea. Sarah sipped her wine, I gulped mine, and before she had finished her second glass I had finished the bottle. I realised that in calming my nerves I had got myself drunk before I'd even left the flat. Then Sarah had a battle on her hands to get me ready. She overhauled my wardrobe and found my favourite black mini-skirt and a sexy chiffon blouse. I thought maybe I looked a bit obvious but, then, I was too drunk to argue. I looked OK before I left but Sarah told me to drink slowly and have something to eat. I wasn't legless or anything, but I was a bit tipsy and giggly, and my legs didn't feel very strong. The problem when I get drunk is that my legs seem to lose their ability to hold me up. If I can mentally hold it together I usually fall over, which is a bit of a giveaway. I hoped I wasn't going to fall over. Before I got into the cab to take me on my first date since Ben (God, that sounded weird), I apologised to Ben for what I was about to do. I told him, silently, that I still loved him and wanted no one else and I wished he was with me. Now, as well as concentrating on not falling over, I had to concentrate on not crying.

In the cab on the way to the bar I felt truly awful. I began to wonder why I was putting myself through this ordeal, why I had drunk so much beforehand, why I was going. I should have stood up to my friends, told them I wasn't ready to date. I was such a wimp, I was gutless, I was at the bar.

It was a large, noisy, modern place, full of young professionals in huge groups, not a quiet romantic-date place, but that was probably a good thing. Simon was waiting for me and kissed my cheek. He was gorgeous, tall, with blond hair and blue eyes. And his legs (I'm a legs woman) were pretty amazing. He ordered a bottle of Chardonnay and we managed to find a table.

Simon was very enthusiastic, the opposite of Ben. He spoke of everything with such excitement. I was drunk, dizzy and exhausted. And he didn't stop talking. He told me about his job in sales, on a car magazine, which he loved. He told me about Manchester University, where he had recently graduated with a degree in history. He told me about his older brother and his older brother's wife and his younger sister and his parents and his dog, called Bobby or Bobble.

And while he talked I drank. I drank and drank, and finished my second bottle of wine. Looking at him through the bottom of my empty wine-glass, I realised that Simon was what I refer to as a 'catch'. Not only did he have looks, but he had another quality imperative in a husband: Simon was a gentleman. He went to get me another bottle of wine. I had to hold on to the edge of the table to keep upright. I wondered if he noticed. When he came back, as I was drunk and as I had decided that this could be my man, I decided to impress him. I told him loads of funny stories about my university days ('you won't believe the time I stole a traffic cone'), I told him about Clapham and my odd friends, I told him about my shit job and John the geek and Mr Motivator my boss. He laughed a lot so I must have been funny. I flirted, I pouted, I drank.

Then I told him about Ben. I was drunk (have I already said that?), and I got tearful, which was inevitable, really. I always cry when I'm drunk. Then I asked him if he thought Ben was a low-life bastard and he said he was. Simon said that he'd never treat me like that.

I woke up. My head hurt. I was in bed, but it wasn't my bed. I looked and saw Simon. I was in Simon's bed. I was also naked. I felt sick. I'd slept with Simon, and I didn't remember doing it. I knew I'd done it: there was a condom lying on the floor. I felt sicker. I'm no nun and I'm no moral judge, but I draw the line at sleeping with a guy I've only just met and not even remembering. What if I'd passed out in the middle? God, what if I'd passed out before the start? I felt really sick. I wasn't used to this situation. Where the hell were my knickers? I hated not knowing where my knickers were. I was so embarrassed. I could see my top, my bra and my trousers, but not my knickers. I looked at Simon. He was sleeping, I really didn't want to wake him and ask him. What was I supposed to do? Do I leave? Do I have breakfast with the guy? God, no, I didn't want breakfast. I needed an escape plan. I got out of bed quietly, decided to leave my knickers wherever they were and left.

I didn't even know where I was. I found a cab and went home. There I had a long bath and, still feeling hungover and mortified, I went to bed. I woke at midday and my absence from my bed had been duly noted. Everyone knew of my conquest. Even Thomas had come round to share in my victory. They said this was the first step in getting my life back together. They were all really proud.

Until I told them what had happened. You should have seen their faces.

They were dumbstruck. I had rationalised what had happened and decided it had been Simon's fault. I had been drunk and vulnerable and he had taken advantage of me. What a bastard.

This theory was not shared by my friends. They thought it was my fault: 1. I shouldn't have got drunk. 2. I shouldn't have got so drunk.

Then when I told them how I'd left, I faced another attack.

'God, Ru, that's what horrid men do,' Jess said, and the other girls agreed.

'Do you realise you've probably destroyed his confidence in the sexual department? His life is ruined,' Thomas said.

Any defence I had was in vain. They made me so miserable I swore I would never date again. I also made a vow to get some more sympathetic friends. I had changed from being a monotonous bore to being a monotonous boring slut. It didn't feel like a step in the right direction.

So, I couldn't get over Ben and I couldn't replace him, which left me in a bit of a pickle. I could cry a lot (I did) and I could live with my huge sense of loss, but those seemed to be my only options. Simon, well, the Simon débâcle proved everything to me, really: it proved that I was right to love Ben and I was right to want only him, and I was right to feel so completely miserable. Simon had fucked me up and proved me right. But this didn't make me feel triumphant. Feeling vulnerable didn't bother me, being taken advantage of didn't bother me, but my betrayal of Ben did. For some bizarre reason I felt as if I'd been unfaithful to him. I would never, ever be unfaithful to Ben. Although he wasn't here.

You know, sometimes you try to solve a problem but you're stuck in a never-ending circle so you keep coming back to the problem. That's how I felt. The problem was, I had had sex; the problem was, I hadn't remembered; the problem was, Simon had taken advantage of me; the problem was Ben. Ben, Ben, Ben. I screamed at him in my head, 'How could you leave? How could you make me like this? How could you screw up my life?' And again I was crying. Drink. That explained it. I was unhappy, I drank, I was stupid. Being drunk with Simon, for a while, had made me forget who I was. Actually it had made me forget everything. Perhaps it was just sex. But sex had always meant something to me. Ben was much better in bed than Simon: I always remembered sleeping with Ben. And I cursed Simon for being a typical insensitive-ruled-by-his-penis man, who had used my crisis to get a shag. Are some men born without conscience or is it something they get taught to ignore at school? I stopped crying. Simon was a low-life rat and if I ever saw him again I would stick a red-hot poker so far up his backside he would be sorry for ever (if I had a red-hot poker handy, of course). And at the same time, perhaps I'd stick one up mine.

Jess was the third member of our family to go on a date. She went out with 'someone in PR', which was all she told us about him. It didn't go well. 'Opposites do not attract,' was her only comment on the evening. We knew better than to push for details. Sophie was in a relationship, if you could call it that, and Jess and I had both had a disastrous date, but Sarah hadn't been out with anyone. I felt sorry for her; not one bit of testosterone had been flung her way since she'd moved to London, but I didn't want to mention it. I mentioned it instead to Jess, who thought about it, agreed with me and, not having my sensitivity, brought it up one night.

'Sarah, I've been thinking, you haven't had a date in ages. How about I fix you up with someone I know?' Ever the subtle Jess.

Sarah looked at us. 'No, thank you.'

'But I know a number of suitable men,' Jess pushed, and

I wondered why she'd never offered to fix me up with one of them.

'I'm sorry to disappoint you, but the reason I am not dating, or have not dated, is because I've decided to become celibate.'

We all looked at her.

'Why on earth would you do that?' I asked. I had never understood voluntary abstinence from the one good thing in the world.

'Because I want to concentrate on my career and men only complicate things. You guys illustrate my point beautifully.' Sarah was getting stroppy.

'I hope you're not including me in that. I do not let men complicate my life, nor do I let them take over my life, not like those two.' Jess was stroppy too.

Sophie and I looked at each other: we both knew better than to try to defend ourselves against those charges. For one thing, they were true, and for another, both Jess and Sarah could be scary when riled.

'No, Jess, I didn't mean you, although you did spend a fortune on a DKNY top when you had that date with the Opposite,' Sarah conceded.

'OK, but I'll wear that top loads. I did not buy it for my date.' Jess had calmed down a little.

Then I remembered what had started this. 'Sarah, are you sure you don't need any male comfort, not at all?'

Sarah giggled. 'You don't need a real penis to have a good time,' she said.

'Don't you?' asked Sophie. We all laughed. Sophie went pink.

'How's the Porsche?' I asked, to make her feel better.

'I don't know what I'd do without James, he's so great.' She went pink again. 'I think I've met The One,' she declared.

We all cringed and hoped she didn't mean it, but none of us said anything: we were all trying to be good friends.

'He's taking me away this weekend, to Scotland, for a

romantic break. I'm so looking forward to it.' She was still pink and happy and, to be honest, the fact that he was a wanker was irrelevant. It would be irrelevant until she realised it, too. She jumped up excitedly. 'Ru, come and help me choose what to take.' So for now we left Sarah and her celibacy and went to pick clothes.

Later, when Sarah and I were alone, I asked her why she was so anti being part of a couple. There's nothing wrong with wanting to be on your own (even if I didn't understand it), but it is rare. Even Jess, the biggest independent career woman, likes the idea of having a man around. But not Sarah. Even at university she would meet guys, see them for the bit, and lose interest. Ben decided once that she must be a lesbian, just because she wouldn't go out with one of his hockey mates, but he was just being horrible.

'Sarah, why are you so intent on being single?' I asked.

'Oh, Ru, I know the world seems to revolve around couples – you don't even need to be a heterosexual couple, just a couple. And I don't see what the big deal is. You know how organised I like my life to be and I'm scared of disrupting that. I think that's what men do, they disrupt you, and sometimes it may be a good disruption, but most times it seems bad, and at the moment I don't need any disruption in my life.'

'But what about fun? What about sex, romance, all those things? It can be magical, Sarah, it really can.'

'I'm sure it can. But at the moment it's not part of my game plan. I know Jess is always the outwardly ambitious one, but I want to start my own business and I think in a few years' time I'll be able to. Then I'll have to work all the hours to get it off the ground, and when it is, maybe I'll be able to think about romance. But that's my priority. It's the most important thing in the world to me. I know you're the opposite, and that's OK, because we have something in common.'

'We do?'

'Yes, neither of us believes the bullshit that we can have it all. If I fell in love now, I know that my plans wouldn't be half as easy to achieve. Once I'm up and running, maybe I can have everything.'

'Sarah, if because of your career you end up manless and lonely, you can come and live with me and be a rich auntie to my six children.' I laughed.

'Do you think I'm mad?' Sarah asked.

'Do you think I'm mad?' I asked.

We looked at each other 'Yes,' we said.

Chapter Three

A Perfect Husband.

The perfect husband will be a perfect gentleman. He will be courteous and complimentary. He will dress well, be handsome and slim. He will be intelligent and widely read, with a good grasp of current affairs. He will engage only in gentlemanly pursuits, such as riding and hunting, and he will have an engaging appreciation of the arts.

I decided to make my perfect-husband list. After all, you can't be too careful in this day and age and I didn't want to end up with just anyone. Even though I wasn't actively looking at the moment, and even though I knew Ben was my perfect husband, making the list seemed like a good idea. Just in case, of course.

Height, over five feet nine; build, slim; hair, yes; eyes, blue or brown. He needs to be clean and relatively devoid of obscene bodily functions – i.e. farting and burping should only occur when absolutely necessary. He needs to be under thirty and have a job, ideally a well-paid job and a car, but not a rubbish car. A good sense of humour is essential, and he will enjoy making me laugh. An ability to drink and smoke excessively without falling over or being sick. Sporty would be nice, but not obsessed. He must maintain short fingernails. Clean driving licence. He will have great manners – open doors, pay for dinner, never say that you're overweight, your boobs are saggy or that his ex-girlfriend was better in bed than you are. As a lover he will be attentive to my needs and won't think that foreplay is a bottle of cheap wine and a pizza. Most importantly, he will not believe that women should work. Oh, and he will be very sexy.

You must understand that if I was being unrealistic I would ask for a James Bond type, smouldering good looks, huge amounts of money and lots of gadgets, but without the eye for the ladies. However, as I was hoping to find a husband I was willing to compromise. I didn't think I was asking too much, was I?

Chapter Four

'There is only one suitable career for a woman: marriage. With marriage comes motherhood. In many ways they are the same. Girls need to learn at an early age how to take care of a man. It is the only valuable lesson we can teach.'

'But surely, Miss, women are capable of more than just marriage. Surely we should encourage their talents.'

'Talents in girls are merely instruments for enchanting men. An accomplished young lady is so much more appealing to a gentleman than one who cannot do a thing. Music, painting, reading poetry, dancing – these are the talents we must encourage in our girls. The only talents girls need.'

'But, Miss, what if our girls have other ambitions? What if they would like to find some kind of employment? Something to stimulate them.'

'Oh, my dear girl, employment is only for the poor. Rich girls do not need to work, therefore they do not want to work. Working is an unfortunate consequence of one's station in life. It is neither attractive nor fun. No, the young women we teach will have no desire to do anything but catch a suitable husband. And that is what we must teach.'

'Please tell me, I work due to my station in life. Will I ever be able to attract a husband?'

'Oh, I should say that you will be able to marry well, in

the circumstances, fret not. I will teach you how to attract a husband and then you may give up work.'

'Miss, I would very much like a husband, but I also enjoy working here. I would like to marry, but is it not possible to keep my employ?'

'Oh dear. I see we have some work to do. If you want to get married, then why would you want to keep working?'

'I enjoy my work.'

'Oh, is that all? Do not worry, you shall enjoy being a wife very much more.'

Do you know what it's like to be born in the wrong time? A basic mistake in the year of my birth and the rest of my life was ruined. I should never have been born now. The Jane Austen times would have best suited me, I thought. I would have spent my days playing the piano, sewing, reading and walking. I would have waited for dashing men to court me, I would have married well. Life would have been perfect. I felt as if I had been held in a womb for a hundred years or so. I couldn't believe that someone had got it so wrong.

There was one silver lining in my cloud, though: I was still convinced that the life I found myself with was not permanent. In fact, it was very, very temporary. The house was nice, Clapham was nice, my friends were nice, most of the time, but I still expected Ben to come back for me, I knew he would. I knew, being realistic, that he wouldn't come back straight away. When he left and I was still at home, I would jump every time the phone rang and rush every time I heard the doorbell, expecting him to be there, but that was just wishful thinking. After a month or so, I knew he'd realise he'd made a terrible mistake and he'd rush back to me, begging my forgiveness. Although the small sane part of me knew that I was living in Fantasy Land, it wasn't big enough to kick me into reality. I was firmly ensconced there, and I had no intention of leaving. That was how I coped with my day-to-day life; that was how I coped with London. I got through it by knowing that Ben would rescue me soon, and we'd ride off into the sunset together.

Then it happened. I got a postcard. A postcard with a picture of Ayers Rock, Australia, on it, a postcard from the other side of the world. A postcard telling me that now Ben was further away from me than ever. It came via Thomas and it said, 'Dear Ruth, having a great time, weather is hot, beer is cheap, lots of culture, from Ben.' Not even 'Wish you were here', not whether he'd climbed Ayers Rock, or even if he'd been there. When that came, I felt I'd hit rock bottom yet again. He wasn't coming back and he hadn't realised he'd made a mistake. To him our relationship was a cheap postcard. I felt such anger towards him. How dare he not come back for me? How dare he subject me to this life? He was to blame for everything and I almost hated him. But I couldn't hate him because all I wanted was for him to be here, with me, and I had to face for the first time that there was a strong possibility that that was never going to happen.

'Why?' I asked, I was weepy.

'Why what?' Ben said.

'Why are we over?' The tears sat still in my eyes but I was ever aware of their presence.

'Because I told you I'm going travelling.'

God, this man was one pain in the arse. He couldn't even do a decent job of breaking up with me. God knows how he ever passed a law degree. 'Ben, I know you're going travelling and I hate that you're leaving, but I don't understand why we have to break up.'

'What?' Ben looked confused.

My strength was returning. I loved Ben, I really did, but he wasn't the brightest man on earth. 'Listen, Ben, we've been together for over two years and now you want to throw it all away. What about me waiting for you?' I'm not sure what logic in me produced this, but I guess it was that I wanted to stay with Ben, I wanted to be his girl, and if it meant a year without him, well, that would be what it took. A little ray of light returned to me. Ben and I didn't need to be over, not at all.

'No,' Ben replied.

I took a deep breath. This was either going down in history as one of the most difficult break-ups or the longest. 'Why, Ben, why? Don't you love me? Why don't you want me?' I was tired and I felt a little tear escape. The silence lasted for what seemed forever. I was concentrating on not crying: I looked at the sky, so clear, so dark, so enveloping, so warm, so cold, so big, and I looked around the steps we stood on, steps we had stood on a thousand times before – I think we even kissed on these steps. I could hear shrieks of laughter in the distance as the graduation ball was still in full swing. I could hear music. But none of it felt real. All that was real was Ben, my love and me, and even that wasn't real any more either.

'We're young, Ru, too young to settle down. I wasn't ready for all your plans, they scared me, and I don't want to go away for a year and come back to find things still the same. I need to go away and I need a fresh start.'

I was fast running out of energy. I still wanted to know why he hadn't told me before, or why he felt this or when he felt this, or if he even loved me, but I didn't seem to have any strength left. It was shock I was feeling, momentous shock and I just didn't know how to deal with it. I didn't know how I'd ever deal with any of it.

'So, you don't want to be with me.' It was time to cut the crap.

'Ruth, I just need to be on my own. I'm young.'

'Yes, Ben, you are.' The tears were rolling down my cheeks and everything looked hazy. I couldn't focus on Ben, on anything. I felt scared and I felt nauseous.

Ben looked awkward but he moved towards me.

'Did you ever love me – do you love me?'

'Yes, I did, Ru, course I did, but it's just . . . Do we have to do this?' Ben looked so out of his depth, but I guess that was because this was one of the longest conversations he'd ever had.

'Yes, we do.'

'Sorry.'

'I want to kill you.'

Ben turned from his fashionable purple colour to a green shade of white. 'I want us to stay friends.'

That did it. Those were the last words I heard before I threw up all over Ben's shoes. I didn't even realise what I'd done until it was too late. He jumped back, looked horrified, turned greener. He kept looking from me to his shoes to me again. I stood still, recovering, taking deep breaths and trying hard not to be sick again. We stayed like this for ages. All I could hear was my breathing.

'I'm going now. I need to clean up.' Ben looked at me with a sort of smile, a scared, sad smile. He walked away, just like that.

'Ben, don't, please don't.' I don't know if he heard, I don't know if I was whispering or shouting because I couldn't hear myself. I watched him go, walking the way he always did, the way I loved, slowly, with his head bowed. I guessed he was still looking at his newly decorated shoes. I sat down on the step and I stopped fighting as I let a torrent of tears cascade down my face.

I knew that there had been crises far worse than mine, unimaginably worse. I knew that there were a lot of people in this world with a zillion more problems than me. But this was my crisis and to me it was serious. I might feel guilty about those other people, but I was still damn well going to have my crisis. Once it was over, if it was ever over, I might look back and think I overreacted, or behaved really stupidly at times. Then I did not want to have to admit that I was a mad, obsessive cow, nor did I want to be told that. When I was feeling really bad, and letting everyone know, Jess always said, 'At least you're not starving and homeless and friendless and familyless,' and I'd look at her as if she was the most evil person in the world, because one thing you don't want to do when you're in a crisis is feel sorry for anyone but yourself.

And to end the crisis, what would I need? Ben, an official status as a non-career woman, a home and some money. That was all it would take. I wanted the world to say, 'It's OK. Just because you're a woman, you don't have to have a career.' I wanted men to say, 'If you want to work, fine, but if not, then we'll take care of you.' Anyway, that was all I needed. I knew my wishes weren't shared by everyone and that was fine. I thought that if that was the case I might have more chance of getting them. Less competition, that sort of thing. Jess didn't think I was an individual, she thought I was a wimp. I always ran after men and I always did as I was told. She said that was what happened with Ben. But I knew that was not how it was. Our relationship was never like that. Jess and I always disagreed over things like that. She wanted me to be like her. I wanted her to stop being quite so like her.

It was time for me to start the process of forgetting Ben. He was gone (can you believe I'm saying this? No, nor can I), I had to start accepting that and to make matters worse I still hadn't sold anything at work, I wasn't even close to it, and my boss was starting to get a bit worried about me. My motivation was at an all-time low. I decided to seek help from my friends.

'You see, the thing is I hate my job and I hate working. I've got no desire to make a go of it, I want to leave and I want never to have to work again.' That just about summed it up.

'Ruth, I thought that by now you might have got some ambition. Even if your first job isn't right, don't you want to find something you do like?' Sarah was obviously appalled by my attitude.

'No. I want to get married,' I said.

'God, Ru, people like you put the women's movement back a million years. People fought for the rights you've got. They burned their bras, chained themselves to railings and you just want to get married.' Jess was quite cross.

'I didn't ask them to,' I said.

Jess gave me a dirty look. 'That's a stupid thing to say.'

'I thought the whole thing was about giving us choice, Jess. This is my choice. I just want to get married,' I defended myself. Jess gave me another dirty look.

Sophie tried to pacify things. 'Some people are not meant to be ambitious. I think that's OK.' She got a dirty look too, and promptly shut up.

I didn't feel like the others at all. Maybe I was the odd one, but I still thought I had a valid point. I didn't have a thing I loved, like them, and I didn't want to devote my life to something just because that was what I was supposed to do. 'I work to earn money, but I don't really want a career. I want to find someone to love and take care of him. That's my ambition,' I said.

'Ruth, we're approaching the millennium, I wish you'd stop behaving as if it was the 1950s,' Sarah said.

The horror expressed by everyone was based on a view totally opposite to mine. I was a minority. Being a minority can make you feel very alone.

As far as I could see, working held little attraction. So you got a job, you worked really hard, they gave you promotion, you worked even harder. Your colleagues were your competition, your boss your aspiration, and you had constantly to pay attention so you didn't get left behind. For what? A good salary and a company car. Where was the fun in that? You spent your life stressed, worried and with ulcers. You see, in my world, work wasn't stressful. I didn't get worried. If I got fired I'd have a party. But, like I said, I was a minority. Jess said my forte in life was to start the women's regression movement, extolling the virtue of looking after men, the whole thing women had worked so hard not to do. Women had value now, they had independence, self-esteem. Apparently I was trying to destroy all that was good. But I thought that was a little harsh. I didn't want to make women want to stay at home, just make it not so bad for the ones who did. Like me.

'I blame men,' Sarah said.

'For what?' I asked.

'Everything. The reason women have to work so hard is because men tried for so long to keep us in the kitchen, and now we've proved ourselves, they still make us work twice as hard as them.'

'You're so right. Men used to have it all and they still do. We've come a long way, but we still have a long way to go. That's why you really aren't doing us any favours, Ru.' Jess was excited.

'Oh.' I felt suitably chastised. Then I thought about it. 'I blame men too,' I said.

They looked at me.

'Really?' Sarah asked.

'Most definitely. When we were fighting so hard for the right to work if they'd told us that working is a shitty existence and really stressful perhaps we'd have listened to them. But instead they fought us, we won, and now we have no choice but to earn our own living because men spend their money on fast cars, slick clothes and womanising. They could at least have given us a warning,' I said.

Jess looked as if she was going to kill me.

'How can you talk such crap?' Sarah looked pretty much the same.

'Ru, you're not being remotely amusing. OK, we've accepted that at the moment you have no ambition, but please do not belittle the women who do. Now, go and make some coffee.'

I slunk off to the kitchen. Even I knew when I'd gone too far.

We are supposed to want it all. In theory it should have been easier for me. I didn't want it all, just a little bit. But the little bit I wanted seemed to be the hardest to get. Society had high expectations of me, but in return I was offered no assurances of happiness. It wanted me to achieve, but would not guarantee my reward. I didn't think I'd ever live up to those expectations but, then, society hadn't lived up to mine.

I returned with the coffee, but the conversation was still going. I was beginning to regret ever having said anything. My chat about my job crisis had turned into a lecture about how odd I was.

'Ru, I made my list today,' Jess said.

'What list?' I asked.

'My aims list, my list of things I want to do by the time I'm thirty.'

Sophie and Sarah congratulated her.

I was confused. 'So is this list thing common?'

'Yes, of course. We've all done one,' Sarah said.

'Even you, Soph?' Sophie nodded.

God, this was bad.

'Anyway, I've done mine and I think you should do one,' Jess said.

'Come on, Jess, tell us.' Sarah looked excited. She sat up straighter on the sofa.

Jess beamed. 'Well, I'd like to be promoted from junior account executive to account executive at my six-month review, then after a year senior account exec, then account manager by the end of the next year, or six months if I move companies, and by my third year I'd like to be a senior account manager. Then I want to move swiftly to account director. I plan to move companies and have picked out my next two. By the time I'm thirty I'll have a board position. I'll drive a flash sports car, have men flocking around me and I'll own my own flat, somewhere nice, like Fulham, and I'll have a wardrobe full of designer clothes.'

'That's great, Jess, really focused,' Sarah said.

I thought it sounded complicated and exhausting, all those different 'account' titles, God, it sounded awful. Jess looked smug. But I hadn't got a list and everyone was looking at me accusingly. 'Ah,' I said triumphantly, 'you've all made a list because you know what careers you want. Seeing as I haven't got a clue what I want to do, you can't possibly expect me to make one.' Now it was my turn to be triumphant.

'Um, that's true,' Jess concurred. She and Sarah looked at each other.

'OK, so we have to go back a stage with you. What we can do is make a list to identify your chosen career.' Sarah could be determined sometimes. My heart sank. 'Listen, Ruth, now that you know your current job isn't right, before you leave we have to find you one that is,' she told me, and went to get a pen and paper.

We started making a list of everything I enjoyed. Then Sarah crossed out any references I'd made to Ben and going to bars. It was a thin list. 'For God's sake, Ruth, there's nothing here. Unless you count watching TV and cooking as career options. And you can't even cook.' Sarah was angry.

'Ruth, you've got to make some effort. You may think you can make a career out of missing Ben but you can't. You've got to get on with your life.' Jess was angry.

Sophie came and put her arms around me. 'Babe, it will be OK, we'll help you, promise, we'll find you something.'

I decided then I liked Sophie best.

'I know, I've got it.' Sarah jumped up.

'What?' I was scared now.

'I know this woman — she's a career counsellor.' Sarah looked smug.

'What's a career counsellor?' I asked. It sounded awful.

'A professional who helps you focus on your abilities and

what you enjoy in order to find out what job you'd be suited to. She's very good, she's bound to be able to help you. I'll make you an appointment.'

'So she won't ask me about my childhood?' I asked.

'No, silly, she'll just talk you through what you enjoy. Then she'll give you some career options, maybe some you didn't know existed, and she'll help you to get a job in the area you're interested in.' Sarah was looking determined.

I really didn't want to see this woman. 'You know something, I made a mistake. I actually quite like my job, I think I'll give it a bit longer. If it really doesn't work out then I'll see the career counsellor. Thanks, you guys, you've really helped me loads.' I ran from the room before anyone could say anything.

After upsetting Sarah and Jess, I thought I'd do the grown-up thing and work things out for myself. Everyone else had, so I should have been able to. First I gave serious consideration to my current job. There was no one in the office I liked, apart from Brian and he wore cardigans. I hated selling, I was bad at it. I hated my boss, especially as lately he had devoted his day to motivating me and, well, that was it. I couldn't stay there much longer. But I would stay until either they fired me or I had worked out where I could go from there. I had to lie down. I had to think. Do I really want a career? Well, perhaps. I mean, it's not as if I've given it much thought. I picked up Ben's photo. 'Did you take my ambition away?' But, as nice as it would have been, I couldn't blame Ben. I couldn't remember when I was ever interested in doing anything other than men. Ha, not even as a baby. When I was a baby I spent hours eyeing up boy babies in their prams.

Perhaps I shouldn't have dismissed being a career woman. Perhaps somewhere buried deep inside I had some ambition. After all, I used to watch *Dynasty* and I always wanted to be Alexis. Alexis was style, shoulder-pads, hair, perfect make-up, long, painted nails and a string of men in love with her. And she was a great bitch who owned her own corporation. You see, I liked that idea. Although the shoulder-pads and being a bitch were a bit *passé*, perhaps there was still something in my love of Alexis that meant I should consider the career thing. Perhaps I could have it all, I thought. Perhaps I would like to have it all.

She wakes at six in the morning, feeling wonderfully refreshed from her sleep and dreams. She reaches out to the man beside her, who, after all this time, still fills her with desire. He smiles at her sleepily, kissing her tenderly. As happens most mornings, they make love passionately. At half past six the bedroom door opens and their two children rush in. They hug and kiss their mother and father, whom they love and by whom they do not feel at all neglected. Mother and father, wife and husband, their lives are wonderful. They go downstairs and prepare breakfast. She puts the toast on, he makes coffee; the children's cereal had been laid out the night before. The children eat their breakfast and chat to their parents about the day ahead at school. She drinks her coffee and eats her toast while mentally planning her day. Her husband looks at her lovingly and thinks how lucky he is. At a quarter past seven she goes to take a shower and he starts to get the children ready for school. Once dressed and perfectly made up, she takes over the children and he gets ready for work.

At eight they all leave the house together, dropping the children off at school with loving kisses. Then she drives her husband to the station and she goes to her office. He is a highly successful businessman, she a highly successful businesswoman. The day is wonderful, she loves her job. She does everything she has to. Her husband phones to tell her he loves her, she does the same to him. After a very successful day in the office she leaves at half past five and drives to the station to pick up her husband at six. They discuss their respective days, he asks her advice on a problem, she gives it.

When they get home the children rush to greet them, the nanny leaves. The house is spotless, the children have done their homework, and now she prepares dinner with her husband. They have a glass of wine. Dinner is at seven, the food is home-made and healthy. It is a family affair. At eight the children are put to bed, after kissing their parents and telling them how much they love them. Then they sit down, with some wine and talk. At eleven, unable to resist each other any more they go to bed and make love for the second time that day.

It didn't sound so bad, sort of the modern-day *Waltons*. But, then, was it attainable? The problem I had was that I still hadn't named her job and I couldn't think of one I'd enjoy. The second problem was, what if I couldn't find a modern man as a husband, one who would be willing to split the home tasks? I mean, Ben wouldn't, would he? Not ready to dismiss this idea, I called my mother.

My mother had always worked full-time, but she also took care of the house. I asked her how she managed to come home from work, cook dinner, supervise my homework and keep the house clean. She told me she just did. I then spoke to my father and asked him how come he came home from work, watched TV, went to his study and watched more TV. He asked me if I'd gone mad.

I was not convinced that although women had the chance to move into a man's world men had accepted that the traditional roles in the home had changed. I didn't want to have to be a superwoman. I was worried that women having it all meant women doing it all.

Perhaps here was an opportunity to create a modern day housewife, a role that would be attractive to some women, but more importantly it would be fantastically appealing for men because they would have to pay for it. I knew that not every woman wanted to be a housewife and I didn't think they should have to, any more than I should want to be a career woman. But it would be nice if being a housewife, or wanting to be one, didn't have a huge stigma attached to it.

The housewife gets up for the second time at about ten in the morning. She'd already got up to get her husband off to work and make his breakfast, but she then went back to bed to read the paper, or just to have a nap. She does her exercise video — must look good for her man. She then showers and dresses. She has breakfast and deals with the mail, all complex household issues, like bills, are her responsibility, and she makes sure that the household accounts are up-to-date. Her husband phones at eleven to tell her how much he loves and values her; she tells him the same.

She goes out to get the shopping. At home again, she puts it away and cleans the house. She calls her friend, who comes over for lunch. They gossip and drink lots of tea. In the afternoon her husband calls again to tell her he loves her. She bakes for the weekend, all her husband's favourites. At four she goes to her Spanish class, which she attends twice a week; the other days she does pottery and dressmaking. She will soon be able to speak Spanish, have lots of pots and actually make a dress.

At half past five she begins to prepare dinner. She opens the wine. At seven, when her husband returns home from a hard day in the office, she puts his dinner on the table.

Now I didn't think that sounded too dull. Liking the idea, I tried it out with Jess.

She looked at me. 'If that's the life you want, you really need to see Sarah's career counsellor.'

I was upset. 'It doesn't have to be dressmaking,' I tell her.

I returned to work with the aim of giving it one last go, and my friends gave me a reprieve. They went back to their lives and left me to mine. The good thing was that Jess had met a man and said she really liked him. His name was Sam, he had a job in corporate finance, whatever that was, and he was very, very driven. Jess had invited him round for drinks. Unlike Sophie, who needed her friends' approval, Jess wanted her friends to intimidate her men early on in the relationship.

He arrived and seemed nice, friendly, not too flashy. He was tall, with very short, neat hair that seemed to be sort of dark grey. I thought he probably looked older than thirty. He asked the usual what-do-you-do-for-a-living? questions, and everyone gave him their replies. He was interested and asked polite questions, then it came to me.

'I'm working until I get married and become a housewife. Of course I need a husband and a house first, but as soon as I find them my working days are history.'

'Really?' He looked surprised. He continued, 'That's great, it really is. God, I wish more women felt like you.' Jess lost all the colour in her face. Sam obviously didn't know her very well, and it looked as though he might not get to know her any better.

'You don't mean that,' Jess said.

'I do. I think that if a woman wants to stay at home, looking after the house and the children, that's lovely. When I marry I'd like my wife to stay at home – definitely when we have children.'

Jess went purple, Sophie looked ready to do a runner and Sarah drank her wine in one.

I decided that as this was my fault, I'd try to defuse the situation. 'Sam, I'll marry you.'

Everyone laughed, apart from Jess who was getting more purple by the minute.

'How could you be such a pig? God, men like you should be made illegal. I don't believe you. What if your woman doesn't want to be kept barefoot and pregnant? This is 1999. Even if Ruthie doesn't realise it. And you have no right to expect women to stay at home. Who the hell do you think you are? You're a bloody stupid old-fashioned tosser.' She was screaming.

Sam laughed, which wasn't a good idea because just as it looked like Jess couldn't get any more purple she did. 'Jess, I just said that I'd like my wife to stay at home. I don't expect you to. We don't all have to share the same views, and we can't all embrace the modern world. Anyway, sugar, I think it's great that women are doing so well, I really do.

I just don't want to marry a career woman.' He flashed her his best smile.

It didn't work. 'No, of course you don't. You don't want to marry a career woman because she won't have enough time to dote on you, wait on you hand and foot, take care of your every sodding whim. You are just a typical lazy, egotistical, ignorant, chauvinistic, bloody-minded male. I want you to leave,' Jess replied.

Sam left. Which was really no surprise as, in his place, I would have left too.

We all looked at Jess, who was returning to her normal colour. She had probably overreacted, and if Sam had been dating me she would have been quite calm. In her eyes, though, Jess was dating a Neanderthal. That was the worst thing in the world to her: she was dating someone who didn't understand how important her career was to her and, even though they weren't close to getting married, he had committed the worst crime. He wanted someone who was everything Jess wasn't. He wanted someone like me.

'What a wanker,' she said finally.

'Are you all right?' Sophie asked.

'Yes, I'm fine.' Jess burst into tears, and she never does that. 'I shouldn't have made such a big deal. You know how I feel, but I shouldn't have made such a fool of myself.'

'Jess, you didn't make a fool of yourself, I think Sam looked the fool there.' I gave her a tissue.

'Did you see his face when you called him an egotistical, chauvinistic whatever? He looked really embarrassed.' Sophie laughed.

'I quite liked him,' Jess admitted.

'I know, hon, but, well, I think it's obvious you weren't really suited,' Sarah said.

'I wish I'd found him first.' I laughed. Everyone laughed.

'It's not too late. I'm sure if you run you can catch him,' Jess said. We laughed more. 'Why are men so difficult?' she asked.

I thought about it. 'I think we made them that way.'

Jess was not upset for long, as Jess never is, but she did say that she would be more careful about whom she dated in future. I said I would too, but as I never met any men there was really no need. My social life was as interesting as Peter Stringfellow: not at all interesting. I needed to go out more.

My social life in London had consisted of a date with Simon, a couple of nights out in the Sun in Clapham and a lunchtime drink with Cardigan Brian. That was it. No wild parties, not a single club. It was pitiful. I was twenty-one years old and my social life was dead. I decided to do something about it. I told my friends they had to take me out. The only times I spent with them was when they were in and we'd drink wine and eat pizza. We never went out, really: they reserved that privilege for their other friends. To persuade them, I sank to new depths of emotional blackmail. I told them how being in all the time was making me miss Ben more. How I hadn't met anyone new in ages so how was I expected to get over him? How my work didn't provide me with a social life the way theirs did. Then I cried and begged, so they agreed to reserve the next Saturday night for me. I thanked them profusely, and felt that at least I had something to look forward to for once.

Ingredients for a girls' night out: take four girls, some sexy (but not tarty) clothes, a lot of make-up and a bottle of wine to get ready with. Mix it all together and you get me, Sarah, Sophie and Jess ready to hit London. We all felt differently about the purpose of a proper girls' night out (apart from the fact they were only doing it because they felt sorry for me). It wasn't exactly 'tarts on the town'. I wanted to find a man, but I always wanted to find a man; Sarah wanted to remind herself that she wasn't missing out on anything by staying single; Jess liked to laugh at everyone, and Sophie just liked to be with us. For me it was the biggest event in ages.

'Jessie, can I borrow your little black top?' I was intent on wearing my favourite blue hipsters, and I needed a little black top to reveal what cleavage I had. Jess's top provided cleavage.

'OK, but, Ru, can I borrow your satin shirt?' Jess had decided to wear a hip-hugging velvet skirt, so short it was almost obscene. I had to admit that my satin shirt, which was deep red, looked pretty hot with her big brown eyes.

'Deal. Sophie, can I use your new eye-shadow?' I ran into the bathroom where Sophie was expertly applying her make-up. She looked sensational in tight cropped black pants and a little cropped top. We mock-fought for space in front of the mirror as I took out the blusher brush.

'Yup. Have you got any mascara?'

I passed it to her. 'Here you go.'

We curled, blushed, lip-lined and generally slapped on the makeup.

'Sarah, have you opened the wine yet?'

Sarah appeared wearing her uniform baggy black trousers and white blouse. She had swapped her glasses for contact lenses but was wearing very little make-up. 'I'm just doing it.' She blew me a kiss as she swept downstairs.

I followed, trying to stay upright in my high heels, Sophie followed in her flatties, and Jess clomped behind us in her new black mules.

'Well, I'm ready and it only took me half an hour,' I said, as I flopped down at the kitchen table.

'What about the hour you spent in the bathroom? What were you doing? Shaving your legs and armpits in case you get lucky tonight?' Jess giggled as she took her first sip of wine.

'Don't be mean, Jess. I'm sure Ruthie isn't the sort of girl who lets a little body hair get in the way of true love.' Sarah giggled and poured another glass for Sophie.

'Will both of you stop taking the piss? I'm getting some more wine.' I went to refill our glasses. 'Sarah, if you meet a really gorgeous fellow tonight, will you give up your vow of celibacy?' I asked.

'No. I told you, I'm not getting involved. Men and sex bore me, and before you say anything, I'm not turning into a lesbian. Living with you lot has put me off women too.'

'Ha, ha. I don't know how you manage it. I mean, I don't sleep with men because I'm still heartbroken but, well, you could,' I said.

'You don't sleep with men because you don't know any,' Jess laughed, 'and not everyone is sex crazed.'

'I am not sex crazed!'

'Yes, you are,' everyone said.

Sophie stood up.

'Wow, Soph, you look gorgeous. It's a shame you're already taken.'

Sophie giggled. 'Yes, I am.'

I wished she would try harder not to look smug.

'I have a feeling I may meet someone tonight,' Jess said, the Sam incident well and truly forgotten.

'I hope I do,' I agreed.

'I think we should go before I realise what a bad idea this really is.' Sarah grabbed her coat and, after applying the last layer of lipstick, we left.

Jess had said that we were going to The Cellar Bar. No one dared argue: since her life in PR had started, Jess only went out in Fulham, South Kensington and Chelsea. We got there at nine, it was downstairs and looked a bit dark and dingy, but quite funky and littered with men. We ordered drinks. Then I did the thing I always did at university. 'I'm just going for a pee,' I said.

'Liar. You're going to check out the men,' Sarah said.

'OK, I'll come with you,' Jess said, and off we went.

We did a subtle circuit of the bar and I spotted a group of four who didn't look so bad. I tried to catch their eyes, but they seemed intent on not looking my way. 'Jess, what about those four over there?'

She looked. 'Where?'

'Over there – keep your voice down.'

'What – those four? Don't you think they look a bit young?'

I looked again. 'No younger than us.'

'Oh, I just thought I might try to find an older man tonight.' We made our way back to the others and I saw Jess's ideal man. 'Look, Jess, at the bar, he must be at least fifty.'

'Piss off, Ru.'

'What have you found?' Sarah asked.

'Four lovely men over there, but Jess wants Granddad at the bar.' Jess hit me. We had a couple more drinks.

Jess took the piss out of every outfit that every girl was wearing. 'Oh, she shouldn't wear that with her figure,' she said, about an overweight girl in knee-length boots and a mini skirt. 'God, if she had real friends they'd never let her go out in public like that.' I looked at Jess, all hips and boobs, and thought that maybe we should have said something to her. Well, if we'd lost the will to live. Then she pointed to four girls who looked about six and were wearing tiny little dresses. 'You need to wear a cardy with those.'

We all laughed.

Then I decided it was time to make our move. 'Let's go and stand near those guys.' They all followed me as I stalked my prey. When trying to attract the attention of men, while still being subtle, you can do one of two things. The first is to sound as if you're the funniest person on earth: you laugh a lot and get your friends to laugh a lot too. The trouble is my friends refused to do this. The other is to make Sophie stand somewhere prominent. In about five seconds flat she is surrounded by men. My plan never failed.

The four boys made their way over and the nicest-looking went straight up to Sophie. As she wasn't interested it was a shame, but then I got to talk to a guy called Andy, who was good-looking in a sweet kind of way. He was quite tall – well, taller than me – he was slim, or skinny, really, he had nice short brown hair, brown eyes, and he was definitely under thirty. He didn't tell me what he did for a living, so I couldn't rate him on the job scale but, then, he didn't ask what I did, which pleased me. Jess was talking to another guy who looked terrified, laughing and saying, 'Fab,' a lot, and Sarah had terrified the last one, who had slunk off to the bar. Sophie made her excuses, and she and Sarah went to dance on the tiny dance-floor. After a while Jess left the guy she was talking to and went to join Sarah and Sophie. He slunk to the defeated corner with his other friends. I was getting on well with Andy. I was at the very drunk and very flirty-bordering-on-sluttish-behaviour stage, standing very close, talking in my best sexy voice and giving my come-to-bed looks, which seemed to be working, he seemed absolutely overawed by me.

He went to the bar to get a drink and Jess came over. 'There's something you should know.'

'Not now, I'm pulling.'

'Yes, you are but, Ru, there's something you should know.'

'What?'

'Do you know what he does for a living?'

'No, I haven't asked yet.' I was annoyed.

'Well, he doesn't do anything. He's at school, he's doing his A levels and he's not even old enough to drink alcohol!' Jess could no longer suppress her giggles.

I was totally stunned. 'Get me out of here.' We escaped from the bar leaving Andy holding two drinks and looking devastated.

Once outside we burst out laughing.

'Ruthie, it was obvious they were young. I mean, they were so awkward and out of place.'

I was indignant. 'Actually, Andy was quite sophisticated.'

'Yes, for a seventeen-year-old I'm sure he was. I wonder if their parents knew where they were.'

I hadn't seen Sarah laugh this much in ages. 'I'm glad you find it so funny. I don't. Where now?'

'We'll go to the Fez club, I'm sure we'll find you someone there.' It was also dark. I guessed that Fulham revolved around being dark. We paid at the till, handed over our coats and walked in. The first thing that struck me as soon as I regained my eyesight was that it was very full. It was also hot and sweaty. Couples littered the outside of the room and men littered the dance-floor. We bought drinks, which cost a week's income. Even Jess flinched as she handed over her money. Then we stood near the dance-floor. In the Fez club Jess was worse than anything: she was manic and went around talking to every man she saw, asking them where they came from. She moved from one as quickly as she found another. After half an hour, she had asked every single one where they lived and apparently none lived in Fulham, which made them big no-nos in Jess's eyes. 'I can't believe I came to Fulham to pull and every single man I meet lives in Shepherd's bloody Bush.'

We all giggled at her snobbery.

'Perhaps you should go out in Shepherd's Bush,' Sarah suggested.

I hadn't met any more men but by this stage I didn't care. We drank more and had a good dance, and Jess abused every man she met. We fell into our flat sometime in the middle of the night. I was snogless and manless, but too drunk to care.

Saturday night had been fun, but on Sunday the gloom of the impending Monday hit. I couldn't stop thinking about work. I figured out that the reason I couldn't be a salesperson was that I felt guilty pushing people to buy. If I detected any reluctance I had to stop, retreat, because I was too embarrassed to try to persuade anyone that they really wanted my product. That was not the sales mentality. My boss said that at the beginning of a conversation they might be a little reluctant but that was because they didn't yet know they wanted that product, but with a little pushing from us they would realise they couldn't live without it. I didn't believe him. Apart from the fact that I was bored to tears by the product (the magazine), selling was just not in my nature. Salesmen don't feel guilt, they don't say, 'I'm so sorry to have bothered you, 'bye,' when they detect that someone is uninterested. They always arrange to call again to see if the person has changed their mind. I got the hang of calling again, but I'd hang up when they answered. I was scared of selling, so I turned into a nuisance phone caller.

From the word go, my sales days were pretty much numbered. My boss had even got fed up with giving me cheery motivational pep talks every morning, ('Sell, sell, sell, positive attitude and you're so hungry for the deal I can hear your stomach rumbling'). Actually, he probably *could* hear my stomach rumbling, I never had time for breakfast. I thought it was quite sweet of him to be so persistent, but then I learned that sales managers took it as a personal insult to have a new trainee fail.

In desperation, he came up with a new strategy. I was to go out to a meeting. He said that the problem might be the telephone and with face-to-face contact I might fare better. He arranged for me to take a client to lunch. The client turned out to be the son of a client, but important all the same. He was Mike Woods of Woods Construction. A son, so he must be young, father owned a big company, so rich. I was beginning to feel a little excited by all this.

The next day at work, Steve gave me a pep talk on how to handle a lunch. He told me it was a big responsibility, but he was sure that I would rise to the challenge. I was not to drink too much, to keep asking 'open questions', to bring the magazine into the conversation as much as possible and to come away with an order for more advertising. What could be simpler?

We had booked a restaurant in Soho. Mike Woods was from Yorkshire, so Steve seemed to think he would be impressed by Soho, don't ask me why. I turned up at the restaurant at noon. It was quite a trendy place, all white tablecloths and French bread. Mike turned up shortly afterwards. 'Hello there, you must be Ruth.' He shook my hand and I noticed that he had short clean fingernails. He was tall, not gorgeous but not ugly, broad, healthy complexion and quite young — well, I think he was under thirty anyway. He had white hair and baby blue eyes — actually they were quite small and I *think* they were blue. The only really bad thing was his prominent ears. Still, not bad . . . not bad at all.

'Yes, Mike, nice to meet you.' I put on my best businesslike voice, with only a hint of flirtation.

We sat down, and straight away Mike ordered some wine. 'Don't know about you but I fancy getting drunk,' he said.

I laughed, worried about not drinking too much. 'So, you run a construction company?' I asked.

'Yes, it's me dad's, really, but he's old now so I do all the work, pull all the strings, have the power, y'know what I mean.' He winked at me — well, I think he was winking, he might have had a squint.

'Well, you're a very valued customer of the magazine.' I squinted back as I flattered him.

'What? Oh, yeah, sure. You ready to order? I'm famished.' We ordered lunch and started on the wine.

'The magazine is growing very fast. Its circulation figures have doubled recently.' Steve would have been proud of me.

'Oh, we don't want to talk about that now. Tell me about yourself, Ruth.' I gave up. He obviously was as interested in my magazine as I was, so we discussed other things. Like me and London and Yorkshire, and how powerful Mike was, and then we had another bottle of wine. I was feeling a little tipsy. I'm not the best drinker but at lunchtimes I'm even worse. After lunch, he ordered port and we sat smoking and getting drunk.

He could certainly drink and smoke excessively. I couldn't. I was wasted.

'I don't know about you, but I've had a lovely time.' Mike took my hand.

'Oh.' I was pleased, yet a little surprised. 'Me too.'

'So, how about we go back to my hotel and continue the party?' He winked at me again.

I remembered all Steve had said, and as I had broken every rule already I decided to go for it. I knew I shouldn't but reason had left me. 'OK,' I said.

We got to his hotel room, which was huge and expensive. Mike headed straight to the mini-bar. I thought as I walked in that the receptionist must have thought I was a prostitute, and actually, in a perverse way, I preferred that to his thinking I was a slutty salesperson. Mike told me I was sexy, then I giggled and told him he was. Actually, he *was* sexy but, then, I was drunk. He touched my hair, and my stomach churned. I touched his and he kissed me. It was an insistent kiss, verging on the harsh, bruised-lip kind, but it was so nice just to be kissed. I lost control. I pulled myself out of my jacket and undid my blouse, the whole time watching him watching me. He kissed me again and, with one hand, expertly undid my bra. He took off his jacket and I undid his tie, which took me quite a while. He undid his shirt while I kissed him and pushed my breasts into his face, he took them in his mouth, one after the other. My nipples hardened and I could feel he did too. I wanted him so badly.

It was his cufflinks that put an end to the smooth seduction. We couldn't get them undone. First he tried, then I tried, then we both tried. He was getting frustrated and I worried about what might not happen if he couldn't undo them. Then I remembered that he could keep his shirt on as we made love.

'Leave it,' I commanded, in my best sexy voice. I made a mental note only to sleep with men who had buttoned cuffs. I pulled off my skirt and he pulled off his trousers to reveal a pair of Y-fronts. I averted my eyes until he had taken them off, then gasped as I saw him naked. He had a really nice penis. He pushed me on to the bed, took out a condom from the bedside table and, without any foreplay, he made love to me. He was amazing. He started on top of me, slowly at first, then more quickly, more urgent. Then I climbed on top of him, pinning his arms down, teasing him, taunting him. I felt like I was in a movie.

Mike was an enthusiastic lover: he kept making whooping noises, saying 'Bloody 'ell,' 'Blimey,' 'By 'eck,' and, well, lots of words beginning with B. Then he got back on top and we just rolled over and over again fast and furious, until he suddenly collapsed on top of me. It was over before I was ready, but I tried not to mind. I had never had sex with a northerner before, but Mike was great, he was fantastic, he was totally 'by 'eck'.

We had an afternoon of wild sex in a hotel, I felt like a rock chick and I could see myself married to Mike with lots of wild afternoons like this in my future. I must have dozed off thinking about our future because when I awoke it was five o'clock, my hair was stuck to my face and I had a horrible headache. 'Shit!' I screamed.

'What?' Mike looked the worse for wear too. Actually, he looked horrible.

'I've got to get back to the office.' Frantically I pulled my clothes on.

'OK, 'bye now,' Mike went back to sleep. He didn't even kiss me goodbye. I felt sick, and my head was pounding. I got a cab back to the office.

Steve was in his office when I walked in. 'Where the hell have you been?'

I thought quickly. 'Um, Mike was really ill, something he ate, I had to take care of him,' I said, as I realised my hair was still stuck to my head.

'Really? Then why has his father been calling me all

afternoon, saying that Mike was supposed to be at some important appointments and hadn't shown up?'

Oh, shit. 'Well, he was ill, I guess he forgot.'

'His father is the organ grinder, it turns out, and Mike his monkey. Ruth, if you've messed this account up I'll kill you,' Steve shouted.

I went home and took a bath. I felt awful. Hung-over, tired and upset at Steve. He had obviously known I was lying. I put on my dressing-gown and went into the lounge. No one was at home. I cried.

I was just pulling myself together when Sarah came home. She looked at me. 'What's happened, Ruth?' I burst into tears again. 'Tell me,' she commanded, and handed me a tissue.

'I had a client lunch today, the one I told you about.' I had to stop, I was crying so hard.

'Look,' Sarah said, 'if the client didn't like you, it's not the end of the world. Not all my clients liked me at first. It took a lot of work.' Sarah had her best sympathetic voice on.

'He did like me, that's the trouble.' Part of me wanted to tell Sarah what had happened so that she could tell me it wasn't that bad, but part of me knew she'd say it was incredibly bad.

'I don't understand. Now, take a deep breath and tell me what happened.'

'I met him for lunch. He was young and northern and nice and he ordered wine and we ate and he ordered more wine, then port and I was drunk and he took me back to his hotel and we, you know, and it was five o'clock and I went back to the office and I told Steve that Mike was ill and he shouted at me because Mike's dad owns the company and he'd been calling all afternoon because Mike had missed loads of appointments and everyone thinks it's my fault.'

Sarah looked stunned. 'You slept with your client?' I nodded. 'My God, you really had sex with him?'

'Yes, and I'm really sorry.' I knew she'd be shocked. Now, even I was shocked.

'Ruthie, hon, do you know what you've done?'

'Yes, I broke all the rules and now I'm going to get sacked. I'm *sooo* stupid,' I sobbed.

'I'm not going to lecture you. You look like you need some food — I'll make some pasta.' Sarah went to the kitchen.

Jess arrived home. 'What the fuck happened to you? You look dreadful.'

'Sarah's making dinner. If you tell her you're back, she'll probably make you some too.'

Jess gave me a funny look and went to the kitchen. After what seemed like ages, they reappeared with food. I tried to eat, but it was the last thing I felt like doing.

'You really slept with your client?' Jess asked. I nodded. 'My God, Ruthie, what happens if your boss finds out?'

I looked at her. 'I get sacked.'

Jess looked thoughtful. 'Well, it depends. I mean, I don't approve of women using their bodies to advance their careers, but if your client had a good time he might increase the business.' Jess smiled.

'It hadn't occurred to me that I was advancing my career. I was drunk. That's why I slept with him. I was drunk and lonely, no other reason.'

'All right, but let's look at damage limitation. Tomorrow you call him, tell him you had a great time, he'll give you some orders and you'll be a hero.' Jess was trying hard to be helpful.

'It's not that easy,' I wailed. 'I think my boss is already suspicious and it turns out the client is not really the client but the monkey.'

My friends looked at me confused.

'He's a monkey?'

'No, his father is the client, Mike was just his son. Oh, God.'

Jess and Sarah exchanged glances. 'It's worse than I thought,' Sarah said.

I burst into tears. 'What am I going to do?' I asked, but they just shrugged. I'd really defeated them this time and it had defeated me.

Sleep can sometimes offer clarity. I woke feeling positive and decisive. I went to work. There were two significant events at the magazine that day. I handed in my notice, and Henry Woods called to cancel all future advertising with the magazine.

I had opened Pandora's box and nothing good was in there. All I could see was despair, depression, disease. Hope was nowhere. I looked hard, but the box was just full of bad things. I closed it. I was glad it was Pandora's box and not mine. I could see him up ahead, the man in Armani, and I could make out it was Ben. Ben was my man in Armani. I started running towards him, I could see him clearly now, but he was so far away. He was smiling. The faster I ran the further away he seemed, so I ran faster and faster, but no matter how fast I ran I couldn't reach him. Then all of a sudden he was gone. I was too slow, he was tired of waiting for me. It was my fault he was gone.

I have never been one for analysing dreams. I think there's too much in life we need to interpret, and dreams can be magical so they should be left alone. So, whatever you dream shouldn't worry you, because when you're awake you can snatch back the control of your imagination you temporarily lost. But that dream bothered me. Sophie was a dream expert. Well, next to me she was — she'd read a couple of books anyway. She told me that there were certain things we could look for in our dreams that help explain them. For instance, running was significant, so was Ben, so was the fact that I couldn't get him, but more significant than anything was that he was smiling and I ended up blaming myself for not reaching him. Sophie said that logic would say he could have met me half-way, but my dream was telling me that Ben was gone, he wasn't coming back no matter how hard I tried, and I still blamed myself for his going. Also, the smile indicated that he was happy. I wished I'd never asked.

'Sophie, what does the Armani suit mean?'

'Um, I think that's just wishful thinking,' she replied.

So, the fact that I was now unemployed, or about to become so as soon as I'd worked out my week's notice, (still on probation, luckily, so I didn't have to wait a month), and that I'd had this horrible dream left me feeling rather restless.

Sarah and Jess decided it was time I thought seriously about my career. Jess gave me another long lecture on the joys of PR, but I told her I really didn't think PR was for me. Sarah agreed and again brought up the career counsellor. Sophie (Judas) agreed with Sarah, and Thomas said he couldn't think of anything I'd be good at, but not to worry because they let women do most things these days.

'Ruth, PR is the best, most fulfilling job in the world. It stretches you, but it also gives you a social life, I could talk to some people for you.' Dear Jess.

'Um, that's really kind, but do you think that maybe I should see Sarah's woman first?'

Sarah looked triumphant, Jess looked confused and Thomas said, 'Right, now we've sorted out Ruthie's career, can we talk about sex?'

Sarah had made me an appointment for the following afternoon – she'd already done it. She'd won. I was going to see a career counsellor. I went to the appointment, as told. Sarah had armed me with two warnings. The first was that if I didn't turn up, she would make my life a misery, the second, that if I didn't behave myself, as it was a business contact of hers, she would make my life a misery. I decided to try to be positive but, then, I couldn't promise anything, could I?

I walked into some posh offices, and realised that these careers counsellors were not doing this from the goodness of their hearts. My appointment was with Rosalind Parker and she met me almost straight away. I hated her instantly. She was tall, very thin with a pointed nose. Her suit was so impeccable it didn't look worn at all, and she had a thin-lipped smile, the kind you should never trust. She led me into her office where I sat down in a big armchair (not a couch in sight) and suddenly I felt angry at having to do this. I felt I had failed, I couldn't sort things out on my own, I was reduced to this.

'So, Ruth, why have you come to see me?' she asked.

'Because Sarah made me.' I had resorted to sulky-child mode.

Rosalind looked at me, then smiled. 'Let's start with a few basic CV details, shall we?' She took out a pad. 'Name?'

'Ruth Butler.'

'Age?'

'Twenty-one.'

'Driving licence?'

'Yes.'

'Marital status?'

'Um, single, recently singled, but never married, not even engaged to be married, not living with someone. *I don't have a man.*' I was a little upset by that question.

Rosalind looked a bit shocked. 'OK, fine, good. Now, let's talk about your career history. How many jobs have you had?'

'One.'

'OK, and what was it?' She was now patronising me.

'I was selling space on *Nuts and Bolts Monthly*. I don't expect you've heard of it. I recently had to leave because I didn't sell anything and I slept with a client's son and he cancelled all the advertising and if I hadn't resigned they would have sacked me and they're making me work out my notice as punishment for not getting to sack me.'

Rosalind went a bit white. 'Can you get a reference from them?'

I laughed. 'After the trail of destruction I left?'

She tried a different tack. 'What do you think a career counsellor does?'

I was tempted, but remembered Sarah's threats. 'Helps people decide what career they'd enjoy, then helps them to get a job?' I said helpfully.

'Yes, sort of. I mean, we try to help you decide what you're looking for and then we give advice on how to get into your chosen field. Some people come to us knowing what they want, but feeling a bit unsure of how to go about getting it. Others come thinking they don't know what they want. Which category do you feel you're in?'

'If I have to be in a category, as you put it, I would be the second, but not even that. You see, I don't want a career.'

Rosalind went white for the second time. 'What do you mean?'

'I'm just working to earn a living until I get married. I told you, it's only my friends who think I should have a career.'

'I don't understand.'

I almost felt sorry for her: she looked confused. 'Can I ask you, Rosalind, are you married?'

'No.'

'Well, when you get married, will you cook for your husband and do the laundry and clean the flat, or will you share the chores?' I asked.

'We'd share the chores.'

'OK, so you find a man who'll share the chores. What about when you have kids, will you work fewer hours?'

'I don't see what this has to do with anything, but I suppose I'll get a nanny.'

'OK, so you'll have a demanding job, run a house, have a healthy relationship with your husband – who, by the way, I wonder if you'll have time to meet, and spend enough quality time with your children.'

'Ruth, lots of women do just that and the children don't grow up dysfunctional. But I still do not understand what my marital status has to do with you not wanting a career.'

'Well, I believe that love is the most natural and important thing in the world. I want to fall in love, get married, have children and spend "my career" looking after the things that are most important to me. Not in some crummy office working all the hours God sends.'

'Fine, but you said you don't even have a boyfriend, let alone a husband. Have you considered the fact that you might enjoy a career until you get one?'

I felt she was being a little sarcastic now. 'Do you have a boyfriend?'

Rosalind was losing her cool. 'I really don't see why you need to know this, but no.'

'OK, so you don't get much chance to meet men, being so career-focused. I'm sorry, but I don't want to miss my Mr Right just because I'm busy.'

Now she looked pissed off. 'Did you have a normal childhood?'

I looked at her. I had thought she wasn't supposed to ask me that. 'Oh, no, you're a career counsellor, not a sit-on-my-couch-and-tell-me-about-your-mother counsellor.'

'Well, Ruth, it's just that I'm trying to understand you so we can move on to your career options. At the moment I don't know where you're coming from.'

I was certain now that we were at war. 'I didn't have a dysfunctional childhood. In fact, I had a very functional one. The only mental cruelty my parents inflicted on me was when my mother insisted on me wearing a ra-ra skirt. However, I have forgiven her for that – well, after she burnt all the photos anyway.' I gave my coldest smile.

Rosalind sighed. 'OK, let's move on. You said you liked children. Have you considered working with them?'

'What?'

'Become a teacher or something like that.'

'No way. I don't like children that much – of course I'll love mine, but teaching, no. It's a noble profession and everything, and you do get a lot of holidays, but it's also bloody hard work and you don't get much money.'

'Would you consider yourself lazy?'

'Yes.'

'Do you have any hobbies?'

'I like cooking and wine.'

'Great. You could become a cook, or a caterer, or go into restaurant management.' Rosalind gazed at me desperately.

'Oh, no, I only cook for my friends, and I'm not even that good yet.'

'What about the wine business?'

'I only like drinking it.'

'I think, Ruth, to be honest, you refuse to explore any avenue apart from the romantic ideal you've set yourself. I can't help you if you won't help yourself.'

'Can I go now?'

I had defeated her. She nodded and I left. I knew full well I was being awkward and, well, a bitch – but, come on, she wasn't really trying to help. It was a load of twaddle.

Sarah was eager to know how I'd got on and I told her, leaving out certain details, the parts where I'd insulted Rosalind, had been sulky and intrusive ... and generally all the details. 'She said I should just get an administrative job or something, because I'd be happiest being a housewife.'

Sarah was puzzled. 'Really?' she asked. I nodded. 'Well, that's the last time I give her any business.'

For a moment I felt guilty, but then again, less business meant Rosalind could devote more time to finding herself a man.

Chapter Five

The heroine of our story licked her bright red lips. 'I defy any man to resist me,' she said, as she pouted in the mirror. She had a plan. It was the most elaborate of all plans. It involved seduction, deceit, cunning and a Harvey Nichols store card. She laughed as she thought of her prey, men waiting to be captured. Our heroine couldn't fail. She had the looks, she had the lipstick. She would find her man and he would be powerless to resist her. He would fall at her feet and stay there for ever more. He would be under her spell, he would be hers.

The heroine must go now, she has men to catch. They'll be tall, handsome, with a very large wallet. Those are the credentials. Love doesn't come into it. Love doesn't matter when you're a *femme fatale*.

Sarah was almost defeated. She had tried to pull her best hand, Rosalind, and it hadn't worked. I was no nearer to becoming a career woman than she was to having sex. I felt empowered. Privately, Rosalind had helped me; she had helped me to find focus. A career was not going to happen for me. It was obvious. The evidence pointed to one thing: Ruth Butler was not, in any shape or form, made to be a career woman. Ruth Butler was not meant to be without a man. Ruth Butler had to take control of her own destiny. I decided myself what my next career would be. I was going to go out and get myself a husband. My job title would be 'husband-hunter' and I would not fail. Oh, no. I was going to put an end to this career nonsense once and for all.

I decided that, with my new-found confidence, my plan was going to work with a little help from my friends. I pounced on them that evening as we all sat in front of *EastEnders*. 'Now, let me tell you what I want to do, as you're all so interested in my life. First I want to get an administrative job, something not too stressful — and, Sarah, I expect you to help me get one. Second, I'm going to find a husband and then become a housewife and, Jess and Sophie, I expect you to help me do that. If you meet single men, you keep me in mind. OK? Do you understand?'

They just stared at me as if I had flipped, and perhaps I had. Sarah was the first to speak.

'OK, I'll get you a job. Come into my office on Monday and we'll find you something.'

God, that had been easy. Jess and Sophie were still silent.

'But before I get you a job, I just want you to consider something.' She was almost defeated, but not quite.

'What?' I replied. I couldn't understand how I had gone from being in control, to Sarah being in control.

'What do you want from life? Do you want Rubber gloves or Jimmy Choos?'

'What?' Sarah had flipped, I didn't have a clue what she was talking about.

'You know, do you want a pair of washing-up gloves or a pair of lovely Jimmy Choo shoes?'

'Why can't I have both?' I still didn't follow.

'You could, if you could pay for both. What I'm trying to say is, sure, you may be able to find a man to support you totally, even in this day and age. But is he going to be rich? Unless he is, you'll be confined to wearing washing-up gloves and cheap shoes for the rest of your life.' Sarah smiled triumphantly.

I was indignant, I hadn't really considered money. 'This isn't about money, it's about me and what I want spiritually. Of course, I may not find a rich man, but if he loved me I'd be happy with my rubber gloves, honestly I would, and if money was really a problem, I suppose I'd have to work, but only if I had to. I don't need Jimmy Choo shoes to make me happy, I just need love.' I looked at her pleadingly: reality was butting into my life again.

'You're completely and utterly bonkers. The thing is, Ru, that I have aspirations, for myself, for me. It's about what you want from life. Like I said before, I want a flat in Fulham.' Jess was eager to jump on the latest Sarah bandwagon.

Sophie looked at her. 'What's wrong with Clapham?'

'Oh, Soph, there's nothing wrong with Clapham, Clapham's great, but, well, it's not Fulham, is it?' No one could argue with that. Jess got a dreamy look in her eyes. 'You see, Fulham is wonderful. The sun shines more in Fulham, the streets are cleaner, sort of sparkling. You get nicer people there, less crime, even a better class of homeless people.' Jess looked serious.

I now thought *she*'d finally flipped. I had a vision of clean homeless people sitting under their John Lewis duvets and looking pretty, while the nice people of Fulham gave them money and food from the local deli.

Jess carried on. 'It's an area I feel I belong in. Where I know I'll be among like-minded people.'

I made a mental note never to live in Fulham.

Unfortunately this madness had merely irritated Sarah further, and she was still on my case. 'Ruthie, love may be enough for you, I hope it is, but you need money in this day and age to live. Perhaps you should remember that you won't be happy being poor. You can't rely on other people to give you all you want. You have to be prepared to work for it yourself.'

'I won't be poor. I told you I'll work if I have to and, yes, money is necessary, but the chances are I'll marry a professional, so I'll be all right.'

'OK, but in the meantime don't you want to earn money

for yourself, to save, buy nice clothes, have holidays, a good life?'

'Yes, maybe, but can't I do that without a career?'

'Perhaps, but if what you say is true and you want to attract a husband, and preferably a rich one, you need to look nice. All the time. Looking nice costs money and you have to work for money. Also, I don't think you've considered the fact that professional men are attracted to professional women. That's the truth, hon.' Sarah was determined to win, and she was dangerously, dangerously close.

'I'm not looking to attract a husband,' I stated.

Jess and Sophie stared at me. Sarah flung her arms in the air. 'Why the fuck are we having this conversation, then?' She looked thunderous. I was doing my usual backtracking.

'OK, I am, but, well, you just don't understand. I'm going to find a man and he'll be rich and you just don't have to worry about it.'

All of my friends were dumbstruck. Of course I hadn't considered money. All I knew was that I had been working hard on getting over Ben, and to do that and have a good life, I needed someone else. But if Mr Nearly Right was poor and I had to work anyway all my dreams would be shattered. I had two options. Either I could go down the love path and be prepared for whatever happened, or I could just hunt men with enough money to keep me. As much as I am a romantic, I decided that if I had to sacrifice something, it would be love that went. After all, I still wasn't convinced I could love any man but Ben. So, I'd find a rich man, marry him and learn to love him. Oh, no, Sarah is *not* going to put me off this time. I will become a *femme fatale*, a fortune-hunter. Or, at least, a girl looking for a husband with a little bit of disposable income.

Even I knew that by society's standards I was far too young to consider myself a spinster. But I also knew that at a certain stage in life, thirty, thirty-five, forty, women were suddenly given the 'on the shelf' stamp and considered a failure. Not because they didn't have a great career, a sports car, their own flat, but because they didn't have a man. Now how modern was that? I'm sorry, girls, but you're never considered successful unless you have love. Of course, a man would never be judged this way, but that's a different story. Although not yet a spinster, I was not going to be fooled into becoming one. As my friends (bar Sophie) might. They would climb the ladders of success and achieve more and more, and just as they reached the top they would be turned against because they hadn't had time to find love. 'So what if you have a great career? Aren't you lonely? Don't you want babies? Are you gay?' society would scream at them, and then they'd feel cheated because they had just done what they were supposed to do. Society is evil sometimes and unfair. Oh, I recognised the unfairness of the situation: being single is not a crime at any age, but at the same time I don't make the rules. I'm sorry. I wouldn't be caught out like this. I wouldn't let society cheat me. I'd defy it and spend my time finding my mate, not building a career. I'd let it laugh at me now, rather than later. I would outsmart it. Perhaps I was more a product of my time than I gave myself credit for.

All happy endings involve falling in love. So love brings happiness. Even in modern novels every happy ending involves a man and, come to think of it, normally a rich, successful one. I wanted a happy ending, therefore I was only doing what I had to do.

I left my job on Friday and no one threw me a party or wished me luck, but I didn't care. I had what I needed now. I had worked out my future. On Saturday I decided that my plan would be put into action. I found Jess reading. 'Jessie, what are you doing today?'

'Nothing. I thought I'd just chill and read.'

'How boring. Don't you think it might be more fun to go shopping?'

Jess looked interested. 'Where?'

'Harvey Nicks.' I'd got her.

'OK, but we have to look smart.'

I sighed. She was probably worried she'd bump into everyone she worked with. Jess put on a black trouser suit; she looked as if she had money. I had grey trousers and a shirt, Jess chose for me. Then she grabbed her sunglasses.

'Jess, why are you wearing those? It's November.'

'I'm wearing them on my head – they all do, you know. Here, you'd better take my spare pair.'

Harvey Nichols was Jess's favourite place in the whole world. She loved it more than anything, she was such a PR stereotype. I loved it too, because rich men shopped in Harvey Nichols.

We shopped for hours, surrounded by women wearing sunglasses on their heads. I understood now. We started by looking at the cosmetics counters, testing the latest perfumes, or I did because Jess insisted on spraying them on me – she didn't want to smell like a whore's boudoir. Next we went to the women's designer-clothes sections where I found a pretty crochet top, it was white and I thought maybe I could treat myself, until I spotted the price tag. I dropped the dishcloth-like thing. 'Christ,' I shrieked.

'What?' Jess said. 'Is it a spider?'

I shook my head, picked up the string vest and thrust it into her hands. 'Wow, that's quite reasonable.'

'Reasonable, Jess? Reasonable for what? A month's rent? That would be reasonable. A lace hanky? I don't think so.' I was in shock.

'Ru, you're so funny.' Jess dragged me to the shoe department.

I couldn't bring myself to look at prices after that, so I just watched Jess try on shoe after shoe after shoe. This wasn't helping me find my man. 'Jess, can we go and get a drink?'

'Good idea.'

We went to the bar, but I was disappointed to find there weren't many men in there. 'Where are the men?'

'What men?'

'You know, the rich men who always come here.'

'No, they don't.'

'Don't what?'

'They don't come here, not much. I think this is more of a place for fortune-hunters, so the fortunes stay away.'

'No.' I couldn't believe it. Why hadn't she told me before?

'Ru, it figures. Rich men with their wives and girlfriends come here and rich single men do mail order. It's total logic. Sorry, you won't find Mr Right here.'

We went home with an addition to Jess's lipstick collection and sore feet.

So, where did you go to find men? Why was that the best-kept secret of all time? Due to my lack of social life, I had to hunt during the day. How the hell was I going to meet someone?

'Thomas, fix me up with one of your friends,' I begged, when he came over that evening.

He looked at me over his glasses, 'You've got to be joking. You went out with my best friend and now he's left the country.'

I hit him. 'Sarah, do you know any single men?'

She looked at me over her glasses. 'I wouldn't have a clue if they were single or not.'

'Jess?'

She didn't even look at me. 'I don't have time to match-make.'

'Soph?'

Sophie smiled. 'Well, I could probably introduce you to one of James's friends, he's got loads and I think they're all rich – well, they talk about money a lot anyway.'

On second thoughts, 'No, thanks, Soph.'

She looked offended. So on my list of places to meet men, I had struck off Harvey Nichols, my friends and bars. That left one. The supermarket.

I remembered reading that the supermarket was a real pulling place. I knew that wasn't a sign of wealth, but I still thought it might hold potential. And I could go there on my own.

Sunday afternoon, that was bound to be a good time. I prepared carefully: I dressed nicely, put on my makeup and left for the local Sainsbury's. It was not full of single men. It was full of families. I bought some salad and left. I went back that evening – single men, Sunday evening, it made sense – but it was closed. My plan was not as foolproof as I had first thought. Of course, not one to give up easily, I planned to go every night the next week – I was determined to find singles' night.

The job Sarah had got me was as an administrative assistant in the marketing department of a small animal charity. I began with an attitude even less enthusiastic than for job one. Although I considered that if I had to work I might as well do some good but, then, rich men/animal charity, it just didn't tally. Sarah said it was a good job, with prospects, but I didn't want prospects. What good were prospects to me? I promised Sarah I would try hard, but it wasn't easy. There was a problem. My boss was a woman called Annalise and, well, if I'd thought Steve was bad, he had nothing on her. Annalise was a bitch. You could tell just by looking at her. She was the marketing manager and the office rumour was that she had slept with just about everybody important to get her job. I didn't believe it, of course: even I knew that in this day and age men didn't exploit women like that and women didn't need to sleep with men to get good jobs. Jess had taught me that. But I could also see why they said it about Annalise: she was so horrible.

Janie, the department secretary, told me that Annalise had got my predecessor to do all her work while she just chatted to her friends then took all the credit. Apparently this had driven the said predecessor to a nervous breakdown, hence the vacancy. This didn't worry me. After all, I felt I was in the midst of my own breakdown. But as I left the first day, having lost count of the times Annalise had shouted at me already, I felt that perhaps things would get worse.

Sainsbury's, Monday night. No nice young men. I went to work the next day feeling more despondent. But I didn't see any of this doing-all-the-work thing. Annalise seemed to be giving me only little tasks, so although she shouted it was fine.

Sainsbury's, Tuesday night. Lots of men but in pairs. It was either gay night or male-bonding-over-a-tin-of-tomatoes night. No one even looked at me.

Work the next day was great. Annalise was out of the office all day so I just gossiped with Janie. She said that Annalise was only going easy on me because I was new and that in a couple of days, she'd be having me working really hard. I just brushed this off. No one would ever expect me to work hard.

Sainsbury's, Wednesday night. Finally spotted a cute guy and breathed a huge sigh of relief. I met him in the fruit department as soon as I walked in, good sign. I took my basket to him. He chose apples, I chose apples, he chose bananas, I chose oranges. Then we moved to the tinned produce, we both browsed at the soups. He still hadn't noticed me. I pushed close, then apologised. He smiled. He picked up a can of mushroom soup, 'Good choice, I love mushroom soup,' I cooed. He nodded. I picked up tomato soup, feeling a little bit of a moron. Then we went to pasta, I dropped back a bit and met him later in the deli. 'Should I get streaky or not?' I asked. He shrugged. This was not proving as easy as I'd thought. I was following a man through the supermarket, I was buying everything in sight, and he still hadn't spoken to me properly. When I'd started I'd have put money on us having a conversation by Condiments, but no. And my basket was getting heavy. We went to Bread and Cakes, Cereals and Frozen, but we didn't buy much in Frozen.

Then, to my immense relief, we went to Alcohol. At the beer section I, like him, picked up four cans of Stella. 'What a coincidence,' I said. He looked a bit scared. I don't know how but I think he'd figured out I was following him. Oh, well, it had to come out at some point – he had to know I was interested. I just had to convince him I wasn't mad. I decided to go to the checkout next to his: that way we could leave together (having the same amount of food), and I would laugh and say something like 'You must think I'm following you,' and he'd say, 'Yes, I did a bit,' and I'd say, 'I'm sorry. Let me buy you a drink to make up for it,' and then we'd go for a drink and get on really well and then we'd see each other the next night, spend all weekend together and after a three-month whirlwind romance we'd get engaged to be married and I'd be happy. This was fun. It was working. Until the woman in front of me started questioning the cost of grapes and my man was being served. I started panicking. I willed the woman to go, but she wouldn't. By the time it was my turn, my man was signing his bill. I had to do something. He couldn't leave – I'd been here five times waiting for this man. I shouted, 'Wait for me.'

He looked at me. 'You're fucking crazy,' he screamed, as he ran out of the door.

Everyone was looking at me. I wanted to die. He was right, I was crazy, and I realised that madness wasn't that attractive. I left Sainsbury's alone and thirty pounds poorer.

On Thursday, Janie turned out to have been right about Annalise. I worked like a horse. She sat me down and said that I had responsibility for just about everything, from press cuttings to advertising and all sorts of marketing things I had never heard of. I had lied on my CV and told them I had worked in the marketing department of a publishing house. Sarah had told me to do this. She said I could learn as I went along. I couldn't. I didn't even really know what marketing was and Annalise had no intention of helping me. She chatted to her friends and went to lunch. I did all the work. And there was a lot of work. By the end of my first week, I had been working until seven at night to finish things and then I wasn't sure if I had done them properly. The only good thing was that I was more distressed by my job than I was about the Sainsbury's episode. I told Sarah what was going on and she said that I should report Annalise to the marketing director because she was a waste of resources. I knew I couldn't do that: I was far too much of a wimp to do something so brave.

Until the following Thursday. I had been working really late, I hadn't had time for lunch, I wasn't enjoying the stress. I'd reached the end of my tether. Then Annalise shouted at me; my work wasn't up to scratch, I was inefficient and if I wanted to keep my job I had to improve. I went mad. I marched up to the marketing director, told him I did all the work in the department, that Annalise did nothing and that she was a waste of resources. The marketing director promised to look into it but went red. The next day I was asked to leave. The rumour about Annalise sleeping with the bosses turned out to be true.

After this experience I actually felt better. Sarah was totally defeated and said she'd no longer meddle in my career life.

I was brooding about the failure of my supermarket plan more than being sacked. Then it hit me so hard I nearly fell over. The one place I would be sure to find a man was at work. You see? Simple. All I had to do was get a job in a male-dominated environment (according to Sarah, there were loads of them), become a secretary, find my man. It was beautiful, it was simple. Having been sacked by Annalise the Sleaze, I knew what I had to do. I would put conditions on my employment: only work in those industries known to contain men, only work for a man and wear short skirts. Watch out, the male workforce of London, I am out to get you and get you good.

My friends couldn't figure out what had brought about this change in me. You see, I was excited, confident, and I felt I had started to put Ben behind me. Although I still missed him I'd come out of the denial stage that Jess constantly told me I was in when I had continually talked about Ben coming back. Well, I wasn't there any more. I knew he was never going to be mine. I didn't like it, but that was another stage apparently.

'Ru, you seem different, more confident, I'm so proud of you,' Sarah said.

'Thanks.'

'I mean, we didn't expect you to deal with things so well,' she continued.

'What things?'

Sophie explained. 'Well, we were worried after Ben, then Simon, and you hated your job, and then Mike and quitting and then Annalise. Well, it's been pretty horrid for you, hasn't it?'

'But, look, Ru has come through. She's positive, I knew you'd stop being a wimp and a bore one day.' Jess slapped me on the back.

I wasn't sure whether to thank my friends or scream at them. Sometimes their kindness was confusing. 'I'm OK. Things haven't been great, but I'm surviving. And, no, I'm not happy, but at least I think I may be happy again one day. Sarah, did you get me a new job?'

'Yes, I think so. It'll be confirmed tomorrow. There's a secretarial vacancy in a management consultancy. It's for two months and it pays well. But, Ru, it's going to be boring, I hope you realise that.' I nodded solemnly. Boring? *Boring?* A company full to the brim with men? How could that be boring?

'Look on the bright side. Ruth may get so bored it spurs her on to get a proper job,' Jess offered.

Sarah nodded, and Sophie said, 'I think soon Ru will realise her destiny and everything will fall into place.'

'Oh, girls, I couldn't agree more,' I said.

The job was confirmed, but after much persuasion. Sarah said I'd have to be able to type and use a computer. I assured her I could — after all, this was the computer age, wasn't it? Actually, this time I wasn't lying. I had used a computer when I had spent two weeks solidly typing Ben's dissertation; this also meant I was quite a good typist.

I looked in the mirror. I was starting my new job and this was the first chance to put my husband-in-the-workplace plan into action. I didn't look bad in my navy suit, but even though the skirt was short I was hardly sizzling with sex appeal. I guessed I would have to accept that I'm Ruth and I'm not really a *femme fatale*. I left for work with a smile on my face and a sparkle of optimism in my pocket.

At first glance, my excitement about this job proved correct. The office I walked into was a husband-hunter's paradise. It was fabulous. Men everywhere, young, old, fat, thin, lots and lots of men. A few women were scattered about, but this was definitely male-dominated and I loved it. My boss, Colin, was fiftyish, balding and had pictures of his wife and kids in his office. He was nice, but not really in my market. I started to work, but was really trying to formulate my plan. I had two months to find one man, out of lots, which didn't seem impossible. But I knew I'd have to pay attention. I was sitting opposite another secretary and I decided to become her best friend.

Samantha was nice; she worked for Colin's boss and had been there a while. She showed me around and told me all the gossip. She then said we should go to lunch together. Brilliant. Obviously my strategy had to be subtle, but at the same time it had to be quite quick. I decided that the direct, but not too direct, approach was called for. At lunch I took the bull by the horns.

'Samantha, I couldn't help but notice the number of nice-looking men in the office. What are they like?'

'Well, I've got a boyfriend, but if I hadn't, I'd know what you mean. Not that I notice, I'm totally in love, but there are eighty men in the whole office and about twenty are young good-looking men. The rest are old or ugly, I guess. But out of the nice ones, be careful. Ten are untouchables because they're married and you really don't want to get involved with a married man.'

I liked Samantha: she was being incredibly helpful.

'So, ten available, nice, good-looking men,' I summed up.

'Weeell, not exactly. You see, out of those ten, five are real womanisers. I mean, you wouldn't believe some of the stories. They chew women up and spit them out. Not like my boyfriend, Dave. He's lovely.' She looked all dreamy.

'I'm really glad for you. Now, we're down to five men who are eligible, is that right?'

'Yes. Five are OK. But I have to say that I do think out of the five, two are gay.'

'Is there hard evidence of this?' I was getting a little impatient.

'Well, they were caught snogging at the Christmas party.'

'Who were they snogging?'

'Each other, of course.'

'So, out of an office of eighty men, three are single, straight, good-looking and nice?' Please let this be right.

'Yes, absolutely. Darren, Justin and William. All very nice, single and gorgeous. Would you like me to point them out to you?'

'Yes!' I practically screamed.

We returned to the office and I made coffee. Then I persuaded Samantha to give me a guided tour. She, being either dim or just a pain in the arse, introduced me to every single person before Darren, Justin and William. She saved them until last. Was it worth the wait? Well, no, if I was normal, but yes, as I was desperate. Darren was quite good-looking, with dark brown hair, a nice physique and lovely eyes, Justin was short but he made me laugh – he definitely had a GSOH – and William was posh: he looked like he had money. Put them together and we'd have had my perfect man.

One good thing about being a new girl is that your value increases hugely because of your novelty. After speaking to the three guys, I hinted heavily that an after-work drink would be nice and they obliged me – well, me and Samantha (William especially seemed interested in her obscene cleavage). Undeterred, I felt that perhaps I could conduct a group interview with them, or get drunk and hope one of them picked me. A sort of Ruth's *Blind Date*, but with a contingency that if I couldn't think of enough good questions, I'd just have anyone who wanted me.

At five thirty Samantha and I went to the pub. The guys were joining us at six. I had to listen to half an hour of Samantha going on about Dave to whom she constantly referred as 'my boyfriend'. He was a rocket scientist or a car mechanic or something, and she loved him and they were going to get married soon. Etc. After the men turned up, Samantha's boyfriend, mysteriously, was unmentioned. At one point they were talking about some guy from work, who had recently got married. I said, 'Sam may be next,' and she kicked me.

Justin made me laugh a lot, Darren was intelligent, the type of guy you'd want on your team when playing Trivial Pursuit. William was rich. William was not only rich but edging closer to Samantha, who was pushing her cleavage at him suggestively. Justin and Darren gave each other knowing looks. At nine we left. Justin was going home, Darren had to meet a friend, William and Samantha left together, and I went home, feeling I'd achieved a hell of a lot more in one day than I'd ever hoped.

My friends were delighted to hear what a good day I'd had and how I'd made friends, but of course I omitted to tell them that I'd tracked these 'friends' down better than a sniffer dog and that I was preparing to go in for the kill. I went to sleep that night, dreaming of which man to choose. Gorgeous Darren or funny Justin, I really didn't know. I knew I had to choose carefully because this was the rest of my life.

The next day I invited Justin to lunch and laughed all the way through it. I decided that he was the one. The day after, I had lunch with Darren and we had a great conversation. I thought he must be the one. By the end of the week, I was totally confused. Until Friday. William asked me out. William the rich, William the besotted with Samantha. William the rich. I said yes, because, well, he asked. I didn't tell Samantha, but I asked her if there was anything between them.

'Of course not, we're just friends. I have a boyfriend,' was her annoying answer. By this stage I knew how rich William was because Samantha had told me he had a large trust fund. Then something strange happened. I pictured myself married to William, living in a huge house, nice cars, surrounded by Jimmy Choo sandals. I'd never have to work. At that moment I fell in love with him.

We went to the same pub as we had on the first time we went out. That felt romantic to me. William had impeccable manners. He held the pub door open for me, he sat me down before asking what I wanted to drink, he lit my cigarette for me and he even stood up every time I went to the loo. Even his conversation was polite. He asked me about my family, my school, which he was surprised to find he hadn't heard of, and about me. His voice was like cut glass: he sounded like a member of the Royal Family. I flirted, I tried to be as funny as I could, and I drank. William laughed at me, bought me endless drinks and flirted back.

I found out that he was twenty-four, had grown up on a farm in Gloucestershire – well, actually I think farm is the wrong word. While I conjured up visions of William in his wellingtons, chewing straw and mixing pig swill, he was talking about being a member of the landed gentry. He went to Harrow, then Oxford, then got himself a 'jolly little job' as a consultant, on account of being the youngest of three sons. All the time he spoke he dribbled, which made me wonder if he was the result of inbreeding, but I quickly quashed the thought when he suggested going to dinner. I was delighted and drunk, or the other way around, I'm not sure.

We walked to a 'nice little Italian' he knew. I knew this wasn't strictly a date, but it was nice being taken out by a gentleman. The restaurant was small, romantic and fairly empty. We were led to a table that sat in an alcove and was quite secluded. William ordered a bottle of red wine while I stuffed the fresh olive bread into my mouth in the hope that it would soak up some of the alcohol.

As the waiter delivered the wine I caught William staring at me. 'What?' I said.

William flashed me a toothy grin. 'You really are beautiful,' he said.

I turned red. 'Thank you,' I mumbled, not knowing what else to say. Now it was a date. I guess I should have sent him a compliment back but I wasn't sure how – 'Oh, William, I do like your Savile Row,' or 'Oh, William, I do like your obviously expensive watch,' or 'Oh, William, you do sound like Hugh Grant,' which I wasn't sure was a compliment. Instead I smiled and sipped my wine.

'How do you enjoy working with us?' William asked.

I filled him in about Colin, the boss who spent most of his time doing his children's homework, about the clients he liked, the ones he didn't and I sort of got my Miss Chatterbox head because I didn't stop talking. I talked through my mozzarella and tomato salad, my seafood pasta and my ice-cream. William ate, smiled and nodded. By coffee I had moved on to Samantha and told him, in my most amusing way, how she called Dave a hundred times a day, wore padded bras and dreamed of living in Essex. I knew I was being bitchy but I wanted to get across that Samantha was unavailable and common. Compared with me: I was available and verging on classy. William, to my relief, laughed with me.

When he summoned the bill and signed his credit-card slip he looked at me. 'How about another coffee at your place?'

Wow.

I smiled shyly. 'OK.'

We held hands as we left the restaurant. William was still holding my hand as he hailed a cab, still as he asked me where I lived, still as I said Clapham and still as we climbed into the taxi. When seated he put his arm around me and pulled me to him. My heart was fluttering like crazy. As he kissed me I turned to jelly. For someone with so many teeth he was a great kisser. We kissed all the way back to my house and it felt so right. When the cab stopped so did we, and William paid the cab driver as I searched my bag for the keys. I opened the door, led him into the lounge and, as we were alone, I kissed him again.

'What about coffee?' I teased eventually.

'Where's your room?' he asked.

I led him there feeling excitement build. This was the first time I had had a man here and I was thankful that there were no dirty knickers on the floor. I pulled off my jacket and sat on the bed. William did the same. I groaned inwardly when I noticed he wore cufflinks but was distracted by another kiss. He took off his clothes, neatly folding them, and expertly undid the cufflinks. He stood in front of me wearing only his boxer shorts (cotton) and his socks. He grabbed my hands and pulled me to my feet.

'Get undressed. I need the bathroom,' he commanded.

I nodded and pointed him in the right direction hoping that none of my housemates would see him. Then I undressed. Once naked I felt vulnerable and unsure. I sat on the bed to await his return but that felt and looked awkward. Then I lay back but that looked too provocative. Then I stood, sat and decided on lying propped up against the pillows with my knees up towards my chest. I stayed in this position for what seemed like ages, and just as I contemplated going to find him he arrived back. He leaped on the bed and started smothering me with kisses. I lost all inhibitions as he licked my nipples until they were hard and

I was aroused. He eased himself out of his underwear. I ran my hands down his body, his stomach, his hips, his penis, stroking him. He explored me with his hands, slowly, surely. His eyes were half closed as he groaned with pleasure. 'Now,' he said, 'now.'

I searched my bedside table and found a condom. I gave it to William. He entered me and I groaned. We moved together slowly at first, then faster, more urgently. I was so wet and he was so good, although he insisted on staying in the missionary position. I had my first orgasm since Ben and, boy, it was great. When William came he turned so red I thought his head would pop off. He removed the condom, tied it in a knot and gave it to me. I put it on the bedside table, unsure what to do with it. Then he put his boxer shorts back on, climbed under my duvet, kissed my cheek and went to sleep. It was only when I got up to get a T-shirt that I noticed he was still wearing his socks.

I awoke to find his hands between my legs and I kissed him again. Thank God he still wanted me. I had worried that perhaps he wouldn't want to marry me because I'd slept with him so easily. I tried to reward his loyalty by bringing my lips to his penis but he pushed me away. We made love again, in the missionary position, and I fell in love.

Afterwards I offered him breakfast, but he said he had stuff to do, he'd see me on Monday.

Wow, he wanted to see me again! God I was so lucky. The fact that I had to see him at work escaped me, for the time being, as I basked in being liked by a man I'd had sex with. I felt sure William was the one.

A weekend had never felt so long as that one did. I was excited and told my friends about William. They were impressed by the fact that he had a good job and money, and he sounded nice. I had been in London for three months, and although he wasn't Ben I had found the nearly-man of my dreams.

Or the man of my nightmares. I went into work on Monday to be met by a hysterical Samantha. 'How could you?' she screamed.

It transpired later that William and she had been having a fling behind the wonderful boyfriend's back. William had told her about us. He had used me to make her jealous or something. Darren and Justin were distant, and I knew that I was now being seen as the easiest new girl on the block. It was awful. I felt as if everyone knew what had happened, I felt cheap and dirty and humiliated. Imagine thinking he'd be my husband. I hardly knew him, for God's sake, and he didn't even speak to me now. I had been so stupid. I got through the day somehow, but it took everything I had.

I went home and poured out my heart to Sophie. She told me not to go back to work. This made me feel slightly better. Then Sarah came home and I was still crying and she said I didn't have to go back, she'd find me something else. She also said that William should be shot and so should Samantha. Jess came home and I was still crying and she agreed I couldn't go back. I felt safe again. They did say that perhaps it would be a good idea not to sleep with people connected with work in the future. I said I'd never sleep with any man ever again.

I cried that night and allowed myself the luxury of a thought about Ben. And I dreamed about him but he kept turning into William. I realised that having a plan to get a husband might not be as easy as I had first felt. I also realised that I'd had three bouts of casual sex and it was about time . . . not to abandon my plan to find a man but not to sleep with them so easily. That was it. It wasn't my plan that was wrong, it was my approach to it. That could be changed.

Chapter Six

———◆———

It was one of those pieces of gossip that everyone was talking about. The wicked witch had somehow put a curse on a beautiful girl and now she would have to sleep for a hundred years. Apparently it had something to do with a talking mirror and sex appeal. I decided to hunt down the wicked witch, and over a cup of homemade broth, I asked her if she would consider putting me to sleep for a while. It didn't have to be a hundred years, just one would do. I was so tired. The witch cackled and said she would have to consult the mirror. I waited patiently for her return, praying that she would do this thing for me.

On her return she looked at me almost sympathetically. 'I can't put you to sleep, I'm sorry, you're absolutely no threat to me.' She then showed me out.

Just after the William experience I got flu. In that state of sorrow I felt that I was being constantly reminded that just as I thought things couldn't get any worse they did. I lay on the sofa wrapped in my duvet, surrounded by tissues, pills and cough medicine (courtesy of Sarah), magazines (courtesy of Jess) and videos (courtesy of Sophie). I ate packets and packets of Tunes until I felt sick, I put a Vick's inhaler up my nose until I felt dizzy, and drank more than twice the recommended dose of cough medicine. I felt secure, almost as if I had everything I needed. This way, under my duvet, I didn't have to face the world. The sofa was the world. I was tempted to stay there for ever.

Sometimes truth reared its ugly head. Truth let me know that I was not going to find a husband easily, or even a boyfriend. Truth said that the reason everything went horribly wrong for me was that I still wanted Ben. Truth said that I was falling into bed with every man I met because I was lonely, and loneliness was no foundation for a lasting relationship. Truth said that I had to stop, think and wait for love to happen. When truth shouts in your ear like this, there are two things you can do: take notice and act, or bury your head back in the sand and ignore it. I told truth to butt out of my life.

Flu passed and Sarah got me yet another job. This was as a secretary in an accountancy firm. At first I tried to protest. 'Accountancy? Sarah, is that the best you can do?'

'What's wrong with that?' Sarah replied.

'Well, aren't accountants all terribly dull, polyester-suit-wearing people?'

'And, Ruth, tell me why that would make any difference.' Sarah looked at me sternly.

'It wouldn't, doesn't, but I'm just worried I might get bored.'

I had dropped myself in it again.

'Bored? But, Ruth, you told me you didn't care what job you had because there was nothing you'd be interested in, nothing you wanted to do, so why all of a sudden would you be worried about being bored?' Sarah smiled sweetly.

'Cow. You did this on purpose. You got me this job so I wouldn't be tempted to sleep with anyone.'

'Well, babe, it did cross my mind. Seriously, so far I have shit relationships with two of my clients, thanks to you, and I can't afford to lose any more. This job is only for two months and it's compulsory that you stay for the whole time.'

'Christ, two months with a bunch of accountants. I'll come out of it wanting to be celibate like you.'

'That wouldn't be a bad thing.' We both giggled.

'Or I'll come out of it having had sex with an accountant.'

'Don't think about doing that. I mean it.'

I laughed again, and decided that just for her sake, and nothing to do with the fact that all accountants have to give up their sex appeal when they qualify, I wouldn't sleep with anyone in my next job.

It was just as I had imagined it. Grey, quiet and boring. The boss was OK, he was a puffy-faced man who needed me to file things and make him tea a lot. He was called Nick and he was boring. But he didn't look like the shouting type, so that was something. He even tried to tell me what accountants did, but I found it too boring to listen to.

However, I had done something positive. I had started to learn to cook. Yes, I had bought myself *The Conran Cookbook* (no girl should be without one) and I had read it diligently. I knew how to gut fish and skin a rabbit, although I hoped I wouldn't need to do that. I gave all my friends different food when they were around, and Thomas started coming round more often. He loved my cooking. Even Jess and Sarah were impressed, and I enjoyed it. I thought back to the career counsellor, but knew that I wouldn't like to cook on a grand scale, just for my friends and, of course, my future husband. I was making myself more marketable to the male race. The way to a man's heart and all that.

I had become useful, as Jess discovered. Jess had been spending a lot of time with her PR counterparts, the other graduates who had started with her. Of course she couldn't stand them: they were her enemies waiting to stab her in the back at any given time. Jess believed that you should keep your enemies close. They had all had dinner parties in turn. Jess called it 'team bonding', but it was just another way for them to outdo each other. Now it was her turn. And, in true Jess style, she wanted to impress.

'Ruthie, darling, I was thinking, this dinner party, we're a girl short so would you do me the honour of coming?'

I looked at her, Sarah looked at her, Sophie looked relieved.

'Me?' I asked.

'Yes, it will do you good to meet new people. It'll be fun and there'll be men there.'

'OK.' What did I have to lose? Apparently nothing, but I had a lot to do.

'I thought perhaps we could choose the menu out of your *Conran Cookbook*.'

'OK,' I said.

I was still in a state of shock. I couldn't think why she had chosen me. Sarah would have been far more suitable; Sophie would have scored her Brownie points. But instead of wooing her colleagues with her career-minded friend or her beautiful friend, she had decided to woo them with me. I was her . . . her – I don't know what friend.

She went to get the cookbook and we spent hours poring over the recipes.

'Oh, no, too easy,' she said, or 'Oh, no, not pretty enough.'

I wanted to kill her. Sarah was looking amused. Jess tried to pick the most impossible recipes but I persuaded her to compromise. We were to have homemade French onion soup with homemade bread to start, Normandy pheasant with apples and Calvados for main and crème brûlée for dessert. It was quite a tall order but Jess insisted, and although I knew she couldn't cook, well, I'd help.

'OK,' I said, 'fabulous menu – but, Jess, are you sure you can do it? It doesn't look that easy.'

She smiled sweetly. 'Well, Ru, I was sort of hoping you'd help me, sort of a joint effort.'

'OK,' I agreed.

Sarah laughed really loudly.

'What?' Jess snapped.

'You'll get Ru to do it all.'

'No, I won't.'

Sarah shrugged.

I was a little worried: I might have been a good cook, but I hadn't had much practice. I knew it had to be perfect and I wasn't sure I could cope with so much pressure. I looked at Jess, pleadingly.

'Ru, of course I won't. Like I said, it'll be a joint effort. Relax.' I felt slightly better.

The dinner party approached. Jess went shopping. She bought the food, the wine and a new outfit. I donned my apron and asked Jess where she wanted me to start. 'Wherever.'

'But what should I do first and what are you going to do?'

She flashed her sweetest smile. 'Actually, I'm going to the hairdresser.'

Sarah had been right. I was on my own. With expensive food and Jess's PR people to cook for. I panicked. I had to do it all. I spent the day cooking, baking bread, preparing. Jess returned at three in the afternoon with lots of flowers, which she arranged around the house. She gave me no help. I was so angry, but I didn't have time to be angry: I had soup to make.

At four in the afternoon it dawned on me what I was doing. Up to my elbows in pheasant, I realised that if Jess's colleagues were anything like her, which they apparently were, and there were going to be six of them plus us and me the only non-PR person, I didn't want to be there. It was going to be a total nightmare. I couldn't think of anything I'd hate more. Oh, how the gloom descended on me. It would be the dinner party from hell.

While I was immersed in reality, Jess started panicking about things being perfect. I realised, although I was very cross with

her, that this was incredibly important to Jess. If she produced
a perfect dinner (or I did) and the house looked lovely (which
it did), and she looked perfect (she'd been to the hairdresser
and got a new outfit), then they'd be impressed, or worried that
she was actually Superwoman. God, this office politics thing was
hard work and bloody expensive. I decided that as I had been
such a pain to Jess in the last few months, this was my penance.
Although I had previously been won over by the idea of four
guys, who were all single, coming to dinner, now I realised that
there was a reason for them being single. The idea of dating
the male version of Jess was horrific.

Jess looked perfect: her hair gleamed, her new outfit, an
incredibly short, tight red dress, emphasised her lovely curves
and huge cleavage, and her lipstick matched perfectly. As I had
been chopping, cooking, cleaning, I didn't.

Jess looked at me. 'Oh, my God, we have to do something
with you.' She dragged me off to get ready.

I saw that as her friend I would also need to impress these
people, or my life would be hell. I also knew that although I
might be her best friend on the cooking front I would be the
worst at impressing.

While getting me ready, she dropped another bombshell. 'I
told my friends you were a writer.'

'What?' I'd never written anything in my life, apart from
the odd letter.

'Yes. To make you more interesting, I told them you were
writing your first novel and had high hopes of being published.
I told them you were really talented.'

'Thanks,' I grumbled. Although I had realised that I wasn't
interesting enough, I resented Jess reinventing me. But the word
penance kept popping into my mind and Jess was my friend,
although I disliked her sometimes. I reluctantly said I'd carry
out the charade, but if I forgot at any time she wasn't allowed
to shout at me. We had a deal. She did my hair, put me in one
of her glam, tight black dresses and smeared so much lipstick on

me I couldn't feel my lips. By the time we opened our pre-guest bottle of wine (I had also been told not to get drunk), Jess was happy. She had a perfect house, a perfect dinner, a perfect her and a nearly perfect friend.

The two girls arrived first. Fennula and Henrietta. They were as awful as they sounded and they looked like the Ugly Sisters on a bad-hair day. Of course they oohed and ahhed about how wonderful everything looked, but they made every compliment sound bitchy. Jess became just like them. Everything they said had a bitchy undertone and everything was about one-upmanship. The evening was turning out worse than I had first thought.

The four guys arrived together, and the last one to walk in was Ben. My Ben. As my heart flipped, I did a double-take and realised it wasn't him – well, not unless he was masquerading as a Julian and had started wearing tweed jackets. But he looked just like him. I hardly noticed Rufus, Charlie and Marcus, I couldn't take my eyes off Julian. I cornered Jess in the kitchen. 'Why the hell didn't you tell me he looked like Ben?' I was quite shaken up.

'Who?' she asked.

'Julian, of course. He's identical to my Ben.'

'I hadn't noticed. Ru, how much wine have you had?' She swept back to her guests and that was it.

Henrietta the Horrible gave me a horrible smile. 'So, Ruth, I hear you're writing a book.'

'Yes, I am, and it's taking for ever, but I'm very excited about it.' I beamed back.

'How interesting,' said Fennula, who made it sound very uninteresting. 'What's it about?'

Oh, God, I didn't know. Jess hadn't told me what it was about. 'It's a tragic love story,' I said, Jess shot me a look, but then the questions flowed at me from all angles.

I started to panic, but Julian saved me. 'Writers never divulge their secrets.'

I could have kissed him, literally. He then indulged me by telling me how much he admired me for taking on such a project and I got caught up in it. I promised he could read it as soon as I'd finished. After a while even I started to believe I was writing this novel. It was great.

We ate and drank and I concentrated all my energies on Julian. But he was as full of himself as the others. He was arrogant, vain and too confident. Dinner consisted of everyone trying to talk about themselves as much as possible, even me now that I was interesting. The conversation was mainly about PR, work and the whole evening was dull. I was short-lived as the centre of attention.

Dinner was over and everyone congratulated Jess on her cooking skills. I didn't mind; she was my friend. When everyone was about to leave I asked Julian for his number. It was a spur-of-the-moment decision, based on drunkenness (I'd been bored) and that he really did look like Ben. He gave it to me then asked to see me next week. We arranged to meet on Wednesday for dinner. To be honest, I knew that dinner alone with him would be an ordeal, but as usual my hormones were out of control.

I came up with a theory that if Julian annoyed me as much as I suspected he would I might be able to get over Ben. It was so logical: go out with a man who looks like your ex but is horrible and you'll end up hating your ex and anyone who reminds you of him. Pure brilliance. I just didn't know why I hadn't thought of it sooner.

When Jess found out about my date with Julian, she was thrilled. 'Find out as much as you can about him. His weaknesses especially.'

'Jess, I'm going out with the guy for my own reasons, not

to become your spy.' But she didn't listen and she even tried to work out if she could fix Thomas up with one of the girls.

Sarah, Sophie and Thomas were horrified that the person I had chosen to date after Ben (we'd eliminated Steve, Mike and William from my records) looked like him. Sarah said I was a masochist, I seemed to get myself into more and more situations that ended up with me getting hurt. She assured me that this would end in tears. Sophie told me, in the nicest possible way, that it was weird and even questioned my sanity. Thomas said I should be locked up and never allowed to go out in public. Actually, Thomas was quite cross with me and he never gets cross with me. These views might have upset me, but Jess defended me, which was nice: it was the first time I'd been defended by anyone. As I had become a total pain in the arse, I took more pleasure in being defended by someone rather than indulging in indignation at being attacked.

On Wednesday I was excited at work. Really excited. I'm not sure if it was the thought of Julian or the thought of going out, but I didn't care. I breezed through the day, smiling at Nick and making him extra tea, and I couldn't wait until half past five.

I met Julian in Covent Garden. He looked so lovely, more like Ben than I remembered. He kissed me on both cheeks. 'Ruth, lovely to see you.' We went to a bar, sat down and ordered drinks. After the initial God-what-do-I-say-to-him feeling, I decided that I would do the thing men like most and asked him about himself.

'Tell me, how did you end up in PR?' I tried to look as if I cared.

'I've always been quite creative, really, you could say an ideas man, ha ha. So someone suggested PR to me and I thought, Well, PR makes the world go round, really, everything's based on PR, it's a powerful tool, you know, a powerful tool. And there you have it. Tell me about you and Jess.'

I looked stunned. 'Me and Jess?'

'Yes, how did you meet?'

'At university.' I couldn't think why he wanted to know.

'What was she like then?'

'The same as she is now.'

Julian nodded thoughtfully. 'What does she do in her spare time?'

'I don't know – she sometimes goes to the gym.'

'Does she have a boyfriend?'

'No, I don't think so.'

On and on he went. He wanted to know what she said about work, what she said about her bosses and her colleagues, and it dawned on me that I was being used as a double agent. In a way I was glad: it would be much easier to hate this guy than I had first thought.

'How about dinner?' Julian suggested, so we went to eat.

The conversation turned back to him. 'Which university did you go to?' I asked.

'Bristol. It's a pretty good university. I got a first, made loads of friends and played hockey for the first team.'

Oh, my God. 'Hockey?' I asked, spooked.

Then he went on about what a fantastic hockey player he was and how the girls adored him (not sure how we got around to that), and on and on he went. Time flies when you're being talked at by one so arrogant, so when Julian paid the bill I felt that six months of my life had just passed.

'Would you like to come to a party with me on Friday?' he asked. I nodded, too tired to speak. So that was the end of the first date and this plan was sure to work. A few more dates with Ben-like-wanker Julian and I'd be over Ben the Beautiful. It had to work.

Friday came and we went to a party. This was the first party I'd been to since I'd moved to London. It was a good feeling. I felt that perhaps I had a life again. Well, sort of. Julian might be good for me: he would give me a much-needed social life, even if it was a crap one, and I was hoping he might take my mind off all that career stuff too.

The party was in Islington, held by an old schoolfriend of Julian's in an impeccable flat, all white carpet and white sofas. I couldn't help thinking that it was the sort of place that should host poetry readings not parties. Then I noticed that no one was smoking and no one looked the type to throw up over the floor, so it was more like a poetry reading than a party anyway, but without the poetry.

Julian introduced me to everyone he knew. 'This is Ruth. She's a writer.' Everyone was impressed and I had to talk about the non-existent book all evening – a drawback of going out with Julian I hadn't thought about. As long as I was with him I had to keep pretending I was writing a book. It might prove hard work.

After the party, I went back to his flat. He lived in West Kensington, which apparently was nearer than Clapham. In the cab, it suddenly dawned on me that I was going home with him. I was expected to sleep with him. Although so far during my time in London, it had not proved difficult to part me from my knickers, I suddenly wanted to keep them well and truly on. Even though I was drunk. Panic gripped me, my chest tightened, everything closed in. I didn't want to sleep with Julian. Julian was supposed to get me over Ben. He could bore me to death, he could patronise me, he could talk about how wonderful he was, he could do all that. But, and it was a big BUT, I did not want to sleep with him. Because sex with someone who looked like Ben – no. It was twisted, it made me feel sick. Sophie was right: I was weird.

My plan was not so great – trust me not to have thought of the details. I was going to have to think fast if I was to be saved. I started to calm down as we approached the flat. After all, there was no law that, just because I was staying there, sex had to be involved. We went in and Julian put on the lights. It was a nice flat, very clean, not really manly but not girly either. It was sort of modern and co-ordinated.

'Nice flat,' I said, as I sat down on the Habitat sofa.

'Thanks. It's all right, I suppose. I mean, of course it's not ideal, but as soon as I get promoted I'll probably buy one in Fulham.' I thought for a moment that I was with Jess. I just nodded.

'Coffee?' Julian asked.

I was saved. 'Oh, God, yes, please. Could I have a large mug?' Julian gave me a strange look and went to the kitchen. I could stall for time.

'Julian, where's your flatmate?' There was no sign of another person here.

'Away this weekend. It's just the two of us.' Oh, great. I decided to have a look round. God, it was so tidy. Men aren't supposed to be tidy. I went to the bathroom. It was like my house: pots and potions littered the shelves; Clinique for men was prominent, with expensive shampoo and conditioners, bubble bath, shower gel, and I'm sure I saw some waxing strips. I went back to the sitting room.

'Julian, is your flatmate female?'

'No, Ruth, I told you, I live with Duncan. He's in corporate finance.'

'Of course he is.' I sipped my coffee slowly. We watched TV, had more coffee, but Julian was getting tired and every time he tried to get close to me, I jumped up and ran to the bathroom. He must have thought I had the weakest bladder in town. In the end he could endure no more. He nibbled my ear. 'Let's go to bed, baby.'

Oh, God. I decided I had to be assertive. 'Listen, Julian, I just have to tell you something. I'm not the sort of girl who jumps into bed with every man she meets. In fact, I don't intend to have sex until I feel we have an established and steady relationship. If that never happens then fine, but I need time before I take that step.' Not bad, if I say so myself. I just hoped I'd be forgiven for the lie.

Julian smiled and stroked my hair. 'You know, I wanted to make love to you tonight, but I wouldn't have respected you in the morning. I think you're quite right to wait.' He took my hand and led me to the bedroom. Actually, I thought that was what he was going to do but we went to the bathroom, where I soon found out who owned the beauty products. 'Here, I always keep a spare.' He handed me a brand new toothbrush. Then he cleansed, toned and moisturised – what a woman! – before taking me to the bedroom. I borrowed a T-shirt, we got into bed, we kissed and cuddled then Julian fell asleep. Thank God. I lay there thinking how alien this all was. It was the first time since I'd been in London that I'd been in bed with a man and not had sex. I looked at him, and when he was asleep I could almost convince myself he was Ben. I stroked his hair and thought about how much I would give for him to be Ben. I then thought how much I would give for Julian to be just anyone nice.

If I had been honest with myself, I would have realised at this point that I should have given up this plan quick smart. Before Julian, I had reduced my thoughts of Ben to an almost acceptable volume. Now, looking at him, the obsession flooded in. I was back to square one. Ruth the boring, pain-in-the-arse moron. And I couldn't believe Julian's double standards. First he wanted to sleep with me and if I had he'd have got what he wanted, but then he didn't want me to sleep with him because he'd have lost all respect for me. And men say that women are complicated. I would have loved to be in a situation where I had had a one-night stand with a man and in the morning I would say, 'That was great, but you'd better leave now.' He'd say, 'Can we see each other again?' and I would say, 'No, I never see anyone again who puts out so easily,' and that would be that. Huh, never call me anti-feminist again. It was time we developed the same double standards as men.

*   *   *

I left after breakfast, I wanted out. Julian told me to call him and suggested going to the movies on Sunday. Which wasn't a bad idea — at least he wouldn't be able to talk. So I agreed. I know I'd just spent a sleepless night but no one else would take me to the movies and although he wasn't much he was all I had.

At home no one was in, which was great. I had a long bath, a long think. If being with Julian didn't get me over Ben, at least I was going through some sort of self-punishment, self-destruction, more penance, which is all I felt I deserved. Sarah was right: I *was* a masochist. I lay on the sofa and started daydreaming. Julian wasn't like Ben, whose beauty routine was soap and water. Clothes were jeans. He was a real man. Thomas was the same. I don't know if it was just Julian, or were all men turning into girls? Will the Millennium be remembered as the time when you couldn't tell the difference between straight and gay men?

Great Britain is in a state of confusion. Women are losing their femininity and men are losing their masculinity. Men are scared of women. Women are scary. Penis envy has been replaced by boob envy, men want to be women. They have started growing their hair into styles. They wear attractive underwear. They consult skin-care and make-up experts. At the end of the year 2000, men have spent as much on beauty products as women.

Men don't hold doors open, they expect women to hold doors open for them. Shorter men wear heels, more adventurous men wear dresses. They try to be glamorous at all times and many men will not be seen in public without mascara. They have lost interest in working, lobby Parliament for the right to have breast implants and demand research into how men can have babies. Men always take the contraceptive pill now. There are two reasons for this, the first being that the male pill keeps you looking young, the second that women cannot be trusted with something so important: women spend too much time drinking after work, they will probably forget. Men cry after sex.

Men are not frequently found in managerial jobs. The majority of secretaries are men. A survey found that men made great secretaries because they were natural typists. The reason for this was that, despite trying, they never got the hang of growing their nails. In surveys when asked what their ideal job would be, eighty-six per cent of men said they would like to be housewives. Asked if they were in a happy relationship, seventy-nine per cent of men in a relationship said they felt downtrodden. Asked if they would object to the woman paying the mortgage, bills and housekeeping, ninety per cent of men said they would love that.

Men's favourite hobby is dieting. They take care of their bodies ruthlessly, but women are finding less and less time for exercise. Women take thirty minutes in the hairdresser's, men take hours having cuts, styles and colours. Men go shopping twice as much as women. They buy three times the amount of clothes. Women's favourite films are action, men prefer romantic comedies. Women don't like men. The make-up, the clothes, the silly emotional attitudes, the breast envy make them unattractive.

Lesbianism is growing in popularity. Women surveyed said that the most useful thing that men do is the cooking, ironing and cleaning.

'Ruthie, I got shagged senseless by this right nympho last night.' Thomas bounded in and interrupted my daydream. I kissed him. He didn't have a dress on. Oh, I loved men just as they were. Thomas wore his oldest jeans, a rugby shirt and a victorious smile.

'Thomas, do you think that this, um, girl, who slept with you just after meeting you would be an appropriate girlfriend. I mean, will you see her again?'

'God, yes, she was amazing.'

'You don't think she's cheap.' I loved Thomas.

'Ru, of course she's bloody cheap. She came up to me in a bar and told me she wanted to sleep with me. She didn't even ask my name. I'm so fucking lucky.'

'But if she was cheap and you think she does that all the time, why sleep with her?'

'You can be really stupid. Because she was female and gagging for it. I'm going to make some tea.'

I *did* love Thomas, even though I didn't always know why. 'See, the sexual revolution has caused many problems, Thomas. Women are allowed to enjoy sex and be sexually active outside marriage, but still, as has been the case for the whole of time, men are seen as cool if they shag a lot and women as sluts. Where's the justice in that?'

'There isn't any. But I'm bloody glad I'm a man.'

'Thomas!' I hit him. 'Think yourself lucky it's me you're talking to and not Jess or Sarah.'

Before I had had time to recover from my last date, it was cinema-with-Julian time.

'So, Ruth, are you going out tonight?'

'Yes, Jess, I'm going to the cinema.'

'Oh, who with?'

'Julian.' Who else?

'Oh. Tell me about his flat again. How much Clinique does he have? I called Henrietta to tell her about the wax strips. She wasn't surprised. Can you try to find out what he uses them for?'

'Jess, for God's sake, you can't go around telling people those things. I told you in confidence. And, for the millionth time, I am not seeing Julian so I can spy for you. I don't tell him things about you.' I was upset; this had been going on all weekend.

'Calm down, it's just a bit of information-gathering — although you may be right, I shouldn't tell anyone else. Why should I share? What I'll do is accumulate, and when I have enough damning information I'll destroy him.' She was gleeful, she was serious. She was scary.

'Jess, stop. I mean it. I know I don't like him very much but I won't have you talking about destroying him and trying to get me to help. No way. And in future I won't share any information with you.'

'We'll see.' She smiled sweetly and left. I knew she was right. I loved Jess, I told her everything, she was my friend. I gave her all the ammunition she needed.

After the cinema I told her he gobbled his popcorn like a turkey and fiddled with himself throughout the film. After our next dinner date I told her how he thought he was doing better than anyone else on the graduate scheme and would be promoted first. I also told her that I had found out he had his back waxed at a beauty salon. I told her he ironed his shirts for hours and only wore Calvin Klein underwear. I told her he plucked his eyebrows, colour-coordinated his wardrobe and starched his shirts. He thought he had a great body and always asked me to feel his muscles. And he had athlete's foot. I told her all that. Perhaps none of this sounds too damaging – he hadn't killed anyone or anything bad like that – but it lost him any respect he might have had, because when work found out he plucked his eyebrows and waxed his back, I don't think they would see him in the same light as before. I was giving Jess exactly what she wanted.

Apart from Jess's interrogations, having Julian made me feel good. Well, it did when I wasn't with him anyway. You see, I had a boyfriend, a live one (well, a half-live one anyway), and he was mine. Now, you might call me sad, but how many girls at some stage in their lives have gone out with someone they weren't exactly mad about? Yup, nearly all of you. You see, my confidence had been dented and having a Julian was going to repair it for me. And I had the added defence that the man-not-of-my-dreams was going to enable me to get over the man-of-my-dreams. So it made perfect sense.

And, of course, now that I was working in an accountants' office, well, Julian could at times look positively interesting.

Sometimes I really looked forward to seeing him, usually after a day spent listening to my boss drone on about balance sheets, when even Julian talking about himself was a welcome release. If you want to torture someone put them in a room full of accountants and soon they will be begging for mercy and totally under control. Well, the normal weak person would. I, however, was different. I knew that Sarah was expecting me, firstly, to crack after a few figure-filled days at Accounts Are Us and beg her to find me an interesting job, and then to decide to become a career woman and the person they all wanted me to be. Well, I wasn't playing ball. No, I was not going to crack. I would spend the whole two months, or what was left of it, in the office, and when I left I would get another nice little admin. job without too much stress. And I would have won.

'Ru, how's the job going?' Sarah asked, looking up from the magazine she was reading.

'Fine.' I was suspicious and on my guard.

'Good.' She went back to her magazine.

'Actually, it's really good.' Huh, that would throw her.

'I'm pleased.' Now I'd got her on the hop.

'Yeah, and I really like my boss, he's a scream.'

'Is he? Great.'

'Oh, I'm just sorry I have to leave after two months. It's such a shame.' I was enjoying myself.

'Yes, isn't it?'

'Oh, yes, it is.' I was trying hard not to laugh. Sarah's plan had backfired so horribly.

'Don't worry, I've got loads of accountancy firms on my books. I'll get you a job in another one just as soon as this one finishes.' She beamed at me.

Bitch! Does she never give up? I went into my bedroom to sulk.

Later she came in to see me. 'Are you sulking?'

I was lying on my bed daydreaming about my wedding day. 'No, of course not. Why would I be sulking?'

'I know you don't love the job.'

'How?' I thought I'd been convincing.

'Because, Ru, if you did you wouldn't be you. You probably dislike it as much as all the other jobs you've had and I wouldn't blame you.'

'It's not as bad as some.'

'I guess that's something.'

'Yeah, but you're right, it's not as much fun as I made out. My boss isn't really very funny, you know.'

'I kind of figured that too. But, Ruth, this wasn't a plan of mine to get you some ambition. I still think that you *will* get some, but I know it will come in your own time. So I didn't get you this job to be horrid, it was just a two-month contract and I thought a short-term job might be good for you.'

'I didn't think that.'

Sarah laughed. 'Ru, you always let your imagination run away with you. That's exactly what you thought.'

I was chastised. 'Sorry.'

'It's all right. So, tell me, do all accountants wear polyester suits?'

'Yes, and most are grey, although the discerning accountant wears navy.'

'I bet they're pissed off that grey is fashionable now. They'll need to find a new colour.'

'I may suggest green to my boss.'

'Purple would be better.'

'Sarah, you won't always make me work for accountants, will you?'

'Nah. I guess I could elevate your interest levels by getting you a job in a morgue.'

'I might prefer that.'

'Are you going to ditch Julian?'

'Where did that come from? We were just talking about my "career".'

'I just thought that now you'd stopped being delusional about your job, you might do the same about your love life.'

'Never.'

'Fine, you keep kidding yourself, but Christmas is coming up and the Millennium. Afterwards, I expect you to do some serious thinking, madam.'

'OK.'

'Good.'

Sarah was right as always but there was no way I was going to let her know that. Not in a million years. I hugged her. 'Fancy a beer?'

'OK.'

We left the dangerous territory that was my love life and headed for the sanctity of the local pub.

''Tis the season to be jolly.' Apparently. December is the time when everyone, or at least everyone I know, is overtaken by a festive feeling, even at the beginning of the month. Everyone was talking about presents, parties, going home, real excitement. And, of course, everyone was talking about the biggest new year to hit since ... well, since the last millennium, I guess. To me the whole thing was just another nail in my coffin.

This was my first Christmas in London, or pre-Christmas at any rate. I'd be going home for the actual event. Although I tried very hard to be depressed, I couldn't help being a little bit excited. Julian took me to see the lights in Oxford Street, and London was at its most beautiful. Although we couldn't move for people, even the cold was warm: roasted chestnut stalls gave off delicious aromas, and the lights were amazing. London sparkled and, wrapped in my warm coat, gloves and scarf, I had never wanted so much to be out of doors. Every street seemed special, every person seemed to smile, and I smiled too.

We got a little tree for our house and we decorated it – well, Jess and Sarah did, and we were only allowed bows and baubles from John Lewis, red and gold. Tinsel was banned. Although Sophie and I managed to add one piece to the mantelpiece when no one was looking.

We were planning our Christmas dinner before we all went home, I would do the cooking. It was just us, Jess, Sarah, Sophie, Thomas and me. We didn't invite Julian or the Porsche, for obvious not-wanting-the-evening-to-be-shit reasons. It was even festive at work. Nick gave me an afternoon off to go shopping. He also asked me to decorate the office, lots of tinsel, and I was invited to my first office party. It was in a restaurant and all twenty of us in the firm were going. Me, the receptionist, two other secretaries and lots of accountants. Not exactly my dream evening, but still . . . Everyone was happy, Christmas brings out the best in people. I had even stopped calling Julian a boring wanker to Jess. But I still hadn't slept with him.

Most of December passed in a blur of fun and parties, wine and mince-pies. Then the real thing arrived and I got ready to go home. The evening before I was leaving, I went out with Julian to do a present exchange. I resented having to get him anything and I was cross that he had to give me something – it was bound to be awful. I went shopping with Jess and bought him a pair of gold collar-stiffeners. Jess wanted me to get him something horrible, like a willy-enhancer, but I decided against it. I knew he'd like the collar-stiffeners – he'd probably wear his collars turned up so that everyone could see them.

We were meeting at his flat and going to dinner. I wasn't exactly thrilled at the prospect, but I went with my usual mixed feelings. I liked going out, but I didn't like him. However, the festive season was not a time to dwell on this matter: I had decided it could wait until next year.

'Hi, gorgeous, you look great.'

I did a double-take. Was Julian talking to me or to himself? 'Hi, are you OK?'

'Yes, I've missed you.'

'Really?'

'Yes, Ru, I have. I feel our relationship is going somewhere, don't you?'

'Um, shall we go to dinner?'

'Of course, pumpkin.' Pumpkin?

We walked to the restaurant, conveniently situated near Julian's flat. I felt panic rising again. I might be dim, but even I had figured out the reason for this attentive behaviour. I had managed to push it aside for so long, but now it was back. He wanted to sleep with me.

'Ruth, has anyone told you what beautiful eyes you have?'

'Shall we order?'

'I could die in your eyes.'

I almost wished he would. 'I think I'll have the fishcakes and a bottle of white.'

'You're so beautiful.'

'Julian, order, I'm starving.' He did and I went to the ladies'. I didn't want to sleep with him, but I also didn't know if I minded so much. I was confused, and I was too lonely to lose him just yet. I didn't like him any more than I had at first, but I needed him. It was crazy, but I started panicking at the thought of losing him. I did what I always did; left the decision in the hands of the drink.

By the end of the meal I was plastered. And Julian was still showering me with annoying compliments.

'Julian, let's go.' The drink had made its decision.

'OK.' He jumped up, paid the bill and made me run home. When we got in we went to the bathroom (of course) and when we'd cleansed, toned and moisturised we went to the bedroom. Julian started undressing, so I did the same and when he was naked he started kissing me. I kissed him back. We lay on the bed, and he told me he loved my tits. I tried to think about football.

Foreplay was undressing, sex was brief, post-coital affection was a kiss on the cheek. It was over before it had begun. Julian had met all my expectations in the bedroom department. He was completely crap.

In the morning I felt foul. I was repelled by what I'd done and by Julian grinning like a Cheshire cat.

'Darling, last night was wonderful.' He nuzzled my neck.

'Sorry, but I am strictly a no-sex-in-the-morning woman.' All I could think about was how I had to get home and catch a train. I gave Julian my present, he gave me three. I told him we had to save them until Christmas Day. I couldn't bear to have to pretend to like whatever he'd given me. As soon as I sat down on the tube I opened them. The first present was a fondue cookbook, the second was a Clinique gift set, and the last was a packet of flavoured condoms. I cried all the way back to my house.

On the train home I put Julian out of my mind and, in a childish way, I couldn't help but be excited by the prospect of Christmas. When I got home it was festive, the Christmas decorations were old friends, and I was really pleased to be with my parents. Although they gave me the usual what-are-you-doing-with-your-life? I still loved them.

On Christmas Eve my parents had a party to go to and I was left alone. They asked me to go with them, but I declined. I wanted to drink wine and think about the year that was coming to an end. It had started well, Ben and I were together. Then Ben and I weren't together and, well, you know the story. For a year that had started so well, it was going to end badly. And it was not just the end of the year, it was also the end of the century and of the millennium, or something like that. It was a very dramatic time to be having such a bad time.

Julian had called me. Sex hadn't put him off; it seemed

to have made him keener. He wanted us to spend New Year together, with some of his friends in Scotland. Unable even to entertain that idea, I told him I'd already promised Sarah and Jess that I'd be with them. Which I had.

I was spending my first Christmas without Ben. Technically it wasn't – I'd had about eighteen Christmases before I met Ben, but I don't count them. And I'd never actually spent Christmas Day with Ben, but when he was my boyfriend he had made Christmas special. My first Christmas without Ben would be followed by my first New Year without Ben. I was reverting to monotonous-bore mode and I decided to see how many firsts-without-Ben I could think of. In my usual perverse way, this game amused and depressed me at the same time.

Christmas Day. My parents and I had a nice breakfast, then we opened our presents. They had given me a briefcase and an electronic organiser. I couldn't think of more useless presents but I tried to be grateful. My father loved the power-tool I had got him although I didn't know what it did; my mother loved her Germaine Greer books, but they scared Dad. He had bought her some beautiful earrings and she had bought him golf clubs. Everyone was happy.

My new social mother had invited another family for lunch. The Butler family is small: it consists of a long line of only children, so we were it. The family joining us was Mum's charity friend Amelia, her husband and her twenty-two-year-old daughter. I was looking forward to it; I would have a playmate. My mother cooked, my father and I watched Christmas television and ate chocolate. Then, at about one o'clock, our guests arrived. The daughter was called Sally and she was really girly. Giggling and dumb and boring. She spoke about her boyfriend constantly – he was in the army – and she was a teacher. She seemed middle-aged. And she looked it. But then I realised that, although not quite as dull, I was the same. The difference was that she had a boyfriend and a tweed skirt and I was still looking for a boyfriend and I'd never wear tweed. She made me realise that I had been so worried about the future I had forgotten about the present, and now that the present had gone, I would carry on worrying about the future. It's a trait of today. We all do it. We need to know what will happen, that we'll have a pension plan or a man or whatever. We lose our youth because youth is just a stage on the ladder to growing old. We plan for when we get older, we forget about when we're young. I thanked Sally and Christmas for making me realise it was time for my youth.

After Boxing Day I had to go back to work. Although I begged my parents to let me stay, I was kicked out, armed with my briefcase and my electronic organiser. Although I had seen it was time to start living my youth, I still cried on the whole train journey back to London. I know people who would rather die than cry in public, but not me. Crying had become second nature and I didn't care where or when it happened. The elderly woman sitting opposite me handed me a British Rail napkin. 'What's wrong, love? You just had to leave your young man?' I shook my head. 'Oh, bless my soul, you just split up with him?' I nodded. 'I'll go and get you a cup of tea,' and off she went. She returned with the tea and a muffin, for which I was grateful – I had tried to persuade my parents to let me stay at home by refusing to eat. It hadn't worked but it had left me hungry.

'Oh, men, I dunno, they don't deserve girls like us, do they?' I smiled. 'When I was your age, many years ago, I fell in love. He was a GI, but the handsomest man I ever saw. And, of course, I was married. Well, we were, in those days, and my husband was in the war. Didn't know if I'd ever see him again, it was like that. But this Yank, we had a love affair – oh, don't look shocked, in those days you didn't know when you'd get it again.' I nearly choked on my muffin. 'Anyway, he had to go back to the States and my husband did come home, after all.

I've often wondered what happened to the soldier. But, well, I was pregnant, of course, and what could I do? Abortions weren't handed out like sweeties then. No, we women had to be resourceful. So, I seduced my husband then told him I was pregnant. I bribed the midwife to say the baby was three months early. He believed to his dying day that Sam, the baby, was his. I always said men knew nothing about babies. I mean, Sam was ten pounds and three months early, and no one else believed it, but my husband did.'

I smiled at her. She was great.

She told me more about her wartime exploits and the Yank, who had no name and Sam, who is a criminal now – it must have been the American genes – and Jean, that was her name, kept me entertained until we got to London.

'Why are you going to London?' I asked.

'Oh, I thought I'd see the New Year in. I've got a gentleman friend there, you know.'

'I have to go back to work,' I told her.

'It's such a pity, pretty thing like you. You shouldn't be working – you need to find a nice young man to take care of you. Listen, I'll tell you a secret. It doesn't matter how many women work, the only work that will ever make you truly happy is looking after the man you love. You mark my words.'

I smiled, I didn't think she was right about most women but she was right about me. I hugged Jean when we got off the train and I went home smiling.

Chapter Seven

Sissy looked at her sister as she was getting ready for the New Year's Eve ball. 'I have made my New Year resolution,' she declared proudly.

'Oh, really? That's a very good thing,' Lilly replied.

'Yes, my resolution this year is that I shall find a husband and I shall marry well.' Sissy smiled, but Lilly frowned.

'But, dear sister, was that not your resolution last year?'

'Yes, it was,' Sissy answered, 'and it will be my resolution every year until it happens.' She reached for her gloves and swept stubbornly out of the room.

If I hear Robbie Williams' 'Millennium' one more time I am going to scream and throw something. Every single radio station in the country seems to be stuck on this one song. Even my parents had been walking around the house humming it, and I'm sure my father doesn't even know who Robbie Williams is. I used to like it before it was rammed down my throat billions of times a day. Now it just annoys me, which is sad because I fancy Robbie in a taking-care-of-him sort of way. Anyway this song was bugging me for a reason. You see, it's nearly the new Millennium, only days away. And this is the only change of Millennium I'm ever going to see, and I guess I'm lucky because not everyone gets to live through one. And I wonder if things will change hugely now that there's a new thousand years. Or will the world end, as so many predict? Oh, there's just so much to think about. I blame Robbie Williams. In fact, Robbie has become the new target for my obsessions.

You see, he wrote a song that is played and played and played and what it represents for me is the fact that not only is the year and the century ending and the new thousand years coming, but also that I have to go to Jess's PR party and I don't want to.

The four glamorous options I had for this most important occasion were: Edinburgh with Julian and his tossy friends; Pat and Ken's fancy-dress party with my parents; staying in on my own, by invitation of myself, or going to the PR party of the year with Jess, Sarah and lots of PR people. Jess made her invitation compulsory so, had I been tempted by any of the other options, I wouldn't have been allowed to take them up. I was resigned to a night with the *Ab Fab* brigade and I couldn't help but worry how many times they'd play Robbie. And I only had a couple of days to go.

When I arrived at the house it was quiet and dark. I wasn't really scared of staying there on my own, but I don't like being on my own for too long. When I opened the front door the smell of pine hit me, or the musty smell of pine, anyway, and it was so cold. Ice cold. I rushed to put the heating on before I did anything, pushing the thermostat as high as possible. Then I dragged my belongings into the sitting room. I faced one of those depressing post-Christmas scenes. The tree stood bare, its needles decorating the carpet; the baubles that had looked so shiny now looked sad and lonely. The lights seemed out of place and even the bows drooped. The rest of the room had lost its festiveness – even the piece of tinsel that Sophie and I had insisted on hanging on the mantelpiece was shedding. Still cold, I decided to make a cup of tea. I switched on the TV and felt weird at being on my own so I decided to make a start on the cleaning. I took the tree out, put away the decorations, Hoovered the carpet thousands of times and dusted. I stopped briefly to watch *EastEnders* and to take a phone call from Julian, which I kept brief and to the point.

'I miss you,' he said.

'Really?' I said.

'It's the Millennium, Ru, we should be together.'

'Yup, but we can't be.'

'Are you busy, sweetie?'

'Yes, a bit. I ought to go now. Happy New Year.' Bless him, he really wasn't very bright. I'd already slept with him and he still thought he had to be nice to me.

By ten o'clock I was bored. I had run out of cleaning, good TV and trying to think of Julian's good points. I thought it might be interesting to visit my friends' rooms, because I missed them. First I went into Jess's where I admired her huge shoe collection and counted her lipsticks. When I got to a hundred I gave up. She had a great room: pencil drawings in wooden frames scattered the walls, shoes were lined up along one side, her huge bed was filled with bright orange and green cushions. It looked as if it was out of an interior-design magazine and it probably was. She had four shelves full of make-up and her lipsticks were organised by colour, starting with the palest and finishing with the brightest, I wondered how she had found time to do that. I opened her wardrobe and laughed at how she had organised that too: suits first, then shirts, then single skirts, trousers, then her party clothes. All of her fashion disasters were there too: the hot pants she had bought at university, which made her look huge, the fake Gucci flower-print dress that made her look like your great-aunt Ada, her Utility-chic outfit, which made her look like a cross between a Boy Scout and a mercenary, the boob tube that didn't even cover her boobs. I said a little prayer to the fashion god not to let them bring back anything short in the next millennium, then Jess might stand a chance.

I reluctantly left Jess's room and crossed the hall to Sarah's.

I opened the door and gasped at how tidy it was. Sarah was the true Wonderwoman. Her walls were decorated with Matisse and Monet prints, the same ones she had had at university. A couple of old teddy bears were propped up on her pillows and her stripy pyjamas were neatly laid out. Under the bed were a few shoe-boxes full of letters and postcards but I knew better than to look through them. I'm not a terrible friend, you know. Instead I decided to hunt for her vibrators, of which I was sure she had many. I'd eliminated under the bed so that left the underwear drawer. I opened her drawer and found than even her knickers were neatly folded, as were her socks and T-shirts. And not a vibrator in sight.

The one part of Sarah's room I always loved was her pinboard, which she had filled with pictures of us from when we were at university. I was always sneaking in to take a look. There we were, Sophie, Jess and Sarah and me, at our first toga party, the house we'd lived in, Thomas and Johnny, me and Ben looking lovingly at each other, or me looking lovingly at him anyway, and our graduation photos. There was a new addition: us in our Clapham home. Sarah might be totally anal but she has a good sentimental side too. I closed her door and opened it to check that I hadn't left anything out of place. That's the trouble with snooping: you get paranoid about getting caught.

I climbed the stairs to Sophie's attic room. I just loved it – it was so messy, clothes strewn everywhere, her dressing-table sprayed haphazardly with makeup, more perfume than I had ever seen. She had a bean-bag on the floor – of which little was visible – with all her nail varnishes arranged around it, and lots of brightly coloured sarongs on her walls. It was the coolest room. I lay on her bed and looked up at the skylight. It was romantic watching the sky from your bed. On the table next to the bed was an alarm clock and a picture of her and the Porsche. She looked gorgeous and flushed, with her hair hanging loose, and he looked smug. I decided against looking in Sophie's wardrobe as she kept most of her clothes on the floor, so I ran down the stairs and into my bedroom. I smiled to myself as I went to sleep that night.

Work was quiet, and the only reason I had been asked to come in was in case the phone rang, which it only did when my boss asked me if anyone had called. I read my book and wished that work was always like that. It wasn't like working. Anyway, it passed quickly and before I knew it it was New Year's Eve.

New Year's Eve. One year ends and another begins, just like that. I didn't want 1999 to end, but also I did. I mean, I was scared that somehow it made Ben seem even further away. Part of me didn't want it to be a new year because the old one hadn't ended satisfactorily, and ends and beginnings should be just that. I didn't want an end and I didn't want a new beginning. And it was such a big ending and beginning; never again would I refer to the year as nineteen something, and that felt weird. On the eve of the Millennium, the last-ever day of 1999, I decided to do something to mark the occasion. Memorable, anyway. I bought a newspaper, *The Times*, read it from cover to cover, wrote a diary type thing of my life so far (well, it was the brief version on three sheets of A4) and went to the hairdresser. One thing I knew for sure was that Jess would be disappointed if I did not have very big hair on this very big New Year's Eve. Armed with my big hair I was almost convinced that I'd have a good time. And Jess and Sarah were returning, so I would have my playmates back. I painted my toenails, chilled the champagne, painted my fingernails and all by half past two when the door opened and Jess burst in.

'Happy Millennium, Ru.' She hugged me. 'God, you look sensational.'

Sarah followed Jess in. 'Christ, Ru, she's unbelievable. I think she's caught what is known as the Millennium bug.'

As Jess and Sarah got showered, I remembered last New Year's Eve, when I had gone to stay with Ben at his parents' house in Oxford. We had gone to a horribly crowded pub, got drunk on pints and snogged at twelve thirty because Ben went to the loo at midnight and fell asleep. One of his friends woke him up and he stumbled back, looking sleepy and gorgeous, and I gave him his first kiss of 1999. I could still picture him. I formulated a survival plan. I would go to the party and pretend to have fun and at midnight when everyone says, 'Happy New Year,' I'd just pretend to say that. For me this would just be a normal night. I wouldn't let this year end until I was good and ready.

We changed into our dresses and drank the champagne, Jess amuses us with about a hundred resolutions that all seemed to be about losing weight. Sarah was talking about her new-year career plan, and I just smiled and kept quiet. I have to admit we looked gorgeous: my mother had given me a short purple silk dress from her shop, which was beautiful, and with my strappy black shoes I had an outfit fit for any Millennium celebration. Jess was wearing a long, straight, Audrey Hepburn-type black dress with a feather boa, and Sarah had opted for a cream shift dress, which would have been more appropriate for a wedding than the Millennium, but she looked nice anyway. We went to the party — funnily enough it was in Fulham. Jess had booked a taxi before she left for Christmas — and she had even booked one home. I guess her foresight was the reason she was so good in PR. Taxis in London at the turn of the millennium were like gold dust.

The party was in a huge club-type place. When we walked in, it took my breath away: it was decorated in gold and the theme was a Roman orgy — well, that was what it was supposed to be. Banners saying, 'Welcome 2000', adorned every wall, which was the main unRoman thing about it, but the ice statues were Roman-like so that made up for it. Instead of chairs *chaise-longues* were scattered about the place and the dance floor was huge, lit with gold. 'Dan's Disco' was also a little unRoman but there you go. I guess Roman discos don't exist any more. Waiters and waitresses dressed in togas handed out champagne and canapés, and it was a pretty good show. Sarah and I, hungry because we hadn't eaten, followed them about, taking as many canapés as we could. We also had a fair few glasses of champagne. Then they seemed to disappear, leaving us with the huge gold bar, which was sort of half Roman.

'Ru, I'm not snogging anyone at midnight, and as you're seeing Julian, though God knows why, I don't think you are either, so if we lose each other we'll just find each other again,' Sarah ordered. Then she changed her mind. 'On second thoughts, don't leave my side.'

'Fine, although I'd forgotten about Julian.' I really had.

Jess found us again as Fennula walked in. She looked more of an Ugly Sister than ever in a puffy pink dress – well, I think it was a dress.

'Fennula, you look wonderful, darling,' Jess gushed.

'Oh, thank you, darling, so do you.' Fennula looked us up and down.

'Henrietta, you look divine,' Jess gushed, which was a blatant lie because Henrietta was wearing what looked like a hessian sack.

'You look fab,' Henrietta gushed. And they all cheek-kissed.

'How was the hols?' Off they went playing Who Had the Best Christmas. Sarah and I exchanged glances. Jess, Fennula and Henrietta the Horrible were all caught up with gossip, bitching, gushing and seeing who could make themselves heard the most. Sarah and I went to get drunk.

'Let's drink doubles.' Sarah looked quite scared. I raised a questioning eyebrow at her. 'Ru, I just need to survive this evening. It's going to be a nightmare. I could have gone to a party with Thomas but, no, Jess made me come here. Come on, let's get drunk.'

I ordered double vodka-and-limes. 'What party with Thomas? Why wasn't I invited?'

'Thomas was going to some party full of lawyers and friends of lawyers. He said there'd be loads of men and they needed more girls. I guess he didn't invite you because of Julian. He probably thought you'd be with him.'

I scowled. 'Why does Julian seem to be ruining my life?'

'You know you're going out with him because he reminds you of Ben and, yes, he does look like him, but you're never going to get over Ben by sleeping with Julian. Ru, I know I already told you I disapproved but, well, I really do.'

I ordered more drinks. 'For your information, I've only slept with him once.'

Sarah's jaw dropped. 'But, Ru, you've seen him loads in the last month.'

'I'm not a total slut, you know. Anyway, I thought that sleeping with him would be like sleeping with Ben, which would be really weird, and then when I gave in and slept with him it wasn't like sleeping with Ben at all. It was really crap.'

'Another drink?' And another and another, and then I stopped counting.

When Jess found us we were laughing at a group of men on the dance-floor, who shouldn't have been on it. 'What the hell are you two doing? Come and meet some people.'

We followed her. We met Fiona, who was big in PR — actually, she was big full stop, and Sarah nearly exploded trying not to laugh because she kept saying, 'One day you, too, can be as successful as me,' and she was serious. Then we met Harvey, who wore a cravat, and Sarah said he was a closet gay even though he tried to kiss her. Then we met Dave and no one knew who he was but he was on drugs. We met loads of people. Jess pulled a photographer called Ollie, who was really tasty, and Fennula fancied him, which was why Jess did it. Ollie didn't really have a choice. We chatted, we danced, I even danced to Robbie's 'Millennium', which they must have played a thousand times. At midnight, I told Dave the druggie to piss off when he tried to kiss me and Sarah and I toasted the event with another double vodka.

Sarah doesn't often let herself get very drunk, but when she does she gets really sentimental. At midnight on New Year's Eve, as the new millennium began, Sarah was plastered.

'Do you remember when we first met? Oh, I do, like it was yesterday. In the kitchen, you and Jess, me and Sophie. I bet you didn't know then what great, great friends we'd become.' I nodded. 'You, Sophie and Jess, you're my best friends. I love you and Thomas. I love Thomas. This year is going to be better, Ru, I promise it will be better.' Sarah hugged me and I felt like a selfish witch.

Jess, with Ollie in tow, came and rescued me from being told any more how much I was loved, and we all got our cab home. As soon as we got in Sarah passed out. It was the first time in living memory that I had known her to go to bed in her make-up. Jess dragged Ollie straight into her bedroom and I sat up alone, thinking about the good old days and Ben, of course — well, it was a special occasion. Perhaps it was time for me to move on properly, make it my New Year resolution. But somehow I couldn't. On the first day of the year 2000, months after Ben had left, I still wasn't quite ready to face the truth. I wasn't ready to face the thought of life without Ben.

Chapter Eight

The big fat frog was sitting on a lilypad near the side of the pond. 'Hey, you,' he croaked, as I passed by. I stopped to look: after all, it wasn't every day that a frog spoke to me.

'Who? Me?' I asked.

'Yes, you. I'm really the prince of a vast kingdom,' he said. 'An evil witch put a curse on me and now I'm destined to remain a frog unless a beautiful girl kisses me.'

I looked a bit horrified. 'With tongues?' I asked.

'Yes. If you do this for me I will marry you and make you my princess.' The thought of kissing a frog was revolting, but the thought of marrying a handsome rich prince was not.

'OK,' I said, and I kissed him. Nothing happened. As I kissed him he remained a horrible fat frog. I felt like I'd failed. He needed to be kissed by a beautiful woman; I was not beautiful enough.

I turned to walk away in shame, but I heard the frog giggle. 'Works every time,' he croaked. I vowed that would be the last time I ever kissed a frog.

January was the month of bleak. I was bleak, my job was bleak, Julian was bleak and my friends were bleak. A scene of us looking bleak greeted everyone who came our way. It wasn't pleasant. If I had accepted that it was a new year, I would have observed that we couldn't have got off to a worse start.

Jess was close to a nervous breakdown. Her six-month review was coming up and if she didn't get a glowing report or a pay rise or promotion and anyone else from her company in the same position did, she was planning murder. She had worked her heart out for the past six months and she had seemed to love every minute of it. But now she was so stressed. And she was hell to live with. She shouted at everyone, even Sophie, and no one shouts at Sophie. She accused me of stealing her clothes, Sarah of stealing her cigarettes and Sophie of generally being in her way. We realised how important this was for her so we put up with it, but she had become even worse than me to live with. Poor Jess was going through hell. So was Julian, although he never let on. But all the people on the graduate-trainee scheme were constantly calling her to discuss the imminent reviews. I don't know what they said, but after she came off the phone from any of them she would go to her room and throw things around. It was carnage.

Sophie was having a really bad time with the Porsche. She spent most of the time either in tears because he hadn't called her or they'd rowed, or elated because he sent her flowers or turned up unexpectedly. The tragedy was that he was a wanker and she wasn't. There should be a law against it. Jess told Sophie to dump him, she had her own problems, which upset Sophie even more. Sarah agreed with Jess, which left me to be nice and sympathetic. Not the easiest job, I can assure you.

We were not sure what was wrong with Sarah. She didn't say anything, she just looked miserable and didn't want to talk to anyone. She had taken to spending hours alone in her room and she never seemed to go out. I suggested that her vibrator had run out of batteries, but then I was accused of being a heartless bitch. To stop being a bitch, I braved the closed door of Sarah's room. She was sitting on her bed reading. I sat down, but she ignored me.

'What's wrong, Sarah?' I asked.

'Can't you leave me alone?'

'No, I can't. We know about Jess, Sophie and me, but we're worried about you.'

'Right. Like you're not all totally self-absorbed.'

'God, is that what it's about? I'm sorry, I know I can be selfish, but I hate to think I'm hurting you. I feel horrible, we really are worried.'

'Sorry, no, it's not that. There's a new guy at work, Daniel. He's such an arsehole, he's making my life a misery. He tries to use the fact that I'm a woman to win over my male clients. You should hear his sexist jokes. I do all the sodding work and he walks in and gets the glory. It's really bothering me but I don't know what to do.'

'You need to say something. I know I'm not an expert on office politics but I know you're the best and if this Desperate Dan character is causing problems tell your manager. You have to.'

'I know, but I'm scared.'

'You're what?'

'Scared, Ru. I know it's a surprise, but I'm scared that this guy is going to ruin all I've been working for.'

'Christ, where's the Sarah I know? You don't give up without a fight, especially a fight you know you can win. Remember Annalise? You told me to stand up for myself, didn't you?'

'Yes, and you got sacked.'

'Oh, yes. But that's not the point. I was new, you're not, you've earned respect, they know you're good. I think you should either go to your boss or take Daniel to one side and threaten to cut his balls off.'

'That sounds tempting.' Sarah looked really sad. 'Thanks for the advice, I guess I have to do something, it's driving me mad.'

'That's the Sarah I know and love.'

'This must be a first for you.'

'What?'

'Giving advice. You don't get to do it often.'

'Yeah, well, I think I'm quite good at it. I may just do it more often.'

Sarah hit me with her pillow and rewarded me with a rare smile. I hugged her. I hoped I was right because this was not a Sarah emotion: Sarah was never scared.

However, my instinct had been right. I felt better that for once I had been a friend to her.

So what was wrong with me? Oh, nothing new. I missed Ben, I hated working, I was seeing a guy who could win the Biggest Prat in the World competition, so everything, really. The problem was, now that I was surrounded by misery I felt like a fraud. I had no new problems so largely I kept quiet and tried to be the cheerful one. We weren't a happy household. When Thomas came round, in his braver or hungrier moments, he said it was like being with four girls who had constant PMT.

Jess's big day arrived and I was worried. Not just about the murder Jess would commit, but also about Julian. If he won whatever it was they were trying to win, I'd get the blame. If he didn't, he'd be even more of a pain in the arse than usual. While Jess was still at work the day before the review, we discussed what we'd do if things didn't work out for her. Sophie said thoughtfully that we'd take her out and listen to her, be sympathetic and loving, tell her that she was better than anyone else and her company didn't deserve her. We'd build her ego and pander to her. That sounded awful. Sarah said we'd persuade her to get another job with another company because she was so good at what she did. Sophie was taking the motherly approach; Sarah was being practical. I said that I'd remove all the knives from the house, pack away all my breakables (Jess had none left) and dig a tunnel so I could make a fast escape. Sarah said that sometimes I could come across as a really rotten friend.

The evening after the review we were all at home, waiting for Jess. But Jess wasn't there. She hadn't called any of us during the day and we were worried. Sophie thought that we should maybe phone Julian, then the police. Sarah thought it must be bad news; if it was good, Jess would have let us know. I said I was going to start digging my tunnel. At eight, Jess swept in with a bottle of champagne and a great big smug smirk. She announced that she had been given the highest accolade of her group, the one precious promotion. She was now above all her competition and she could look down on them. No more inviting *them* to dinner: she had a new circle of competition to court. It made me realise how evil she could be. Sarah demanded to know why she hadn't called as we'd all been worried. Jess gave us a blank look and said, 'I can't think why you'd worry. It was a foregone conclusion. I knew all along I was going to win.' There are times, and this was one, when I thought about killing Jess. She had put us though hell, had forgotten all about it and instead of apologising she gave us champagne and acted like the Queen of bloody Sheba.

One good thing that came out of her promotion, apart from the champagne, was a solution to the Julian problem. Although I feel embarrassed to admit it, I had slept with Julian on a number of occasions since Christmas. And it didn't get any better. Something about his personality screamed, 'I am a crap screw.' I had waited before I slept with Julian, and if I'd known what he was like, I'd have waited a whole lot longer. Our fumblings were brief, foreplay rushed (on my side), lovemaking rushed (on Julian's side), and no passion was ever aroused in me. My heart didn't flutter, I didn't turn to jelly, I just found the whole thing dull. For once I had stopped deluding myself and faced the truth. My plan of using Julian to get over Ben wasn't working, and although I should always have known that, at least I knew now.

I didn't like Julian. How could I? He bored me; he talked about himself, he loved himself. Once again, I had behaved like a complete moron. Jess set me free. When I had first started seeing Julian, she would wait for me to get back. She'd be sitting in the lounge, which had become the interrogation room, with a glass of wine and a cigarette, if it was the evening, or orange juice and croissants if it was the morning. She was always there. I'd sit down and then I'd have to answer endless questions about him. I tried not to, but Jess could wear anyone down. She'd have a great future with MI5.

I saw him on the Friday after Jess's big win. And, of course, he spent the whole evening moaning about the injustice of it all and even suggested that Jess was sleeping with the boss, who was a woman. I got really angry with him. I refused to give him any sympathy but he was so depressed that he didn't notice. He didn't even want sex with me. That was the only good thing about the evening.

When I got home, Jess was in the kitchen.

'Where's my breakfast?' I asked.

'What?' she said. The free croissants and orange juice were no more. Instead Jess told me she'd had a date last night with some guy from an advertising agency who had been determined to argue the merits of advertising over PR. 'I think that's the reason he asked me out, to convince me that advertising was great and PR was crap. Of course, I put him straight on a few things and by the time he went home he was seriously considering a career change.' We giggled. 'So, you were out with Julian last night?'

'Yes.' I took my interrogation position under the lamp.

'Ru, when are you going to dump him?'

'What?' I hadn't been expecting this.

'Well, darling, you know, going out with him isn't helping you. You're so miserable, I can't bear to see you like this.'

'But, Jess, you wanted me to go out with him in the first place.'

'But not if it made you unhappy. Dump him.'

'No, I can't.'

'What do you mean you can't?'

'Well, he may not be great in bed and he's got a small penis and he bores me, but at least I go out now.'

'Ruth, I'll take you out. There's no point in you seeing Julian. How come you didn't tell me before he had a small penis?'

'Because it's none of your business. I wish I hadn't told you at all. Listen, Jess, what about helping your career?'

'Well, I've been promoted, Julian isn't important any more. Dump him, although I would like to be there when you do.' So Jess wanted me to dump Julian, not for my own good but because she didn't need to destroy him any more. Bless her.

'Ruthie, you're a wonderful friend, the best. Come on, I'll buy you lunch.'

Jess was right. I couldn't keep cheapening myself by sleeping with someone I disliked so much. And now that the free breakfasts were over, there was no point. Apart from my fear of my ailing social life. I decided to do as she said and get rid of him. But one thing I have had little experience of is dumping people. In fact, I've had no experience. I was a bit slow off the starting-blocks in seeing men. Before Ben, I had had a few boyfriends, but only the hand-holding, snogging kind. Yes, Ben was my first. And I hate the word dumping: it makes the whole process sound so inhumane. I wish there was a nice way of saying it, but I can't think of one. Dumping will have to do.

I arranged to see Julian on Sunday evening. I had convinced myself I was letting him go, setting him free. But I didn't know how to do it. I was really quite nervous. What could I say? I asked my friends.

'Well, just make sure you let him down gently. He may

not be the nicest guy in the world, but he still has feelings,' Sophie said.

'You got yourself into this mess, you'll just have to accept the consequences. I did warn you,' Sarah said.

'He'll probably be glad to see the back of you, ha, ha. No, seriously, tell him early so you don't ruin his whole evening.' Thomas laughed.

'Start by picking holes in the things he says, then tell him he looks really rough, criticise what he's wearing, tell him he has a small penis, pull apart his sexual performance – oh, and make sure he's crying before you leave,' Jess said. Not very helpful.

I decided to deal with this the way I deal with most things. I got slightly drunk before I left to meet him.

In the cab I thought about what I was going to say and I felt quite nervous. I could tell him I was moving to Australia (that drew on the only real experience I had had at being dumped), or that I had a rare contagious disease or that I used to be a man. I told myself to be more realistic. No, I would tell him that my book was putting too much pressure on me, that he was distracting me too much, that I really liked him and liked being with him, but at this time in my life I had to prioritise my writing. Not bad, Ruth Butler, not bad at all. And, of course, I would say that I hoped we could remain friends.

We met in a pub near his flat (my one concession). Julian ordered the drinks. He was still moaning about Jess's promotion and the unfairness of it all.

'Are you sure she's not sleeping with Camilla?'

God, the guy had a serious ego problem. Once again he was boring me to death.

More drinks followed and I was well on my way. It was time.

'I don't think we should see each other any more.' Hooray, good start.

'Don't be absurd, of course we should.' Wrong answer.

'Julian, I mean it. I like you a lot but I need time to myself, for my novel.'

'Darling, I know the problem. You're falling in love with me and you're scared I don't feel the same. Feelings can be scary. But although I don't love you at the moment I may grow to. Don't worry so much.'

Where had that come from? All my good intentions flew out of the window and my old friend Drink took over. I was mad. 'How dare you, you arrogant, conceited self-centred wanker? I am not in love with you, I don't even like you very much. You look rough, you bore me, you've got no dress sense and you behave like a woman. The only reason I went out with you was because you look like my ex-boyfriend. He was more of a man than you'll ever be. You're crap in bed and you've got a really small penis.' For the first time, Julian was speechless. I grabbed my coat and ran out of the bar.

I would have liked to blame Jess, but I couldn't. I would have liked to blame the drink, but I couldn't. I felt so bad: no one deserved the dressing-down I'd given him. I decided I wouldn't tell anyone what I'd done.

For a few days I tortured myself about Julian. I hated myself for what I'd said. If only he'd accepted it was over, if only he hadn't said I was in love with him. No, on second thoughts, he probably deserved everything. I felt as if a great weight had lifted. Dumping Julian had been therapeutic. I was a bit more cheerful, Jess was happy again and so was Sarah, who had taken my advice. No, she hadn't cut his balls off, she had discussed the situation with her boss. Danny-boy was given a huge ticking off and he knew now not to mess with our Sarah.

That left Sophie. The Porsche had been getting worse lately, if that was possible. Sophie was destroyed: her self-confidence was at its lowest possible, she said she was ugly, fat, boring, stupid, all the things he made her feel. I really hated him.

Sophie, the most beautiful, wonderful girl in the world, was being stamped into the ground by a complete bastard.

I got home from work a few days after letting Julian go, and Sophie was lying on the sofa in tears. Floods and floods of tears.

'Oh, my God, what's he done now?' I looked at her puffy face. It reminded me of something.

'He's finished it, it's over, he doesn't want me any more.' Sophie ran to me and grabbed me.

'Oh.'

'He said he was falling in love with me and he didn't want to.'

'Oh.'

'He said we had to stop seeing each other before we did any more damage.'

'Oh.'

'What am I going to do? I loved him so much, and I know he felt the same, he told me, why did it end?'

'Oh, come here.' I hugged her again. 'What a bastard.'

'No, he's not.'

'I don't understand. *Why* did he end it?'

'Because he loved me and he was too scared to love me – well, that's what he said. He couldn't cope with not being able to control his emotions and now he's gone for ever.'

Sophie was crying really hard, she had mascara running down her face and she didn't look good. I knew just how she felt. 'Well, perhaps that's just it. He's the sort of person who needs to be in control of his emotions.' Constructive, perhaps?

'I don't care. I just want him back. Ruth, tell me how to get him back.' She looked at me pleadingly.

My heart broke. The worst thing was that I knew I could do nothing. My best friend was distraught, her confidence had left her, her life was over. I did the only thing I could in the circumstances: I called Sarah and Jess's mobiles and summoned them home. When they arrived, things looked bad. Sophie was sobbing, two loo rolls had been used, I looked close to a nervous breakdown. I had already done the comforting thing, then I started crying because I'm an emotional wreck and, well, I was responsible for half a loo roll. I wasn't helping matters.

Sarah took charge. She hugged Sophie, ordered me out to get wine and chocolate, tidied up the loo roll and got Sophie in a semi-calm state. 'Tell me what happened,' she commanded.

'He ended our relationship. He said he couldn't cope with his feelings for me, he was falling in love and he didn't want to.' She stopped crying.

'Oh, baby, I know you feel shit now, I know how much you loved him, but we're here for you, we'll get you through this, I promise.'

Sophie nodded. Wine and chocolate followed. Sophie, although still in pieces, had not started crying again. This was a good sign. I hadn't stopped crying for five days, not even for chocolate.

'Soph, you need to get away. Why don't you visit your parents this weekend?' Jess suggested.

Sophie nodded, again.

'Good idea,' Sarah agreed. 'Just to get you away for a bit. You may be able to think more clearly.'

I'd known they'd sort it out, at least the immediate situation. Get us over the crisis, keep Sophie going until she could start to get herself together. Jess and Sarah were good at that. I was useless. Sophie went to bed with some of Jess's sleeping pills and we finished the wine.

'It's so tragic,' I said.

'What?' Jess asked.

'Sophie and the Porsche. It's awful she had to get so hurt.'

'Yes, I hate him for hurting her, but I'm glad it's over. He made her so unhappy. She'll get over him,' Sarah said.

'I know he was awful, I hated him too but, well, I hate seeing Sophie like that.' I was cross and I was nearly in tears.

'Babe, I promise you that one day Sophie will learn to hate the Porsche. She'll see him for what he really is. And one day you'll probably be able to do the same with Ben.' Jess hugged me, and I was sobbing. I felt so selfish, here was one of my best friends with a broken heart, and all I could do was remember mine. I vowed to stop being such a terrible person.

The thing you have to remember about a broken heart is that it loses all rationality. It takes over the strongest of us, and turns us to jelly. It can't just be glued back together. It can take days, months or a year to heal, or sometimes it never does, not properly anyway. People so afflicted should be treated kindly and not told to pull themselves together. For non-sufferers it is easy to underestimate the seriousness of such an illness; sufferers find it difficult to imagine anything worse.

Sophie came back from her parents' house rather more cheerful. Within the next week she had started calling him 'bastard' and 'dick-head'. She swore. Once she even kicked something. She was well on the way to recovery – she even talked about taking acting classes. She still cried for him and she still hurt, but she wasn't a victim.

We went for a drink, just the two of us. I decided to try to be a proper friend.

'The thing is, I miss him, and I know that's not going to pass for a while. We hadn't been together that long but I really fell for him, you know.'

'I know, Soph, and I'm really sorry.'

'Yeah, but you understand. I mean, Jess and Sarah have been great, but they don't need men like we do. I hate being on my own. I love having a boyfriend. That's not wrong, is it?'

'Well, I don't think so, but if it means we always get hurt and meet the wrong type of men then I guess it is. I don't know, I think the way to be is not to need men but just to like them and enjoy having them around. Do you think we can do that?'

'It may take a bit of work, but we could try,' Sophie suggested. We laughed.

'OK, deal,' I said. 'We're a funny mix. Jess and Sarah put careers above all else, I put finding a man above all else and you put equal importance on both of them. You've probably got it right.'

'I hope so, but then maybe I'll just keep falling into bad relationships. I don't think my confidence could cope with another James.'

'No.' I wasn't going to push it.

'Ru, I know he was bad, selfish, arrogant and mean. I know now why you guys hated him so much. I mean, I don't hate him yet but I'm on my way. I wish I hadn't let him do that to me. Next time I'm going to get a man who dotes on me and is always nice.'

'I'm not sure if that's not just as bad as dating a bastard.'

'Maybe, but at least I won't get hurt.'

'No, Soph, you won't.'

At that moment I knew that no one would hurt Sophie again. I'm not sure how I knew it but I did.

Her recovery threatened to send me into depression, but then I realised that if she could do something about her crisis, I could do something about mine. I just didn't know what.

I had become an official clockwatcher at work. Can you believe that? All these years I'd heard of this group of people called 'clockwatchers' and I'd thought they were like trainspotters, but no. Because I was one now, I understood. Clockwatching is an occupation, not a hobby. Arriving at nine every morning, the clock starts to tick. You watch the minutes as they pass, you watch the hours as they pass, you will the clock to move more quickly. As with any occupation you get a break. At lunchtime you stop watching the clock and you have a rest. But you resume an hour later then watch, watch, watch until half past five. Then you have watched the clock enough and you are allowed to leave. Clockwatching isn't the most interesting profession, but it's the only one I'd got.

I was feeling barren. After Julian my social life had gone back to nothing. I didn't go out. My friends were always busy – even Sophie filled her evenings at acting classes now that she didn't have the Porsche. I had no life, which meant that I was unlikely to meet a man and I would probably get old and die never falling in love again. I couldn't shake the feeling that I'd never meet anyone and I'd end up alone. I had panics about being alone, panics that gripped me in the stomach and made me feel nauseous. One step forward and five hundred back. That was Ruth Butler.

One good thing about no social life was that I was getting good at television. I had become a walking, talking TV guide, and my new knowledge gave me a certain popularity at work.

'So, Ruth, what's on TV tonight?' they would ask.

'*Emmerdale* at seven, *EastEnders* at seven thirty,' and so on until about eleven. I had value now. Of course, the fact that none of these work people ever asked me out for a drink had added to the start of my TV knowledge, and now they never asked me out because they thought I liked staying in and watching TV. It was a vicious circle. I was now a soap queen, *au fait* with the goings-on in Albert Square, Coronation Street, Brookside Close and Emmerdale. I was a little upset that I missed *Home and Away* and *Neighbours*; then I would have had a full house. I had no life so I lived my life through the soaps. I cried with Peggy Mitchell, I laughed with Jack Duckworth, I sulked with Jackie Dixon and I drank pints with Seff. Actually, Seff drank pints and I drank wine.

I was lonely. I told Jess what was happening to me. She looked thoughtful.

'Ruth you're twenty-one years old, nearly twenty-two. You're young. You've just come out of a two-and-a-half-year relationship, and you're worried about being left on the shelf.

Is that right?' I nodded. 'God, I didn't realise things were so bad. Julian and everything, the messes you keep getting into, it's all because you're scared of being alone?' I nodded again. 'Ruth, why didn't you say something?' I burst into tears. I had been saying things, I had. Jess looked worried. 'The main problem is that you think a man will solve all your problems and, well, he won't. Maybe you should see someone.'

'Who?'

'A counsellor, someone who can help you.'

'No, not another counsellor, I don't want to see one.'

'OK, but you have to learn to control your panics. I don't want to see you make yourself unhappy and you have to try to stop being so obsessed with finding a man. It's ridiculous. Oh, it's my fault, isn't it? I should never have pushed you towards Julian. I'm to blame. God, I'm a rotten friend. I'm sorry. Can you ever forgive me? No, of course you can't. I need to lie down.' Off went Jess. Perhaps it was her fault about Julian but, no, it was my fault.

Later that evening Jess recovered and told Sarah about our conversation.

'Your only problem is that you think a man will solve everything, and he won't. You need to make yourself happy.' Sarah was quoting from the same book as Jess.

I had come to a life decision, dramatic but true. I was going to stop crying and moaning to my friends, I was going to stop being a pain, I was going to solve my problems on my own. Of course, I knew I needed a man to make me happy, but I just had to choose more carefully in the future. I would find one, social life or no social life.

We ordered pizza. Pizza solved everything. I ordered pepperoni, Jess vegetarian, Sarah and Sophie ham and pineapple. Jess put in the order, Sarah and Sophie supplied the wine, so I had to open the door to the deliveryman. That was the worst job. I hated it: I never knew if I should tip and the men always kept their helmets on, which was scary. I tried to swap jobs but no one would.

The bell went. I opened the door to a tall, skinny man in a helmet. He handed me the pizzas, and I checked them. Sarah had told me I must always do that.

'Oh, my God,' I screamed.

'*Ummmph,*' came the reply.

'These pizzas are wrong.' I had pepperoni and pineapple, and the ham had come alone. Only Jess's was right.

The pizza man removed his helmet and his dark hair cascaded down his back. It was long and glossy. He had dark brown eyes, a chin decorated with recent stubble and kissable lips. God, he was really quite cute. 'Um, sorry. What if I don't charge you?'

I smiled and fluttered my eyelashes at him. 'But I hate pineapple and Sarah will kill me.'

'Yeah, but you could, um, take the pineapple off and put it on the other one,' he suggested.

I clapped my hands. 'You're so clever, Yes, I can do that, but I expect a discount.' I pouted at him.

'Yeah. Only pay for one – six pounds forty.'

I smiled again. 'What do you do when you're not delivering pizza?'

'Huh?' He had a deep, sexy voice.

'In your spare time. You must do something?'

'I play pool.' He looked confused.

'Oh, I love pool, I used to play all the time.' Actually I've never played, but I spent a lot of time watching Ben.

'Oh,' he said, putting out his hand for the money.

'Why don't we go out sometime to play pool?' I said suggestively.

'OK,' he said, still holding out his hand.

'Tomorrow. Are you working?'

'No.' Now he looked terrified.

'Well, why don't you pick me up at half past seven, then we'll go hustle?' I laughed.

He looked stunned. 'OK.'

'Great,' I said, giving him the money. 'See you tomorrow, then.' I waved him off. Who said you need to go out to meet men?

It wasn't until I got back to the living room that it dawned on me. What the hell had I done? *I had just picked up the pizza guy after having spoken to him for two minutes.* God, you don't go around asking out every man who comes to your front door, do you? What was I thinking? Why wasn't I thinking?

'What took you so long?' Sarah asked.

'They got the order wrong. Only Jess's was right.'

Sarah groaned. 'I hate it when they do that. Ruth, these are cold.' I looked guilty.

'You were out there for a long time, it doesn't take that long to sort out a wrong order. What were you doing?' Jess asked.

'Nothing.' I went red.

'What's going on?' Sarah asked.

There was no easy way to say this. 'Well, um, I kind of arranged a date,' I mumbled.

'WHAT!' they all said in unison.

'You arranged a date with the pizza-deliveryman?' Jess asked. I nodded.

'You're going out with the guy who delivered our pizza on a scooter?' Sarah asked. I nodded. My three best friends proceeded to wet themselves laughing.

I went even redder. 'He was really cute,' I defended myself.

'Ruth, he delivers pizza, how could you?' Jess said.

'Jess, you're a horrible snob.'

'What's his name? How old is he? This could be his after-school job,' Sarah said, and they all started laughing again.

'I don't know.'

'What don't you know?' Sarah looked at me.

'His name and I don't know his age. I only know he plays pool.'

'Oh, my God, you're going out with a pool-playing pizza-deliveryman whose name you don't know.' Jess was horrified.

'I can't believe you accepted a date from him without knowing his name,' Sarah added.

'I asked him.'

They all looked shocked.

'Where are you going?' Sophie spoke for the first time.

'To play pool.' I cringed. This was worse than I first thought. They were right, all of them. 'I'm not going,' I announced.

'You're going to stand him up?' Jess was laughing again.

'Yes, I bloody well am,' I replied.

'So, where are you meeting him?' Sarah asked.

Oh, shit. 'Here.'

My friends all carried on laughing until they could laugh no more. I could see why they found it funny: I had picked up a stranger, I'd asked him out, I'd told him I could play pool, and then I'd eaten the pizza he'd delivered. I'd said I was going to find a man, but hadn't I also said I'd be more discerning in the future? Whoops, blown that resolution already.

The next day at work I thought about what I'd done. Really thought. Although I could see the amusing side, I also knew it hadn't been the most sensible thing in the world. I had a one-way ticket to self-destruction. I was so embarrassed, I was bright red. Nick asked if I was ill and wanted to go home early, but I declined his kind offer. For once I never wanted to go home. I had visions of turning into a middle-aged woman in a pink négligé and pink fluffy slippers spending my time seducing the postman, the milkman, the gasman, the plumber, the electrician, Jehovah's Witnesses, everyone. God, I was turning into a tart, or maybe I already was one. This was not the future I had pictured for myself.

It was Thursday, and all my friends went out on Thursdays. Not this Thursday. They were so amused by my date, they had decided to stay in. They were so cruel. I tried to be uninterested. I wore jeans and a shirt, no make-up. Jess said she'd never seen me look so casual in my life. The desired effect. 'Look, I know I have to go, but I'll be home early and I'll never see him again,' I told them.

They laughed.

'If you say so, but I think you'll get drunk and screw him.' Jess was such a bitch.

'We'll see.' The bell rang. Everyone ran to the door, but I got there first. I grabbed his arm and dragged him out as quickly as possible. I could hear my friends still shrieking with laughter as I walked down the road. I took a look at him. His dark hair was tied back, he was wearing jeans, a blue shirt and a beige cowboy jacket with tassels. I gathered he didn't go on many dates.

'By the way, I'm Ruth.'

'Wayne.' Oh, God. Just as things couldn't get worse, they did.

'Wayne. How long have you been delivering pizza?'

'Oh, about three months. I'm saving up to travel the world.'

There, I knew he was going to be interesting. 'Great. Where are we going?'

'Um, the Five Bells. It's a sort of pool place.' I'd forgotten momentarily about the pool.

We reached the pub and walked in. Everyone was male, and they stopped and stared at me. I turned red. Everyone was dressed like Wayne, and I realised that if I had been wearing tassels I would probably have been OK. I wasn't, so everyone kept staring silently. I felt as if I was in *American Werewolf in London.*

Wayne put up our names for pool and he bought the drinks. I thought it strange that he didn't ask me what I wanted, just gave me a pint of bitter. I'd never drunk bitter before. It was foul. The next round I went to the bar and asked for lager. The barman laughed, then informed me they only served bitter, five kinds, mind, but only bitter. I had bitter, funnily enough,

People had stopped staring now so I was able to regain my normal colour. It was my turn to play pool. Have you ever thought you'd get to live out your worst nightmare? Well, I was in mine. I'd watched the game, so I knew the theory, white ball pots the other balls. It couldn't be that hard. Actually, it's much harder than it looks. At first I couldn't even hit the white. Then when I managed to hit the white it didn't hit anything else. Every time I used the cue it veered skywards as I had so little control. Wayne was appalled and I tried to say my cue was too long. I don't think that excuse held up. Wayne could play – he potted everything. I potted the white. I whooped with joy until I realised that potting the white was a bad thing. I could feel everyone staring again. When he'd won by potting all his balls while mine stayed firmly on the table, he mumbled something about winner stays on. My ordeal was over and I went to the bar. I'd had two pints and I was getting drunk. I asked Wayne, who was still the winner staying on, if we could get something to eat. His brow furrowed and he got me another pint of bitter and a packet of peanuts. Then he went back to the game.

After four pints, I couldn't drink any more. I asked Wayne to take me home. He looked peeved, but I apologised and he got his jacket. We walked home. Well, Wayne walked and I leaned. He made me feel quite secure. We got to the front door and, as I felt guilty about making him leave the pub, I asked him in. He smiled and followed me. I ignored the stares of my friends as I led Wayne to the bedroom. Once again, I was too drunk to care.

I didn't really fancy Wayne and I hadn't enjoyed the evening. But I felt secure with him. I probably had an over-inflated opinion of myself and thought that I could dominate him or something. I hadn't even spoken to him all evening. I still didn't know the first thing about him; all I'd done was sit at the bar being stared at, drinking bitter while Wayne played pool. It had hardly been a romantic date. There was a certain appeal in this. Not only did I feel I could dominate him, I also felt I could seduce him properly, like a *femme fatale*. I had an opportunity to be someone I wanted to be. I was getting quite turned on by the idea. I got undressed. So did Wayne. We hadn't even kissed yet. I was torn by the need to feel intimate and wanted, and knowing that I was making yet another mistake.

I got carried away with him. I felt beautiful, I felt in charge, I felt like I could turn this guy on as much as I wanted, he was putty in my hands. I felt powerful, I felt wonderful, I gave him a blow-job. Wayne was enjoying himself. I liked the feeling of reducing him to jelly. He kept saying, 'Ruth, Ruth,' over and over. I was in control.

It was so sexy, like a scene from a film. I was the sexy woman, the wild woman. Wayne was my pawn. I could make him feel wonderful. I had that power. But then it happened. I started to feel sort of sea-sick. Then, all of a sudden, my mouth filled with vomit. God, what should I do? I had a mouthful of vomit and a penis. God, what should I do? Let go (yuk) or swallow it (yuk)? Why did this have to happen? Fuck, fuck fuck. I was about to choke when I pulled my mouth away from Wayne and threw up all over his manhood.

Wayne screamed, really screamed. 'Where's the bathroom?' he yelled.

'Straight through the lounge, up the stairs,' I said quietly. He ran out. After a couple of seconds I composed myself. I had failed at seduction like I failed at everything. I couldn't believe what had happened. I was so disgusting. When Wayne returned from the bathroom, he put on his clothes and left without looking at me. He didn't see the tears that were rolling down my cheeks. The next day, I called in sick to work and I was sick. I kept having visions of what I'd done, Wayne's face, my friends' faces, oh, the humiliation of it all. Now, if I'd never been there before, I really was at rock bottom. I made two decisions that day. I would never tell anyone what had happened, and I would never pick up a deliveryman again.

Chapter Nine

A wise man once said that money can't buy you happiness but it can buy you food. Food can make you happy. He said the same about shoes.

I went to bed early on the Friday after my disastrous date with Wayne. Luckily my friends were out, although I'd had calls during the day from all of them asking me why Wayne had run naked to the bathroom last night. I had forgotten that they must have seen him. I said he was mad and I didn't want to talk about it. They laughed.

I woke on Saturday feeling horrible. You know that feeling when you keep thinking about what you've done, cringe and can't forget it? That's me. I decided I needed to go out. I went shopping. I hadn't been shopping for ages so I decided that it might cheer me up. It worked for Jess. The trouble with going shopping when you're depressed is, as with men, you should stay away when you're vulnerable: people are out to get you — they see you coming and, like vultures, they pounce on you.

I walked into the department store and went to the beauty counter. An orange-looking lady asked me if she could help.

That was it. I told her I knew nothing about all these products and asked her to explain them to me. She told me that the most important thing for me to do was get rid of cellulite, protect my skin from the damaging environment and keep myself young-looking. 'Don't you think I'm too young to buy an anti-ageing cream?' I asked.

'It's never too early to start using it,' she replied, shocked. Then she launched into a description of Ahas and CC-somethings and then listed loads of anti products. It was far too much for me to cope with. I tried to concentrate but I was distracted by the line where her face stopped being orange, just above her neck. Then, out of guilt for not listening, I bought everything — well, not everything but a lot of things, anti-cellulite, anti-wrinkle, anti-oxidant, and I didn't even know what that was.

Then I went to the shoe department, determined to buy something nice, glamorous, something totally opposite to me. I looked at the shoes on the shelves, rows and rows of them. I wondered if they missed their partner, with only one of them being displayed. Did the right miss the left and vice versa? And did they have conversations to pass the time? Did they comment on the people who tried them on? 'Oh, God, please don't let her become my next owner, she has really ugly feet.' What would they say about me? I was going mad. I found a pair of high black shoes. They were beautiful: they extended my five-foot-seven height to six foot. God, they made me feel like the tallest, sexiest woman in the world. They also made my legs look good. I had to have them. I knew I'd never be able to walk in them but, hell, I could just stand. I took the shoe to the counter to reunite it with its partner and on the way I spotted it. A lonely brown suede mule that had been reduced. And it was a size five and a half, my size. It looked so lonely and neglected sitting on its own that I just had to have it. I bought my two pairs of shoes and, for a minute, I felt great about it.

Of course, the euphoria I experienced when I left the shop

with my packages was short-lived. The cold afternoon delighted in making me realise I had been conned by the most evil of con-artists: the beauty-counter sales woman. I had also been tricked by a pair of shoes.

Today is about cosmetics. It's not just vanity, it's insecurity and fear. An obsession with beauty is something that seems to contradict the modern fuck-you woman, but it's important to us all – and not only to those trying to hook a man. Self-image is important; looking the best you can makes you feel good, simple and true. If the cosmetics industry were a man, it would be called a bastard. It's the sort of man who plays on your vulnerabilities and exploits them. Oh, God, excuse the lecture. I'm just bitter and on the verge of bankruptcy. Because I was not going to be able to go shopping for a while, a long while I went, and bought a bunch of women's glossy magazines and decided to hibernate.

I went home, to find my friends lounging around.

'What's going on? You guys are normally out.' I threw my packages on the floor.

Jess picked them up. 'Blimey, you must be depressed.'

'Thanks, Jess.' I flopped on to the sofa.

'We're here because none of us has any money so we're staying in. Let's all have dinner tonight,' Sarah said.

'As long as it's not pizza,' Jess said. Sophie hit her. But I did laugh.

'I hate to tell you this, Ru, but these products don't work.' Sophie looked very upset. We all laughed.

'I didn't really expect them to.' I distributed the magazines and we all started reading.

'Oh, my God,' Jess exclaimed.

'What?'

'There's a diet here I haven't tried.'

We all looked at her in disbelief. There's no diet Jess hasn't tried.

'Are you sure?' I asked.

'Yes, I just have to eat cabbage soup for about a month.'

'Yuk,' Sophie said, looking at her perfect figure.

It seemed that the cabbage shop was about to make some money.

Sophie doesn't ever diet. She exercises but she doesn't diet. Most girls hate Sophie on sight – she's tall, slim, and she eats whatever she wants. But she's nice, so you can't mind too much. Jess, however, is always on a diet – the hip and thigh, liquid diets, WeightWatchers, the F-plan, food-combining, pills; she tried not eating but she fainted. She tried the cigarette and coffee diet, and every designer diet on the market. And she goes to a gym three times a week. Jess is obsessed. She isn't overweight, it's just that now the term overweight seems to refer to anyone who is bigger than a size eight. Jess wants to be the same size as Sophie and she will do anything in her power to get what she wants. I tell her regularly that no one is as slim as Sophie, apart from Kate Moss – and, anyway, Jess couldn't be like Sophie, she's built differently. It really annoys me that fashion and media try to make women the same shape (thin) and convince other women that they have something wrong with them if they don't conform. I think I'll put them on trial along with the cosmetics industry.

Jess has size twelve bones, not fat. That's her build and it suits her. Jess couldn't be a size ten, although it's not worth trying to tell her that. Her mother once told me that no matter how much she dieted Jess would always be size twelve, she can't change her bones. As I've said before Jess doesn't like to be defeated: at the moment she's saving up for liposuction.

When Sarah left university she was overweight, not fat but bordering on it – too much beer. As soon as she started her job the weight just fell off and she became slim and normal for a girl of five foot three. Jess went berserk. She followed Sarah around, ate what she ate and even called her at work every lunchtime to find out what she was having. Sarah said her diet was just 'sensible eating' and she said she had to lose weight because fat women are discriminated against in the workplace. I took her word for it. She also said that when she was overweight too many strange skinny boys had paid her too much attention. Sarah got sick of Jess trying to work out how she lost weight, so to get her own back she told Jess that toothpaste was high in fat content and had loads of calories. Jess flew into a rage, called Boots and screamed at them to invent a low-calorie one. Sarah found it hilarious, but when she told her the truth Jess refused to speak to her for a week.

I don't think for a minute that I have the perfect body – I'd be hugely deluded if I did – but I have a good reason for not being like Jess. You see, I'm as paranoid as the next girl about my body. I held my stomach in every time I slept with Ben – every day – I hate my thighs and have a huge bum, but the alternative to paranoia for me is even worse; diet and exercise. I have tried dieting a couple of times, but it's like giving up smoking: impossible. I ate cottage cheese and crispbreads, but then I'd have to have chocolate because I was still hungry. I realised I was too lazy to diet, so I gave up. Then came the exercise. Sophie and Jess went to aerobics at university, so I joined them once. It was awful. I hadn't known how uncoordinated I was until I tried aerobics: my arms wouldn't move at the same time as my legs and I didn't know what I was doing. The next day I ached so much I couldn't go again.

Ben used to run every day and he persuaded me to go with him once. By the time I reached the end of our street I was huffing and puffing and Ben got really cross because I wanted to go home. He tried to get me to run every day to build up my stamina, so I had to hide my trainers and say they were lost. I made a choice: I would accept the way I was and just live with it, no guilt, no misery. That was my sensible choice. I think you're only allowed one obsession (more is unhealthy) and I was obsessed with love.

Jess went to buy cabbages and I continued to read my magazines. I have to admit I'm not a faithful buyer of women's mags, so reading them was a real revelation. I wasn't a very good woman. I wasn't a very good twenty-first-century woman. My life wasn't how it should have been at all. And my bottom was definitely too big. I qualified on only a few points: I had an education, I had a sense of humour and I had friends. But I didn't have a great career or aspire to one, I didn't have a boyfriend or a fast car or a shit-hot apartment. I was a failure. I read articles on how to have twenty-five orgasms in five minutes, female circumcision, which made me feel sick, how beauty queens get taken advantage of, how to tell if your best friend is after your man, how to tell if your best friend is really your best friend, how to spend a million pounds on cosmetics (already done that), how to get promoted, how to ask for a pay rise, how to tell if your boss is your enemy, how to improve your career prospects, how to spend thousands of pounds on a holiday, how to diet without cutting out food, how to diet by cutting out food, exercise of the month, how to make your boyfriend fall in love with you, how you can tell when he doesn't want to commit, and I also looked at a hell of a lot of clothes. It was exhausting.

I looked at Sarah, who was reading how to make a million by the time you're thirty. 'Sarah, are women really like this?'

'No, Ru, most of the women who read these mags are like us, but with aspirations to be like that.'

'But I'm not like that. It sounds awful,' I said.

'Me neither,' Sophie said, although she was often in these magazines herself.

'It's OK, you don't have to be. I mean, the have-it-all image is the perfect life. Most of us have more realistic visions.'

'It's just a myth, isn't it?'

'Yup.'

'So no woman is going to have twenty-five orgasms in five minutes?'

'No.'

'And I don't have to look or behave like these women in here?'

'No.'

'Thank God. I think I'll write and suggest some more appropriate articles.' I went off to get a pen. Sophie and Sarah exchanged glances. Jess bounded back in.

'Jess, what do you think of these magazines?' I asked.

'Invaluable. I would never be able to live my life without their guidance.' She looked hurt as we all collapsed in giggles.

I started thinking of making my list of things I wanted to find in a women's magazine. Rules for women to abide by when having safe sex. The first is that you always hold your stomach in until the man marries you, the second is use a condom. Of course, if you have a flat stomach and don't need to hold it in then you don't deserve to have sex. Instead of investing in an expensive Wonderbra, fold your arms across your chest, just like you'd do if you were really cold, it has the same squash-together, push-up effect. An article on eligible men not afraid of commitment and where to find them. No matter how fashionable it becomes, never wear brown tweed. Which famous people are looking for love and where to find them. Fad diets and pills don't work. Only diet if you're really fat. Beauty doesn't come in a tube, babe. Being single is not a disease. Not wanting a career is not a disease. Then I would read it regularly.

I tried out my list on my friends. They were a little unimpressed, apart from Sophie, who agreed with me.

'Ru, you're just not thinking about catering for today's women. We don't want to read that stuff, we want to know how to have it all.' Jess looked stern.

'Oh, God, here's an article for you, Ruthie, one about house-husbands.' Sophie passed me the magazine she was reading.

I read about men who stayed at home, looked after the house and the kids and did the shopping. 'I think the idea of having a house husband is horrific,' I said.

'Me too,' Jess agreed.

'Really? I thought you'd appreciate the concept of a down-trodden man chained to the kitchen sink.' I was surprised.

'Oh, God, no. I want a successful husband with an interesting job. No one will be impressed by me having a house-husband.'

'Well, I don't want one because then I'd have to work,' I said.

'If having a house-husband is dull so is having a housewife. Equality, Ru. The only people who should be in your house during the day are housekeepers.'

'But I don't think the majority of the population can afford housekeepers,' I pointed out.

'Oh, I'm sure they're quite cheap.'

If I live in my own little world, God knows whose world Jess lives in.

I carried on to read a debate about whether to take your husband's name when you got married and should you be Ms or Mrs.

'Jess, you're Ms not Miss, aren't you?'

'Of course. Women should not be status-graded according to their marital status. I refuse to be judged like that.'

'OK. Sarah, are you Ms?'

'Yup.'

'Same reasons as Jess?'

'Yes, Ru. The point is that my name is Ms Sarah Rogerson. When, and more to the point if, I get married, my name will be Ms Sarah Rogerson.'

'So as well as not adopting Mrs, you're not going to adopt your husband's surname?' I asked.

'Why should I change my name?' Sarah asked.

'Exactly. Men are Mr and that hasn't changed ever, I don't think. Also the man gets to keep his surname. It's so unfair,' Jess added.

'OK, so what happens when you have children?'

They looked at me blankly.

'Which surname do they take?'

'It's so unfair. Men keep their name, then they get the woman to take it, then they get to pass it on to their children. What do women get, huh? A bloody raw deal, that's what. I mean, the only way to solve the problem is to give them both surnames, but that means hyphenating them and that's just tacky.' Jess was on a tirade now and I was beginning to wish I'd never started this.

'I totally agree. Ru, we have to give up our identity when we get married. Even in this day and age we're expected to. It's unfair. Men give up nothing and gain everything,' Sarah added.

'Oh, I'm sure you're right. But do you think that the majority of the people who call themselves Ms are married or single?'

'What?'

'Well, I'm interested to know. Calling yourself Ms is supposed to stop people from knowing your marital status. Do you think that the people who don't want their marital status known are single or married?'

'Both, of course,' Jess said and Sarah nodded.

I think the majority of people who call themselves Ms are like Jess and Sarah.

After reading all the magazines, I needed a lie-down. My education had greatly improved with what I had read, but I felt like shit. It was definitely time to live. I'd said it a thousand times before but I hadn't done anything about it. No, I'd just let myself get into loads of irritatingly awful situations and that didn't count as living, it counted as disaster. It was time for me to stop suffering from Miss Havisham syndrome and become an embracer of life. Yes, that was what I needed to do.

Chapter Ten

A gentleman's guide to post-date etiquette. After meeting a young lady at a party or taking her out for a date, a gentleman will always help her into her coat and escort her home. He should take her to her front door, but if this is not possible then he must put her into a taxi. It is correct and necessary to telephone her the next day to enquire if she reached home safely. A law is about to be passed to ensure that this takes place.

With my new-found optimism, or nearly optimism, I embraced, or sort of embraced, the first day of the new month. I think I'm ready for a new year, so here we go. My new life starts right now. My girlfriends weren't around and I needed to go out to celebrate so I called Thomas.

'Thomas, it's Ru. I need you to take me out tonight.'

'Why?'

'Because no one else is here and I want to go out.'

'Where do you want to go?'

'I don't care, I just want to go out.'

'Is this the pizza-guy thing still?'

'No.'

'You're not going to cry, are you?'

'Only if you don't take me out. Please, I need some fun and

you're the only friend I've got and I promise I won't talk about Ben all night and I promise I won't cry.'

'OK, I'll be there in an hour.' I hung up and thought how much I loved Thomas.

He turned up on time and I hugged him. I was going out.

'Listen, let's go to the Windmill, then maybe we can get a curry or something,' Thomas suggested.

I agreed. 'So, how are you?' I asked.

'Fine, you?'

'I'm OK – I'm trying anyway. Come on, let's get a drink.'

In the pub, with our drinks, I felt safe. I decided that I would be positive tonight and for once not bore people to death with my problems.

'You have had a run of bad luck. God, Ruthie, I can't believe what a disaster you are.'

So much for that. 'I know.'

'It's not about careers and stuff, it's about your personal life. You need to get that bastard friend of mine out of your system, you really do. You don't deserve what he did to you, and Johnny and I both told him that, but we can all be horrible and I'm sorry.' Thomas looked apologetic.

'It's nice not to be lectured on careers for once; come on, tell me more about how horrid men are.' We laughed. I liked the honesty I knew I'd get with him and I also liked knowing that we would never sleep together.

'You say you don't understand men, but we're simple, really. We like beer and girls and sometimes we're ruled by our penis, but we do have brains – some of us – and we can be nice and even sensitive. But women, well, I'll never understand women. I mean, you wanted equality and you got it, but it's never enough. Women want to be on top, they want more than equality. I think women nowadays are scary.'

'Only because you know Jess and Sarah. Not all women are like that. I know some see men as the enemy, which is stupid, but most still think you have a valuable place in this world. We still have deep emotions and we always will. That stops us from becoming really scary.'

'Maybe, but I don't think you'll stop until you've got us as slaves. You'll treat us as badly as we treat you. God, what a nasty thought.'

'I didn't realise you were so bothered by this.'

'I'm not, I'm just saying, that's all.'

'Yeah, well, you sound terrified.'

'I just don't know about you girls. I mean, what is it you want?'

'Do you really have to ask?'

'Not you. Women in general – and you, I guess. What do you want from us men? I mean, I'll be fucked if I know.'

I smiled at him. 'We want what we've always wanted. Tall, handsome, considerate, funny, not too smelly, good dress sense, good job, good in bed. That's all.'

'Christ, I must be bloody perfect, then. I fit all that.' Thomas beamed.

'Yes, you do.'

'Why do women get periods?'

'What?'

'Because they deserve them!' Thomas chortled all the way to the bar.

'Are you still in love with Sophie?' I asked, when he returned.

'Ru, you can't say that.'

'I can.'

'Yes, of course I am. What sane man wouldn't be? But she's a mate. How scary would it be, me being with her with Jess and Sarah around?'

'Yeah, it must be scary for any man, but Ben did it.' I still felt a pang when I said his name.

'But I'm sure they've got scarier since then.'

'Probably.'

In true Ruthie tradition I got very drunk and Thomas

and I went for a curry. 'I love a curry. I've missed it, you know,' I said.

'I know.'

'I mean, the guys were rowdy, but I loved going out with the boys. I really miss him, Thomas. I know I'm being a pain and I promised myself I wouldn't do this any more, and I know I'm boring and stupid, but I still really miss him.' I managed a sad smile.

'I know, baby, and I wish I could do something.' Thomas shrugged, and we ordered our food.

I knew that one day the pain would go away, but now I wanted that day more than anything.

I had a job interview to go to. I was on the verge of leaving the accountants and now, according to Sarah, I was ready to take on a permanent job – one I couldn't leave quickly. Actually, I wasn't as horrified by this idea as I'd thought I would be, I quite fancied some stability in my life. Perhaps that was what I needed. The job was PA to one of the partners in a property-management company. I was to be interviewed by Tom Fulhurst, of Fulhurst Properties, my potential boss.

I went to their offices in South Kensington, which were really smart. Tom shook my hand enthusiastically and looked kind. We went through my CV, then Tom explained that Fulhurst Properties was owned by him and Charles his brother. I asked politely what a property-management company did. Tom said, 'We buy, sell, develop, rent, renovate, search, all sorts, really, but we're not estate agents.' He smiled at me and I still didn't know what they did but, then, I wasn't sure he did either. I decided I wanted the job. I liked the idea of working for a man who owned a company but didn't really know what it did. I turned the charm on full blast. It worked. I was offered the post of Tom Fulhurst's PA, and I was to start on Monday.

✳   ✳   ✳

I got to the company at half past nine on the Monday morning. A very nice girl called Jenny showed me around. 'There's the coffee machine, there's the photocopier,' and so on.

She had just introduced me to my desk when in bounded another girl. 'Bloody District line. Stuck in a tunnel for fucking ages,' she said.

Jenny gave a tight-lipped smile and introduced us. 'Katie, this is Ruth. She's working for Tom and I'd appreciate it if you showed her the ropes.' She didn't wait for an answer, she just left.

Katie had long dark hair scraped back in a ponytail. She didn't have on much make-up, but she looked smart in her pencil skirt, cardigan and flat shoes. She looked at me with one eye open and the other shut. 'I haven't got a squint, it's just that I've got a hangover and only one eye works,' she explained. 'I'll get you a coffee.'

When she came back, I tried to show keen by asking about the job and the company. 'Well, there's not much to tell, a bit of typing, a few calls, it's really cushy. Both Tom and Charles spend most of their time out of the office. I work for Charles. Tom's last PA was really old. She used to do my head in, always moaning and bringing in plants and telling me what to do. I think it'll be much better now.' She smiled.

I smiled. 'I don't have any plants,' I said.

We chatted for ages. It turned out that Katie had been working there for a year, and although she'd had to work with this woman she didn't like, she'd stuck with it because it paid quite well and allowed her to keep up with her social life, which I discovered was the equivalent of four normal social lives. She also told me that there had been nothing wrong with the District line. She'd woken up to find a man from last night in her bed and it had taken her half an hour to wake him up. She also told me that Jenny was the office manager. She was really superior and always looked like she'd got a very sharp pencil stuck up her bum. I was warming to Katie: she was funny, uninhibited and, although I was quite sure I hadn't met anyone like her before, I thought we could become friends. If I played my cards right, she might even be kind enough to share her social life with me.

During the first week I discovered much about Katie's social life, but not much about Katie or the job. I saw Tom twice: he came into the office for about half a day each time; Charles came in twice at different times. It was Friday and I wasn't sure who would be in today. In fact, neither was. I booked a couple of restaurants, tickets for the theatre, typed four letters, all personal, and ordered Tom some new golf clubs. I still didn't know what he did, apart from eat, go to the theatre and play golf. I discovered that Katie was a law unto herself. She was always late, not by much, but always late. She was always hung-over. She had stories to tell from the night before, always involving men, usually involving drink and the odd drug. She didn't mind telling me these things, although at first I was shocked, and she wasn't boasting either; she thought her life was normal.

Katie had always lived in London, she didn't mention her family, she had dropped out of art college, due to lack of inspiration, and decided to become a full-time party girl. Katie knew everyone in London, or so it seemed, could get into any club for free and was always being invited to parties. I called her Katie Party and I thought she was trendy and cool, as opposed to me, a sad loser. Although I knew nothing about her past, I wanted to be like her.

'Katie, it must be fantastic to know so many people,' I said.

'Not really. They're just people.' That was all she said. I told her my unglamorous story. How I had moved to London, how I had only four friends, how I never went out and that I wanted to meet men (sorry, I couldn't help it.) I told her how I had recently lost the love of my life – God, I sounded really sad. I poured out my heart to her. She looked a little shocked.

'That's, um, really bad,' was her response. Not the one I was after either. I decided to take a different tack.

'What are you doing this weekend?' I asked.

'There's a new club opening tomorrow night.'

'Really? Where?'

'Soho.'

'That sounds great, loads of fun.' I pulled my best smile.

'It'll be all right, I suppose.' This wasn't proving easy.

'I don't have any plans. I'll probably stay in and dye my hair or something.'

'Really?' Now Katie sounded surprised.

'Yes. All my friends will probably have plans, so there you go. It'll be all right, I'll have a bottle of wine and a takeaway.' She had to invite me now; I'd given her my best sob story and my best smile.

'If you want you can come to the club.'

'I'd love to, thanks.'

'It's no big deal.' Yes, I wanted to scream, yes, it is a big deal, well, it is to me.

At the end of the day I took her phone number, arranged to call her the next day, and went home excited. I was going out somewhere cool. I was going out with someone cool. It was fantastic.

All Saturday morning I was feeling hyped up. I can't tell you how much I was looking forward to going out with Katie. That girl had already bewitched me to the point where I wanted to be her. She didn't worry about anything, she did what she wanted, she didn't care what people thought. She was also intelligent and down-to-earth. Her view of men was that they had been put on this earth to amuse and pleasure her, and they were quite good at mending cars. She said there were so many about that she couldn't entertain the idea of just having one. She equated settling down with a man to getting a mortgage, buying a sofa and admitting you were too old to party seven nights a week.

I was so excited about going out that it didn't dawn on me until lunchtime that it was also very scary. I mean, apart from the fact that I didn't get out much, when I did I was hardly a hip, slick, millennium chick. I did not qualify as trendy, or cool, or interestingly quirky, which I guessed everyone else Katie knew did. What if I looked wrong? What if I sounded wrong? What if I danced wrong? Actually, I was bound to dance wrong. I had bad nerves. I also had about seven hours of bad nerves to look forward to until I was due to meet Katie.

When I called Katie, she suggested meeting me in Soho, but I persuaded her to let me go to her flat. She couldn't understand why I'd want to do that, but I didn't know Soho very well and I knew I'd feel safer going with her. I told her she was on my way so I might as well pick her up. I was still nervous when I hung up: I felt like I had the Kirov Ballet performing *Swan Lake* in my stomach.

To distract myself I thought I'd decide what to wear. I trawled my wardrobe for something suitably cool. When I had eliminated my work clothes, my student clothes and my fashion mistakes, I was left with two pairs of black trousers, three boring short skirts, a silk blouse, a chiffon blouse and my evening dress. And I couldn't wear my evening dress. My drawers yielded no better. The stuff was OK but it hardly screamed 'trendy', 'cool' or even 'marginally interesting'. I was in despair and I was alone. There was no one for me to turn to. I lay on my bed in best thinking position.

The only member of our household who was trendy was Sophie, and the only part of my anatomy I could squeeze into her size eight clothes was perhaps my foot. Sarah's wardrobe, even if she had been my size, was in an even more dire state than mine. Which left Jess.

Jess was a follower of fashion, but not a very good one. She bought whatever was the thing of the moment, even if it looked dreadful. Cropped tops that barely covered her boobs, trousers so tight they left nothing to the imagination, dresses so shapeless they left everything to the imagination and only a creative imagination at that. The other problem with Jess's wardrobe was the keep-out notice pinned to it — figuratively speaking, of course. Jess loved her clothes and did not love other people stealing them. In fact, if I borrowed from her without asking and she found out, I would be killed, a horrible-slow-death sort of killed.

But I was desperate and Jess was away. Even if everything in her wardrobe made me look hideous, at least I would be dressed in the right century's fashion. So I did it. I walked calmly into Jess's room. There was a lot of pink, which isn't my best colour, but who was I to be choosy? I pulled out a pink crocheted top with a big gape at the front and tiny straps. It looked like a leaves-nothing-to-the-imagination top. I tried it on. It showed a bit more flesh than necessary but it was my only hope. When it was time to get ready, the pink top with my black satin trousers and my high-heeled boots seemed to work. I clipped back my hair, put on as much make-up as possible and surveyed the results.

So, I looked like a Spice Girls' fan, but at least I didn't look like a Spice Girls' fan's mother. With my stomach still churning I grabbed my jacket and left the house.

I went to Katie's flat in Victoria — she had said living centrally was essential to her lifestyle. When Katie opened the door I thought for a minute I'd come to the wrong flat. The girl who stood there did not look like the Katie I saw every day at work. The first thing I noticed was her hair: it had somehow become very big and stuck straight out from her head. On closer inspection I saw that it was also decorated with glitter. Her top was glittery too: she was wearing a silver sparkly boob tube. Luckily her boobs were quite small so she could get away with it. Then I looked down and noticed her belly-button ring, looked up and saw her pink fairy tattoo on her shoulder, then looked down again and saw her black suede patchwork skirt, which was so short I could almost see her knickers. Despite it being the middle of winter, her legs were bare from thigh to mid-calf, and ended in bright blue platform boots. They made her almost as tall as me.

I tried to regain my composure as I went in but, God, compared to her I was like a Spice Girls' fan's grandmother. She had a nice flat, very neat, which surprised me: for some reason, I had expected her to be messy.

'Ruthie, have a glass of wine.' I took it and was also handed a joint. I smoked – after all, I'd done that at university, I wasn't totally green. The trouble was I knew I shouldn't smoke much because I always pass out if I do.

'Do you want to go to a bar before we go to the club?' Katie asked me.

'OK.'

We left.

Unsurprisingly the bar we went to was trendy – glass everywhere, sofas instead of chairs, and low tables. It was stark and looked bigger than it probably was. Even the bar staff looked as though they were made of glass. Once we were seated in a huge sofa, me drinking wine, Katie drinking red wine and Coke, I started talking. In fact, I didn't stop talking – the effect grass had on me. I told Katie about my horrible lack of ambition. 'You see I haven't got a clue what to do with my life.'

'Most people haven't, Ruthie. They all think they do but they don't think at all. You'll find it one day, but until then, just relax about the whole thing. I know I'm never going to have a career and I can't see myself married and I don't know what I want to do with my life, maybe travel, maybe go back to art college. But what you must remember is that there is always more than one option in life, and whatever you choose to do, you can do. If it doesn't work out, so what? You just go and do something else.'

Katie was usually a little wild, but now she had become the most sensible person I knew. I tried to find out more about her and art college, but she wasn't forthcoming. Although she cracked jokes and made me laugh, it was going to be hard work finding out who she was.

It wasn't long before she was surrounded by people. There were so many and although she introduced me to them I couldn't keep up. Most of the men were gay, which she had to point out to me because I was trying to flirt with them, but I didn't mind. It was so refreshing to meet new people, talk to new people, just to see new people. When the crowd had dispersed I turned to her. 'You're so lucky to have so many friends.' I was impressed: she knew more people than I had met in my life.

'They're not exactly friends.'

'But they were so friendly and nice, Katie. What do you mean they're not friends?' Katie almost scowled, and I was annoyed with myself for upsetting her before I had had the chance to make her like me.

'Ruth, I go to parties, that's what I do. These people do the same. We have that in common. We talk, laugh, joke whenever we see each other, but they don't have my telephone number, they don't know where I live, they don't even know my last name.'

'Why not?'

'They don't ask and I don't tell them. That's the way I am.' Katie indicated that this subject was closed by grabbing her jacket and ushering me out of the door.

We went to the club. Katie had put us both on the guest list — being such an unhip chick, that made me really happy. I felt important and I felt special and I also felt a little bit smug when I saw that the queue was about a mile long.

The club was huge and light: it looked as if it was owned by the same people as the bar. Mirrors everywhere, which I found a little disconcerting, chrome bars and the biggest dance-floor I had ever seen. It was fairly full of people. A few were already dancing, more were at the bar and some sat at small chrome tables that ran along the side of the room.

The people were wild, wearing outfits I couldn't quite fathom, cheek-kissing and seeming to know everyone else — women looking sexy, drag queens, men looking sexy all in one room, mixing and having a good time. I was overawed by the scene but excited at the prospect of becoming part of it. I wanted to be part of it. We drank, danced and Katie took some pills, but when she offered me one I declined. I met more people and I was really enjoying myself.

'Katie, baby,' a guy shouted, and ran over to her. His friend followed. Within seconds Katie and this guy were playing Swap the Tongues. I looked at his friend, who shrugged.

'They're old friends,' he said.

'I'm Ruth,' I said.

'Philip. Ruth, can I buy you a drink?' He led me to the bar and I looked at him properly. He looked nice, tasty even. Tall, long blond hair and slim. He was wearing blue velvet trousers and a sweater vest, although I guessed it wasn't called that. It turned out that he worked in advertising, he was a creative something, and he did look quite creative. I told him I was between inspirations at the moment and left it at that. I thought that sounded a bit more interesting than the truth. We got drinks then Philip led me to a table in the corner. Katie and his friend hadn't come up for air yet.

I was really pleased, a little drunk, and sure that Philip was going to seduce me. Instead he started lining up cocaine. I was shocked. I mean, it was dark, but we might get arrested — *I* might get arrested, and what would my mother say? I kept looking around to see if anyone was coming but they weren't. I tried to calm down; being cool was going to be harder for me than I had first thought.

Philip offered me some cocaine, but I declined. Actually,

I'd only smoked grass and I didn't want to risk making a fool
of myself with a handsome stranger. He snorted, and I tried
to concentrate on not being paranoid. After a couple more
lines, Philip grabbed me and started kissing me. It was very
nice actually, and he seemed to enjoy it. He invited me back
to his place and there was no way I was going to refuse.

I insisted on finding Katie to say goodbye and we left.

We got a cab to his place, which was somewhere in north
London, I wasn't exactly sure. Philip was a bit fidgety in the cab.
He kept clanking his teeth, smiling and touching his hands. I
thought he might be nervous until I remembered what he'd been
putting up his nose. I smiled back at him. Despite the alcohol
I felt nervous. Philip was so unlike the men I'd met before.
He was ... well, I guess he was more cosmopolitan. When we
reached his flat we got out of the taxi. 'Eleven pounds forty,'
the driver said.

Philip searched his pockets. 'Ruth, I don't seem to have
any cash.'

As he bounded to his front door I pulled the money out
of my purse. Great. This could not be the man of my dreams. I
followed him through the door, which at least he held open for
me, then walked up a hundred stairs until we reached his flat.

As I followed him in I was struck by how small it was. And
messy, unbelievably messy. We walked into his lounge, which
was tiny and filled with junk. He sat down on his sofa – well,
I think it was a sofa but I couldn't tell: it looked more like a
rubbish tip. Oh, well, I sat on top of the tip. Philip grabbed a
mirror and started lining up his cocaine. He snorted. I declined
again. He was an obvious expert, I was an obvious square. After
he'd finished he lit two cigarettes, passed me one – well, at least
he had lit it for me – and started talking. And talking.

He told me his whole life story. How as a boy he'd eaten
dirt, or worms, how he'd grown up in London or Essex, or
gone to college in one or the other, how he was a Goth, a
punk and a hippie in that order. How he'd dabbled with both

men and women and decided he liked women. And while he
talked, I smoked. I felt a little out of my depth, or a lot, and
I grabbed hold of a pile of rubbish to steady myself. This was
going to be a one-night stand, a long one-night stand. Just as I
thought I must be in the twilight zone he kissed me again and
I remembered why I was here.

The kiss was long, slow, exploratory, damn gorgeous. When
it ended I felt as if the breath had been knocked out of me. My
stomach was in tatters. He moved closer to me, I moved closer
to him, I tried not to think about what I was sitting on and
whether it would collapse. We kissed again and I was so turned
on. I pulled at his T-shirt as he removed my top. I kissed his
nipples and he kissed my neck. Then he stopped and he started
talking again.

I groaned inwardly, as did my libido, and he gave me yet
another cigarette. This time he took me through his love-life
history. From his first kiss with a girl named Claire aged five,
to him losing his virginity with his cousin aged fourteen, to his
first real love and everyone else until now. And there was a lot.
Then eventually he kissed me again and I put my whole self
into it to ensure he didn't start talking again. Ever. The tactic
was simple. I pushed my breasts into his mouth, I wiggled out
of my trousers. I pulled him out of his and started licking his
legs until I reached his small but adequate penis. I took it into
my mouth and basked in his pleasure. He moaned sexily, and
I licked and teased until he was about to come and I pulled
away. He looked at me with his eyes half closed and I kissed
him again.

'Condom,' I breathed at him, and miraculously he pulled one
out from beneath the rubbish tip. He put it on, turned me over
and entered me from behind. I couldn't help but yelp loudly.
This was the best I'd felt in ages. He moved back and forth,
his hands gripping my hips, pushing and pulling me with him.
'Oh, yes, Philip, yes, yes, yes.' I couldn't help myself. This was
heaven. It was almost worth the hours of chat I'd had to endure.

He worked harder and harder and I was on the brink of orgasm, real-life orgasm. 'Philip, Philip, Philip,' I screamed, then I came. A few seconds later Philip joined me and he collapsed on top of me. Me and the rubbish tip. After another cigarette, during which he remained unusually quiet, I asked to go to bed. I fell asleep as soon as my head hit the pillow, smiling at the memory of that orgasm. And, boy, it was good.

When I awoke, Philip was sprawled across the small double bed. I lay there basking in the feeling of last night until I could no longer feel my legs. I got up and found the bathroom – not hard in such a small place – but on seeing the state of the shower and the towels I settled on splashing myself with cold water. Once I had located my clothes, marvelling at how much worse the flat looked in daylight, I woke Philip. He groaned as he opened his eyes. 'What?' he mumbled.

'I'm going, Philip. Thanks for a lovely evening.'

'Bye,' he said, which I took as acceptance of the situation. I kissed his hair, because that was the only part of his body still available to me, and I left.

I realised that this had been a traditional one-night stand, which saddened me a bit. I mean, I'd been hoping he'd ask for my phone number and that I'd see him again, but still I was almost proud of myself: I had managed to sleep with a very nice man without losing my memory, my knickers, my job, or being sick. It was a shame that I wouldn't see him again, but I felt it was a step in the right direction. And, of course, he was a drug addict. I smiled all the way home. Of course, I felt slightly cheap but I'd had fun and, on the whole, I had colour in my cheeks and a spring in my step. Of course I did. I'd just been laid.

When I got home, everyone was waiting to question me on what had happened last night. Normally I share everything with my friends and they with me. But, for some reason, last night felt like a step forward in changing my life. I felt that I might now be able to enjoy myself again, things were moving. I didn't feel ready to share, not just yet. I told them I'd had a fab time and that I had stayed at Katie's. They looked disappointed at no disaster story, but I thought they'd get over it.

That afternoon Thomas came over, saying he had a crisis. We all lay in wait: nothing like a good crisis to brighten up a Sunday afternoon, especially if it's not yours for once. He sat down, looking forlorn, so Sophie ran to make him tea, Sarah gave him a biscuit, Jess grinned at him like a vulture and I held his hand.

'What's wrong?' Jess said, getting down to business.

'It's Andrea, this girl I'm dating. She's giving me the total runaround, not returning my calls and I'm calling a lot. When we do go out we have a fantastic time, but in between it's hell. I don't know what to do.'

'Welcome to my world,' I said. Thomas looked more horrified than ever.

'Perhaps you should be a bit cooler. Play hard to get, don't call her,' Jess suggested.

'But if I don't call I'll never see her and I really like her.'

'She sounds like most men,' Sarah said.

Thomas looked indignant. 'I'd never treat a woman like that.'

'What about that sweet girl at university – Catherine? You slept with her and then whenever you saw her you'd hide and she knew because you were so obvious about avoiding her,' I reminded him.

'OK, but that's the only time I was a bit mean.'

'And gutless. What about Annie, the girl from your law course? You told us you were in love with her, then you took her out, called her, took her out, slept with her and never called her again. And you kept your answerphone on constantly so you never had to take her calls,' Jess said.

'But she was really clingy. I wouldn't do that normally but she made me feel claustrophobic.'

'Thomas, you're such a liar. Remember last month? You really liked some girl you met at the Hanover Grand. You spent all night pursuing her, ages getting her number, you took her out, slept with her, told us you didn't want a relationship and never called her,' Sarah added.

'I was confused.'

'More like you were running out of excuses. Face it, babe, you've been treating women really badly and the worst thing is you're dishonest about it. You're gutless, selfish and a complete bastard. Now you have the cheek to complain when someone does the same to you.' Jess wasn't about to let Thomas get away with anything. If he was looking for sympathy, he'd come to the wrong place.

'Yeah, but I really like Andrea, and I promise I'll never treat anyone like that again as long as she stops avoiding me. I really do like her.'

'Only because you can't have her,' I suggested. 'Fancy a pint?'

Thomas soon forgot about his love problems and got drunk. He stared at Sophie lovingly all evening and crashed out on our sofa. Poor Thomas, he's bad for women and I don't condone his behaviour, but he is my friend, after all, and puts up with my habits, so I guess it's only fair that I do the same for him.

For the first time ever I didn't shudder at the thought of going to work on Monday. I had badly wanted to talk to Katie on Sunday and swap stories, but her answerphone was on and, although I left a message, she didn't call me back. I was looking forward to seeing her.

In my second week I had two missions. The first was to make Katie my friend, the second was to find out what Fulhurst Properties did. Katie and I sat outside the two offices of Charles and Tom. We were separated from the rest of the office by a glass partition. The rest of the office consisted of a receptionist, the office manager (pencil-up-her-bum Jenny), ten property consultants and two secretaries. The only information

I could get was that the property consultants were running the show. Tom and Charles never seemed to do any work.

I began to think that maybe this was just a front for a crack house, or gun-smuggling or something really bad. I looked for clues, but found nothing, not one bit of crack or any guns. I was getting more convinced that something was going on, but then one of the property consultants came to see Tom and Charles and told me they'd just struck gold on a bunch of property that had doubled in price, so it might have just been property.

I started work at half past nine. The one boss whose turn it was to come to the office that day would arrive around half past ten. I'd open the mail and I would answer the phone occasionally. When my boss arrived, if my boss arrived, I'd make him coffee. We'd go through the mail and put made-up appointments in his diary. He'd make loads of phone calls and then at lunchtime he'd leave, saying he had a business lunch, and he'd be gone for the day. Hardly anyone ever called for him.

It might sound boring, but it wasn't. I had Katie, and we chatted most days. Although she wasn't exactly calling me her best friend, I felt she was warming to me, probably because as we had so much time she knew more about me than she did about anyone else. I thought I could stay in this job until I got married.

Jenny hated that Katie and I had fun. She was always poking her nose in and trying to give us work, which Katie would refuse. 'If you want us to do any work for you, you have to get Tom or Charles to give it to us.' This put Jenny in a horrible mood and she sent a memo to the brothers saying that they didn't need two PAs. Tom – it was his turn in the office – asked me to reply. I showed him what I'd written. It read: 'How dare you suggest that people as important as us do not need a PA each? We have a very complicated and confidential business, and therefore require people we can rely on. If you are so desperate to cut costs, get rid of one of the other secretaries.' Tom laughed, said, 'Quite right, on the ball,' and signed it. I quite liked Tom, although he was obviously mad.

Jenny was fuming. She came in to us waving my memo. 'I was trying to do them a favour. One of you could do this job quite easily.'

Katie shook her head, 'I'm afraid that Tom is quite right. We do a lot of confidential work here and you don't even know about it, because that's how good we are at keeping quiet. One of us would definitely not be able to cope.'

Jenny narrowed her eyes. 'What kind of confidential work?'

'We can't tell you that. We've taken an oath.'

Jenny looked distraught and slunk off to shout at the other secretaries.

Over the next week I continued to try to build a friendship with Katie. I had fallen in love with her instantly. This was what I knew about her: she had no career aspirations; she had a couple of tattoos and a navel ring; she had the hugest social life, she knew loads of people, but according to her she didn't have any friends.

My friends immediately thought she would be a bad influence, but she wasn't. She was a good influence: she was going to teach me how to live again. She understood about Ben – she'd been in love once, although she didn't go into detail. She didn't care about conventions, she was just herself: a good-time girl having a good time. My new plan was for me to become a good-time girl too. I felt almost happy for the first time in ages. Almost, but not quite.

Tomorrow was Valentine's Day, my first Valentine's Day without Ben. Valentine's Day is the day for lovers, so as I didn't have a lover I planned to spend it lamenting lost love. I'd been good lately so I felt I deserved a relapse. I was not the only one upset. Sophie was miserable, because she hated being alone, and although she'd had plenty of offers she hadn't met anyone since the Porsche. Sarah was still firmly celibate, didn't believe in Valentine's Day, and Jess was manless. As she had no certainty of cards coming her way she became very revolutionary: she said it was a load of bollocks, and St Valentine was a villain or unpopular or something, and a card being unsigned just added to the confusion in dating we already had to endure, and it was evil to dent people's self-esteem when they didn't get any cards, and the whole day should be made illegal. I agreed.

Thomas was the only one of us looking forward to Valentine's Day. He had given up on the elusive Andrea and found a nice girl who followed him around. It was the early stages and he asked us what he should get her. Jess told him not to bother, Sophie started crying, Sarah said he should get something useful because flowers die and she couldn't see the point in giving someone something that died, and I wondered how anyone could have a relationship and spend any amount of time with us, so I took control. 'Send her flowers, a card and take her out to dinner somewhere nice.' Everyone gave me a dirty look. 'Well, Thomas is the only one here who is having a remotely healthy relationship and I think he should do all in his power to keep it that way.'

'Yeah, but flowers, chocolates and dinner – that'll cost me a fortune.'

'Thomas, it will be worth it. Just think how good you'll look, a real romantic, a man who knows how to treat a woman. She'll love it and it'll be worth every penny.'

Thomas thought about it. 'For once, Ru, I may take your advice. With all that I'll be guaranteed a good shag, won't I?' Luckily Jess hit him hard before anyone else had the chance to.

Valentine's Day came and the mat was bare. Sophie got a rose from some guy in her acting class, but she didn't know which one and was miserable about that. 'I bet it's the one I don't even like,' she said.

Jess came home from work fuming because Henrietta the

Horrible had flowers delivered to her at work, and she didn't cheer up when I said she'd probably sent them to herself. Sarah just said that it was lucky no one had sent her a card because she'd have ripped it up.

Katie got a few cards, but she wasn't bothered. 'Men only like me because I don't want to see them again. It's nothing personal to me,' was her view on her appeal. I liked her lack of arrogance; I wanted her success with men.

I bought a card for Ben and in it I told him that although I was better I still loved him and missed him and hoped he was safe and well. I told him how I hoped he was happy, which I thought was bloody nice of me. Of course I didn't send it – I didn't even know where he was – but I sealed the envelope and put it in my drawer. I felt better for doing it, although I knew it was stupid and I didn't dare tell anyone else. I felt close to him, or as close to him as I'd ever be again.

Although I will probably be classified a mad cow over my Ben antics, there were reasons for me being hit so hard. The first was that Ben was my first love and my first . . . you know. They say that the first love is always the hardest to get over, so on that point I have justification. The other was the lack of contact. I knew that seeing him might not make things easier, but if I bumped into him occasionally, or heard about him, or just saw him from a distance, I felt I could have started to get him out of my system. Because his departure from my life had been so absolute, my last image of him was of Ben as perfect. Does that sound crazy? I didn't know any more, but I just felt that if I could hear from him, or about him, then he would become real to me again. At the moment he was my fantasy man. There's no way you ever get over your fantasy man.

I knew that Thomas got letters from Ben and Johnny, but diplomatically he never mentioned them or showed them to me. Actually, I begged him to show me them a couple of times but he refused, brushing them off as boring. I knew then that if I wanted to get over Ben I had to find out what he was doing. I'm not sure of my logic in this, but I had to read those letters.

I devised a plan. Sophie and I went to visit Thomas. It was Sunday, I called him and told him we were bored, he said so was he and I said we'd visit him.

'Soph, we have to visit Thomas,' I said.

'Why?' She looked comfortable reading a playscript and lying on the sofa.

'He's really depressed,' I lied.

'Oh, God, what's wrong?'

I'd known she would be immediately concerned. 'Well, I'm not sure, he just said depressed.'

We got our coats. You might think me devious, playing on the unrequited love of one friend and the good heart of another, but I was desperate. I had to do it.

When we got to Thomas's he didn't seem depressed, but I had told Sophie that she shouldn't mention it under any circumstances. God, I was good at this.

Thomas went to make us tea. 'Sophie, I need you to keep him talking in the kitchen.'

'What?'

'Please, Soph, talk to him about Chelsea Football Club, for a while – please. I really need you to do this.'

She looked at me. 'I don't know anything about football.'

'Just ask him how they're doing and take it from there. You're an actress, just improvise.'

'Why, Ru?'

'Please, just do this for me, please.' I was also good at begging.

'OK,' she said, and off she went.

I snuck into Thomas's room and easily located the letters. There were about four. Of course I didn't think about invasion of privacy, I just started reading them. I knew I was wrong, but somehow it didn't matter. The thing I had to remember about friends was that they don't keep things from you without a reason. The reason Thomas didn't want me to read Ben's letters was because all Ben talked about was all the 'birds' he had pulled, how gorgeous they were and, God, there were loads. Travelling for Ben was not about seeing the world, it was about seeing how many clitorises he could discover. He wasn't doing badly.

I was mortified. My Ben. I couldn't stand the thought of him with one other woman, let alone half of the world. At the point where I started wailing, Thomas and Sophie had obviously run out of the Chelsea conversation and came in to find me on Thomas's bed. I was bawling my eyes out. Thomas didn't shout at me, he just tutted and hugged me and said that Ben had probably made up half the things to impress him. Sophie hugged me and started crying too, because she's like that, and Thomas hugged us both, called us silly and generally tried to calm us down.

I stopped crying. 'He's moved on, hasn't he?'

'Yes,' Thomas said.

'He moved on even before we split up, didn't he?'

'Yes.'

'Our relationship meant nothing to him, nothing,' I spat.

'It did, Ruthie, it did.' Sophie had glistening tears in her big eyes.

'Ru, he loved you in his own way, he really did, but he was young and he couldn't handle it. He didn't know how. None of us do, really.'

'I do, I bloody do. I loved him so much. I could handle it.'

'I know, babe, I know, but Ben, well, he couldn't and now he's gone and, yes, he's moved on, and I didn't want you to read those letters. I couldn't bear the thought of you being hurt any more, but now you have and maybe you can move on too.'

I felt like I was five years old again, being comforted by these kind people. And they were right, I could move on – I had to. I had to try, at least.

'You're right. I'll try. I need to go now.'

Sophie took me home and we didn't speak. I knew what Ben was doing now and I knew he was happy, and I knew he didn't think about me and I vowed that I would make sure now that I got over him. This was the beginning of the end of Ben.

Chapter Eleven

The Trojan Prince, Paris, was chosen to judge a beauty contest between three goddesses. It was to be held to solve an argument that had broken out between Hera, queen of the gods, Aphrodite, goddess of love, and Athene, goddess of justice, about which of them was the loveliest.

Paris had a reputation as a womaniser, so it was thought he would make a good judge. The goddesses paraded in front of him in their swimwear and evening wear, but he was reluctant to choose: they all had their merits. To get the matter settled, each offered him a bribe. Hera offered him rulership of the world, Athene offered to make him the mightiest and most just of warriors, Aphrodite promised him the most beautiful woman in the world as his bride.

Tough choice? Not for Paris the womaniser. He chose Aphrodite without a moment's hesitation. His reward was Helen, Queen of Sparta, an already married woman. The result was the Trojan war, which was started by Helen's spurned husband and ended in the destruction of Troy. The moral of the story is, men shouldn't be ruled by what they keep in their trousers.

Monday again. I couldn't believe the cruelty of Sundays: they last such a short time and propel us to Monday without a second thought. I was a classic sufferer of Monday-morning blues. Katie had a great way of beating Monday blues; she had them on Tuesday instead. Monday was always a good-mood day for her. But although I hated Mondays I didn't hate them as much in this job as I had in the others. I can remember towards the end of my time at the magazine pulling the duvet over my head and sobbing. This was fine compared with that.

When I got in Katie was already there. A first. She announced that Charles and Tom had decided to go to Portugal for a week so effectively we had a week off. Although I wasn't sure it would make much of a difference, it was a nice thought. Jenny, who by now I couldn't stand, kept coming up to our desks asking if we had enough work to do. 'Of course. Are you trying to suggest that the Fulhursts would swan off without priming us first?' Katie asked.

Jenny went red and went off as usual to shout at the other secretaries.

'Do you think she's a huge pain because she likes to boss people around, or is she threatened by us, or is she a job'sworth?' I asked.

'All three. She likes to make her authority known with all the secretaries and she hates us because we don't take any notice of her and she thinks she's important, which of course she isn't, she's just a pain in the arse,' Katie replied.

'Let's play the worst-boss game,' I suggested.

'What's the worst-boss game?'

'Oh, we just tell each other worst-boss experiences. It's simple, really.'

'OK. I used to have a boss called Trevor, Trev for short. Anyway he was young, fat and thought he was God's gift. He used to pick his nose and call me darling. I was working as a receptionist at the time and he was so ugly. Actually, he might just have been the ugliest boss – no, he was the worst boss too. He asked me to dress more sexily and wear more make-up as we had clients coming in a lot. I told him I wasn't a slut, but he said that as long as I worked for him I was for sale. That did it.

I might not have many morals, but being treated like a whore? No way. When I left I told him he was the crappiest pimp in the world – he'd never made me sleep with any men and he'd never hit me. Although he almost did when I said that to him.'

We laughed.

'My worst boss was a woman called Annalise. She had slept her way into her job and she couldn't do it. I was her assistant but she made me do all her work and then took all the credit. She spent all day on the phone to her friends.'

'What a bitch.'

'Well, yes, but the worst thing was she complained about the standard of my work, said I was making mistakes so she was getting flak. I reported her to the director, who had obviously slept with her because I got sacked instead of her. I didn't mind that too much.'

'Tom and Charles are great bosses.' They really were, although a little unusual.

Katie, although friendly and great, had been proving a little tougher than I first thought. I still knew hardly anything about her and, apart from one night out, she hadn't been forthcoming with social invitations. I knew she went out all the time and I wanted to go too. This was becoming serious.

'Katie, what are you doing this weekend?'

'I think I'm going to some party.'

'Oh. Listen, you can say no if you want but, well, can I come?' God, Ruth, subtle as ever. I could write a book on how to lose a friend before you've even made one.

Katie looked at me. It was surprise, not anger I saw in her face. 'If you want. Listen, Ruth, I go out all the time. If you ever want to come, just say. To be honest, I thought you'd do your own things.' She shrugged.

'I wish. I told you I didn't have a social life.'

'Wow, when you said that, I thought it was just that you were having a quiet time – you know, that guy and everything. I didn't know that people didn't have social lives. Ruth, you're the first person I've ever met without a social life. Weird.'

Katie giggled, and I felt a bit stupid. Actually, I felt really stupid.

But feeling stupid passed as it always does and the thought that now I could ask Katie to take me out (she said that, didn't she?) filled my head. It would be only a matter of time before she and I were friends, good friends, and then I could start to become like her. What were the qualities I wanted from her? Her ability to attract men would be nice, and her ability not to get hurt, her happy-go-lucky nature, her dress sense, her I-don't-give-a-flying-fuck attitude. That would do for starters. Then I'd really be moving on, wouldn't I? That would show Ben.

But I was still looking for love (just in case you thought I'd changed my mind). I always have been, since I first learned about its existence. I thought it would be easy, but it wasn't. Love is the most elusive thing in the world: it has no definition, no colour, no texture. How do you find it? Perhaps love is one of the great mysteries of the world. It's harsher than the rain, warmer than the sun, colder than the wind, more beautiful than the snow. It can make you feel the best you'll ever feel, or it can make you feel the worst. It plays games with people, cruel games. Love is the one thing everyone wants; it's the one thing not everyone has. Why are we so obsessed with falling in love? I knew I was top of that tree. I knew I regularly made a fool of myself in pursuit of it. And I knew I bored my friends with my obsession.

I couldn't help it; that's what happens when you're obsessed. Being single, panic-stricken and miserable is not the privilege of the thirty-something. Oh, no, contrary to popular belief the feeling of needing a relationship, wanting a relationship, being a failure for not having a relationship can strike at any age. It wasn't as if my biological clock was ticking or anything. I didn't want children yet, just a man. It was my heart that was ticking, tick-tock, tick-tock — and would go on ticking until it shrivelled up and died without love to wind it up. I don't think we're meant to be alone, I think we need to love, to give, to receive. Hands up everyone who doesn't want love, hands up all you women who don't start wearing extra make-up when you meet someone you fancy. Hands up all you women who feel that if you're single it's socially unacceptable, hands up all you women who have a boyfriend and don't feel smug. Hands up all you women who went to the supermarket looking your best when you heard it was a good pick-up place. Hands up all you women who found a man at the supermarket. Society does not help. Society still puts people into couples. But who is Society to dictate what is right and wrong? Who is this cruel person who encourages our feelings of insecurity and loneliness? It is one of the most influential people you know. Although everything else about life has changed, as far as love is concerned the only thing that seems to have changed is that men are harder to come by, these days. Well, they were in London, anyway.

I wanted to fall in love. Really in love. The whole thunder and lightning, *Romeo and Juliet* kind of love. I wanted a man to start the Trojan war over me, I wanted the intensity that only lovers know. I wanted magic. I wanted to devote my life to the man who came for me on a white horse, not the man who had sex with me and had to ask my name in the morning. I always hoped my knight in shining armour would turn up. Realistically I hardly expected him to have a white horse, maybe a Ferrari, or just any car. I was paying attention to finding my Mr Right. Every day when I walked to the tube I had a fantasy that a gorgeous man would give me his seat, we would smile, introduce ourselves, then chat, and when I had to get off, he would run after me and ask for my phone number. It hadn't happened. I hadn't met any man on the tube willing to give up his seat for anyone.

But at the weekend, I'd be with Katie and there would be men.

It was Sophie's birthday. We were going out for dinner and I'd baked her a cake. We all rushed home from work to get ready and sing and give her the cake. We had clubbed together and bought her a handbag she'd fallen in love with, and as hers was the first birthday we'd had in London, we were all excited. Sophie was pink and flushed as she opened the champagne.

'There's something I should tell you,' she said.

'What?' we asked.

'Well, you remember that rose I got on Valentine's Day?'

'Yes.'

'I found out who sent it to me. It was a guy called Nick from my acting class. He came up to me today and told me. Said he couldn't bear to keep it from me any more. He also said that he'd die if I didn't let him take me out for a drink.'

'Wow, how romantic,' I said, wondering why that never happened to me.

'Yes. Anyway, I told him it was my birthday and I invited him to come along tonight. He's really nice, not at all like James, much nicer.'

'Great, can't wait to see this one,' Jess said, with as much enthusiasm as she could muster. We drank the champagne, got ready and waited for Thomas and the new boy, Nick.

'Will you promise not to be horrible to him?' Sophie asked.

'As if.' Jess laughed. 'Unless he's as horrible as the Porsche.'

'God, you girls are like teenagers whenever a man's involved,' Sarah said. 'It's called regression.'

'Yes, and it can be bloody good for you. You should try it sometime,' I suggested.

'Only when I'm guaranteed not to become like you three.'

Jess threw a cushion at her: we couldn't help but get excited when a man became involved. That's what girls do, even twenty-first-century girls.

Nick and Thomas arrived. Poor Thomas was confused and mortified to see that Sophie had another man. We left for the restaurant. Nick looked quite nice: tall, brown hair, brown eyes, stocky, quite sexy, really. I decided I'd try to be nice to him.

'Nick, you're an actor,' I stated the obvious.

'Yes, well, trying to be, ha-ha. Actually, it's still very new to me. I recently finished my Ph.D. in physics, but then something amazing happened. I realised I hadn't been born for physics but for the stage. In a flash, like a vision, I realised I was born to act.' Well, he was certainly dramatic. Jess choked on her wine.

'So, well, that's great, really. What did you do? I mean, didn't you have a physics job lined up?' I encouraged him.

'Yes, I was going to work for a huge lab, doing something incredibly dull. Now, from a young age I knew that I was good at physics, but I didn't realise that I didn't like it until recently. Luckily I had my vision just in time. I told them I wouldn't be taking the job, joined an acting class and changed my name.' He changed his name. Nick wasn't his real name? God, what a prat.

Sarah choked. 'You changed your name to Nick?'

'No, I changed my name to Nick with a K.'

'You mean K-N-I-C-K?' We were all confused.

'No, not Knick, N-I-K. It was N-I-C-K before.' He looked really proud. Jess's mouth was so wide open she was catching flies, Sarah was trying not to laugh, Thomas was looking pleased, Sophie was oblivious to NIK's stupidity, and I wondered which village was desperately missing its idiot.

'And I've got an agent,' Nik said.

'That's good.' Sarah had composed herself.

'Yeah, first I get an agent, then I get to come out with Sophie. Life is good. I'd like to propose a toast. To Sophie, happy birthday.' We all toasted her. Nik continued, 'The most beautiful girl in the whole wide world, I adore you.' God, did he realise this was their first date?

He was romantic, that's for sure. He asked the restaurant to put a candle in her dessert, he bought roses from the flower lady and he kept telling her how much he adored her. He was a little over the top. I mean, he was better than the sort of men who think romance is ten pints of lager and a kebab, but he was a bit of a joke.

When we went home, minus Nik, Sophie didn't ask us what we thought of him.

'Sophie, don't you want to know what we thought of N-I-K, Nik?' I asked.

She looked at me. 'OK, but I don't care this time. He's nice to me.'

'He is nice to you,' I said.

'He's very nice to you,' Jess said.

'He's incredibly nice to you,' Sarah finished.

'Sophie, do you think he's ... Well, do you think he knows what he's doing with this acting business?' I asked.

'Yes, he's quite good. I know he's a bit dramatic, but that's what actors do.'

'Of course they do,' Jess said.

'Well, I've got a new name for him.'

Sophie looked at me. 'Ru, don't be horrid this time.'

I had been going to call him the Village Idiot, but that was mean. 'I'm going to call him the Thespian.'

'Oh, that's not nasty,' Sophie said, relieved. So the Thespian he was.

On Saturday I got ready for the party. This time I wore a safe black dress and a cardigan. Again, I didn't exactly look trendy but I looked OK. Once again I had invited myself over to Katie's. She didn't exactly fall over herself with joy at the idea, but she didn't say no either. She looked amazing. This time she was wearing a sari, I think. It was Paisley print, wrapped around her like a halter neck and reaching her knees. With it she was wearing her blue platforms.

Predictably we drank, we smoked, I talked. I made a mental note to try to control my verbal diarrhoea, then perhaps I might learn something about Katie. I promised myself I'd do that next time.

We went to a party full of trendy people. The clothes were outrageous — fluffy trousers, skirts with bottoms cut out, heels taller than me, feather boas galore. Had I not recently become a little more cosmopolitan I would have been really scared. Katie knew everyone, so I snuck off to find men.

One I met was called Nathan. But Katie didn't really know him. He was lovely, tall with cropped dark hair and wearing trousers so tight it was almost obscene. I looked into his deep blue eyes and I fell for him. Nathan was a chef. I told him about my love of cooking and he told me he worked in one of the trendiest restaurants in London. I was impressed. He had a few drinks and he told me funny stories about the famous customers he'd cooked for. Of course, he never mentioned names. One very famous man lost his hairpiece in his dinner when he was drunk. One famous woman tipped the soup over her boyfriend for shagging her sister.

I was smitten. He was gorgeous, funny, intelligent and he cooked. I thought I was in love. He was polite, always ensuring I had a drink. He was also interesting, talking about things that showed a wide-ranging knowledge. He really enjoyed making me laugh. He was definitely husband material, especially in those trousers. After a while he said, 'Ruth, I'm a bit bored. Fancy having our own party?'

'OK,' I said. Then I went to find Katie.

'Ruth, take care,' was all she said.

We went back to his flat in Soho. This guy was cool. He led me to his living room, which had a lot of satin. I thought satin must have been the new thing.

'Beer?' he asked. I nodded. We sat down on satin cushions on the floor, he leaned closer and I was sure he was going to kiss me. My heart started beating fast. 'Do you want to shoot up?' he said. He didn't kiss me.

'What?' I asked.

'Let's get high.' I didn't know what he was talking about. He disappeared and came back with some stuff and I understood what he meant. The last guy I met sniffed cocaine, and this guy had a needle. I started panicking. This was way out of my league. I wanted out.

'Actually, Nathan, I'd rather not,' I said

'Why not, babe, it's great?'

'Um,' I had to think fast, 'actually I'm allergic to it.' Nathan looked confused, then proceeded to shoot up or whatever they called it. I was scared. I was in a flat with a man I didn't know who was taking dangerous drugs. I'd seen *Trainspotting*, so I knew. It's really not nice to find out that the man you were planning to fall in love with is a heroin addict. He put stuff in his arm. I looked away, appalled. Then he relaxed back into the cushions and closed his eyes, I didn't know what to do. He stayed there for what seemed like hours and showed no signs of getting up. Here was my chance. I checked that he was breathing, and when I was sure he wasn't dead I ran from the flat and hailed a cab.

I was crying really hard and I gave the driver Katie's address between sobs. I was scared out of my wits. Why didn't I learn? Anything could have happened to me. Katie was in, but she wasn't alone. She answered the door, took one look at me and let me in. She handed me a tissue then went into her bedroom. Five minutes later a guy emerged, glared at me and left. I sat on her blue sofa. 'I'm sorry,' I sobbed.

'Is it Nathan?' I nodded. 'Oh, God, I feel like it's my fault, but I didn't know, honest,' she said.

This was the first time I'd seen Katie look worried. 'Didn't know what, Katie?'

'Well, he takes heroin like a trooper and he's gay.'

I looked at her. Somehow nothing shocked me any more.

'He's a well-known closet case. He was going to come out but then it stopped being so cool. He picks up girls from parties, gets high, they leave, just like you. He's weird.'

'But I was going to fall in love with him.'

'I thought you were going to stop all that nonsense.'

'I was, but did you see his eyes and, more importantly, his trousers?' We laughed. 'Katie, I was scared, really scared. I don't want to be your responsibility but I feel green, you know, like a hick. I just want to be cool, I want to have fun, I want to be more like you. I'm not doing a very good job, am I?'

'Ruth, I don't understand. You're a lovely person, you have friends and family who love you and you want to be like me?'

'Yes.'

'Why?' Katie lit a cigarette, perching herself on the arm of the chair.

'Because you're carefree and you always have men and your social life is brilliant and you never cry or bore people, or end up in stupid situations.'

Katie laughed. 'Ruth, I'm not sure what's going on here. All I can say is that you don't want to be like me and you're lucky. It's about time you started enjoying being you.'

'I do want to be like you and I'm not lucky.' Now I'd stopped crying about Nathan I realised how drunk I was.

Katie stood up and started pacing the room. 'For God's sake. Listen. I don't have any friends. Not one. That's my choice. People don't get close to me, I don't get hurt. That's my story. You couldn't be like that and you shouldn't want to.'

'I'm your friend.' Katie sounded pissed off, I sounded drunk.

'No, Ruth, you're not. I don't have friends.'

'Katie, everyone needs friends, even you. Okay, so the people you hang out with aren't your friends, but I am. I know I'm selfish and everything, but I would like to be your friend.'

'Ruth, you're drunk and upset, that's all.'

'Maybe I am. Why are you so reluctant to talk to me?'

'I'm talking to you now.'

Katie was pissed off, but I was on a mission. 'Fine, so where do you come from? What's your family like? Why don't you see them? Why don't you talk about them?' I looked at her.

'Why do you want to know?' Katie stood up, lit another cigarette and stood still.

'Because that's what friends do. So far you've listened to my life story, you've let me come out with you, you even kicked a man out for me. That's what I call friendship. But it works both ways, you know.'

'Ruth, I haven't been a friend to you. I let you come out with

me because you ask, I like working with you, we have fun and I was
worried about you tonight, sure, but that's because, well, I don't
know. I'd make a rotten friend, trust me, I don't understand this
attitude of yours. Why do you need to be my friend?' She stubbed
out her cigarette with a vengeance and didn't move.

I gazed at her face: she looked strong, closed, she displayed no
emotion.

'Because although you're trying hard to be a hard-arse bitch,
you can't. Because you don't even know what friendship is and
now you have it. You let me depend on you and now you want
to back away. Well, I know you care about me. Katie, you can't
hide from people all your life, never trust them. That's a lonely way
to live.' Katie lit another cigarette and walked to the window. She
had her back to me but I could tell she was pained, her shoulders
were hunched.

'Believe me, I know it's lonely. But I also know that people let
you down, so this way, the hurt is less.'

'Who did this to you?'

'Did what?'

'Made you so scared of people.'

She turned round to face me. 'What is this, Ruth? You're
trying to counsel me? God, don't you dare start any psychobabble
nonsense.'

'It's not nonsense, it's called caring.'

She started pacing again. Then, to my surprise, she stopped
and waved her arms in the air. 'OK, I give in. You win. This is
me, Katie Parry. My mother is a lush. She drinks all day and sings
Frank Sinatra songs. I think she just managed to stop drinking
long enough to give birth to me. My father knows she's a lush
and encourages her. When I was a kid he came home from work
every day with a bottle of something, whatever was on offer at the
supermarket. My mother would drink, my father would watch
TV. Then when my mother nearly burned the kitchen down, as
happened every evening, my father would go out and get us a
takeaway. My mother would pass out on the bed, my father and

I would eat, then I'd go and clear up the mess in the kitchen while my father resumed his position watching the television. That was the Parry family life. When I was sixteen, as I'd always looked after myself anyway, I decided that I might as well lose them and live on my own.'

'That's awful.' Although Katie exhibited no emotion in relaying this story my head was buzzing and I didn't know what to say.

'Yeah, well, it's in the past.' She sat down.

'Where do they live? Where did you grow up?'

'Mill Hill, north London.'

'If they're so close, don't you ever wonder how they are?'

There was a silence. Eventually she spoke. 'No. My mother is probably dead and decaying in the bedroom while my father eats fish and chips and watches the football. I don't care. I really don't.'

I looked at her. She showed no emotion. Her parents had stopped her from having feelings – no, I knew that wasn't possible.

'But it doesn't explain why you have no friends. I mean, your home life sounds dreadful, but why don't you confide in people? It helps, it really does.'

'Of course I had friends, not so much at school but at college. I was careless with them, which is why I know I'd make such a rotten one now. Friendship comes with a price. Listen, Ru, in your idealistic world friends are great, love is great, but that's not always the case. I got close to someone once – actually I gave them everything, that's what true friendship is about, you have to give yourself. I got very hurt, and I decided I'd never get attached again. But that's another story, OK?'

Katie looked angry, although I wasn't sure if she was angry with me or her memories. I still had so many questions. Why was Katie really like she was? Why did she party? I mean, with a background like that you'd be more likely to join the Mormons than take up drink and drugs. And the friendship thing: who hurt her so much? But Katie didn't look as if she wanted to pursue it.

'Why don't you ever tell anyone now?'

'Because it's none of their bloody business and it's my problem and I'll deal with it my way.'

'It doesn't sound as if you deal with it at all.' That was bit bold, even for me.

Katie sprang to her feet. 'What the hell do you know? God, Ruth – in your perfect world with your perfect parents, perfect friends and perfect ex-boyfriend! And you have the nerve to accuse me of not dealing with things!'

There were two ways I could have responded to this. I could have protested that I didn't live in Cloud Cuckoo Land, although that line of defence was a little weak, or I could have screamed at her to stop being a bitch.

I thought of a third way. 'Katie, stop being so defensive. This isn't about me, it's about you.' Not bad. However when I saw the anger in Katie's face I realised that it was bad.

'Christ, where did you learn to be such a pain in the arse? You sound as if you're quoting from some mumbo-jumbo fucking useless book and it *is* fucking useless.' Katie was mad and she was beating cushions.

I cowered slightly hoping I wouldn't be beaten next. 'Calm down.'

Oops! As soon as the words escaped from my lips I knew I shouldn't have said that.

'Yeah, right, you take my life to pieces because you're "interested" in me, you want to be my friend. Well, fuck you, Ruth, I don't want this and I don't need this. Your interest in me is totally unwelcome and I would like you to leave now.'

I looked at the girl I wanted to make my friend, the girl I wanted so much to be like, and I think I saw Katie for the first time. What I saw was someone who was frightened and, even more surprising, frightened of me. I did what anyone would have done in my place: I left the flat. But as I glanced back at Katie I saw a tear in the corner of her eye.

I went home and tried to think of what Katie was going

through now, what she had gone through then. I kept wondering what it was like to have a mother who didn't make you fish-fingers and invite your friends over and take you to buy shoes. I couldn't imagine what it was like never to argue with your mother, not because you were wonderful but because she was incapable. I wondered what it was like to move away from home before you were ready, out of necessity, not to play jolly hockeysticks at university. I wondered how you could suddenly find yourself alone and cope with that. Most of all, I wondered how Katie managed to be so nice, because she was. She had just thrown me out of her flat, but I still knew she was special.

And she had been right about my life. I was lucky and, despite that, I lived in a land with fairies. I still felt as if I was the victim of a number of huge injustices when I was the victim of very little, apart from a dramatic streak and an overactive imagination. And when I said I was devastated, I was, but I just didn't know what real devastation was. So when I said that tragedies were very personal things I was right; what I forgot to mention was that they were also selfish, and when you opened your eyes and saw people worse off than yourself you felt guilty, a little stupid and, well, like you needed to make amends. What you needed to do was stop being so selfish and horrible and help other people.

I decided that when she was ready I would do all I could to make sure that Katie didn't feel so alone. And I would teach her the value of having friends. Before sleeping I did something I hadn't done for a long time. I thanked God for my life and I asked him to help Katie.

I woke with the horrible realisation that either I wasn't talking to Katie or she wasn't talking to me. She had asked me to leave and she had been angry with me. I was such a kipper. Storming in like a bull in a china shop demanding friendship from someone not ready to give it, giving friendship to a person not ready to receive it. Once again I had managed to mess up and last night even my saintly thoughts had been pretty self-indulgent. There was nothing good about praying for someone who didn't want to be prayed for. Last night had been long; part of it seemed like a million light years away. I needed a penance so I decided that, once dressed, I would spend the day cleaning the house from top to bottom. Out came the Marigolds and the bathroom cleaner. Then the doorbell rang. I went to open it.

Katie stood on the doorstep.

She looked like she hadn't slept much: her hair was dishevelled and her eyes were red. She looked as if she had been crying. Her hair was scraped back, she was in her old jeans and a huge cardigan, her face was devoid of makeup and she looked pale. For a minute I looked at her, not knowing what to say, and she looked at me. 'Can we talk?' she asked.

'Sure, come in.'

'No, I'd rather not. Can we go for a walk or something?'

'OK.' I was surprised: I'd never thought of Katie as much of a walker.

I grabbed my jacket and we set off in the direction of Clapham Common. At first we were silent. I looked at the common, still hazy from the early-morning mist and empty, apart from a few people walking dogs and children. Everyone was there for a reason, going about their usual Sunday-morning business, but we weren't.

'I'm sorry,' she said.

'So am I.'

'But you have nothing to be sorry about.'

'I shouldn't have pushed you. I had no right to extract information you weren't ready to give, and no right to upset you.'

Katie pulled her cardigan tight around her as a gust of wind hit us full on. 'Who does?' We walked in silence again, me unsure of what to say and Katie . . . I didn't know what she was thinking. The haze lifted slightly, giving way to the cold, grey day that awaited us.

'The last time I cried was when I was seven and the kids at school said I was dirty and smelly.'

'Kids are cruel,' I replied weakly.

'Then I learned how to use the washing-machine. From then on I'd wash my clothes and although I was creased I was never dirty.'

'Your mother?'

'She didn't even wash herself.'

'Your father?'

'He sometimes helped me, and I know he bought my clothes but, well, I don't remember why I had to do the washing. I used to love going shopping with him because then it was just the two of us and I felt happy. But that didn't last. When I was twelve or so he just gave me money and I did my own shopping. You know, my father never left us and I couldn't understand why he stayed. I couldn't believe he would want to live with my mum. I sometimes wished he would take me away, then I wished that she would go away. I used to pray to God that they would take her away and then my dad would love me. When I grew up I realised that he should have done something to help her, and me. Even though I don't always remember how he neglected me, it gets hazy. I ate and I grew. But I don't think he ever loved me.'

Katie stopped and looked around her.

'Was your mother always like that?' I asked.

'No. When I was fourteen I asked my father once to help her. He said there was nothing he could do. I asked him if she had always been like that and he said, no, that before I was born she was fine, and he couldn't remember when it started or why. I guess he knew why but he'd never tell me. It was pathetic. Dad was so gutless. I often thought that if he made her better she would leave him so he didn't. Isn't that horrible, to think of him like that? They were both waiting to die and I was the only thing that lived in that house. Or tried to live. I was lonely, Ru. When I left I had never had a friend. It was too embarrassing to make friends. As I grew up the kids didn't call me smelly any more but they gossiped about my mum being a lush and about how my house was the house most visited by the fire brigade. My family life was a joke to them, but it never was to me. So I retreated into myself. I chose a sixth-form college in south London and I moved away. I got a grant, a part-time job and some cheap accommodation. A bedsit. My first home. It was pretty grim but my parents weren't dying around me.'

'Christ, Katie, your life sounds positively Dickensian.'

'Ru, you're so dramatic sometimes. My life was shit, which was the only thing I had in common with Dickens's characters. At least the bedsit was in a student house, so everyone was my age.'

'So you made friends?'

'No, I made *a* friend. Anyway, I stayed with my parents until I passed my GCSEs and then I was off. Am I confusing you?'

'A bit, you're jumping.' My head was reeling. Katie sat down by a tree. Although I was aware of the cold and that the grass was wet, I did the same. A small dog ran up to us brandishing a stick. Katie greeted it as if it was an old friend and threw the stick. We watched as a middle-aged woman and a child ran after it.

'OK, I moved out at sixteen. It was funny because before that I felt a childish tie to my father, which evaporated as soon as my brain developed. I was so filled with bitterness that I planned to shout at him to ask him why. To tell him what rotten parents they were and how angry I was, but when it came to it I just ran away. I couldn't face him so I wrote a letter saying I was leaving and that they would never see me again. I don't know how I did it, but I was so determined and I never did see them again. I went to my new life. I decided that I would make proper friends who didn't know my parents. But even that didn't work out.'

'Why?'

'Matty. But I can't talk about that now.' We got up. Again we walked in silence, Katie hugging her cardigan and me with my hands stuffed into my coat pockets trying to keep warm. It was a cold, crisp winter's day, my head was awash with thoughts. I tucked my arm through Katie's, pulling her gently towards me. 'I'll buy you a coffee,' I said.

'You're on,' Katie said, and smiled.

Chapter Twelve

There was a little boy around town, he was called Cupid and everyone was saying what a naughty little boy he was. Apparently he would hit everyone he came across in the chest with his arrows. Posters warned people to keep away from this boy. But he was cunning: he would disguise himself and trick people to get to them. Everyone was despairing, everyone was falling in love. I decided to track this Cupid fellow down. I saw him sitting on a rock, looking a little forlorn.

'Cupid, Cupid, hello.'

'Hello.' He sighed.

'What's wrong?'

'People are trying to avoid me and my little arrows. It's very sad.'

'But I'm not. Look, Cupid, I would very much like you to hit me in the chest with your arrow.'

Cupid smiled. 'Really?'

'Yes, look, I shall stand here and be your target.' Cupid picked up his bow and arrow and aimed at my chest. The arrow hit me in the arm.

'Ow, that hurt,' I cried, in pain.

'Sorry, I'll try again.' Cupid fired another arrow, which hit me in the leg. Then another, which hit me in the head, and another, which missed altogether. He sighed again. 'I'm sorry, but I guess it's just not going to work when you're so willing. I'm going to find someone else.' With that he picked up his bow and arrows and left me nursing my wounds. People were right about Cupid; he was a bloody pain in the arse.

After our conversation, I felt I was beginning to know Katie, but I had a long way to go, which was fine. I felt I had taken down one barrier, and to become friends with Katie I was prepared to wait until she was ready. I had also broken down one of my barriers: I had stopped wanting to be her. Of course, I still wanted to be like her, but now I didn't want her life. I was sad for her past and I was sad for her lack of friends, but I didn't feel sorry for her. She didn't need me to feel sorry for her. She had reluctantly become my friend. I was determined to teach her that friendship didn't have to mean hurt, but I had to do it her way. This meant that I became part of her life, and her social life. I knew we were both hiding, but that was the way it had to be.

Katie divided her social life into two scenes: the rich people and the 'cool' people. Apparently these groups were kept separate because you couldn't really be rich and cool – or not really cool anyway. The cool people were very scary, always trying to be individual, which meant each person was more outrageous than the next. They were also too cool to talk to most people, and definitely too cool to be your friend. I was in awe of these people. Katie wasn't: she said they were just people, which seemed to be her favourite saying. Walking into a room full of cool people is the most intimidating experience I've ever had.

The rich people were just that: too much money, not enough to do. And they all behaved as if they were still at boarding-school. However, I was almost as intimidated by them as I was by the cool people, although it was among their ranks that I was hoping to find love. Where did Katie fit into these two scenes? I don't know. She said that she just went to the parties because she was invited, and the clubs always had a mixture of people anyway. Katie went because that's what Katie did. She admitted her life was hugely shallow, but that was just the way it was.

Sometimes I wished my life could be a little more shallow. Or perhaps it was. Although I seemed to have a catalogue of disasters as long as the M4 where men were concerned, I hadn't met many. That was the problem I had identified. I just needed to meet more. The more I met, the more luck I was bound to have.

We went to parties, we went to clubs, we went to bars, we went everywhere. It was exhausting, it was exhilarating, it was amusing, and it was sometimes disastrous. I embarked on a voyage of discovery: a voyage to discover all the eligible men in London. And discover them I did.

One night, at a party full of rich people, I met Guy the Fascist. I had learned that to attract a rich man the best stance to take was one of the adoring but dumb woman. I was trying hard to do this as Guy told me he was in the army, 'Gosh, you must be so strong;' he came from Buckinghamshire, 'Oh, that's my favourite county,' and that he collected classic cars, 'Cars are so fascinating.' I was doing a very good job, if I say so myself. But then he had to ruin it by saying that he thought all homeless people should be rounded up, put in a concentration camp and made to work producing things for the rest of society. It would solve the problem of people having to see them, it would clean up the streets and they'd be useful. I had been listening to this man for hours. I had given him my best dumb-bimbo act, and now I was ready to chop his balls off. In response I suggested using them to help the armed forces, sewing uniforms, making bombs, cheap labour for people like Guy. Of course, I said this in my best non-bimbo sarcastic voice. Guy missed the sarcasm, and told me that my idea was wonderful. He asked me if I fancied getting together to discuss it further.

'Well, Guy, perhaps I'll see you in hell.' Leaving him looking confused I went home alone.

At a trendy bar opening I met Sebastian. He wore black and looked like a tortured soul, creative, attractive. I decided that this time I would play interesting and amusing: creative people need stimulation. I spent all night talking about London, my jobs, Katie, me. He looked so amused, I was definitely giving the desired effect. Anyway, I was rather drunk and he was very flattering so when he suggested going back to his flat I almost ran there. Sebastian started to seduce me, and I was trying to get into it, but my head was spinning a bit. I could feel him stroking my leg, kissing my ear, undressing me. Then he got undressed. I tried to focus and I saw him naked. He had the biggest, most magnificent penis I had ever seen.

My eyes widened. 'It's exquisite,' I squeaked before I passed out.

When I woke the next morning I was on the sofa with a blanket over me. There was a note on the coffee table, which read, 'Hope you're OK. You were so out of it, I decided to go out again and see if I could get luckier this time. If I'm not here, you'll know I did. Love, Seb.' I slunk home.

When I told Katie about this, she found it hilarious. Especially when I told her about the size of his penis. 'You were faced by the biggest penis you've ever been close to and you passed out?' She couldn't stop laughing. She said that I must be the worst person she'd ever met for attracting disaster. She was probably right. But I wasn't to be deterred.

At a club I met Toby, who was a bit older, about thirty. I decided that a nice mature man might just be what I needed. He was very slick: he said he drove a Lotus something, and I guessed I should be impressed so I was. He also said he ran his own company and had a house in Chelsea. He was perfect. Determined that this one wouldn't get away, I flirted like I'd never flirted before. We danced, we chatted, we danced, we drank. I was having the most fun. At the end of the evening he asked if he could come back to my place. I thought about it, and decided that I would much rather see his house in Chelsea, so I said so. He went very quiet and said, no, that wouldn't be a good idea. When I pushed him he admitted that his wife and baby were there. I made a swift exit.

Then I met Neil, who was shorter than me, but never mind. Neil, who was the only man I'd met so far who seemed to want to have a future with me. Neil who told me, two hours after having met me, that he thought he might be in love with me. Neil, who had ginger hair and was really unattractive. I was desperate, but I did a runner anyway.

At a 'cool' party I met Oliver, who said he was into bondage and asked if I would wear nipple clamps for him. Although I had no idea what a nipple clamp was, I declined the invitation.

Due to my complete inability to find a man, Katie took matters into her hands and set me up on a blind date. Actually I think she did it to salvage her own sanity and who could blame her? God, I was excited. I asked Katie if I should carry a newspaper or wear a carnation, but she just shook her head. 'I've told Barney what you look like. He'll recognise you.'

Barney was lovely, really lovely. He was cool, he was in TV, he was pretty damn gorgeous. And he became my first success in a while. He came back to my house, we had a great time and in the morning he promised he'd call me and see me again. The phone didn't ring. I begged Katie to call him and find out why, but she said that wouldn't do me any favours. I pleaded, but Barney was history. So were any more blind dates and Katie hung up her matchmaking hat.

I returned to my own limited resources. I was still on a mission. My man mission, my love mission, my sex mission. My husband mission. I met Charlie, 'call me Chaz, like the Daz'. The only thing I could grasp from my conversation with him was that he worked in the City, but would probably have been more at home hosting a game-show. I found him hard to understand: he insisted on speaking in riddles, or perhaps it was another language. I was trying so hard to concentrate on what he was saying, I had stopped thinking about my reason for being with him. Until he said to me, 'Women love me, throw themselves at me. If you play your cards right, it could be your turn tonight. Do you feel lucky?' I told him I felt very unlucky and beat a hasty retreat. I was doing what I wanted, I was meeting men. Unfortunately I wasn't meeting the right sort of men.

Rupert tried to talk to me about God. Robert tried to persuade me to go home with him and his friend. John told me I'd been his mother in a previous life, and would I let him suck my nipples? Brian was called Brian and I just couldn't.

Four weeks and five thousand men later, I was still well and truly single.

Chapter Thirteen

The handsome prince was appearing in an advert on television. It had been so well publicised that all the available women in London were told to watch at seven o'clock on Monday. At the appointed time, I took my position in front of the television set. When the prince appeared I could hardly believe my eyes. He was so gorgeous. He said that he had been at a trendy club and spotted a woman with whom he had fallen instantly in love. He had tried to get close to talk to her but she disappeared and the only thing she left behind was a shoe. Silly cow, I thought.

Then the prince held up the shoe. Wow, it was made of glass and I recognised it. It was my shoe. When trying to catch the last bus home on Saturday night, I had lost it. Then the handsome prince said that he would marry whoever the shoe belonged to. The girl had to come to the palace on Tuesday and try it on. I took down the details. I went to get the other shoe to make sure, but I knew it was my shoe, and now I was going to be a princess.

On Tuesday I dressed in my best outfit and went to the palace. Hundreds and hundreds of girls were lined up. I took my place in the queue. I wasn't worried, I knew I'd be the winner. When my turn came, hours later, I went to put my foot in the shoe and it didn't fit. This could not be.

'Next,' the footman shouted.

I tried to protest. 'It is my shoe, it is,' I pleaded. But I was waved away.

I went home shoeless and princeless. What could I do? It turned out that some stupid tart of a girl had made it fit her anyway and now my handsome prince was marrying Sharon from Essex.

I was exhausted. The social life I had coveted for so long was making me tired and, believe it or not, more miserable. On the up-side I had Katie; on the down-side I had a permanent hangover. Katie was wise. She had started to value me, which made me feel good about myself for the first time in ages.

She knew that she wouldn't want to party for ever – 'The shallow life will lose its appeal, believe me.' She thought careers were pointless – 'Why waste my life striving for something I'm going to have to give up when I'm sixty?' And money was just a necessary evil – 'I work therefore I eat and party.' Katie was an education to me. Katie felt you could live your life how you wanted, as long as you could pay for it and you didn't hurt other people. She said, 'It's fine to do what you want. It's just that so many people don't because they don't know what they want. Most people don't think, they just do, and they end up doing what they've been told to do.' Hitting the nail on the head.

'Think about it, I work, I party, I meet men, I sleep with men, I drink, I smoke dope. That's the life I've chosen. But I'm not excessive or an addict, it's controlled. People who start out like me and let things spiral out of control, they're not making a decision to take drugs, they're attracted to drugs because of other problems they have. They're looking for escape. For me they're a choice. People who are addicts will always think they were making a choice to have fun, but in fact, the drugs, or the drink or the gambling chose them. Take my mother, she's a great example. She had problems – she must have done to drink so much – but instead of ever facing them, she drank. I will never be like her. My lifestyle is different. I know people disapprove of me but, then, I disapprove of people who drive Ford Escorts.' The world according to Katie. She seemed so together, but it was time for me to find out more.

'Katie, why do you party – you know, drink and drugs – when you've seen what they can do?'

'I just explained that. My mother was an addict. It just happened to be drink. She would have found something else if it hadn't been that. I can take it or leave it. If I decided I wanted to give them up I could, I really could. That's because, as I said, I make a choice, it doesn't choose me. But, well, if you really need to know, I have to prove to myself that I'm not my mother. If I was the sort of person who refused a drink just because of what it did to her it would show I'm scared of her and scared of it. I'm more intelligent than that.'

'I understand.' I think I did.

'Ruth, you think you know what you want, but you're confused. You want a man and you want love, you don't want a job, you want security, but that's your long-term goal and in the short term you don't know what you want. You kill time by partying with me but one day you'll realise it's not for you, and so will I.'

'You make it sound simple.'

'It is. Life can be as simple or as complicated as you want. If you hate your parents and your friends, get rid of them. If you hate your job, leave it. Too many people spend their time moaning about what they have instead of changing things. They complicate their life and moan about how hard-done-by they are.'

'Sounds like me.'

'No, because you're going to stop doing that, it's just a stage for you. One day you'll wake up and know what you want to do next.'

'I hope so.'

'Trust me. It will happen.'

I know it sounds as if I'm trying to sell Katie to you, but that's the way she was. Confident in an unaware sort of way. Magnetic in an unaware way. Special. Although at first the scales tilted in her favour, we had balanced our friendship. You see, she started to open up to me, told me her fears and her hopes, I was someone she was learning to trust. She told me she was scared that if she stopped partying there would be nothing in her life. She said that her lack of friends scared her – 'although I'm fiercely independent, if I was murdered in my bed I wonder how long would it be before anyone went to the police. Weeks, I think.' She told me she was glad she had me. For once in my life, I felt that someone needed me a bit. Our friendship had become more than just parties.

Of course, my view was not shared by all. As my friendship with Katie grew and my social life grew, I was subject to disapproval from a number of sources. My friends. My mother.

The first line of attack came from Jess. 'Your behaviour isn't normal.'

'Oh, Jessie, what *is* normal? I go to work, I go out, that's what people do, what you all told me to do.'

'Ruth, going out is fine, working is fine, if you do it properly. You do neither properly.'

'Huh?'

'Well, you don't have a career, you just work, and you don't just go out, you go out and get rip-roaringly drunk and leap on men.'

'Well, when you put it like that . . . Jess, I have fun. Can't you just be pleased?'

'Oh, Ru, I'm pleased you're happy, but your lifestyle, well, it can't go on for ever. You need to do something more. Being a party girl can't become your replacement for Ben.'

'Can't it?'

'No. You can use it as a distraction, but it isn't a long-term solution. Not by any stretch of the imagination.'

'Oh.'

'You can't just party for the rest of your life, or work in a cushy job where all you do is be hung-over.'

'I can't?'

'No, and don't give me this nonsense about you'll stop when you get married because the way you're carrying on no one will marry you.'

'They won't?'

'No. You mark my words.' Jess swept out of the room looking triumphant. The trouble was she had failed to realise that advice, although often given, is rarely taken.

The others had their opinions too. Sarah said my work would suffer, Sophie thought I'd been meeting too many undesirable men, Thomas just thought that letting me out at all was dangerous, and they held Katie responsible for all of this. It was her fault. You would have thought that Katie was the devil, and I was the person the devil had kidnapped. They tried to persuade me to stay away from her, but they couldn't. I knew they cared about me, but sometimes they had a strange way of showing it. They couldn't understand that, if I was going to do all those things, I didn't need Katie to corrupt me.

My mother, who knew little about my new life, called me at work and demanded to know why I was never at home. She said it was unhealthy for a young girl to be out having fun. Didn't I know there was more to life? I should be planning my career not chasing men. She said that a woman who preferred a man to a career needed her head looked at. My mother should have given birth to Jess or Sarah. I tried to convince her that the whole point of being young was to have fun. My arguments fell on deaf ears. As a last resort I told her I was sorry to be a disappointment to her but I loved her and she was a wonderful role model and I admired her life. Then she said she loved me too and she was sorry, she just wanted me to be happy. I assured her I was, and told her to stop worrying. We parted well. I decided that I should visit my parents soon and I asked Jess if she wanted to be adopted.

I concluded that I had to do two things. The first was that I would introduce Katie to my friends, poor girl; the second was that I was going to invite her home to meet my parents.

'Katie, I'm thinking of going home for the weekend near my birthday in April. Why don't you come?'

'Well, I'm not sure.' Katie looked terrified.

'Don't be like that, it'll just be a nice normal weekend with my family. And we'll get fed.'

'Is it important to you?'

'Yes.'

'Ruthie, I don't know why I let you do this to me, but OK.' I'd won.

'Oh, and Katie ...'

'What now?'

'I want you to come and meet my friends.'

'God, Ruth, why?'

'Because they need to meet you. You're a part of my life they don't understand and, well, I'm sure you'd like them.'

'Do I have a choice?'

'No.' It was settled.

My friends shared Katie's reluctance, and although they swore they wouldn't like her, they grudgingly agreed to meet her.

'I'm going to give her a piece of my mind,' Jess said.

'I think she's very brave coming to dinner. I'm going to find out just how many drugs she's addicted to,' Sarah said haughtily.

'I can't bear to meet the person who's ruining my friend's life,' Sophie said.

'Is she fit?' Thomas said. I arranged for Katie to come to dinner at our house. I told her my friends were looking forward to meeting her. I forgot to tell her I was feeding her to the lions.

*　　*　　*

I cooked, without any help, and Katie was late.

'How rude,' Jess said.

'She's always late,' I defended her, but I was met by a tutting disapproval.

When she did turn up, she was pleased to meet everyone and for a few minutes they forgot to scowl. I was amazed by her outfit: I was used to seeing her in either outrageous clothes or work clothes – short skirts, saris, sequined cardigans that reached the floor, mad trousers and, of course, the blue platform boots. Tonight she was wearing black trousers, a pink jumper and black boots. Her hair hung straight from her face instead of the scraped-back or abstract I was used to. She looked positively demure.

'Hi, it's good to meet you all.' She said this with genuine enthusiasm. It seemed to do the trick.

'You, too,' Thomas said. Jess, Sarah and Sophie managed a sort of smile. She brought wine, no grass, to my relief, and sat down to ask questions. 'Sophie, Ru said you were an actress, what are you doing at the moment?'

'I'm rehearsing for a new play by a young writer, but I'm not allowed to tell anyone what it's called. I'm playing the lead girl – she's a hooker,' Sophie said proudly.

'God, you don't look much like a hooker, I hope they give you a good makeover,' Katie said. Sophie looked pleased and everyone laughed kindly.

'Tell me about Ruthie at university. Was she as man-crazy as she is now?'

'Worse, if you can believe it. Although she's a darling and we love her, of course, she's still mad,' Jess replied. Everyone laughed again.

'Katie, what do you want to do with your life?' Trust Sarah to play recruitment consultant.

'I don't know. I always thought I wanted to be an artist, but then I wasn't sure, I sort of lost it a bit. Anyway, now I'm drifting.'

'You don't think you'll go back to art?' Sarah was not yet satisfied

'Maybe. It always was my true love. I just think I'm lacking inspiration. I still hope that one day I can make it my career.' Katie smiled. Sarah smiled. *Sarah actually smiled*. Katie had said the magic word: career.

By the time we had finished the starter, everyone was in love with Katie.

'Have you ever thought about working in PR? You'd be great.' Jess.

'If you ever need a new job, just call me.' Sarah.

'It would be nice to go to an exhibition sometime, if you want.' Sophie.

'Name the day and I'll take you both out.' Thomas.

I was gobsmacked. My friends had not mentioned my demise once: they were too busy sucking up to Katie, who kept everyone laughing. They were as mesmerised by her as I was.

When all the food was eaten, the wine drunk and the cigarettes smoked, Katie stayed over and we talked into the early hours.

'I really like your friends.'

'Yeah, they're great,' I admitted, 'and they liked you.'

'Did they? They're a bit different from you.'

'Most people are, apparently.'

'No, that's not true. And the twenty-first century is a big place. There's enough room for everyone.'

I fell asleep oddly comforted by that thought.

The next day my friends couldn't stop talking about Katie: she was wonderful, she was funny and she was smart. They had forgotten what a bad influence she was and what a drug addict she was. I was pleased, it was nice to know that now I had their blessing for my friendship they would leave me in peace.

✿   ✿   ✿

Sophie's boyfriend, the Thespian, was at our house a lot. We all looked on him as a joke, but we did so affectionately. Even Sophie seemed to think so. She didn't make half the effort for him that she had for the Porsche, but he doted on her and she seemed to like it. He was auditioning for a part in a well-known soap opera as a waiter, and he had two lines, 'Are you ready to order?' and 'Thank you'. He was very nervous and asked if he could practise on us. Being the drama queen he was, he needed the setting to help him 'feel the role', so our kitchen was turned into a restaurant, with the table laid, candles, a pretend menu and wine.

The four of us were his customers. The Thespian was a perfectionist and would start all over again if one thing wasn't right. I didn't help; I kept laughing, and in the end Sophie said, 'Nik, I think the last one was wonderful, spot on,' and we all agreed.

'Perfect,' Sarah said.

'The best,' Jess said.

'Wonderful,' I said.

He seemed to accept this and stopped. I was so relieved – we'd been doing it for an hour. I hoped he wasn't going to get any bigger parts in the near future. He made Sophie happy because he loved her and he didn't intimidate her. In fact, he couldn't even intimidate me. Which meant that even if he'd wanted to he couldn't intimidate anyone. When he left us, we were all exhausted.

'Do you love him, Soph?' I asked.

'No, not really, but I like him and he's good for me. I don't think it's for ever but then again I don't know. I like the romance in him, even if he can be a bit ...'

'A bit what?'

'A bit of a wally.' We all laughed.

'Huh!' Jess scoffed

'What?'

'Listen to you two, romance this and romance that. I've bought this book called *The Rules*. If you follow it you're certain to be able to marry the man you want, when you want. It's far easier than all this romance stuff.'

'That's ridiculous. Love is the most natural thing in the world, you can't do it to order and you certainly can't do it by rules.' I was horrified. Although the way my love life had been going lately, perhaps it wasn't such a bad idea.

'Of course you can. I'm going to find my man at twenty-six, I'll marry at thirty, have one child at thirty-four and another at thirty-six. What could be simpler?' Jess was indignant.

'Falling in love is not something you can plan as rigidly as your career.'

'Don't you know it's the new millennium now?' was Jess's curt reply.

Sarah shared Jess's view. 'Love is something I'll do when I'm ready. I don't know when that will be, or even if it will be,' she said.

'No, it doesn't work like that. It will happen when it wants to.'

'No, I'll decide when and if I wish to fall in love, thank you.'

'No, you'll just fall in love when you're least expecting it and when you least want it.'

'No, I won't.'

'Yes, you will.'

'People only fall in love if they want to. It's totally controllable and I don't want to hear another word.' Sarah looked stern. I decided it was best not to argue. I was trying to sell romance, but at the same time I had been trying to manipulate my own love life. I certainly wasn't leaving anything to Fate. I was a hypocrite.

Katie told me she'd only get a permanent boyfriend when she got tired of partying and wanted a man to cook her dinner every night. She didn't care about the big-romance thing as long as he did the laundry and was good in bed. I sometimes wondered if Sophie and I were a dying breed.

I told my mother I would be bringing Katie home to meet her soon, and my friends kept asking when they would see her again, so I was allowed to carry on my debauched lifestyle. Except I didn't really want to. After my man-hunting and my failure, I felt that perhaps I had tired of the social life rather more quickly than Katie had predicted. I loved Katie, but she wasn't really the reason for going out. When we went out, we generally went our separate ways. She headed for the people she knew, I headed for the men. Although I knew that going out would be the only way I could meet men, I just had to remember the men I had met so far to make staying in for the rest of my life seem attractive. Once again, I didn't know what I wanted. I couldn't get a boyfriend, I couldn't keep a boyfriend, I couldn't find a boyfriend, I couldn't even have a one-night stand. I was having a relapse.

I sat in the kitchen drinking tea and feeling sorry for myself. There is nothing better than sitting at a pine kitchen table to make you feel at home. I had just found a packet of cookies, which made everything so much better, when Sarah walked in. She looked tired.

'Where have you been?' I asked.

'At work.'

'Sarah, did no one tell you it's Saturday?'

'Very funny. It's been so busy lately, I've been catching up with paperwork.'

'You work too hard.'

'One of us has to.'

'Thanks, Sarah. Look, all I'm saying is that you work long hours during the week and now you're working Saturdays as well. We all need time off, not just me.'

'I know, Ru. I don't love going to work at a weekend, but

I'm building my career, you know me. Perhaps you could do with a bit more of what I have.'

'Sarah, I'm happy at Fulhurst's. Really, I don't want another job. I thought you'd be pleased.'

'Well, I am, sort of. I'm pleased you've settled down but, then again, the only reason you like it is because you don't have to work very hard and you've got Katie, not because you've found something you like doing.'

'OK, so those are the reasons, but you know I don't want a career and I know you all hoped I'd change my mind, but I knew I wouldn't. I'm just happy the way I am with a great social life.'

'Do you really enjoy your social life?'

'Of course I do,' I lied.

'So you don't find it boring and shallow?'

'No,' I lied again.

'And neither does Katie?'

'No. Anyway, I thought you liked Katie.'

'I do, she's great. But I know you, and don't forget you've catalogued the awful men you've been meeting lately. I just don't think it's making you that happy.'

'Sarah, it's making me happier than I've been in a long time and that's good enough for me. I don't want a career. How many times do I have to say that?'

'OK, calm down. I hope you're happy, you know that.' Sarah left me and I knew she was right, although I'd never tell her that. I knew I wasn't happy. I still hadn't come close to finding what I was looking for.

The next week I stayed in. I caught up on the soaps, spent time with Sarah, Sophie and Jess, and tidied my room. I remembered when I never went out, how I saw this house as my confinement. Now I felt safe within its walls. It was nice to stop for a while. Katie understood: she said that every now and again she took time out and stayed in. I just hadn't seen her do it. I thought perhaps I might do it a bit more often.

*   *   *

It was the weekend before my birthday and I had promised my parents that I would take Katie home with me. I was looking forward to it, a weekend of being fed, pampered, and seeing my parents: I missed them.

We took the train on Friday evening. Katie seemed excited. As we settled into an overcrowded carriage I picked up a magazine and she started reading her book. After a short while the grey buildings of London became green fields, trees, hedges.

'Wow,' Katie said.

I put my magazine down. 'What?' I asked.

'Just look, Ru. Christ, it's so beautiful.'

I looked, I really looked, and she was right, it was beautiful. Katie abandoned her book and craned her neck. It's amazing how special something can be when you've seen it a thousand times before. We smiled at each other. Patchwork fields, cows, forests, lakes. Katie kept her eyes glued to the scenery until we got there. I watched and saw things I'd seen so many times before but had never *really* seen. I caught her awe and liked having found something great I could share with Katie.

'I'm quite looking forward to seeing how a normal family works,' she said.

'I'd hardly call my family normal,' I replied, but they were. Well, if normal meant good, loving, kind and stable they were.

Katie smiled, 'Any family that doesn't drive you away is good enough for me.'

She said it with no bitterness in her voice, but again I felt sad for her. 'I'm sorry.' I didn't know what else to say.

'Don't be. I came to terms with my family a long time ago. Anyway, I'm looking forward to meeting yours.'

Both my parents had come to the station and we were greeted with hugs and kisses.

'Mum, Dad, this is Katie.'

'Hello, Mr and Mrs Butler,' Katie said.

'Oh, no, please call us Theresa and Stuart,' my mother replied.

'I've missed you, princess,' my father said, and my eyes filled with tears.

'You look really well,' my mother said, stroking my hair.

They had decided to take us out to dinner before heading home, so we went to my favourite Chinese restaurant. Katie was asking millions of questions in the car, how long had we lived here, where my father worked and could she see my mother's shop. Like my friends, within seconds my parents were mesmerised.

'You must need a rest, you girls, after working so hard in London,' my father said.

'Yes, we do work quite hard, but I don't mind,' Katie said.

I stopped myself laughing. My father told her about how he had started out in London in a firm of accountants. It's funny, but when I had that job with the accountancy firm, I had never thought of my father as one of them. I suppose that's because he's a nice one. Then my mother told Katie how she and my father had met at a dance, and how it had been love at first sight, which made me want to cry for some reason. We had dinner, which was lovely, and Katie told my parents about her love of art, carefully eluding any questions from my mother about her family. When we got home, I fell into bed exhausted.

On Saturday I woke early and spent some time on my own with my parents. They didn't ask me about my career or my life, they just chatted, which we hadn't done in a long time. My father told me about a new housing development they objected to; my mother told me how well her charity was going. I told them about Jess, Sarah, Sophie and Thomas, whom they knew and loved. It felt more like home than ever.

I woke Katie and we had breakfast.

'I don't remember the last time someone cooked breakfast for me. It's fantastic,' Katie said, and she got extra bacon.

After breakfast we went for a drive. I showed Katie my old school, the town I used to hang out in, the pub where I had my first pint and the fish-and-chip shop where I received my first proper kiss. It was funny because I was showing her my life and I hadn't shown anyone before. Not even Ben had known this much about me. I drove to my mother's shop, but she wasn't there. Barbara, a woman who had worked for her for ever, welcomed us. She told Katie how she hadn't seen me for years. I guess it was a while since I'd taken an interest. I told Katie how, when I was little, I had spent hours in the shop, loving the dresses, and how I always said it was my favourite place in the world. It was lovely to take that trip down Memory Lane. We had lunch in the pub then headed home.

There we flopped in front of the television and just relaxed.

'You know, we must be mad. We go out all the time but this is the life. How about we move to a village outside London and live like this?' Katie suggested.

'OK, so we grow our own vegetables and get a cow, do we?'

'Why not?'

'And you wouldn't ever get remotely bored? Even though there are no men for miles around?'

'We'd just have to get a couple of farmhands to double as gigolos.'

That wasn't a bad idea, and we laughed.

'Maybe I would get bored, but it's peaceful. I haven't felt peaceful in a long time.'

Saturday night my mother cooked dinner and we all chatted. Katie had become part of the family easily, and it was funny to see how she took to being a daughter. She loved asking my mother questions and she loved listening to my father's jokes. I felt sad for her that she didn't have a family she could do this with. Before we left on Sunday, my parents gave me some presents and a card and made me promise not to open them until my birthday.

God, my birthday. In four days I was having a birthday. It was the saddest birthday ever. Not just because it was the first without Ben, although I'd vowed not to drag that one out again, but because it was the birthday after my twenty-first year and I never wanted to stop being twenty-one. It was the age at which you get to be an adult and a youth at the same time. It was the best age ever. And now I was about to say goodbye to it.

On Thursday I woke up excited. Even now I still have those feelings when it comes to birthdays or Christmas: excitement, anticipation, celebration. It is, after all, a celebration of my birth, and although sometimes that does not seem much to celebrate, I was still going to. I woke up feeling twenty-two. Actually I didn't. I wouldn't know how to feel any age, it doesn't work like that. I woke up feeling like it was my birthday, which made me the centre of attention and I loved that. I also woke up without thinking about Ben. I was going to work, which I didn't mind: work was fun. And tonight Jess said that she and Sophie would be cooking me dinner, and Katie and Thomas were coming. I was really looking forward to it.

I opened my parents' presents. I needed to open presents, it made me feel like it really was my birthday. They gave me books, a vanity case and a cheque, much better than Christmas. When I was ready I left the house and headed for the tube station, smiling.

When I got to work, Katie was waiting with a croissant with a candle in it and a large cappuccino. She gave me a book called *A Guide for the Advanced Soul* — you thought about a problem, opened the book and it would give you a wise saying to help. I could see it getting a lot of use. My boss Tom popped in and gave me some chocolates and perfume, which surprised me because Katie hadn't been shopping. Then I remembered he had asked me to buy them the previous week. I thanked him very much. Tom left earlier than usual, so for the rest of the day we ate chocolates, played solitaire and asked the book questions. It was very wise. At lunch we both went out, and when Jenny tried to protest, I just said very sweetly, 'It's my birthday and Tom said we must go out for a long lunch, so if you have a problem ask him.' Jenny scowled after us. We had a bottle of wine then went back to work, Katie knew that if she let me drink any more I'd be ill or asleep all afternoon. My parents called, my friends called. It was nice, I felt special.

When I got home, the smells from the kitchen were of roast beef. Jess had got Sophie to do all the cooking. I changed and went to help her.

'Happy birthday, Ru,' Sophie said, handing me a glass of wine. I took a sip. The wine was cold and lovely, and memories of the bottle at lunch flooded back. I drank it quickly. Shortly afterwards Sarah and Jess came in. They all stood and sang to me, while I turned a lovely shade of red. When Katie and Thomas arrived, the guest list was complete. We had champagne and the best roast beef in the world. They had bought me a new dress, which was figure-hugging, sexy and shocking pink and Jess had baked me a cake, after all. I blew out my candles and wished that my friends stayed my friends for ever. I wished us all happiness and then, if I was allowed another wish, I wished for love, but my friends came first. I felt a warm, happy glow as I fell asleep that night.

The next day I felt hung-over but clear. I had had a fun night with people I cared about, no idiot men, no desperate embraces. I decided there and then to give up one-night stands. My birthday resolution was perhaps the most sensible resolution I had ever made. I told Katie.

'What are you going to do now?' she asked.

'What do you mean?'

'Well, all you do at the moment is have one-night stands, you'll need to find a new hobby.'

I poked my tongue out at her. 'Katie, what I will do is this. I will no longer have to look for my knickers every morning. I won't have to run away. I won't worry that they don't ask me for my phone number. And I won't pass out and leave myself in the clutches of weirdoes.'

'OK. So what are you going to do?'

'I don't fucking know. But I won't feel like a slut.'

'You are a slut, or an ex-slut, now. I understand what you're saying and I'm really proud of you. You've made the right decision.'

Katie wasn't a slut and I couldn't quite work out why. I mean, she slept with more men than I did and she seemed to have been sleeping with men for ever, but she wasn't a slut. She took sex for what it was and had no illusions about becoming some guy's girlfriend. When I had sex I liked to delude myself that each man I slept with was The One. Of course they never were. I was going to give it up. But Katie was right; I felt panic grip as I realised I didn't have a clue what I was going to do now.

I came to terms with my new lifestyle remarkably easily. I still went out with Katie and I still met people, but I chatted and I relaxed a bit, and although sometimes I had to hold myself back from the men, Katie was a great help. She had decided that in the name of moral support we would go home together, without men for either of us. Sometimes I thought she must be an angel.

To take my mind off men, Jess had found one she actually liked. Jess met Jerry the Journalist at a launch party for something. He was there because the product was boring: no one else on his paper would go and he was the most junior.

Jess was there because she was part of the team that organised it. They hit it off straight away.

'When I saw him, I just knew I'd like him. He's gorgeous, tall, dark, intellectual glasses, nice bum, you know. Anyway I just went straight up to him, asked him which paper he was from and he told me he was from the *London News* and I asked him what he thought of our launch, plied him with drink and made him promise to give us some editorial. He's great, funny, intelligent, ambitious, gorgeous – did I already say that? Anyway, I really like him.' We all sat open-mouthed while Jess told us this. 'And, anyway, we were quite drunk. We talked about our jobs a lot, of course – really I was just doing my job, chatting up a journalist, so we spent all night talking. Then he suggested we go on to another bar, which we did, then we kissed and it was a wonderful kiss. Then I gave him my business card and he gave me his and I came home. I know he'll call. Oh, and he lives – guess where he lives? He lives in South Kensington, how great is that?' None of us could move.

'Jess, you like this bloke?' I said.

Jess looked thoughtful. 'Well, he's OK. I mean, I'd quite like to see him again, no big deal.' She wandered off whistling.

'God, I am so glad I'm celibate,' Sarah said

'I think it's so sweet,' Sophie said, although I'm not sure that 'sweet' could be attributed to Jess.

'It just goes to show that no matter how independent and career-orientated you are, when a man comes along we all become gibbering wrecks,' I pointed out.

'But Jess?' Sarah said.

'I know.'

'Yeah, it's weird,' Sophie finished, and once again we sat still and silent, not quite knowing what to make of it.

Of course, Jerry called Jess at work. Of course, they arranged to go out at the weekend. Of course, she didn't have to go through the agony of waiting for the phone to ring. Of course, she did have to go through the what-to-wear agony. There is some justice.

She came home from work with the biggest smile in the world. 'He called,' she gushed. We nodded, we were seriously worried. Jess couldn't do this, she wasn't a girly girl, she was Jess, tough Jess, Jess who had men for breakfast, not pink, fluffy Jess, we didn't know this girl. 'We're going for dinner, in Kensington.' Pink, pink, pink.

'What are you going to wear?' I asked.

'Oh, my God, oh, my God. I've got nothing. Shit. And I'm so fat. I can't go out, ever, I'll have to stop eating for the rest of the week. What the hell am I going to do?' Jess looked really distressed as she flopped onto the sofa. It was a familiar scene, but it never happened to Jess.

'Calm down. You do not need to give up food and you have plenty of clothes. Let's go,' Sarah frog-marched Jess to her bedroom. We heard screams and shouts and banging and crying. Eventually Jess came out, marched past us and into my room. She came out with an outfit. Actually it was my outfit. I didn't mind, she was pink again. She flopped down on the sofa. 'I think I'm in love,' she said.

'I think I need a strong drink,' I said. We all did. Apart from Jess, who had a smile stuck to her face. 'Jess, you told us you weren't going to fall in love until you were twenty-six,' I reminded her.

'You must be mixing me up with someone else,' she replied, still smiling.

Perhaps I was, or perhaps someone had kidnapped the real Jess and put this girl in her place.

The date on Friday was a success. She stayed the night. She was very happy when she came home, on cloud nine. They weren't seeing each other for another week, 'We're incredibly busy people.' Thank God, the old Jess was back. At least she wasn't completely changing into me. Jess resumed her usual persona, but with a glow that hadn't been there before.

I think Sarah was more upset than most of us: she liked the camaraderie that she and Jess shared, the work-before-men rule. But Jess changed. Although she still worked as hard and her job was still her number-one priority, she went to a lot of trouble for Jerry and obviously cared about him. We were all happy for her, but I guess Sarah may have been the tiniest bit jealous.

Jess invited Jerry to dinner on Friday. She looked so happy I wanted to cry. We were told to be on our best behaviour and she refused to let Sophie invite the Thespian in case he acted like an idiot, which he usually did. I wasn't allowed to talk about wanting to be a housewife, Sarah wasn't to talk about celibacy and Thomas could talk about whatever he wanted. As usual I was excited: I was going to meet a man who could turn Jess into a giggling wreck. He had to be very special indeed.

He arrived, he smiled nicely at all of us, he kissed Jess and they looked good together. They sort of fitted. He was nice-looking and just as Jess had described. Part of me felt happy for her, part of me felt suicidal. We sat down to dinner. I had cooked, of course, but Jess had passed it off as her own. It would serve her right if he married her and then she had to learn to cook.

'So you work for the *London News*?' I asked.

'Yes, well, I'm a trainee journalist, they don't let me out on my own much.'

'I think it's really interesting. Are you going to be a news journalist or are you going to specialise in some area?' Sophie asked.

'News ideally. I was lucky to get this job, but I want to work for the nationals eventually.'

'It shouldn't take you long, not with your talent,' Jess said.

Jerry touched her cheek. In that gesture, my belief in love was reaffirmed.

'Don't you have to work odd hours?' Sarah asked.

'Yes, but it's worth it. I've been indoctrinated by my bosses. Their favourite sayings are. "The most important thing is being able to get to a story when it breaks"; "It can make your career to get an exclusive"; "News doesn't stop".' We all laughed. Jerry was cool. Jerry was confident. Jerry was perfect for Jess.

Jerry was relaxed with us and with Jess. He kept us entertained with stories of his birth in journalism, covering school fêtes and pet shows for his local paper. Then the university magazine, which was burnt by anarchists because it was apolitical. And now the *London News*. You could tell he loved his work because he loved talking about it and he was interesting. It was a long time since we'd had an interesting man in this house, apart from Thomas, of course.

The evening was fun, we all thought so. We couldn't fault him. I had no nasty nickname for him, Sophie liked him and Sarah — even Sarah — could find nothing wrong. We all told Jess how much we liked him and she was so pleased. 'I really like him, girls, and it's important to me that you do. Thank you,' she said, and once again we were silenced. Jess never talked like that. It was love. It puzzled me. I didn't think you could have it all, yet here was Jess, proving that you could. But then I remembered I didn't want it all, or not that all anyway. No, of course I envied the love part of Jess's life, but I certainly had no interest in the career side. To me, having it all in today's sense was as appealing as ... Well, it just didn't appeal to me.

Chapter Fourteen

The Greatest Love: Part One

Troy looked at Stephanie, marvelling at her beauty. He thought back to the moment they had fallen in love, able to recall every single detail. They had been at a cocktail party, held in a huge house belonging to Troy's business partner, Joseph Watkins. Troy had been reluctant to attend, having been working hard and travelling extensively due to business but, of course, he could not let down his partner and friend. Dressed in his tuxedo, Troy was the most handsome of men. He had been included in America's most-eligible list every year for the past five, but he was not interested. Although girls threw themselves at him, he declined every offer. Troy was married to his work and no girl would change that.

Until Stephanie. Troy circulated at the party making small-talk and feeling isolated. Then he saw her. Wearing an electric-blue dress, she was not to be missed. Troy was mesmerised as he spotted her across the room, her dress swirling as she walked, her long legs slightly exposed, her long blonde hair cascading around her face. As she got close to him, Stephanie stopped to speak with someone Troy knew. He was able to look at her face. Deep blue eyes the colour of the most precious sapphires, lips full and inviting, skin shining like the stars, she was the most beautiful creature he had ever seen. She was speaking with Dirk, but Troy knew he had to have her. For the first time in his life he knew he couldn't let her get away.

He approached her. 'Hi, I'm Troy.' He kissed her hand.

Stephanie looked into his eyes: the electricity was instant. 'I'm Stephanie,' she replied.

They stared at each other, not wanting to break this most wonderful spell. The spell of love. After what seemed liked eternity Troy took her hand and led her out of the house. 'The rest of our lives starts now,' he whispered, as he took her home.

Troy smiled at the recollection. They had been together ever since and were now planning a lavish wedding. When loves hits, it really hits, thought Troy, as once again he took the hand of his beautiful love.

I had pretty much learned to control my jumping-on-men urges and hadn't slept with or tried to sleep with anyone since my birthday resolution. It was only a couple of weeks, but that wasn't bad going for me. I had even learned to enjoy going out without the sole purpose being men. It's strange, but chatting to people you aren't going to sleep with can be fun too. I felt as if I had discovered a whole new world. And I'd like to add that I had been chatted up by a couple of men. Men whom the old me would have taken to bed very quickly, but not the new me. They had nothing lasting about them, nothing I felt had a chance of doing anything but adding to my bedpost notches. So I was polite and interested, but when they tried to take it further, I declined. Imagine it, I knew how to say no.

I looked forward to parties with a new kind of anticipation, one of just enjoying myself. And in that vein we were going to a party in a club in Fulham, one of Katie's rich friends – Tanya, I think, but I didn't know her. I told Jess, because I thought she'd be impressed it was in Fulham, but Jess had now decided that Fulham was the poor person's South Kensington so she wasn't that interested. Anyway, we were going and I was in control.

When we arrived, the first thing I noticed was that the party was jam-packed with men. Wall-to-wall men. Oh, if temptation was this party, it would be hard to defy. We had a drink, spoke to a few people, including Tanya our host. I couldn't concentrate on anything, amazed at the number of men here. Far more men than girls. Just the way it should be. Katie had been found by a nice-looking guy and I just stood like a spare part, surveying the surroundings. The guy Katie was talking to went off to get us both drinks. Maybe Jess had been right: nice polite blokes in Fulham.

'He seems nice,' I told Katie.

'Um, he's called Duncan.'

'Never mind,' I said, as Duncan came back with the drinks. I tried to nod politely at what Duncan was saying, but my mind was elsewhere. I was thinking how hard it was going to be for me to stay away from these men. Then I saw him. He was tall, with black curly hair. That was all I could see. But I saw enough to know. I was in love.

My mouth dropped open. Luckily Duncan had gone some-where, so I nudged Katie.

'Not bad,' she said.

'I'm in love. Do you know him?'

'No.' She laughed. 'Just go and talk to him.'

'But — but I can't.'

'Fine, don't, then.'

Katie was right. I approached him. Now, I may be quite old-fashioned when it comes to most things, but I can be pretty modern when it comes to chatting up men. 'Hi, I'm Ruth.' Good line. My man turned around. I nearly fainted. He had the most amazing brown eyes and the most amazing smile and the most amazing teeth.

'I'm Mark,' he said. He looked amused as he stuck out

his hand. You know about hearts doing somersaults and knees turning to jelly? Well, that's what happened. I had experienced the sensation before, with Ben, but this was, well, it was more. Bigger somersaults, wobblier jelly. I was in pieces. Everything about him was perfect. I shook his hand, noting his short, clean fingernails. OK, take the bull by the horns. 'Can I get you a drink?' I think I needed to practise my chat-up lines slightly.

'OK, I'll have a Beck's.' Mark still looked amused.

I went to the bar. I wasn't sure what I should do next, but I knew I couldn't let this god get away. I practically grabbed the barman to make sure he served me quickly. I went back with the drinks. Mark was still waiting, still smiling. I asked him about himself. Always a good one. He was a radio producer, he lived in Notting Hill and he had a sexy, slightly posh accent. I told him about my string of disastrous jobs and that I hadn't found anything I liked. I found him amazingly easy to talk to. Throughout the evening a number of girls came up to him. 'Oh, Mark, darling, how are you?' and that sort of thing, which scared the hell out of me, but he gave no encouragement, which made me feel better. So Mark was all mine. And, boy, how I wanted him to be. He made me laugh, he was well travelled, he was intelligent. And he was twenty-seven, which I considered to be a good age for a man. We spent the whole evening together and when it came to an end, he asked for my phone number. Actually he asked if I wanted to carry the evening on, and although my hormones were screaming yes, my head told me no. For the first time in my life I listened to my head. I gave him my phone number and bursting with pride, I went to find Katie.

Katie had ditched Duncan and I told her what happened with Mark. Katie just stood there with her mouth open. 'Katie, close your mouth. I just don't want to ruin things, you know, with my track record. I really liked him.'

'I don't believe it.'

'Oh, come on, I've been so good lately.'

'Only because you haven't met anyone you like. Normally you sleep with everyone. I am proud of you, though.'

'Katie, am I a cool chick?'

'You're getting there.'

I went home. It was about three in the morning, but I was so happy I had to talk to someone. I woke Jess up.

'Jess, I think I've met Mr Right.'

'What the fuck are you doing?'

'Jess, I just had to tell you. I met this guy, he's called Mark, he's twenty-seven and he's absolutely gorgeous.'

'Ru, it's the middle of the night, I was dreaming.'

'Jess, this is important. Do you want a cup of tea? No, OK. Anyway, I saw him across a crowded room, really I did. Then I went up to him, I really did, and I introduced myself and he introduced himself. Did I tell you he was called Mark? Then I got him a drink. He's a radio producer and he asked for my phone number. *He asked for my phone number*, and he kissed me on both cheeks. Oh, he was so polite, a real gentleman, a proper man. Jess, doesn't he sound wonderful?'

'Yeah, whatever.'

'Anyway, thanks for the chat, I'm going to bed now.'

'Uggggh.'

The next morning I woke up early. It was Sunday yet I woke up at seven. I didn't wake up at seven on a weekday without duress. What do you do when you wake up early at a weekend? I cleaned the house. When Sarah got up at ten, it was spotless. I'd been to the shops too and I was cooking breakfast with the Sunday papers in front of me. I made Sarah breakfast and told her about Mark and she was far more interested than Jess had been. Sophie got up at eleven, but I had to tell her quickly about Mark because she was making coffee for the Thespian. When Jess emerged I started making her breakfast.

'You're up late,' I said, and she looked as if she was going to hit me, so I put her breakfast in front of her and she calmed down a bit. I felt happier and more excited than I had since moving to London. I really had something to look forward to.

I wanted to embrace life. I wanted to hug things, anything. I felt alive for the first time in ages. Reborn. And, yes, it was due to a man. A very special man. A very special man indeed. For the first time I was going to be called by a man. I knew he'd call. I hadn't slept with him. According to Jess's rules, he was definitely going to call. Of course, I had to make preparations for being called by Mark. I had to stay in close proximity to the phone. Apart from going to work, which I had to do, I stayed by the phone the whole time. I checked the answerphone for messages as soon as I got home from work and for the next week I waited constantly for the phone to ring. When it did I jumped on it. When it was my mother I shouted at her, when it was the Thespian I shouted at Sophie, when it was Jerry I sulked with Jess, and if it was any of Sarah's friends I gave her a dirty look.

It was hell. On Monday he didn't call, on Tuesday he didn't call, or Wednesday or Thursday or Friday. He hadn't bloody called. My friends assured me he was just playing it cool, but it didn't help. He had asked for my phone number, why would he do that if he wasn't going to call? Katie tried to get me to go out at the weekend but I couldn't leave my phone vigilance so I declined. All weekend I sat by the phone and still he didn't call. Again I was in despair. I called BT to check the phone was working, I wanted to call the hospitals to check that Mark hadn't been in an accident, but my friends wouldn't allow it. I was helpless. I just had to wait by the phone.

After a miserable weekend of waiting, I went back to work on Monday. Katie tried her best to calm me down and stop me worrying, but it didn't work. The only thing that would was

Mark calling, but I had to face the prospect that that wasn't going to happen. At twelve minutes past nine on Monday night, the phone rang. Out of habit I ran like Linford Christie to answer it.

'Hi, Ruth?'

It was Mark.

'Yes.' My heart did a somersault. That voice, that beautiful voice.

'It's Mark.'

Thank you, God. 'Hi, Mark, how are you?'

'Fine, and you?'

'Yes, I'm well.'

'What have you been up to?'

'Um, this and that.' Waiting for you to call, you idiot.

'Well, I'm sorry I haven't called before, but I've been really busy at work, you know how it is.'

'Oh, don't worry, I understand.' He apologised, he apologised.

'Anyway, would you like to go out on Friday?'

'Yes.' Yes, yes, yes.

'OK, well, look, I'll give you a call on Thursday and we'll arrange to meet.' Oh, God, not another call.

'You will call?'

'Yes, of course. I'm looking forward to seeing you. Listen, I'll talk to you then, 'bye.'

''Bye.'

The week and a bit of misery had been worth it. I had a date with Mark, Mark the Gorgeous, Mark the Wonderful. I had a date. I had the biggest smile on my face as I put down the phone. Of course, I had to tell my friends. Luckily, it being Monday, they were all in, so I had a great opportunity for smugness.

'He called,' I told them.

'Thought that was why you were screaming,' Jess said.

'He called.'

'What did he say?' Sarah asked.

'He's taking me out on Friday, somewhere cool, I expect. He's calling me on Thursday to arrange things.'

'Oh, no,' they all said.

'No, he will call, he promised. Did I tell you how good-looking he is?'

'Yes.'

'I'm pleased, Ru, really pleased,' Sophie said.

'Are you sure you know what you're doing? I mean, face it, honey, you've been a nightmare all week, really depressed. Are you sure he's the right sort of guy for you?'

I hated Sarah sometimes. 'He's perfect. Anyway he's very busy, he has a very responsible job. Give him a chance,' I snapped.

'All right, Ru, we're just worried, that's all,' Jess explained.

'Well, can't you just be happy for me?'

'We are, babe, we are.' Sarah was unconvincing.

'But I have a good feeling about him, Sas, he's lovely and he may just be the one.'

'Oh, shit,' Jess said.

'What now?' I shouted.

'What the fuck are you going to wear?'

Horror built up inside me.

'You've got loads of clothes, don't worry,' Sophie said.

Here endeth the don't-get-hurt lesson, and here starteth the panic involved in being a girl and having a date. We ran to my bedroom, emptied my wardrobe, ran to Jess's and did the same. In desperation I did it with Sarah's and Sophie's too, although their clothes wouldn't fit me anyway. Then I started wailing. 'Oh, my God. It's hopeless, I'll have to cancel.'

'Don't be silly. Pull yourself together – we'll go shopping,' Sarah said.

I hugged her. 'Really? New clothes? Nice sexy clothes?'

'Yes, we'll go one afternoon. Can you get time off?' I nodded, and thought that Sarah was the nicest person in the world. For a minute.

'What about my hair? It's a mess.'

'Hairdresser,' Jess said.

'And I'll do your nails and your make-up,' Sophie offered.

'So, I can go out with Mark?'

'Yes, and you'll knock him dead,' Sarah said. I loved all of my friends so much.

The problem with falling in love, or lust, or whatever, is that it is very expensive. First there was the shopping. Sarah and I went on Wednesday afternoon and I bought her lunch to thank her for taking her precious time off for me. After going to thousands of shops we decided on tight black cropped trousers and a sexy low-cut lilac top. Sexy but not obvious. I was planning to wear my black suede high-heeled mules to complete the look.

'What about underwear?' I said.

Sarah gave me a look. 'Ru, are you planning on jumping into bed with him?'

I turned red. 'No, but my mother always says that you feel more confident if you're wearing nice underwear,' I protested. I dragged Sarah into a department store where I chose lacy black knickers and a matching push-up bra. Well, I couldn't rely on folding my arms to give me a cleavage, not when I expected them to be firmly wrapped around Mark. Could I?

Wednesday evening I had my hair done. Sophie came with me as I had insisted on going to her hairdresser, which cost about a million pounds and was hugely pretentious. Antonio was going to cut my hair. He was probably called Tony from London, but he put on a fake Italian accent and was very camp. He walked around my hair a number of times. He touched it and tutted, then tutted some more, said, 'Fluuuffy,' a lot, and after what seemed an eternity he jumped up, said, 'I've *goot* it,' and summoned someone to come and wash it. Once in the chair, he told me my hair was boring, in bad condition and needed lifting. He didn't ask me what I wanted, just hacked away. Then he tried to get me to have it coloured, but I drew the line at that. Antonio told me, 'Bad girls have dullest hair, you want to be a bad girl?' I shook my head and promised I'd get it coloured next time.

Sophie had been sitting reading *Hello* for the last hour and a half, but when Antonio had finished, she came to admire his handiwork. 'God, Ru, you look amazing,' she said. I looked and I liked, and I thought the intimidation had been worth it. I felt a million dollars. It cost me a million dollars.

By Thursday night I was ready for Mark. I sat by the phone with my beautiful new hair and a new-found confidence. He called just as he said he would. Admittedly it was at ten o'clock. And admittedly I had been sitting for four hours waiting and torturing myself that he wasn't going to call. But he called. We arranged to meet in Soho at nine on Friday and, once again, I was on top of the world.

I got to the meeting place early. I had tried to be cool, as Jess and Sarah told me, but I couldn't. I was meeting him in a bar, so I just bravely went in, ordered a drink. Now I was hanging with the cool crowd I could do this. But the bar was hyper-trendy. Full of fluorescent fluffy furnishings, and matching people. Although I thought I looked nice, again I was underdressed. I tried not to feel too out-of-place as I sat down to wait. And wait and wait.

By nine I was getting restless, by ten past I was worried, by twenty past I was a nervous wreck. I didn't know if he'd stood me up, or died *en route*, or had an accident or what. Everyone in the bar was staring at me, or so I thought, and my eyes were glued to the door.

At half past nine Mark walked in and I felt so relieved I wanted to kiss the world. I was secondarily relieved to see he was wearing black trousers, a bright shirt and designer shoes. Not fluorescent fluff. He came over, smiled, kissed my cheek and went to buy drinks. He didn't seem to notice that he was late. I relaxed with him quite quickly. I was even cracking jokes and Mark laughed in the right places. The problem was that everyone in the bar seemed to know him: he was approached by about a hundred people. The girls came up and flirted brazenly with him, the men came up and wanted to talk about business or clubs or whatever. No one was interested in me. When we were alone I decided to ask him about these girls.

'How do you cope with those girls all the time? I mean, they may look nice, but they don't seem to have a brain-cell to rub together, and the way they giggle at everything you say, it's so annoying.' God, I was brave.

Mark laughed. 'Yes, I suppose they are silly, but they're harmless. They just want to hook a man with the right connections, that's all.'

'They obviously think you have the right connections. Do you?'

'Yes, I guess so.'

'Oh, well, that's a relief, I never date a man who doesn't have the right connections.'

'Ruth, you're so funny.'

'Why?' I was a little offended.

'Because you are and I think it's great and maybe we ought to go to this party now, otherwise I won't want to go.' He kissed me. He kissed me on the mouth, no cheeks and I felt all the tremors of a thousand earthquakes. God, he was so sexy.

The party was a repeat performance of the bar. Girls, men, everybody wanted to talk to Mark. He was like some hero. I was hanging on to his arm, because due to lack of attention I was a little drunk and my legs felt quite weak. I was in love. And I wanted Mark to myself. I didn't want to have to share him for a minute more.

'Mark, I want to go to your place now,' I said seductively. He looked at me and we left.

His flat was in Notting Hill and it was clearly a bachelor

pad. The kitchen had no food, the lounge housed a huge TV and
stereo and little else. But I didn't have time to study it in detail,
I had more important things to do. Mark's stereo was huge and
he went straight to it and put a Neil Diamond CD on.

'Beer?' he asked, coming so close to me I felt weak. I just
shook my head. He was teasing me, moving slowly towards me
until I had had enough. I grabbed his bottom and kissed him.
The kiss that almost killed me. We moved to the sofa, still
kissing and eased ourselves down. Mark took off my shoes,
kissing my toes, which was almost orgasmic. He then peeled
off my top and bra. I tried to do the same to him but he shook
his head. 'Wait,' he commanded.

Although I tried to do as I was told, there was a bomb in
my knickers and it was about to go off. He started licking my
neck, kissing my shoulder then moved to my breasts. The way
he sucked, kissed and bit my nipples brought me to my second
almost orgasm. I was losing control, I didn't know if I could
take much more. He moved his tongue down my body until
he got to my trousers. Within seconds he had removed them
and my knickers. I was begging him, 'Please, Mark, please.'
He just smiled as he found my clitoris with his hands and
tongue simultaneously. It was only a matter of seconds before
I came for real.

But as he kissed me I knew I wanted more. I pulled at his
shirt insistently, I fumbled with his trousers easing him out of
them, I practically ripped his Calvin Kleins off him. I started
kissing, teasing, licking the way he had with me. Mark had a
half-smile on his face the whole time, which graduated into a
full smile as I brought him to climax. He lit a cigarette, passed
it to me and we sat in silence. I sat naked on his sofa, he sat in
front of me on the floor.

'Let's make love,' I said, when the cigarette was nearly
finished. He stood up and disappeared. When he came back
into the room he had attired himself in a condom.

'Come with me,' he commanded and, powerless, I followed

him. He led me into the kitchen, lifted me on to his plastic kitchen table. I lay there, feeling slightly exposed as he went to the fridge, pulled out a bottle of champagne. He opened the bottle, poured champagne over me and licked it off, everywhere. Then I did the same to him. Seeing Mark spread across a table, naked bar a condom turned me on more than I'd ever been turned on in my life. And as I devoured the champagne and his body at the same time I had another orgasm. Finally he took me to the kitchen floor, put me on all fours and we started screwing. I couldn't help myself, I was screaming, I was sweating, I was coming again and again. When Mark collapsed on top of me after a few minutes of heaven, I knew I'd had the screw of the century.

We stayed on the floor for a while, catching our breaths, waiting for our heart rates to return to normal.

'Bed?' Mark asked, but I wasn't ready.

'I'd like a bath,' I said. Mark nodded. I just wanted the sexiness to last for ever. We ran the bath, pouring Mark's shampoo into it (he didn't bath much, evidently). The bathroom was stark white, clean and small. He got into the bath and I climbed in between his legs with my back to him.

'You're fantastic,' he said at last. I giggled. He soaped me and I pressed my body to him. Despite everything I was still wanting more. We didn't dry off, we just went to the bedroom where I grabbed a condom from his packet by the bed, put it on him, pushed him on to the bed, mounted him and proceeded to give him the fuck of his life. When we collapsed for the second time, Mark removed the condom, kissed me and we crawled under the duvet. I noticed that it was five in the morning, but I wasn't tired. I was just incredibly happy.

There was more passion than I'd ever given or received. When I'm old and have given up sex, I will remember that night as one of the best. His only flaw was that little smile, which was constantly on his face, as if I was amusing him somewhat.

In the morning I woke to find him doing something very

nice to me. God, he knew how to turn me on. We made love again, then decided to get breakfast at a little café. It was almost lunchtime and I didn't want to leave, but Mark offered to drive me home so we got into his car (which was a sports car) and went to Clapham.

I walked calmly into the house and into the lounge. No one was there. I threw myself on the sofa and lay there smiling. I was so happy. I relived the details of last night in my head. The kiss, the laugh, the smile, the sex, it had all been so perfect. I couldn't believe that something so good could have happened to me. I was well on the way to being totally in love with Mark. I adored him, he was wonderful, I fancied him, he was sexy and we had fun. I was having fun. I had to talk to someone so I decided to go and see Katie. I needed a good gloat – I felt I deserved one.

Katie opened the door looking deathly. She was wearing a tattered towelling bathrobe and the previous night's makeup. She looked really bad – she could even have passed for an extra in *The Rocky Horror Show*. She looked at me, walked to the sofa, picked up the butt of a joint and lit it.

'God, Katie, what's happening? Look at this place! You're surrounded by empty beer bottles and overflowing ashtrays and you – your face, go and clean it.' I looked around. Katie's flat was always so tidy, this was so out of character.

Katie smiled. 'Ruth, this is part of my rock-and-roll lifestyle, you know that. Soon I hope to be waking up in my own vomit.'

'Disgusting! You're disgusting.'

Katie laughed. 'Ruth, I didn't even have a drink last night. I got a bit stoned, that's all. You know Phil who lives upstairs and that weird girl Jiffy he hangs around with? Well, they caused this mess. They drank and smoked for England, then they left. I'm not sure why they came round but I didn't ask them. It was a really boring evening and I was tired so I couldn't be bothered to take off my makeup or tidy up. Why are you so strung up today?'

'I'm worried about you.'

'Fine, Ru, but worry about something that needs worrying about. I know that ever since I told you about my mother you've thought I'm turning into her, but rest assured that I'm not.' Katie stalked off to the bathroom to wash her face.

I wasn't convinced. OK, she wasn't a lush, well, not yet but she was a party girl and when they retire party girls turn into lushes. It's a well-known fact. However, Katie's appearance had distracted me from the real purpose of my visit. To gloat about Mark. Oh, well, Mark-gloating could wait. I had a new project: to sort Katie out.

Katie reappeared. 'Tell me about Mark.'

'Katie, we're talking about you.'

Katie smiled. 'He looked pretty gorgeous,' she said.

'Isn't he? And he's got the most amazing body.'

'And a big thing?'

'Katie, that's really none of your business.' We laughed. 'Actually it's more than adequate.'

'When are you seeing him next?'

'I don't know, he's going to call. But he's got a really busy job so I guess it's back to waiting by the phone.'

'You'd think that the phone was invented so men could avoid using it.'

'Alexander Graham Bell has a lot to answer for.'

He doesn't know how much. I spent the next week in hell. Exactly the same way I'd spent the previous week. Oh, and next time you're asked what heaven and hell are like, heaven is being in bed with Mark 'Sexy As Hell' Watson and hell is waiting for him to call me. It's as simple as that. I smoked twice as much as normal, I drank twice as much as normal, which is no mean feat, and I stopped eating.

Jess was jealous. 'Why aren't you eating?'

'Because I've totally lost my appetite – you know, Mark.' I sighed.

'Bloody hell, I'll have to get Jerry to stop calling me if I'm going to lose any weight. Or perhaps you can ask Mark not to call me too?'

I nodded. 'Well, I will if he ever calls.' Then I lit another cigarette.

Just as I was exhausted from not sleeping, hung-over from drinking too much and weak from not eating, the phone rang. It was Thursday.

'Hello?'

'Hi, Ruth?'

'Yes, Mark, how are you?' It's him, it's really him.

'Brilliant. How are you?'

'Great.' Well, I am now.

'Excellent. Do you want to come to a new bar on Saturday?'

'OK.' Yes, please.

'Right, must dash, I'll meet you at Tottenham Court Road tube station, or the McDonald's opposite.'

'OK. What time?' Thank you so much.

'Oh, about nine.'

'OK.' I can't wait. I'll count the minutes.

'Look forward to seeing you. 'Bye.'

''Bye.' I love you. The exhaustion left and I ate a whole packet of chocolate biscuits. I had another date and Mark liked me after all.

I wasn't so bad about the clothes thing this time, but Jess lent me some really nice trousers without me asking. She understood love now. Jerry was a poppet, according to her, and although they only saw each other once a week, things were going well. He hadn't spent much time at our place since the dinner, but that was because they had so little time together they had to make the most of it. I had visions of us all going to dinner together and becoming a group. Me and Mark, Jess and Jerry, Sophie and the Thespian, Sarah and . . . well, Sarah and Thomas. Nice, cosy friendships.

On Saturday I panicked for the whole day and went back to not eating. I was so excited and nervous at the same time, I couldn't possibly think about food. I just smoked twenty cigarettes instead. I decided to be late meeting Mark, after last time, but no matter how hard I tried I was still on time. At nine on the dot I was waiting outside McDonald's. I couldn't understand it. Of course, Mark wasn't there. I had the same half-hour of thinking I'd been stood up before he bounded towards me and kissed me passionately. I instantly forgave him.

He took me to a new bar, which was very old-fashioned – oak beams, wooden chairs, like ye olde worlde pub. But I guessed it was very trendy because it was full of trendy people.

'Drink?' he asked.

'Um, wine, please.'

'Ruthie, no, we have to drink vodka and Red Bull. Guaranteed to get you drunk and give you energy at the same time. Sort of legal Es.' He had a mischievous glint in his eye that I found irresistible. He came back with a jug of vodka Red stuff and it was really nice. Like punch. I started drinking.

'Marky, hi, darling, where have you been hiding?' A ten-foot blonde girl kissed him on both cheeks.

'Oh, I've been working. Nadia, this is Ruth.'

She looked at me with disdain. 'Anyway, I simply must have you at my next dinner party. You know it's not half as much fun without you.' Nadia was a bitch.

'OK, but only if Ruthie comes. We're together,' Mark said, and I nearly fell off my chair. Together, he said together, oh, my God, this was our second date and we were together. I had a drink to celebrate.

'Of course,' Nadia said, giving me a dirty look. I beamed at her, I couldn't stop beaming. We were together. I decided that 'together' was one of the best words in the English language. It meant so much. Nadia left.

Mark smiled. 'I'm sorry I came on so strong. It's just that I know so many nightmare people and she's one of the worst.'

I smiled back. 'It's OK.'

'Unfortunately the circles I seem to find myself in are very much like that. False, stupid, airhead girls and playboy boys. I hope you don't think I'm like that.' I nearly fell off my chair again: he cared about what I thought.

'No, Mark, it's obvious you're a more intelligent life-form than most of these people, but how do you manage to know so many of them?'

'Well, family, really. It's no big deal.'

I laughed, he was so modest and I felt sorry for him having to know so many awful people. 'What does your work involve?'

'Oh, I could go on all day, but I don't want to bore you. I produce various shows for radio stations. I suppose I'm freelance. I have a company that puts together programmes and sells them to the stations. Now, I think we need to go to dinner.' After a jug of vodka Red stuff I wasn't sure I had any room for dinner, but we went to Mezzo, which impressed me (don't forget, I didn't get out on dinner dates much). With dinner came a bottle of wine. In the true Ruthie tradition I got drunk. I ate the food, but I didn't taste it. I looked at Mark and fell more in love each second. By the end of the meal I just wanted to be alone with him.

'Mark, let's go home.' This was becoming my standard line.

'OK, I'll get our coats.'

We jumped in a cab and started snogging. We kissed all the way back to Mark's flat and continued when we got in. I was in my best seduction mood. We undressed each other and we made love urgently and without foreplay.

'Let's have some fun,' Mark said, with a suggestive glint in his eye. He mumbled something about acting out 'that scene' from 'that film', and as I licked my lips hungrily thinking this was a kinky *9 ½ Weeks* thing and we were going to the kitchen to eat food off each other, he took me to his spare room and I realised I didn't know this film. Then I realised I did. Don't ask me why, but Mark's spare room had a plastic sheet on the floor with a potter's wheel in the middle of it. I had watched enough daytime TV to know it was a potter's wheel. I was filled with horror. Then I remembered *Ghost*. He sat me at the wheel (I was naked), started it up and took a lump of clay from God knows where. I was only glad he was sitting behind me so he couldn't see the look of terror on my face. I mean, I had seen the film a number of times but I'd never done pottery. As the clay lurched out of control on the wheel in a hard slab, Mark grabbed my hands and placed them firmly on it. Christ, it was so messy and I was no Demi Moore. Feeling totally out of my depth I tried to concentrate on making a pot. Mark was getting very excited, kissing my neck, making noises and pushing my hands firmly into the clay. I expected to hear 'Unchained Melody' start up in the background. By the time I'd lost half the clay on the floor and the rest was clinging to me, Mark reached the height of his excitement, pushed me on to the floor into my lost pot and made love to me with a passion I don't even want to understand.

Afterwards I excused myself to shower and Mark, who had now got a fair amount of clay on him, joined me.

'That was the best, baby,' he whispered into my ear, and although for me it definitely had *not* been the best I resolved to take up pottery.

In bed later Mark told me how he loved the scene from *Ghost* so much he had bought the wheel but he'd never made anything. He told me Demi Moore was his ideal woman, he told me he loved having clay-filled sex, and I wondered how the hell I was ever going to get the clay out from underneath my fingernails.

Despite the weird nature of Mark's fantasy, I realised what life was all about. Lying in Mark's arms, revelling in being with him, feeling warm and safe, not worrying about the morning, I knew then that there was life after Ben.

The next morning was a repeat of the previous Saturday. We had Sunday breakfast, we read the papers in the café, it was comfortable. We went back to his place, and he offered to drive me home.

'I don't want to go,' I said. (How cool).

'I know, babe, but I've got work to do.'

'OK, but, Mark, can I have your phone number?' I just had a fear of waiting for another week – I wasn't sure I could bear it.

'Of course you can, baby. Here.' He gave me a card with his home and mobile numbers on it. How great was that?

I rushed into the house to gloat about my new great love-life (again). I told them how it went and was surprised to be bombarded by cautions to calm down and play it cool. Then I made the fateful mistake of telling them that I had his phone numbers.

'Oh, my God!' they all said in unison.

I looked at them innocently. 'What's wrong with that?'

'Ru, you'll call him all the time – you know what you're like. You'll scare him off,' Jess said.

'How dare you? I am not going to bloody well call him all the time. Why can you never give me any credit?' I was having a full tantrum, I stormed out and went to see Katie.

I told Katie about the date and she skinned up. She was happy for me. When I told her about the phone number she pointed out that it was my life and up to me if I wanted to call him. She always made me feel better. That evening, fairly stoned, we went to the chocolate shop. We did buy some lager, but the looks we got for our ten packets of Maltesers, two Mars Bars, a Snickers, some wine gums and a large bar of fruit-and-nut were very strange. I didn't go home that night. I know it seems childish, but I was fed up with my friends always fearing the worst with me. They never seemed able to let me enjoy my happiness without putting dampeners on it.

After work the next day when I went home, I felt a little stupid for my outburst. Sophie was the only one at home and the Thespian was with her.

'Hi, guys, how are you?' I breezed cheerfully.

Sophie hugged me. 'We're fine,' she said.

'I got a part in a pilot,' the Thespian said.

'So did I,' Sophie said.

'Wow, that's fantastic! Oh, Soph, how wonderful, tell me about it.'

The Thespian proceeded to tell me that it was a drama about medical students, like an unqualified *ER*, and he was playing a medical student and so was Sophie. Gripping. Then Sophie explained that it was going to be serious and amusing and fun, with sex, drugs, hard work, stress and intrigue. If it went well they might be regular TV stars. I hoped it did for Sophie's sake.

'Are we celebrating?' I asked.

'Oh, yes, Ru. Let's cook pasta and have lots of wine.' For a change.

'Nik, are you staying?'

'Yes.'

'Oh, good.'

Sarah arrived in time for supper and the fact that we were celebrating meant I didn't get told off for staying out all night. Jess didn't arrive home until ten, she had been working, so I gave her some food and she didn't tell me off either. Sophie looked so happy and we were all happy for her. It was a lovely evening and as I'd been out on Sunday, and doing this tonight,

I hadn't had a chance to call Mark. Who said I'd be straight on the phone?

On Tuesday night I called him. Everybody told me to wait until Wednesday, but I wanted to talk to him, to hear his voice, to see him. I didn't tell anyone I was going to call, I just did. I called his flat and got his answerphone, I left a message.

Half past seven: an hour since I called and the phone hadn't rung. I called his mobile. Got his mobile answerphone. Left a message, but didn't really mean to.

Eight: phone still hadn't rung. I kept checking that it worked and it did, but perhaps Mark's phones were both broken. Oh, God, listen to me, of course they weren't. Maybe he was just out, but if he was, surely he'd have had his mobile switched on and I'd tried that.

Half past eight: I was getting funny looks from my housemates and Thomas, who had appeared. They still didn't know I'd called him. I was trying not to be obvious but when the phone rang a few minutes later I dived for it. It was someone trying to sell double-glazing and I shouted at them to get off the line. When I hung up I thought, What if he tried to call and the phone was engaged? I sat down and tried to behave normally.

Nine: nothing. My friends thought I was still in sitting-by-the-phone mode, so they excused me. I wanted to phone the operator to check there was nothing wrong with his line, but I couldn't without being caught. I thought of going to a phone box and calling him again. I could have told him I'd gone out so I was calling on the off-chance, or perhaps I could have borrowed Jess's mobile. Oh, God, why was I going through this again?

Eleven: the phone hadn't rung and I hadn't gone out. I decided to go to bed. It was obvious that he was just out and his mobile was switched off. Although I was worried in case he'd had an accident. What is the accident-reporting etiquette with someone you've dated only twice? I went to bed thinking the worst about Mark, that he'd gone off me, that he was never going to call, that he was dead. I knew I was being stupidly irrational and I hoped that when I woke the next morning I'd be back to normal.

But I woke the next morning feeling sad. Then I remembered why, that Mark might be in trouble. I thought I should call to check that he was all right. Then I realised what a stupid idea that was.

At work I told Katie about it.

'Ruthie, you know that what you've done is exactly what you were trying to avoid by having his number?'

'Huh?'

'When you took his number it was because you didn't want to go through the sitting-by-the-phone hell of the last couple of weeks. Now you're doing just that.'

'Oh, shit.'

'And answerphones, well, if you leave messages, the ball goes back into their court and you have to chill out a bit. Remember, "A watched phone never rings." You shouldn't wait in for him to call. If you're not there when he calls you can call back. We're going out tonight.'

'Um, I can't. I've got laundry to do.'

'Really? That can wait.'

'No, it's urgent laundry.'

'Ruthie, we are going out tonight. That is an order, not a request.'

I wanted to scream and stamp my foot and say, 'What if he calls? I need to be there for him.' But I knew I was being pathetic and Katie was right on all counts, so I decided not to argue. But I really did have some urgent laundry to do.

We went out and I got home about midnight, although I'd been trying to leave all evening. At one point I had a headache, then I ran out of money, then I felt sick, and by half past eleven Katie admitted defeat and let me go home. But not before she pointed out that it was too late to call Mark. Bitch. When I got in I searched for my message from Mark. There wasn't one. Now I knew he must be in hospital somewhere – I mean, he'd had two evenings to return my calls and I knew he would have rung if he'd been healthy. After all, he had said we were together. I wanted to call, just to check, but it was midnight. I felt myself drawn towards the phone – it was like a magnet pulling me closer and closer. Then I remembered what Katie had said. And I remembered how pathetic I was as I dialled his number. I got the answerphone.

'Hi, it's Ruth, um, just called to check you're OK and you got my message. Call me.' I decided the best thing all round was if I went to bed and never got up.

The next morning I had a slight hangover and a definite embarrassment problem. Fancy calling him twice in a row. Fancy leaving two messages. Fancy being so stupid. As she walked into the office Katie looked at me. I shook my head. I just thought that if Mark had had any intention of calling me he certainly wouldn't now.

He did. He called that night, Thursday, from his mobile. He said he'd come to my house tomorrow night and we'd go for dinner. I gave him my address and he hung up.

He had called and he was coming round tomorrow, he still liked me. I was happy. It was incredible that every time he phoned I could forget the anguish of the previous few days.

I tried to arrange for everyone to be in to meet him. Jess was: she had lots of work to do. Sarah was: she was tired. Sophie said that she'd get the Thespian to come over. I wanted them to see how fantastic he was, how wonderful, brilliant and gorgeous. It was my first opportunity to show off. I called Katie, who also had a date on Friday (Katie doesn't do dates), with some DJ she really liked, or thought was sexy anyway. Sometimes I must remember that there are other people in this world apart from me.

On Friday I arranged my friends in the lounge so that they

looked natural, not as if they were waiting for Mark to arrive. Sophie and the Thespian were having dinner at the table in the lounge, Sarah was on the sofa watching TV and Jess was on the floor surrounded by papers. They couldn't have looked more natural if they tried. I wished I could say the same for me.

Mark was late. Half an hour, as seems to be his trademark. By then Sophie and the Thespian had finished their dinner and were watching TV, Sarah was bored and complaining and Jess said she was getting a numb bottom. They all moved.

When Mark finally arrived I was the only person around. The others came out to meet him, but they were too obvious: as soon as the doorbell went they all lined up in the lounge to receive him. I did the introductions and after half an hour of letting them have Mark's time, I took him away and we went for dinner.

Mark was perfect. We had a perfect meal, a perfect evening, and this time he came back to my house. Sophie and Thesp were still up, so we had coffee and chatted. The Thespian was impressed by Mark working in radio and Mark talked about all his contacts and said perhaps he could help them by introducing them to a few. OK, so he was showing off a bit, but he was so wonderful he was allowed to. He stayed the night, but as I had a full house sex was relegated to the bedroom. I was amazed that although this was our third date I still couldn't wait to rip off his clothes. In the morning we had a wonderful breakfast and he left amid promises to call.

Early relationships suck. I know they're supposed to be full of magic, passion and romance, but really they're full of feeling scared, not knowing when you're next going to see them, feeling misunderstood, nervous, horrible. I had seen Mark three times in as many weeks and I wanted the pace to step up, but how could it? For now I just had to go back to tearing my hair out. God, how long would this last? I've already told you Mark was gorgeous. Even my friends thought so, which was really something because every other guy I'd liked they'd thought not gorgeous at all. Even Ben. He had something magnetic about him, some force that meant he was irresistible, a little like Katie. He was funny and made me laugh. He was clever and could talk about world events with a knowledge far greater than mine. He was interested in me, asking questions about my background, my family, friends, everything. And when I told him I didn't want to be some great career woman, he listened and told me I should always do what I felt was right.

He did have faults: I had not gone into the relationship with my rose-coloured glasses, or not as much as I had with Ben. Mark was a little bad at timekeeping. You'd think after the first couple of times I'd have got used to that but, no, every time he was late I thought he had had an accident or that something terrible had happened. Then when he turned up I was so relieved that I wasn't cross. Not that I could have been cross with Mark. He just had to look at me for me to be under his spell. Was it his strength or my weakness that I fell under it so easily?

He was equally bad with the phone. He never called when he said he would and still I kept thinking something bad had happened and I'd frantically call him. But he was never at home and his mobile was always switched off. He was impossible to get hold of. Actually, it's amazing that we managed to have a relationship. But we did. Isn't that just the best word in the English language, RELATIONSHIP. I could say it all day. But although we only saw each other once a week, that was OK. Mark was busy with his job and I was busy with my life. Actually, it totally pissed me off that I saw him so little and spent the rest of the time waiting for the phone to ring. It also pissed Katie off because I didn't see her as much. She accused me of 'sex before mates', which was probably true, but I begged her forgiveness and she said she'd always be there for me, even though I didn't deserve it. I felt quite intimate with Mark. He was the first man I'd made love with since Ben. And it was great: he was tender and considerate, warm and affectionate. I loved being with him in bed. But he had faults there too. He hated being touched while he slept and I liked to cuddle all night. And when I went near him while he was asleep he would bite me, usually on my head. A little strange.

But never mind, I was about to have a luxurious bubble bath and get myself looking beautiful for my date with Mark. Due to his timekeeping, I had started getting him to pick me up at my house, or arranging to meet him at his. Tonight I was going to his flat. Of course I got there early. I just couldn't get the hang of being late, or even on time, even though I used the Circle line. I walked slowly from the tube station to his flat, but I was still early. After trying to wait, I pressed his buzzer. There was no response. I buzzed again and again and again and again. No, he was not there. Unless – what if he was in the bath and had fallen asleep, or had been murdered in his bed, or what if the buzzer sounded like it was working but wasn't? I ran round the corner to a phone box and called his flat. The phone rang then switched on to the oh-so-familiar answerphone and, no, unfortunately it wasn't the buzzer that wasn't working, although maybe his phone was broken too. Then I called his mobile, which was switched off. I had a cigarette to calm me down. I was so worried: he must be dead or hurt. What if he'd been run over and hadn't made it back to his flat? Oh, God. Another cigarette. And another. I looked at my watch, I had been waiting outside for half an hour.

Just as I was about to call the police, Mark got out of a taxi. 'Hi, baby,' he said, kissing me.

'Where have you been?' I asked.

'I went to score some dope. You haven't been waiting long, have you?' The concern was evident in his voice.

'No, not long.' We went into his flat, which was clean because he had a cleaner but messy because he was messy. I liked his flat: it was manly.

'I got some wine and I thought we'd stay in, get stoned and order a curry or something.'

'Sounds great,' I said. This was a big step forward in our relationship. We were having a cosy night in. He opened the wine and he rolled a joint. When I thought about it, this meant so much more than going out: staying in together, just the two of us, well, that was a couple-type thing to do. This was going to be far more romantic than going out. I was getting used to the idea of a cosy night in when the buzzer went. Mark answered it, and three of his friends walked in.

'Hi, Ruthie,' they said, plonking themselves down.

'Hi, guys.' I had met David, Vic and Mike only once before. Mark got them all beer and they proceeded to get stoned. One of them had brought a video round of martial-arts cartoons and they all watched avidly. I was ignored.

'I'm hungry, Mark,' I said, hoping to cause a diversion.

'Let's have pizza,' David said.

'OK.' Mark went to get the menu. Two bottles of wine, lots of joints, lots of cartoons and a pizza later, it was two in the morning and no one had shown any signs of leaving, probably because they were incapable of it. I was bored.

'I think I'll go to bed,' I said, expecting Mark to join me.

'OK, baby,' Mark said, and kissed me. I went into his bedroom alone. I passed out straight away. Mark came to bed ages later, I guess – I don't know, I didn't wake. In the morning he kissed me lightly and we made love. After we had showered and dressed, we went for breakfast and he walked me to the tube station. I thanked him for a wonderful evening, even though it hadn't been, and he said he'd call me. I arrived home and resumed my normal position of waiting by the phone.

Chapter Fifteen

The Greatest Love: Part Two

Troy looked at Stephanie, mesmerised. 'You've put on weight, you should take more care of yourself.'

Stephanie scowled at Troy. 'You can talk, look at your beer belly.'

'Stephanie, I'm in great shape. You, however, have let yourself go.'

They had been married a year and tensions were high.

'Are you surprised? I take care of the house, I take care of you, and all you can do is criticise.' Stephanie put on her towelling-robe and wished that Troy wasn't such a pig.

'Take care of the house? Take care of me? Honey, from where I'm standing all you do all day is eat, spend my money and cause me major headaches. You can't even cook.'

'Oh, really? And you – you never do anything. You and your "I'm a seriously successful businessman." God, you never stop. You work, yes, but so do I and what do you do around the house? Nothing. You throw your clothes on the floor, you make mess after mess and you never even put the toilet seat down.'

'Stephanie, shut up. You're really boring.'

'And you're a bastard.' Stephanie went to make Troy's

breakfast and Troy went to get ready for work. He forgot about his pain of a wife and smiled to himself, daydreaming about his gorgeous new secretary.

Mark didn't call. I called him, at home and on his mobile, I left messages on both, but by now, I felt I had the right to. I called him on Tuesday, which was as long as I could bear to wait. On Thursday I went for a quick drink after work with Katie, then she had another date with the DJ, so I went home. My housemates looked upset.

'What's going on? Is something wrong?'

'Ru, something's happened that you need to know about,' Jess said. Sophie burst into tears.

'What is it? God, are you OK?' I was worried.

'It's Mark,' Sarah said.

'Mark?' I knew it! He really had had an accident this time.

'Ruth, Mark came here tonight,' Jess explained.

'Why?' I was confused.

'He came to see Sophie.' Sophie was still crying, Sarah was comforting her and Jess looked really uncomfortable.

'Why the fuck did he do that? Why the fuck was he here?' I was confused, angry that they were taking so long to tell me and hoping to God that this was a misunderstanding. Of course it had to be. I was falling in love with Mark. He probably said he was here to see Ruthie, or for coffee or something, and Sophie needed her ears de-waxed or something and had misheard.

'He came round. I was the only one here. I told him you were out and he said that was OK because he was here to see me. I asked him why and he asked to come in. I thought maybe it had something to do with the radio stuff he does, but I felt really uncomfortable. I said could he just tell me what he wanted, as I was busy, I didn't even let him in the door. Do you really want to know?'

I was white. My misunderstanding theory was not holding up but, yes, I needed to know. I nodded.

'He asked me if I realised that you and he were very casual and not serious, and then he said I must have noticed the chemistry between us and he asked me out. I said no, I did, Ru, I said no to him and told him that he shouldn't have done that to you. Then I asked him to leave.'

'Then I got home and found Mark blocking the door,' Jess said. 'I heard him telling Sophie not to tell you, then he left, still smiling.'

'So I burst into tears and told Jess. He was horrid and I need you to believe that I didn't do anything wrong.' I gestured that I knew she hadn't, but I was too shocked to speak.

'Listen, Ru, Sophie told me and she didn't know what to do. She didn't want to hurt you again – none of us wanted that. But we knew he'd end up hurting you if we didn't tell. We did it because we care, I promise. None of us is enjoying this one little bit,' Jess said.

'I know,' I squeaked, then burst into tears. Sophie and I clung together and Sarah and Jess went to make tea. I knew this feeling: desolation, disappointment, anger. How dare he? How dare he do that to Sophie and how dare he do that to me? Bastard, bastard. How could he say we weren't serious? I was bloody serious and I'd thought he was. I'd spent hours waiting for him, to phone, to turn up, to love me. I shouldn't have pinned all my hopes on Mark, yet I had. Mark had become the centre of my life and then he had ruined it. But I had put him in that position. Would I ever learn? I didn't blame Sophie and I didn't excuse Mark. I had come a long way. For once in my life I was not going to make excuses for him, or defend him, or try to cling to him for fear of being alone. I would cry and I'd hurt, but I knew those feelings and I'd get over him far more easily than Ben. I would just bypass the denial stage at the speed of light and take control of my life for once.

I locked myself in my room and cried. I cried for me, for

my loss, I cried for Sophie and what she had been through, and I cried for me again. After sobbing my heart out and feeling those all-too-familiar end-of-the-world feelings, I sat up. I had done this for about a year now and I looked as though I was going to start it all over again. I was going to wrap myself in misery and live my life that way. It made me think. I had been largely unhappy the past year. I had done everything possible to enhance that unhappiness. It was Ben's fault – no, it was my fault. I had fallen to pieces over Ben and I was about to do the same over Mark.

All the time I had felt I deserved every bit of misery I faced. I didn't. I didn't deserve this. I was the good guy here and Mark was the baddy. God, how long had it taken me to realise that I wasn't doing anything wrong? I was just hurting. I had two choices; I could don my I'm-a-sad-loser T-shirt for the rest of my life, or I could stop being a victim and get over it. I had felt I was over Ben when I met Mark, and now I was going to get over Mark too. Oh, how much better I would be without either of them in my thoughts. I went back to the lounge.

'I'm going to call him,' I announced.

'No, Ru, don't,' Jess begged.

'I don't think you understand. I am going to call the creep and tell him he's a creep and get him to stay away from me and my friends.' This was fighting talk.

'Oh, Ru, that's wonderful.' Sophie hugged me.

'I never thought I'd see the day,' Sarah said.

As I walked to the phone I was feeling a mixture of emotions: strong, proud, sad and hurt, worried in case I got the answerphone. I dialled the number. Ironically he answered the phone: the only time he had been there for me was the last time he'd ever be there for me.

'Hi.'

'Mark, it's Ru.'

'Hi, babe, how are you?'

'I'm fine, Mark, but you're not. You're a twisted little fucker who must be really stupid if you thought for a minute that Sophie wouldn't tell me what happened earlier.' Not bad.

'What do you mean? Oh, when I came over earlier, I wanted to surprise you and you weren't there. I told Sophie how much I liked you. What did she say?'

I couldn't believe the bare-faced cheek of the man. 'Oh, Mark, I'm disappointed in you. If you want to behave like slime, then at least have the guts to admit you're slime. I don't think we'll be seeing each other again, ever.' I put the phone down. God, what a cool chick. This was a new feeling. I liked it. OK, I was upset, but I hadn't let him walk over me and I hadn't let him make me a victim. I would get over this and I would do it bloody quickly. I had handled it, and I had handled it brilliantly. Mark didn't know I'd spent an hour composing what I was going to say. I had even sounded natural. I felt good about myself. I felt emancipated.

'I think we should celebrate,' I announced. My friends looked at me, stunned, and Sarah was holding a box of tissues.

'Oh, I don't need those. I need wine and I need to slag off men.'

'Oh, Ru, I'm so proud of you,' Sarah said.

'Were you horrible to Mark?' Jess asked.

I nodded.

'Really horrible?' Sophie asked.

I nodded.

'I'm a cool, mean bitch who ain't never gonna let a penis-holder get the better of me.' We all laughed and opened the wine.

'Let's play the worst-date game,' I suggested.

'What?'

'OK, we'll all say what our worst date was, and then we'll judge with marks out of ten. The winner gets an extra glass of wine.'

'OK, only because you're the girl not to be messed with. But, Ru, isn't it obvious who'll win?'

I laughed. 'I may get to like winning,' I said.

Jess went first. 'I arranged to meet a nice respectable lawyer for dinner. I met him at something I went to with Thomas. Anyway, when I first met him he was smart, wearing a suit and quite attractive so when I saw him in the restaurant I almost didn't recognise him. He was wearing snow-washed jeans, an anorak and a bright orange shirt. He looked so awful, no kidding. I mean, he didn't have to be in Armani, but this century would have been good. I had to have dinner with him, because I didn't know what else to do. We sat down to dinner and I couldn't stop staring at him, he looked so different. I couldn't hold a conversation and I couldn't eat. All I could think about was his bad taste. I was in shock. Jake took my shock to mean I fancied him, so as soon as the coffee was finished, he paid the bill, led me out of the restaurant and tried to put his tongue down my throat. I just ran. I actually ran away, hailed a cab and left him looking confused. Ugh, just the thought of those jeans is almost enough to make me give up sex for ever.'

My turn. 'Without question, I think it has to be Wayne, and I don't need to tell you about that again.'

'It's not fair. Whatever we do, you'll always win with the pizza-man date,' Jess said.

'OK, Soph, your turn.'

'Well, I suppose the worst was when James took me along to one of his work parties. He basically pushed me under the nose of his boss and all his colleagues, he told me which women I should speak to and everything. At dinner I had to sit next to his boss, who was a lecherous old man who kept leering. James was in his element. He was showing me off and when I complained about his boss touching my thigh, or whatever, he told me to chill out and think of his career. Selfish wanker. So I endured an evening of bum-pinching and leering just so James looked good. He made me feel like such a piece of meat. I wish I'd seen it at the time.' We didn't laugh. Sophie looked upset and we were all upset for her. It was easy to see why she was with the Thespian: he'd never have done anything like that.

'Sarah, can you remember far enough back to tell us about your worst date?' Jess joked.

'Actually, I think I have something that qualifies and is recent.'

'What? You had a date? No way!'

'No, it wasn't a date. In fact, it was supposed to be a business dinner. One of my colleagues from another branch asked if I would go for dinner so we could discuss strategy on a new project. Of course I said yes – this was work. Anyway, we went out and it didn't even occur to me that it was a date. We had a nice dinner and wine, and Michael was good company. We discussed work and the project and just chatted. He's very serious about his career too. We talked about our ambitions and they were pretty similar. At the end of the meal the bill came and I offered to pay half. He said no, but I insisted – you know how independent I am. Michael got quite cross and said, "I'm paying, I'm the man," which really wound me up. I said he might be a man but he wasn't my man, and as two friends we were equal. Then he said he only took me to dinner because he wanted to sleep with me – "get in my knickers" was his phrase – and he said I knew that before I agreed to come so I must feel the same. I told him he'd got it wrong. I'd just thought it was a business dinner. He accused me of being a tease and said, "Pay your half, then, you frigid cow," and I said, "No, pay it yourself, you chauvinistic pig," and he looked at me as if he wanted to hit me and then I said, "If you claim to anyone in the company that you slept with me I'll tell everyone that you've got an incredibly dinky penis," and I walked out.'

'Wow, Sarah, you really are Girl Power,' I said. 'But that was awful. Some men are such creeps, aren't they?'

'Yes, but I think women can be bad too,' Jess said, not being able to bear men having the monopoly on anything, even if it was bad.

I had cheered up a little, but I still felt sad and depressed. It was turning into an I-hate-men session for my benefit. 'I always pick the wrong ones,' I said.

'Yup,' everyone agreed.

'I don't know how you can bear to go through all this shit,' Sarah said. She had a point.

'I went through the same with James,' Sophie said.

'The Porsche,' I corrected her.

'Yeah, all right, he might have been a complete tosser but at least he was going to buy a Porsche,' Sophie said.

'Shame he couldn't have bought some balls at the same time,' I said.

'Porsches may be expensive, but it's easier for a man to own a Porsche than to have balls,' Jess said.

'Balls are in very short supply at the moment. I think we're going to have to invent some ball-getting tablets soon.' Me.

'Well, we could, but we have to be careful. I mean, we don't want men getting too many balls, do we?' Sarah.

'No, perhaps we can use the Thespian as a test case.' Me.

Sophie looked indignant. 'Nik has balls, ample balls, so start being nicer about him.' But she laughed anyway.

'Jess, does Jerry have balls?'

'He must have because I like him, but I don't think we've spent enough time together for me to really know,' Jess replied.

'I hope Jerry has lots of balls. Jess, I will do something, you know, and soon. Soon you'll be proud of me and I promise I'll be happy.'

'I'll drink to that,' Sarah said. 'To happiness and balls.'

'Happiness and balls!' We drank some more. The evening was turning out to be a serious female bonding session, the sort that is very dangerous if you're a man.

✻   ✻   ✻

The next day at work, I told Katie what had happened. I have to admit she looked stunned.

'So, the perfect man isn't perfect. Why do they always disappoint?' she said.

'I don't know. But he had all the right ingredients. Nice-looking, fun, good in bed.'

'But he was a cheating bastard. They always have at least one fault.'

'I wish that that fault could have been smelly feet or something. But he's gone now and, to be honest, I know I'll get over it. After all, the whole relationship was pretty one-sided, story of my life.'

'I'm proud of the way you handled it and are handling it. How good in bed was he?'

'Very. I reckon if I spent time with him I'd have to have sex ten times a day.'

'Not bad. I think I may devote my life to the quest for the perfect shag.'

'God, Katie, is that why you sleep with so many men?'

'Maybe. Really, I should have found the perfect shag already. God, I may have found it. I don't know why I have so many men. I wish I did. I think it may have some-thing to do with Matty.' Katie opened up at the oddest moments.

'Who's Matty?'

'You know I told you I'd been in love once. Well, it was with Matty. I was at A-level college with him and he wanted to be a rock star. We were young but we had the most intense relationship, very physical and poetic. Do I sound like a trashy women's novel?'

'Yes, no, go on.'

'OK. Well, we were inseparable, or so I thought. I know we were young, but he practically lived with me. I gave up all my friends for him. I was one of those horrible girls who put sex before mates, but I just wanted to be with him all the time. When we finished our A levels, I went to art college. Matty joined a band, and after a while they started touring in obscure parts of the country. I promised to wait for him, he never wrote, I fucked up art college, lost inspiration due to a broken heart, that sort of thing. I've never had a relationship since. Or a friendship.'

'Katie, I didn't know. It sounds like me.'

'Yes, a broken heart is a broken heart the world over. But, Ru, I didn't want to tell you because, believe it or not, it still hurts a bit.'

'I know.' I did.

'I often wonder what happened to him, I think it's the not knowing. I mean, every great love story has a loved one disappearing and the one left behind spends their life wondering what happened. Huh, I'm just getting sentimental.'

'He's not famous?' It wouldn't have surprised me if Katie's great love had turned out to be a famous rock star: it fitted with her image.

'No, I'd know if he was. He's probably still touring in deepest darkest Cornwall, playing to the sheep, and it serves him right for breaking my heart.'

'So, if you've been in love, why aren't you like me and trying to fall in love again?'

'I don't want to get hurt, not yet anyway, and I kind of lost my belief in love a bit when Matty left. My family, Matty, it seemed safer not to get involved, you know. And there are so many men in the world, why settle for one?'

'I wish I could be like you. I believe the person I'm meant to be with is out there and he'll find me so I should relax, but then I can't help feeling that he may be looking in the wrong place so I have to find him, I have to be alert.'

'Ruthie, you may be a little crazy, but I like your optimism for love. Sometimes I wish I had more of it.'

'Maybe you only sleep with men because you want to be loved?' Is that why I do it?

'God, Ruth the counsellor! Yes, probably, in a way, but I

know that the men I sleep with are for instant gratification, nothing long-term. The trouble is, casual sex can't be exciting for ever — it's very superficial. It gets boring, believe me.'

'Ah, so you're not the sex addict you make out. What about the rest of your life? You're a party girl first and a secretary second. If you give up being a party girl, what will you be?'

'God, I don't know, nothing. Just a secretary and not a very good one.'

'Katie, you always do what you want.'

'Not if you lose sight of what you want. God, you're so right. What am I? Take the parties away and I have nothing. Why didn't I see this? Shit, my life's so fucked.'

'Katie, I didn't mean that. It's not fucked, you don't have nothing.' What had I done?

'Ru, it's true. I've got some serious thinking to do. I need to go home now.' Katie had tears in her eyes.

'OK,' I whispered. Suddenly I was scared. Mark hadn't destroyed me. Katie and I would survive, I'd make sure of it. I was stronger now and she needed me. And, after all, it seemed that without meaning to I was responsible for upsetting her. It seemed that my new strength had made Katie weak.

I saw the Mark incident as a turning-point. It made me look at my attitude to relationships. I had given up one-night stands. Now I was going to give up Mr Wrongs. I had taken back control of my life. Or control of my men-life anyway. Mark had got me over Ben, and now I would get over Mark. I was over Ben. *I was over Ben.* That was the most beautiful thought. I was almost ready to start living my life. I just needed to know how.

Chapter Sixteen

The Times was running a competition, it was the biggest there had ever been. It was called 'The Search for the Precious Present'. The Precious Present was something that gave everlasting happiness, and people were invited to decide what it was. Everyone thought long and hard about what would give them happiness for ever.

One man declared it to be a Ferrari. Another declared it to be a beautiful woman. A woman declared it to be the world's biggest diamond. Another declared it to be the biggest mansion in the world. They racked their brains, thinking what it might be, as answer after answer was dismissed. The village idiot asked if he could have a turn. Everyone laughed. What did he know about happiness?

'I think that the Precious Present is not something anyone gives to you. It is what you give to yourself. It is exactly what it is called, the precious present. Not the past, not the future, but now. If you realise how precious the present is, then you find everlasting happiness.' Oh, how everyone laughed at him. What a dimwit, what a simple fellow. However, they soon stopped laughing when *The Times* declared him the winner.

Katie was officially having a crisis. And I had thrown her into it. The question of her life without parties had tipped her over the edge. Why did I mess up everyone's life? I should have been carrying a danger warning. If Katie's feeling that she was nothing without a party was bad, then what came next was worse.

'If I die tomorrow, what would people say about me?'

'What are you talking about?'

'Well, what have I done with my life? Been in love, dropped out of art college, had a couple of boring jobs, shagged my way through London, made one friend and lost my family. When I'm alive people say I'm cool, but if I was dead they'd think I had an empty life.'

'No, they wouldn't. They'd say you were great and that you made a big impression on everyone you met. You're special, Katie.'

'So what? It's not like I've found a cure for cancer or done any real good. I'm selfish and empty.'

'Katie, don't think like that. Besides, you've still got time to do something great, and I know you will.'

'Huh.'

I was really worried about Katie, I'd never seen her like this. She had been strong when I had been weak; she had been together when I had been in pieces. Now we'd swapped and I didn't know how to help her. I went to see her. She wasn't good: she had decided that her life sucked and it needed changing. Katie had become me. Katie couldn't go to work the following week.

I went to work as usual, but I took Katie grapes and Beck's to help her. She had taken to eating only grapes, sort of fasting but without giving up grapes and she would drink the Beck's. She told me this was her spiritual way and she felt it might help her to find answers. She also smoked a lot of dope. I had never heard of grapes and lager as spiritual, but Katie claimed to know and in her present state I didn't want to argue. I spent my evenings sitting on Katie's sofa watching TV and watching Katie deep in thought. I didn't know how long she was going to be like this, but she wouldn't take phone calls, she wouldn't go out and she wouldn't go to work. I had covered for her at work, by telling them she had the flu, and I told my flatmates she had a virus and was very ill. But I really hoped it wouldn't last much longer. I felt responsible; Katie had been solid before she met me. She had been solid before I taught her how to fall apart.

On Sunday of the first week of crisis, Katie had an answer, sort of.

'I still don't know for sure what I want to do with my life, but I know that the answers are not at work or at the parties. In fact, my life — and yours too now — is incredibly selfish as well as shallow. We need meaning.' She had finally flipped.

'What the fuck are you talking about?' This had taken a week of grapes, Beck's and probably too much grass.

'I don't know the details yet. I just need to find meaning.' I knew better than to pursue her further.

I decided to take matters into my own hands. I would find the answer to our problems. I would find meaning. I would make Katie better just as I had sunk her into depression. I would do something. I really *would* this time.

But first I had to exorcise some ghosts. My thoughts and feelings weren't the answer to my life. Or perhaps they were — I just wasn't concentrating. I spoke to Sarah about it and, well, Sarah told me to make another list. I did. 'Bored' cropped up, as did 'directionless', as did not wanting to work, disliking London, men. Sarah said I was trying to tie myself down with nothing to tie myself down to. I thought that was the wisest thing I'd ever heard her say.

I started thinking about being tied down and realised I wasn't. I had so many things in my favour: I was young, I was not tied to a job, I was free to do as I chose. You see, I had what I said I wanted: I had choice. But I didn't know how to use it. I knew I didn't want to be single and that I wanted to meet Mr Right, but he was out there and I'd find him, or maybe he'd find me, but I couldn't spend all my time scouring London for him. He might not even live in London. I had trapped myself for no reason. I could untrap myself. I was going to do something, I really was, just as soon as I thought of it.

Suddenly it was Jess's birthday. I had been too caught up in myself to be aware of dates, but now Jess would have the honour of joining the Twenty-two Club. As I had drunkenly suggested, I would cook dinner for everyone and this time everyone included the four of us, Thomas, the Thespian and Jerry. The Thespian was only allowed to attend because Jerry was, and I think Jess wanted to show that at least one of her friends could have a relationship. Or that's what she said. Jess also thought this honour would please Sophie.

'If you want him I'll invite him,' Sophie said, surprised.

'Yes, yes, I do, it'll even out the numbers,' Jess replied.

'No, it won't,' I said.

'Won't what?' Jess asked.

'Jess, inviting the Thespian won't even out the numbers. We'll still be one man short,' I pointed out.

'Well, it's not my fault we don't know any more men. Sophie, invite him.'

'Whatever,' Sophie said. Not exactly the down-on-her-knees-with-gratitude act that Jess expected.

Jess, though, was fast falling in love with Jerry. They had increased their once-weekly appointments to twice-weekly, and Jess worked extra hard to make sure she didn't break any dates. She never did. Jerry broke a couple, but he was a journalist and as his job was a little spontaneous he had to. And although this upset Jess, she forgave him, she knew it wasn't personal. How confident was that?

We racked our brains to decide what to buy Jess for her birthday. I mean, what did you give a girl like Jess? In the end we decided on some cool make-up and a make-up bag. It would be something to show off in the office. Jess had taken the day off on the Friday to see her parents and collect her presents; she was due back on Saturday evening, in time for dinner with us. I had made a three-course French meal and it had taken me all day to prepare. It was good for me, therapeutic. Since Mark I had been a little scared of going out, in case I bumped into him, so doing this was helping to keep me occupied. I knew I probably wouldn't bump into him, but I might have been tempted to stray into his regular haunts. You see, I never said I was over him, or that I didn't miss him, oh, no: hating him and thinking him a slime-ball are totally different. I also had Sophie to help me, which kept me entertained.

'How's the Thesp?'

'Um, well, there've been a few problems there.'

'Really?'

'Well, you know we did the TV pilot *ER* for younger, uglier people?' I nodded and laughed. 'Well, it wasn't a huge success and we found out last week that it wasn't going to make us stars. Nik took it quite badly.'

'Soph, I'm sorry. I was looking forward to having my mate on TV.'

'That's the thing. I've been offered to audition for another new TV drama. They liked what I did. And this is going to be a period drama and quite well done – it could be good for me. I'm so excited.'

'Well, that's great.'

'Yeah, I know, but Nik, well, he thinks he should have been discovered, too, and he can't understand why I've been asked to audition. He's really upset about it.'

'I suppose that's a problem when you both work in the same area, especially as it's such a competitive thing. It must be hard for one to see the other have more success.' I couldn't believe I was being nice about the Thesp but I was.

'I know, but I should be happy now and Nik is pissing me off.'

'Gosh.' Sophie didn't get cross.

'Anyway, I'm not sure what I should do about it. Perhaps it will blow over.'

'When's the audition?'

'Two weeks' time. Ru, I think this may be the break I've been waiting for.'

I hugged her. 'Fingers crossed.'

Sarah joined us, and as we had worked so hard, we were allowed an early glass of wine. It was five and Jess was due back at half past six. We'd done well.

'Sarah, what time's Thomas coming?'

'About half past seven.'

'What about the Thesp?'

'Same time.'

'Jerry?'

'Search me.'

'I wonder what he's bought her.'

'I bet it's really nice. Jerry would only buy nice presents,' I said, and the phone rang. I dived for it. Old habits are hard to break.

'Hello.'

'Hi, who's that?'

'Ruth, who's that?'

'Ruth, hi, it's Jerry.'

'Hi, Jerry, Jess isn't back yet.'

'Oh.'

'She'll be back at about half six.'

'Oh, shit, can you give her a message?'

'OK.'

'Well, I've been called to the paper. There's been an emergency of some sort, an accident, and they need me to cover the office tonight. I can't make dinner.'

'God, Jerry, I'm not telling Jess that. You tell her.'

'Ruth, I don't know if I'll be able to use the phone, or when – God, I feel so bad. Look, tell her I'm sorry and I'll call her as soon as I can.'

'All right, but try to call.'

'I will, 'bye.'

''Bye.' I walked back to the kitchen. 'That was Jerry. He can't make it tonight.'

'No,' Sophie said.

'Shit,' Sarah said.

'Who's going to tell Jess?' I asked. We drew straws. Sarah lost and I briefed her on the whole conversation, then carried on cooking. A silence enveloped us, each one worried and trying to predict Jess's reaction. I thought she'd go mad, but Jess had changed a lot since she'd been with Jerry. She'd mellowed a little.

We didn't have to wait long to find out.

'Hi, guys.'

'Happy birthday,' we chorused, with a little too much enthusiasm.

'Thanks.'

'How were your parents? Have a glass of wine.'

'Fine, thanks.' Jess sat.

'There's something I have to tell you,' Sarah said.

I didn't think this was the best time. 'Oh, Sarah, present first.'

Sarah looked relieved, Sophie went off to get it. 'Here, darling, happy birthday.'

Jess opened it. 'Oh, my God, how cool! This is just the coolest make-up in the world! Thanks, you guys.' She hugged us all in turn.

The nice time over, Sarah now had work to do. 'Sarah, you said you had something to tell Jess.'

Sarah gave me a dirty look.

'What?' Jess asked impatiently.

'Jerry called. There's been an emergency at work and he has to stay in the office all night,' Sarah blurted out.

'What? He's not coming?'

'No.'

'I don't sodding believe it.' Jess looked upset, not angry. Upset. This was the new Jess.

'He's really sorry and he'll try to call later, but you know how it is with his job,' Sarah pleaded.

Jess burst into tears. 'Yes, I do know, because I'm always the one on the receiving end. I don't mind that he cancels the odd date, but this is my birthday and I want him here.'

'I know, Jess, it stinks, and Jerry sounded miserable,' I said.

'Yeah, well, I thought I was married to my job, but Jerry really is. It's always going to be like this, I can tell, always.' She stopped crying.

'But you still like him,' Sophie offered.

'Yes, I do,' was Jess's quiet reply as she went into her bedroom. As exchanges with Jess went, that was weird: she had seemed to accept a situation she didn't like, which she'd never done before – she'd fight and kick and scream, she would have gone down to the newspaper office and dragged him out, she would have made him be here. Maybe Jess really had been taken over by aliens, or maybe she had just grown up.

Later she emerged with new mascara and a smile – a sad smile. We poured her more wine. The plan was to get her drunk – it was the only one we could come up with. By the time Thomas turned up, she was on her way. 'Thomas, I'm so glad you could make it, lovely, lovely,' she gushed.

'Happy birthday, Jess.' Thomas looked confused.

Then the Thesp arrived.

'Oh, God, Nik with a K, how are you?' Jess gushed.

'Fine.' The Thesp looked terrified. We sat down to eat.

'Where's Jerry?' the Thesp asked, not knowing Jess as well as Thomas did.

We all took cover under the table.

'Oh, the poor lamb. There's been some kind of national emergency and being a pivotal part of the paper Jerry has to cover it and it will probably last all night, but someone has to give the public the news, don't they? It's such an important profession.'

'Right. What sort of emergency?' the Thesp continued.

'Oh, God, that's a secret. Well, it is until it's reported — journalists never tell before they break a story. They have very high morals and codes and that sort of thing.' Jess was being quite dreamy. 'Jerry is wonderful. Don't you think he's wonderful, Thomas?'

'Um, yeah.' Thomas gave me an odd look.

'Ruth, do you think he's wonderful?'

'Of course.'

'Sophie?'

'Yes, Jess.'

'Sarah?'

'Yes, he's really wonderful.'

'Nik with a K?'

He looked at Sophie, who nodded. 'Absolutely,' he said, much to everyone's relief. Jess started on another bottle of wine. She was drunk, but at least she wasn't throwing things.

We finished the main course, the phone rang. I dived, expecting to get it, but Jess had dived too and Jess won. We couldn't hear but we all deduced it was Jerry, and although I stood as close to the lounge door as I could, I still couldn't hear properly. I heard her say, 'Why?' a lot, but that was about it. I wouldn't have made a good spy. Jess returned and I served dessert. We all looked at her, hardly daring to speak. Jess burst into tears. Jess hardly ever cries and she never cries in front of people — well, people who aren't us.

Sophie noticed the look of amazement on the Thesp's face. 'Nik, you have to leave,' she whispered, knowing that this would save Jess embarrassment.

'I don't want to,' he whispered back.

'You have no choice, just go. I'll call you tomorrow,' she hissed at him.

He looked most put out but then he left. Jess was with her inner sanctum. She could cry with us.

'He's such a bastard,' she said.

'Is he?' I asked.

'No, he's lovely,' she said.

'Jess, what happened on the phone?' Thomas asked.

'He said happy birthday, he said he was sorry he couldn't be with me, he said he's thinking of me and he'll see me tomorrow evening to make up for it.'

'Well, that's all right, isn't it?' Sarah asked.

'Yes, but I want him here now. I need him. And it's not as if Jerry really is important. He has to answer the phone in case anyone from the paper calls, that's all.'

'Well, they obviously need him.'

'Yes, but if he was there and he wrote the story, it wouldn't be so bad that he missed my birthday, but he's not. He's answering the phones.'

'Jess, he's sorry and he misses you. You're so lucky,' I said.

Jess looked at me through tears. 'Ru, it's not meant to be easy, is it? I can't control it. You told me and I didn't believe you, but I really can't control this.' She looked frightened, distraught and, well, my heart went out to her. It was difficult enough having a relationship, but finding out that you're out of control is worse, especially if you're Jess.

'Jess, you can't control your feelings, but this is a good thing, it really is.'

'Then why am I so unhappy?'

I looked at the others. We didn't know. None of us was in love at the moment, and none of us was in love with Jerry. But love had caused me plenty of unhappiness in the past. Perhaps that was what it did.

'I don't know, hon,' was my feeble offering.

Chapter Seventeen

London's latest tourist attraction was a most unusual sight. It was a bus that drove round and round and couldn't stop. The funny thing was that this was not a magic bus but an ordinary everyday number-seventeen bus that had started out as usual on its journey one day and someone or something had put a spell on it. Everyone was puzzled. The bus, which was full of passengers, just drove round and round, twenty-four hours a day and three hundred and sixty-five days a year. It really could not stop. People gathered on the streets for a glimpse of it, photographers took pictures, and journalists tried to interview the driver and the passengers.

After a month of standing on the same street corner as the bus went by, one journalist had managed to put together a story. The driver just said he was very scared and tired. The passengers on the bottom deck said they were used to their lives: nothing changed, they saw nothing any more; they just sat in their seats and, thank God, it hadn't been rush-hour when all this happened. they weren't having a good time, but then they weren't having a bad time either. All in all it was fine. The passengers on the top deck said they were having a wonderful time. Their spokesperson summed it up: 'On this bus, day in, day out, we never know what's going to happen. We see the same sights, but they're different every day. We see the same people who do something different every day, and we don't know what's going to happen tomorrow and the next day and the day after that.' They all agreed it was a wonderful adventure.

Jerry did take Jess out on Sunday evening and Jess had gone back to having a smile permanently on her face. Anyone who underestimates the power of love, witness this: Jess did talk about dumping him, she was scared by the way he made her feel, but when it came down to it she couldn't. Jess had fallen hard, although she would never admit it. I was thinking hard. So hard my head hurt sometimes, but as Katie hadn't made any decisions, I was determined I would. I was trying to find my future and her future, but these things take time. The world was going on around me; I was waiting for something to happen. But when something did happen, it didn't happen to me. It happened to Jess.

Jess came home from work looking triumphant. She was smiling so hard I thought her lips would split her face and she hugged us all. 'I'm in love,' she declared. 'I'm in love, I'm in love, I'm in love.' Then as we all stared at her she did a little dance around the room. I had had my suspicions that she was in love, but never, in a million years, had I thought she'd admit it.

Sarah took it badly. 'How? Who?' Sarah said.

'Jerry, of course. Sarah, you know that.' Jess did another dance then hugged us all again.

'Where is he? Isn't he here?' I asked, confused with the sudden outburst.

'I don't know, haven't seen him. I've been at work, but I did speak to him today.'

'Jess, I'm so happy for you,' Sophie said.

'Oh, Sophie, I'm so happy too.' Jess was behaving strangely; she was behaving like me.

'Jess, how come you've suddenly decided you're in love?' Sarah demanded.

'I just am.' New pink Jess sat down.

'But, how?'

'I don't know. It just happened. I just know.' She went pinker. She was glowing.

'Jess, you belong to the school of thought where love doesn't just happen, you can control it.' Sarah was visibly upset.

'Oh, Sarah, when you fall in love, all those things don't matter. You realise that all that does matter is love.' She left the room, and she left us all unable to speak.

Sarah was upset. Her faith in control had been shaken, because Jess, the most sensible of girls next to Sarah, had gone silly. Sarah couldn't cope with that, or with the thought that, despite all her protestations, this might happen to her. 'I can't believe it.'

'I just can't believe it.' Sophie was also pink. She was happy because Jess was happy. The best thing in the whole world about Sophie is her joy in the happiness of others. She is at her happiest when her friends are at their happiest. She's lovely. 'I think it's wonderful,' she said.

'So do I,' I replied, and I did. Of course I was a little bit green-eyed, but I was also genuinely happy for my friend. You see, I knew now that I'd find my answers. I just had to keep looking.

I told my friends, but not in my usual my-life's-crap-what-can-I-do way, but in a new way: I made sure that they knew I really was trying now and I was being positive. This meant I escaped lectures about careers and that they treated me with new respect. I liked the position in which I had finally put myself. Sophie however still felt that I needed help.

'Ruth, I know what to do. It worked for me,' Sophie said.

'What did?'

'Nik brought me a book on assertiveness.'

'Kinky.'

'No, it wasn't like that. It was for a part I'm auditioning for – the costume drama I told you about. I play a woman ahead of my times. Nik just thought I might need some help.'

'I can see that.'

'Anyway, I'm reading it and it's changing my life. When I've finished, you should read it too.'

'Fine. Will you go and get me some cigarettes?'

'No, go yourself.' I looked at her. Sophie would have gone for me; Sophie wouldn't say that. The second thing happened to Sophie. She changed.

A few days later, Jess asked if Sophie would cook her roast beef when Jerry came to dinner.

'No, I'm not your sodding slave,' was Sophie's answer. Jess was puzzled, so I told her about the book. She must have nearly finished it and I wasn't sure I liked what it was doing to her. Then Sarah asked Sophie if she could help her with turning up a pair of trousers, Sophie being the only one who can sew. Sarah asked nicely, but Sophie got really mad. 'Look, I'm fed up with you guys taking me for granted. Sarah, take your trousers to a tailor and the rest of you can bugger off. I've changed.' I agreed to cook for Jerry and help Sarah with her trousers, which annoyed Sophie even more. She had finished the book. 'Don't you see, Ru? There are two types of people, those who get others to do everything and those who do everything, like me and you versus Jess and Sarah. I would always do what other people wanted, even if I didn't want to, and that's why I became a victim and fell for James. According to the book, I have the makings of a battered wife and so have you. I have decided to change before it's too late, and I want you to do the same. Grab life, Ru, take control.'

'I'm not going to become a battered wife.' Sophie had gone mad.

'Well, tell me that in ten years' time when you call me with loads of black eyes.'

'Soph.'

'Don't Soph me. You need help and I have the help for you. Read this and you'll be better, I promise. Ru, you need this, you need to become independent, empowered, better. I promise you'll benefit.' She gave me the book.

I promised to read it. Although Sophie was scary now, what she had said made sense, but I hated saying no and I didn't want to be like Jess or Sarah. In fact, the idea of becoming assertive didn't appeal to me at all. I read the book: it was hilarious. I was supposed to stand in front of the mirror telling myself, 'I can make decisions,' 'I can be strong,' 'I can say no,' over and over. Of course I didn't. It encouraged me to free myself from slavery and, well, it was all a bit much. I had a good laugh, but it didn't change my life.

I think the only reason it changed Sophie so much was because she wanted to become stronger. She came into my room one day to see how I was going with the book. I told her it was interesting, but not really me. She sat on my bed and sighed. 'Well, it's certainly changed my life. Guess what I did?' I dreaded to think. Had she killed someone? Decided to shave off her hair? Decided to become like Jess?

'What?' I asked.

'I gave up modelling.' She looked pleased with herself.

'What?' I asked.

'Well, I've got the chance of this costume drama and I was only modelling for the money. I've decided to become more confident of my talent so I told the agency to remove me from their books.' She looked triumphant.

'Wow, Soph, that's great, but what about money?' I knew I sounded like Sarah but Sophie was sounding like that damn book.

'Oh, I thought of that. I went to the job centre to sign on.'

I nearly fell off the bed. 'Really?' I asked. Who was this new girl?

'Yes, really. I mean, I know you're not supposed to give up voluntarily but I wanted to do it. I really hate modelling and I need to concentrate on acting.'

'So, what happened?'

'Well, I was so shocked. All those people waiting to see the smug bastards that the job centre employs. When I eventually got to my appointment an hour later than when I turned up, some smug spotty youth told me I had to try to find a job. I explained about being an actress and he laughed at me and told me they didn't have much call for Nicole Kidman there. So I told him not to be so rude and he told me if I wanted to get any of the money that I had previously paid in taxes I had to take any work they threw my way.'

'What *did* they throw your way?'

'He offered selling cheese in a supermarket, jelly-wrestling, and then he asked me if I'd ever thought about modelling.' We laughed. 'So I guess that me and my savings get to do the impoverished-actor thing without any help from our government.'

'Well, Sophie, you're hardly poor. Look at this house, and you have savings. You don't really think you're going to suffer, do you?'

'No, and I am one of the lucky ones. The other people who really need help have to put up with the idiots patronising them just to live.' Sophie had her old compassionate look back.

'I wonder if he suggests modelling to everyone.'

'No, just me. I'm gorgeous.'

'Yes, you are.'

'Far too much so for gits like him.' We laughed. The new Sophie would be just fine without gits like him.

After a couple of days, Sophie mellowed a bit, but she would only do things if you asked her nicely and if she wanted to. The lasting change in her was that she decided to become more independent, and independence meant that the Thesp had to go. I decided that independence was not what I wanted and the book had to go.

The Thesp had been good for Sophie. She admitted that. He'd rebuilt her confidence after the Porsche and he loved her. So it was hard for her to decide to let him go. Actually, there was no decision in it. As she didn't love him – I think she had even stopped liking him, and he was getting serious – she had to put a stop to it. She told us one night, very matter-of-fact, that the Thespian was no longer to be part of her life. We were all shocked and relieved at the same time.

'I can't believe you're going to dump him,' I said.

'Don't say dump, Ruth, I hate that. I'm going to break up with him because I don't love him and I never will. I'm grateful to him, he came into my life at a low point and really helped, but you can't stay with someone out of gratitude. Besides, he's a complete idiot.'

'Are you sure you've thought about it sensibly?' Sarah asked.

'Yes, and I'm not happy about it, you know how I hate hurting people, but I've got to do it. I can't just stay with him for ever to avoid unpleasantness. I need my freedom. My career is taking off, and I need some time for me.'

'You're so right,' Sarah said, as if Sophie had spoken the first words of truth she'd ever heard. The only person without an opinion was Jess, but Jess was busy being in love so it was probably just as well. We were worried, because despite the new assertive her, Sophie was so bad at hurting anyone that we knew this would be hard for her.

'So when are you going to tell him, hon?' I asked.

'Tonight, in an hour. I need to do it quickly so I don't chicken out. You know what he's like, he'll be really dramatic and probably cry and beg. I think I need a drink.' Sarah got the wine and we practised with Sophie what she was going to say. It was going to be the most clichéd break-up in the history of the world. Friends, sorry, unfortunate, lovely guy, too good, etc., all cropped up and Sarah, being clever, told Sophie to treat this like an acting thing, which cheered Sophie up, because then she said how great actors draw on their own experiences and she could do this and it would strengthen her. She had another drink and I told her to slow down: I remembered what had happened with Julian.

She went looking lovely but suitably humble, not her best clothes, not much make-up, hair slightly greasy (nice touch). The rules on dumping are, if the guy is nice, like the Thesp, dress down. If he's horrid, like the Porsche, then look as sexy as you can. But if you're going to break someone's heart, it's important to be dressed suitably for the occasion.

Sarah and I waited for Sophie to return. Jess was singing,

giggling and away with the fairies, so we ignored her. Then she phoned Jerry, and went round there on the spur of the moment, which was highly unusual because they always arranged their dates in advance. We waved her off.

'Sarah, are you happy for Jess?' I had to ask, now that we were alone.

'Of course. I'm not such a rotten friend. It's just, well, unexpected, I suppose.'

'I know, I understand. Jess, well, she was like you. Mind you, it looks like you'll have a comrade in Sophie now.'

'I'm not sure about that . . .'

Sophie came back smiling. Sarah and I had tissues, wine and cigarettes lined up, but she didn't seem to need them.

'Why are you smiling?' I asked. Maybe she'd changed her mind.

'It's amazing, I feel liberated,' she replied.

'What?' Sarah asked.

'You know, *liberated*. I was firm but nice. When he begged I still said no and he even asked me to marry him and I said no. I said he was lovely but I didn't love him and I hoped we'd be friends and all the crap we talked about and when I left we parted on good terms – he'd almost stopped crying anyway. I'm sorry for him, but I feel free and great and, well, if I do this a couple more times, I can play the bitch in any production, not that I was a bitch, but the power – kind of felt good.' She laughed. Sarah and I were dumbstruck.

Sometimes it seemed as if the world had gone mad, usually when familiar things changed. First Jess, then Sophie. I was confused. I looked at Sarah. 'If you do anything out of the ordinary I'll kill you,' I said.

'Me? Now, you know that's not going to happen.' The one thing about Sarah was that I could depend on her not to change. I loved her constancy and I loved that she was here in the midst of this utter madness.

Then I noticed that it was summer. One day I opened my eyes properly and it had been summer for some time. It was July, it was hot and it was sunny. I hadn't noticed the sunshine before, not properly. I was too busy thinking about the future to look at now. I had forgotten to count the months, something I used to do. Actually, I used to count the days, but now I just let them merge into one. It didn't matter to me when it was, or what it was. But it was summer and my friends had spent time sitting on Clapham Common, getting a tan. Apparently this had been going on for a while. How could I not have noticed the weather? I must have been concentrating really hard. June wasn't that nice but July had been lovely, apparently. I couldn't have told you that.

When I noticed summer I tried to join in with the fun. Jess, Sarah and Sophie were loving it, so I spent time with them outside, having barbecues in our small back garden. Thomas had finished his exams and he spent a lot of time with us, as did Jerry now that Jess really loved him. Summer brought a new light into the life of our house. That light even seemed to be shining on me. The common was packed – picnics, children playing football, frisbee, adults watching and getting a tan, dogs finding shade under trees. The streets were emptier, pubs, bars and cafés extending their space to pavements full of people being seen, sipping designer water, wearing sunglasses and looking beautiful. Clothes shrank to reveal almost translucent bodies (the English have no shame when it's hot), and it was so hot.

Jess was so happy, it was lovely to see. She had her work cut out trying to divide her time between her job and Jerry, but I knew she wouldn't have had it any other way. Sophie had got that part in the costume drama and was preparing to be a television star, which I was excited about. Sarah had been offered another job and she was climbing her ladder at a rate of knots. Katie seemed better now she had given up the idea of being a party girl and me, well, I was getting there too, wasn't I?

Although I was better, one thing was not: I hated working more than ever, not because of the job but because of the way

I had to get to it. The tube is a nightmare at the best of times: you take your life in your hands when you use it because people push and shove and kill to get seats. They insist on getting in when it's too full so you have to be intimate with strangers through no choice of your own. You stand under people's armpits, you get your feet trodden on, and people sneeze in your face. I cannot think of anything worse. But in the summer being packed inside a tube train is the most unpleasant experience I have ever had. The London Underground has a culture of its own. I often wondered what people visiting made of it, because I was a visitor in my own way and I found it strange. English people are renowned for queuing, but not on the tube. As soon as the doors open it's a free-for-all, and inflicting pain is allowed. Of course, the aim is clear. The tube is a mode of transport to get you from A to B, but it is so much more than that: it's almost a war game. Once in the carriage the focus shifts to getting a seat. Seats on the tube are coveted more than your neighbour's husband or wife. The prize is golden and people will go to any lengths to get them and keep them. One day, on a particularly nasty journey, I heard a woman, who looked tired and quite fat, say to a man with a seat, 'I'm pregnant.' He looked at her, said, 'Congratulations,' and returned to his book. It transpired that the woman wasn't pregnant, just fat. There are no morals involved in the tube game. Jess should have loved the tube because sexual equality exists there. Men do not give up seats for women, or let them through the door first. There are no favourites there. Getting a seat on the tube in rush-hour is a bit like Musical Chairs: as soon as a seat is empty, you push and shove to get it. One day I was rugby-tackled for a seat by a normal-looking woman, who looked at her friend, slightly embarrassed, as I tried to maintain my balance, and said, 'We have to do this.' Who passed that goddamn law? That's what I'd like to know. 'Leave your manners on the platform, this train is about to depart.' I decided that when I found what I wanted to do with my life, it definitely would not involve tubes.

Chapter Eighteen

'Welcome to the brand new game show — *Self-destruction*.' (Pause for applause.) 'And here's your host, Bernie Butler.' (More applause.)

'Hello, ladies and gentlemen and welcome to the show. As it's new, let me explain the rules for you. Everyone at home, please join in.' (Cheers and applause.) 'There are a number of options as to how you can win. You can either find a partner and let them take over or ruin your life. You can get hooked on drugs, gambling or alcohol, or you can get a bad job with a horrid boss who ruins your life. Or any combination of the three. The winner is the person who manages to ruin their life in the biggest and most destructive way.' (Cheers and applause.) 'And the prize for tonight's winner is ... a brand new car.' (More cheers.) 'I must warn you, though, if you don't want to play this game, be careful. Choose your jobs, your partners and your drugs carefully.'

I couldn't believe it was a year since my life had been torn from me. God, a whole year. I hadn't done much in that time, but now I was ready to let it go. My aims had shifted. First, I had wanted Ben back, then I had wanted to avoid gainful employment, then I had wanted to find a man, then I had just wanted to find something. Now, my main priority was to become a better person. That was the only way I would improve my life.

Then it happened. It had been inevitable but I had pushed it to the back of my mind.

Ben was coming home. After he'd left, even when I stopped believing he would come back early I imagined our tearful reunion. He would tell me he was too embarrassed to express his real feelings for me but now he would like things to go back to the way they were. That was the reunion sketch I had played in my head, and part of me, even after all this time, still believed he would want me. Even though I wasn't sure I wanted him. Actually, I knew I didn't. The him-coming-back fantasy was just another excuse for me to bury my head. It kept reality at bay.

Thomas was at our house. I had been shopping with Katie and I returned to find them all sitting around the kitchen table with a bottle of wine. They went quiet when I walked in and no one would look me in the eye.

'Hi, guys, what's up?' Silence greeted me.

Then Thomas spoke. 'Ben's coming back,' he almost whispered. I can't remember how I felt when he said that – maybe shock, followed by confusion because I was hoping that the news wouldn't affect me. I sat down, poured a glass of wine and lit a cigarette. Then when I couldn't bear the silence, the eyes boring into me, I spoke. 'When?' It was the best I could do.

'Next week,' Thomas said. I lit another cigarette and picked up Jess's wine.

Jess was nudging him, Thomas looked embarrassed, Sophie was staring at the floor and Sarah looked ready to deal with an emergency.

'He's not coming alone,' Thomas said.

I stood up. My heart sank as I picked up yet another glass of wine, I don't know whose, and lit another cigarette.

'I should hope not. I hope Johnny will be with him.' I laughed nervously as my heart fell out of my body.

'Ru, he's bringing a girl.' They all looked at me. I felt myself go very red and part of me wanted to cry, but another part of me remembered all my tears and I swear I took everything I could find inside myself, and more from God knows where, to keep my composure. I did a circle of the room picking up objects, I didn't know what. Sarah followed me around taking them off me.

'Who is she?' My voice was steady, although I felt on the verge of tears. Of course, I should have known that dealing with fantasies was much easier. In my fantasy I heard Ben was coming back and I was strong, uninterested, nonchalant. But when I heard it I collapsed. Then, faced with the added shock of another girl, God, I was just watching my life again. I picked up Thomas's beer, finished it, lit another cigarette.

'She's an Australian called Sam. He met her in Sydney. I'm sorry, Ru, but Ben says they're going to live together in London.'

So, he's coming back with a girl and now he's going to live with her. I decided not to think about that just yet. I managed a sort of laugh as I found a carving knife. Sarah grabbed it.

'Well, is that what you guys have been fussing about all day? I mean, I got over Ben, remember? Really. Remember Mark? Trust Ben. I bet he had her doing his laundry while they were backpacking. How funny.' Where did that come from? I picked up the kettle. Sarah took it from me. I was wandering around the room, picking up things, having them taken from me, drinking everyone's drink, discarding cigarettes God knows where. I needed to calm down. My friends were looking at me oddly. Perhaps it was because I was talking absolute bollocks. But to hold it together I needed them to humour me, to pretend they believed I didn't care. It was the only way I could cope. But still no one spoke.

'Well, we'll have to have a welcome-home party.' I took my seat again.

'Yeah, well, you don't have to see them, none of you do.'

Thomas thought he was being sweet, but he didn't understand. I knew nothing then but that I needed to see him, and her, or just him. I really did.

'Of course I want to see them. I mean, it's been a year, a long time, we could be friends. I know, we'll have a dinner for them here.' Looking at the faces of my friends, I could tell they thought it was a dreadful idea, but my false bravado was still necessary and I needed to see him, here in my home. I had to do it. I put a demon look on my face. 'Don't you all think it's a wonderful idea?' It was really more of a command than a question. I picked up Sophie's wine, drank it, then drank from the bottle and lit another cigarette.

'You don't have to,' Sophie said. She looked appalled.

'A pub might be easier,' Jess suggested. She looked frightened.

'Do you really think it's a good idea?' Sarah asked. She looked in shock.

But I wasn't going to listen to anyone. I couldn't really hear them anyway. 'I've made up my mind. When Ben and this girl have recovered from jet-lag or whatever, I insist they come here, with Johnny. It'll be like old times.' With my final word, I took my last shred of dignity, opened a new bottle of wine, took it into my room and cried my heart out.

Please do not ask me to explain why I was like that with my friends. They had seen me cry many, many times. But I just couldn't fall apart again, not in public. It had been a while since I had cried over Ben, and I had truly thought I never would again. And there was the added problem of the girl. Not only had Ben reappeared in my life, but he'd had to bring some Australian with him. He shouldn't have come back into my life like this. If he was in love then I should have been too. I was the hurt one, I deserved it more than he did. I was angry and jealous, and I wished so much that, just for once, I could have had the upper hand. I remembered when he left me: he told me we were too young to settle down, but now, a year later, he was suddenly old enough. Old enough to fall in love with another girl. I hated her. She had taken my love, she had taken my Ben, she was about to take my flat. I should be moving in with him – I should have done it a year ago. How could he replace me? I had loved him. I emptied the bottle and threw it at the wall.

Anger had come. I had never felt so angry. This girl had stolen my destiny and, instead of killing her, I was inviting her to dinner. I was pathetic. And did I still want Ben? I didn't know. Maybe I just couldn't bear the thought that he couldn't love me but he could love someone else. That hurt, it really hurt. For the first time in ages, I cried myself to sleep thinking about Ben.

For the next few days I was on autopilot. If anyone mentioned Ben I changed the subject. I wasn't strong enough to talk about it. I hadn't told Katie. She knew something was wrong, but she knew better than to ask. My friends didn't question me, and I arranged the dinner party, or told Thomas to do it as planned. It was necessary. Ben was staying with Thomas and looking for a flat for himself and his hussy.

Apparently when Thomas invited Ben and Sam to my dinner, Ben was shocked, and reluctant, but Thomas said I was insistent, which I was. Thomas, bless him, did a good sales job. He said that Johnny was looking forward to it, as were we girls. Ben, still unsure, told Thomas he'd call me. This freaked me out a little. I went back to Mark mode and sat by the phone for a while. I was scared. When he did call, and I heard his voice, it triggered emotions in me. I couldn't stop them.

'Hello, Ru, it's Ben.'

'Hi, Ben, how are you?' I ripped up the telephone pad.

'Fine and you?'

'I'm really good. How was it? Did you have a great time?' My voice was holding up, but I was making the oddest faces.

'Yes, it was great.' He was a little awkward, but he never had been a conversationalist.

'I spoke to Johnny. He told me you both had a wild time. Have you got any photos?'

'Um, yeah, a few, nothing very interesting, really.'

I kicked the skirting-board, it hurt. 'Oh, I'd love to see them and I can't wait to meet this girl I've been hearing so much about.' I couldn't quite bring myself to use her name.

'Yeah, of course.'

'Are you coming to dinner? I'm really looking forward to seeing you. It'll be fun.' I kicked the skirting-board again.

'OK, we'd love to.' My heart sank when he said 'we'. I sank to my knees.

'See you, then. 'Bye, Ben.'

'Sure, see you.'

After I came off the phone, I felt better. I saw the results of my conversation, the shredded pad, the hurt foot, but I had spoken to him, I had heard his voice and I hadn't fallen apart. I had handled myself well. I could do this, I really could. Actually, I was already regretting this dinner but I couldn't back down, I had to go through with it. I picked up the phone and slammed it down, just to prove a point.

The next few days were a blur. I cried a lot, but privately, and publicly I put on the in-control charade, knowing no one believed it. But I got through them and I was still going to cook dinner.

The dinner party was upon me. I visited Antonio the hairdresser, and the hour of telling-off he gave me for not going enough was worth it for the effect he had on my hair. I spent ages planning the menu and I had my nice dress to wear. I was ready. I was also nervous. What would she be like? I wanted her to be horrid. I so wanted to hate her. I wanted everyone to hate her.

Jess, Sarah and Sophie all helped, more than they'd ever

done before. They were terrific, but I could see fear in their eyes and I knew they were right: this was too scary for all of us. Why had I done it? Because I wanted to impress him, to make him see what he was missing – my wonderful cooking, me being the perfect host. I wanted him to look at me again. I wanted him to want me. I kept busy, but the thought, I'm really going to see him, kept creeping into my mind followed by, He'll be with her, followed by, Tonight I will die from jealousy.

I stayed sober, worried about what the drink would do. I got changed, put on some make-up and, by eight, I was as ready as I would ever be. Sarah came up to me. We hugged. She looked great: she was wearing her contact lenses, a short skirt, a little top and high heels. And she was wearing make-up. 'You look terrific,' I said, momentarily distracted from my imminent demise.

'Oh, Ru, shut up.' She *blushed*.

'Thank you for helping me through this.' She was still red, but Ben was in my head and Sarah was invisible.

The doorbell rang. Jess went to get it. She came back and I saw Thomas and Johnny, who kissed me and told me I looked great. I could see the fear in their eyes. I had scared the hell out of everyone, including me.

Then Ben arrived. At first, I didn't even notice Sam, I was just looking at Ben, taking him in again, figuring out if he was as I remembered him. Well, he was more tanned and his hair was a little fairer from the sun but, yes, this was my Ben, in the flesh. He looked terrific. Terrific was not a word I'd ever used about Ben. What I meant was gorgeous, beautiful, lovely, but he wasn't mine and terrific felt more detached. When I saw him, all the hurt of the past year came flooding back. It was as if it had never left me. I looked at him again and still saw him as my happiness. I looked at him some more and saw him as someone else's happiness. I felt as if the knife was twisting in my heart again.

Then I looked at Sam, the girl who was better than me. She was pretty, but not stunning, which might have been a relief but didn't feel like one. She was blonde and quite skinny and smiling, and she was holding his hand. My hand.

'I can't believe you're back.' Jess found her voice. She kissed the boys and shook hands with Sam. We all followed suit.

'Johnny, you look gorgeous,' I said. Then I kissed Ben. He smelt so good. 'How lovely to see you,' I managed.

'This is Sam,' Ben said. He looked terrified.

'Sam, nice to meet you.' I shook her hand. I wanted to cut it off, along with her tits, but etiquette required a shake. I tried not to stare, but it was hard.

To get through the evening, my head had broken it up into parts: the greeting, drinks, starter, main course, dessert and coffee. I would congratulate myself every time I survived a part. Well, Ruth, congratulations, you survived the first.

'Who wants what to drink?' Sarah said, and we could move on to the second part. Why did Ben have to look so gorgeous?

'Aren't you going to tell us about your trip? I don't know, you leave us for a year, and you don't even tell us anything about it,' Jess teased.

'We had a fantastic time, Jess, you'd love Australia. We went to the most beautiful places, met so many great people. It was the best,' Johnny started.

'Sit at the table – it's time to eat,' I interrupted. Johnny raised an eyebrow in surprise but they obeyed. Congratulations, you survived part two.

We started eating. Jess talked about PR and Jerry who couldn't be with us, Sophie talked about her TV show, Sarah talked about her new job, Thomas his exams and Johnny and Ben their travels. I was silent.

'Where are you from?' I asked Sam, trying to be polite while imagining her engulfed in flames.

'Sydney,' she replied.

'I've heard it's a great city,' I said, imagining her engulfed in flames *and* covered with poisonous snakes.

'It is, but I've always wanted to come to London.'

'Really? How long are you planning on staying?' I was becoming a little territorial. Sarah held her breath, but Sam hadn't noticed.

'I don't know — a couple of years. It depends on a lot of things.' She looked at Ben, he looked at her. I wanted to spit, Jess held her breath.

'Oh, well, I'm sure you'll fall in love with England just as much as you fell in love with Ben,' I said sweetly. Everybody let out their breath.

Suddenly I realised that this wasn't about me and it wasn't even about 'us' any more. It was about her, Sam, the girl he loved. I was finding it hard to understand how I had transcended, first, heartbreak about Ben, then being alone, then being over Ben or thinking I was over Ben, then hearing he was returning and feeling back at square one. Only I wasn't at square one, I was now at a different square altogether, because any hurt I was feeling was just about her.

Jealousy is a powerful force and it hit me between the eyes so hard it knocked me down. I just had to see if I could get up again. He loved Sam, he was committed to her, and that made her more special than me. I kept looking for the magic, I listened to try to hear the magic, but I couldn't find it. As far as I was concerned, she was an average girl with an average personality. How could he fall in love with her and not me? This was now about her and me. I wasn't good enough, she was. I was torn between asking her and punching her in the face. I was angry. If life does not naturally provide you with opportunities to kick sand in the faces of these happy people you just have to go and find the sand yourself.

'Ruth, what do you do?' Sam asked.

'Party,' I said.

Ben looked at me, Johnny looked at me.

'She does,' Thomas said.

'I work as a PA, but only so I can go out. I go out all the

time, clubs, bars, parties, hectic, but lots of fun.' I didn't sound like me any more, I sounded like a stranger.

'You never used to like clubs,' Ben said.

I felt sick. He had acknowledged our history, which was unfair, since I had kept from mentioning it to him. 'Things change,' I said calmly. I wanted to scream, 'I have to go out to forget you, you destroyed me, you ruined me, you made me this way.' But I didn't. I survived part three and I served the main course.

I was getting more and more desperate. Everything was going well. The food was appreciated, the drink was being drunk. Sam had started talking a lot and, in a bitch-from-hell kind of way, she was nice. There were a few too many when-Ben-and-I-did-this stories, but I had fixed a smile to my face and it was holding up. Everyone else seemed relaxed, except Sarah who was waiting for the crisis.

'So, Sam, how did you two meet?' I asked. Ben looked at me: he was suspicious and on edge. I wondered for a minute if Sam knew about me, or if I'd been explained as a friend.

'In an art gallery in Sydney.'

'Really?' Jess said, with disbelief. Ben went bright red.

'Yes. Ben came to see a new exhibition and I was working there. He asked me all sorts of questions about the paintings and we got talking. We ended up going for dinner that night.' Was this Ben, or had he been kidnapped by aliens?

'Did you go to the art gallery, Johnny?' I asked.

'No, I was probably in the pub.' It was just Ben who had gone mad. I thought back to when I had asked Ben to come with me to a museum and he said, 'What for?' and I said, 'Because it's cultural,' and he said, 'Bollocks to culture,' and that was that. It now transpired that he had gone to a gallery, of his own free will and he had taken a girl out to dinner. This was too much.

'So, you went to an art gallery, did you like it?' I asked him.

'Yes,' Ben replied.

'Unlike you, isn't it? Normally you'd have been in the pub with Johnny.' I almost said it as an accusation – why weren't you in the pub, you should have been in the pub. Sarah kicked me under the table.

Sam went on, 'So, we went to dinner that night and we've been together ever since. When it was almost time for Ben to leave, I was so upset. When he asked me to come with him, I just had to. I couldn't bear to be apart from him.' She gazed at him again. He looked embarrassed. Was she telling me 'I love him, he loves me, there is no you?' I don't know, but if I'd been her that's what I would have been doing.

My whole world crashed again. It wasn't that I wanted him: I had accepted it was over. But Sam had brought a new ball into the game. He was different, he was nicer, he was in love. I couldn't bear that he had never looked at me the way he looked at her. I hated her and I hated him.

'So, what now?' I asked.

'We're going to get a flat in London. Ben's going to do his law finals. Sarah, I hear you're in recruitment, do you think you could help me get a job?'

Sam was living my life! This was supposed to have been my life! I had to stop myself jumping up on the table and shouting out.

'Sure,' Sarah said. She looked at me apologetically. I smiled – I didn't want to make it awful for her. But I couldn't bear it. It should have been me.

'It's all planned,' Sam said.

'Ben, it's unlike you to make plans,' I said. He turned red. Sophie gave me The Look.

'It was Ben's idea,' Sam said. I couldn't work out if she was genuinely nice or a smug bitch. I decided to go with smug bitch.

'Isn't Ben the changed man? Oh, Sam, if only you'd known him at university, he was so different. Next you'll be telling me he does his own laundry.'

'He does his own laundry *and* he cooks,' Sam said.

We were all dumbfounded.

'It's nice that you've moved into the twenty-first century, Ben.' He was still red and he looked at me pleadingly, but I was on a roll. 'In fact, all Ben used to do was drink and play hockey so I guess he must have expanded his horizons since then. Did you know he used to eat so many kebabs – don't let him drag you into the kebab shop late at night – he always used to order so much chilli sauce and well, it wasn't nice. If it wasn't a kebab it was curry, which more often than not he used to fall asleep in. It was so funny.' Ben looked angry, I had done the bad thing, I had brought myself into the equation. Not that it upset Sam.

'Oh, God, I can't imagine that, Ben. No, we do really interesting things together, galleries, museums, We also both play tennis. I know all about his hockey days – he sounded like such a lad then,' Sam laughed.

This was too much. When he had been with me he was a stupid immature lad, now he had fallen in love and grown up. Ben was different, Ben wasn't my Ben, Ben had been playing when he was with me. Now he was having a relationship. I couldn't stand the battering all this was giving me: I was being deflated. And everyone knew. The air was tense. Everyone was drinking a lot and looking at me. I felt as if I was Ben's inflatable ex-girlfriend. When he left me, he let a little air out of me and now he was back he was letting out the rest. Sam and Ben were taking me apart so they could flatten me and put me in a box, where I would be forgotten about.

'Of course, Josh is very much the modern man.' Sarah choked on her wine, Jess, Sophie and Thomas looked at me.

'Who's Josh?' Sam asked.

'My boyfriend.' Everyone went quiet.

'I didn't know you were seeing anyone,' Johnny said quietly.

'Oh, God, yes, have been for ages. I thought Thomas would have told you. He's in business, very successful, and he's lovely. He couldn't come tonight – he's in Brussels. He works too hard, that's his only fault. But he's very "new man" and very thoughtful, although he doesn't do his own laundry, he has a cleaner.' Thomas looked as if he wanted to kill me. Ben looked at me full of confusion. I think he knew I was playing a game, but he didn't know the rules. Come to think of it, neither did I.

'Oh, perhaps I can meet him some other time – we could all go out,' Sam suggested.

Then, on cue, the phone rang. As I was trained, I ran to answer it. Now, perhaps it was the wine or that I had just told the most stupid lie, but a plan came to me on the way.

'Hello.'

'Hi, it's Jerry.'

I put on my loudest voice. 'Josh, is that you? Gosh, you sound so faint.'

'No, it's Jerry. Can I speak to Jess?'

'You're so thoughtful, but you know I'm in the middle of a dinner party.' I giggled.

'Ruth, is that you? Can I speak to Jess?'

'I know, darling, and I miss you, but you're back tomorrow, aren't you?'

'Ruth, are you all right? Are you mad? Who's Josh?'

'OK, honey, I'll see you then. Take care, love you.'

'Ruth, what's going on? Can I speak to Jess?'

''Bye, sweet dreams.' I hung up.

I knew, because I'd been shouting, that they had heard every word. I walked back in, smiling. My friends were looking astounded and Sam was smiling.

'Dessert, Ru.' Jess dragged me into the kitchen. 'What are you playing at?' she asked.

'I don't know. I, well, I just couldn't stand any more happy families. I needed to balance myself,' I pleaded.

'Don't you think that if you were going to lie you should have warned us? All of a sudden in the middle of dinner you have a Josh. Thomas told both Johnny and Ben you were single, and you've never had a Josh. How stupid have you made us look, especially Thomas? And what about the phone call? Who the hell was it?'

'Jerry. I'm sorry. I couldn't cope. That girl has my life. I had to have a Josh, just for tonight. I'm sorry, it's so awful seeing him with her. Then when the phone rang, well, I guess I was out of control.' I was on the brink of tears.

'Ru, I know it's horrid, we knew it would be. Why do you think we tried so hard to talk you out of it? But you've been brilliant. You've cooked a fantastic meal, been the perfect hostess. You've held it together better than anyone thought you would. You shouldn't have to make up Josh because it's clear you're all right. What did Jerry say?'

'Oh, I think he's a bit confused, you should call him straight back.'

'In a minute. Why did you have to do that, Ru?'

'I just felt so unwanted. I mean, did you hear me? I kept going on about how Ben used to be.'

'He deserved that.'

'But Sam?'

'I don't think she really noticed.'

'Oh, Jess, why have I wasted so long on him?'

'I haven't got a clue, honey. I always hoped he was dynamite in bed.' We laughed.

'I'm sorry, apologise to Jerry for me.'

'Jerry will understand.' Jess hugged me, and I took out the crème brûlée.

I relaxed a little and let the conversation flow around me. I'd said enough. Ben looked at me with embarrassment. I guess I had annoyed him a bit. Or a lot. It was like old times, except I wasn't here: my place had been taken. I was just watching again. The Ben Sam was talking about wasn't my Ben. He was kind and funny and considerate and romantic. He was the Ben I had wanted, but not the Ben I loved. She had the relationship I wanted with the man I used to have.

My ego had taken a huge bashing. It was one thing for

Ben not to love me, but quite another for him to be happy with a blonde Australian. I was hurt and angry. I drank and let everything wash over me. I concentrated on the fact that it would be over soon and that I could avoid seeing them again.

Eventually they thanked me for dinner and left. Sam said it had been wonderful meeting me, I said the same. Ben kissed my cheek awkwardly. I kissed Johnny and Thomas, although they didn't leave. When Ben and Sam had gone, I went to my room without a word.

It was quiet outside; I could hear them talking in whispers. In my room I tried to think about what to do. Should I cry? Should I laugh? Should I just die from embarrassment? Can you die from embarrassment? Should I just climb into a big hole? I lay down. I felt sober although I had been drunk a minute ago. Then the door opened and the light was switched on.

It was Thomas. 'Hi,' he said.

'I didn't mean to make myself look stupid.'

'I know.'

'But I did, didn't I?'

'Sort of.' Thomas sat on the bed.

'But, well, I knew no one would believe I had a Josh, would they?'

'Sam believed it, but I'd told Ben and Johnny you were single and having fun. But I could tell Ben I lied to him to spare his feelings. I mean, it'll make me look like a total tosser but that's better than you being upset, isn't it?'

'Oh, Thomas, you'd do that for me?'

'Only the once, mind.'

I hugged him. 'You said at the beginning of the year that I should be locked up. Do you still think that?'

'Yup. You shouldn't ever be allowed out in public on your own. You're a menace.'

'I quite like the sound of being a menace.'

'Only you could take that as a compliment.'

'Thomas . . .'

'Yes?'

'What do you think of Sam?' I looked at him sweetly.

'Not much. She's pretty boring — art galleries, museums, dull, dull, dull. And she can't cook like you, and I bet she's really messy, and she's not clever. I think she's really thick. You're far more interesting.'

'Am I?'

'Yes, more interesting altogether.'

Thomas looked so sincere, I laughed. 'But is she better-looking than me?' I was enjoying this game.

'What? You're joking! She looks like a hatstand.'

'Hatstand Sam. I love you, Thomas.'

'Oh, God, you girls get so mushy and now my best mate's come back from a year away and he's turned into a poof.'

'Ben? A poof? No, maybe he's learned to use a washing-machine but get him down the pub without the Hatstand and things will be like they used to be.'

'Yeah?'

'Of course. However, for me things will never be the same again.'

'No, babe, they'll be better.'

'You know, Thomas, I think they will.'

When Thomas left, I had a revelation: I had to face my relationship with Ben and work out why it had affected me so deeply. I had adored him, that was clear, and that had set the course of our relationship. I had done everything for him. All Ben had to do was dress himself and wipe his own bottom — I drew a line, you know. My friends used to say I did too much for him, especially Jess used to say that I was behaving like a housewife, not a student. And I was, but I was happy. At no point did Ben ask me to do any of this for him, but I don't expect he would have stayed with me for so long if I hadn't.

I can't accuse Ben of taking advantage of me because I

offered. At the end of the first year when we all moved in together, it was my idea. My friends didn't mind: they liked Thomas and they liked Ben, but most of all they liked me. When the hockey team found out we were going to live together, they said, 'What the hell are you doing getting yourself tied down to a bird?' They said this in front of me. And Ben replied, 'Look, she does my laundry, cleaning and feeds me – oh, yeah, and I get sex every night, more than can be said for you.'

The lads thought he was cool. I knew the pressure he was under so I assumed that he couldn't say he loved me, which was what he meant, he had to pretend he only wanted me for my whiter than whites and my Jif bathroom. I understood, that's what guys were like. But, well, come to think of it, that had probably been the truth, the love thing was only in my head.

Ben made me laugh sometimes, but he didn't compliment me or show me much affection. I loved him, but he never told me he loved me. I would ask him, 'Do you love me?' and he would grunt, which I took as a yes, but it was really no answer at all. I think I wore out the phrase 'I love you' when I was with him, perhaps I said it so much because I didn't know myself. Poor Ben. From the start he didn't stand a chance. I coveted him from a distance, I made him mine. When did he get the chance to love me? He didn't. He didn't even get the chance to know me.

Was Ben ever mean to me? Yes occasionally. Once after a hockey match they'd lost when Ben had played badly, his teammates accused him of playing like a girl. He stormed off and I ran after him, telling him *I* thought he'd played well and everything else nice I could think of.

Ben turned to me with a thunderous look in his eyes. *'Will you stop following me like a fucking sheep. I am not Little Bo-Peep and contrary to popular opinion you are not a sheep. So fuck off and leave me alone.'* Then he stalked away. I cried all the way home, and that night Ben locked me out of our room and I had to sleep in Jess's. Of course, all my friends felt Ben was behaving like a bastard, but I was just worried that he'd never speak to me again. In the morning, Ben came downstairs and kissed me. I looked at him, expecting an apology, but he shrugged and that was that. He never apologised and I didn't want to upset him by mentioning it. When he locked me out of our room I should have been furious, but instead I told myself that he was upset and I accepted his behaviour.

Listen, girls, an imbalance of power no matter who creates it is not the basis for a lasting relationship. God, I had clarity. This was great, why hadn't I done this before?

Another time when Ben and I weren't speaking, I wrote him a poem. God, I didn't shout at him, I wrote him a fucking poem. I gave it to him and said, 'This is how I feel,' and he read it. I still have it:

I saw you sitting on a leaf,
The leaf was green, you were blue
I said come here, come to me
I thought how much I did love you

I saw you sitting in a field
The field was yellow, you were blue
I ran to you, I touched your face
I told you that I did love you

And on it went. I watched him read, and it seemed to take an eternity. I didn't understand the poem myself, and I realised that giving it to him had been a mistake. He had a puzzled look on his face for the first half, and an expression close to amusement for the last bit.

'Ru, what the fuck is this supposed to mean?' I shrugged. 'What do you mean, I'm blue and I sit on leaves? Have you gone mad?' I shrugged, hurt. Ben kissed me. 'You're crazy. Maybe you should think about seeing someone.' I think he was right. I mean, I'm no poet, and Ben certainly wasn't a poetry reader. What I should have done was told him why he'd upset me, not given him something that neither of us understood. I never wrote poetry again.

After every row, I would find a way to apologise; I would take him breakfast in bed, I would give him imaginative oral sex, I would buy him a present, I would promise never to get hysterical again. I would do this whether I was in the wrong or not. The seeds for my dependency were sown. I tried to make Ben depend on me, but somewhere along the way I lost myself.

I behaved quite badly sometimes over Ben. The worst was in the first year, when this girl, Angela, started coming to watch the hockey. I found out that she fancied Ben. Anyway Jess and I used to call her the Virgin, because we're bitches and I couldn't imagine that she'd sleep with anyone. Ben was nice to her and I hated that. I told everyone what a cow she was and I spread some nasty rumours about her. Jess and I were drunk and we told the college gossip queen that Angela believed she'd been impregnated by God. She had to put up with sniggers, and people saying, 'Are you going to call your first-born Jesus?' She hadn't done anything except tell someone she fancied my boyfriend. With Ben I became someone I didn't like very much. After Ben I continued being someone I didn't like very much.

My parents didn't like Ben. In the true tradition of fathers my father thought he wasn't good enough for me, Ben was all wrong: he played hockey, not rugby. My mother didn't like Ben because she said he never spoke. We all went out to dinner once and, well, Ben said nothing, except yes and no, and 'Bank manager' – that was when mum asked what his father did. She said he was the most boring person she'd ever met. I defended him by saying he was shy, which he was. He had no trouble talking when he was with his friends. But, then, as the words 'tits' and 'bums' make up most of their conversation I expect he was a little stuck.

My friends liked Ben – well, at first they did. They liked him because I liked him, but they just got mad when I was upset. I think sometimes, though, they were just as mad at me. Even

Thomas, who was Ben's friend first, would get mad about the way he treated me sometimes. If the words 'stupid cow' spring to mind, well, I was and still am and at last I'm slowly beginning to realise this.

But Ben and I had good times together. I thought I loved him, which meant I did love him. I thought he was The One and he was my first love.

I felt that this was the last stage in my purging process. I am purging myself of Ben. When you're an alcoholic or a drug addict, the first step to being cured is to admit your addiction. That's how it was with Ben. I had been through a number of phases in trying to get over him: denial (he doesn't mean it, he'll be back), depression (my life is over without him), ignorance (other men), confrontation (tonight's dinner). This stage was truth (finally admitting the reality of our relationship), which left rebirth (getting on with my life so that I no longer missed Ben or resented him). Then it would be truly over for me.

Tears were running down my face — tears of relief. I was feeling better, clearer, stronger. I was exorcising my ghosts and I was ready to start living again. Not partying or pulling, not getting a career and becoming a today woman, but learning what I really wanted from life. I needed to learn how to like myself and trust myself before I gave myself to anyone else.

I slept fitfully, and awoke the next morning with a horrible headache and puffy eyes. But I felt better than I looked: I had got rid of Ben, and I could get on with the rest of my life. But first, to make sure, I had to go and see Katie.

Chapter Nineteen

The princess waited for her prince on his white horse, white being the symbol of all that is good, and princes being very nice too. They were both going to rescue her, from evil, boredom, sadness. She wanted to be rescued. But when the white horse came, there was no prince. She was startled: there had to be a prince – how could there be a rescue without one? She waited by the horse, but the prince never came. She waited for a year for this rescue, but now it was time to face facts. Yes, she was to be rescued, but no, the prince was not involved. The princess jumped on the horse and rode off, on her own, into the sunset.

I told Katie what had happened at the dinner party and afterwards: that I had made a fool of myself, the phone call, and then the self-evaluation.

Katie looked thoughtful. 'You're over him,' she said.

I had an empowering dream that Sunday night. I dreamt I was sitting in a huge wooden chair – it was bigger than me, it was throne-like. It was in the middle of a huge and otherwise empty room. I was relaxing in it, thinking, singing to myself, I was happy. Then there was a knock at the door, and in walked Ben. He approached the chair and knelt down. He asked for forgiveness and he asked for my love. I told him that he didn't deserve either and I asked him to leave. He left, crying.

Then Simon walked in. He approached me and apologised for taking advantage of me. He was begging for another chance and he promised he would never ever hurt me again. I told him he was not worthy of me and I ordered him away.

Mike followed. He apologised for lying to me, he said he had some father–son issues, but he realised that was no excuse for making up lies about his importance. He also apologised for taking advantage of me and getting me into so much trouble. I told him abuse of power was the worst way to behave especially with someone as vulnerable as I was. I sent him away with a flea in his ear.

Julian came and asked me to take back what I said about him, about his penis especially. He begged me. I looked at him and told him that that was the price he had had to pay for his arrogance, which is not a quality that deserves praise. He left vowing to change.

Wayne was next. He looked at me with disgust; he didn't need forgiveness. I did. I told him I was sorry to have caused him distress but I hadn't been myself then. He nodded, and I told him he could go.

Philip came and said he wished he'd called me. I told him that it was too late for regrets. He asked for another date, I said no and he left.

Nathan arrived, looking very cool. He said he should have been honest with me about his being gay but he found it hard. He blamed the drugs, they were making him behave like he did, he was sorry for scaring me. He looked genuine and I almost felt sorry for him. I told him to get help for his drug problem then come out of the closet. He thanked me and left.

Then Guy apologised for being a fascist, Seb apologised for leaving me alone, Barney apologised for not calling and the five thousand men said they were sorry for being such idiots. I waved them all away.

Mark arrived. Mark the angel, the beautiful. He apologised for what he had done to me. He called himself all the names under the sun. He explained he was commitment-phobic and wished he wasn't, but now he felt he might be able to give me what I wanted. I was tempted, believe me, but I shook my head. I told him he was a cad who had betrayed my trust. I cared for him, he let me down. I told him to leave in the knowledge that he would never be forgiven.

Just as I thought I was free, Ben came back. He asked for one last chance, he said he loved me. Those words I had so longed to hear. I sighed and told him he was too late, I didn't need him any more, I was all right. I told him I was ready to fall in love properly, equally and happily. I asked him to leave.

I told Katie about my dream. 'It sounds like one of your daydreams. Are you sure you were asleep?'

I thought for a second. 'No,' I replied.

Ben had been the most significant thing in my first year out of university, even though he wasn't with me. For the first part he left me and I spent all my time wanting him back, then in the last part, he gave me the answer I needed, or helped me to find it.

It was a Monday when I decided, a week after the dinner party. I will always remember, because it is very rare for me to make any kind of decision on a Monday. But it was a year and a little bit after leaving university, on a warm day, that I decided. I was going to leave London, England, Ben and my memories. The only thing I wasn't leaving was Katie. I would ask her to come too. When you make a decision of this magnitude and, believe me, I was talking about more than just a holiday, it makes you feel strong, emancipated and shit scared.

But I had decided. Of course, after months of agonising I had made the decision very quickly. It was like doing the crossword: when you cannot get an answer you puzzle over it and it bugs you because you can't find the answer. The next day you're sitting on the loo, or having a bath and the answer comes to you in a flash. The feeling of relief is immense. That's how it was for me. I had finished my own personal crossword: I wasn't on the loo when it happened, I was on a horribly packed tube on my way to work.

I got to the office on a huge adrenaline rush, enough for Katie to ask if I was on speed, but I couldn't tell her. I thought about it all day, not about where we'd go or what we'd do, but just about leaving. The difference between what I was doing and what most travellers did was that I didn't plan to come back. I wasn't going for a year, I was going for as long as it took. Maybe I would come back, and maybe I wouldn't. Was it significant that Ben had been travelling? Probably. He had grown up, changed, become a different person. Now I knew it was time for me to grow up. I think and I hope that I did it more for myself than for him.

I waited until the next evening to tell Katie.

'I know we've been playing at changing things, Katie, but we haven't done anything drastic, apart from not sleeping with every man we meet, of course. We haven't really changed our lives, though.'

'Are you trying to depress me again?' Katie asked.

'No. I'm trying to tell you something, so shut up. What I think we need is to go away. London doesn't hold the key to our happiness door, so we have to leave.'

'What, just leave?'

'Why not? Nothing holds us here. Maybe we'll realise that this isn't the answer, but at least we'd be trying something.' I was very excited.

'Where? Where will we go?'

'Wherever, everywhere, I don't know. I want to see some of the world, really see it. There's so much. It doesn't matter where we start or finish or what.'

'OK, so we plan a trip, or a leaving, and we go. I think we should go to Africa, then South America and then the

USA for starters. If we want to go anywhere else, we can. We need money, though.' Katie was getting excited. Our old friend Money again.

'We'll just have to save every penny. It should be easy now we don't go out. And I've got some savings, if not much.'

'I've got money saved, too, not a fortune but a bit – don't look so surprised. I know I'm not a rainy day type, but money only has so much use. Let's aim for six months. Is that unrealistic?'

'Totally unrealistic, but you never know.' I laughed. 'Anyway, we should be able to get jobs when we're away.'

'Ruthie, you're a genius.'

'Thank you.' I took my praise well. 'Katie, there's one condition.'

'What?'

'I'm only going if you promise not to become a druggie hippie.'

'Only if you promise not to sleep with every guy you meet.'

'Bitch.'

We celebrated with a bottle of Bud, and sat smiling like idiots. We couldn't stop. For the first time I felt really happy and so did Katie. It was the start of our brand new life.

There were many reasons why I decided I wanted to go away. I wanted some fun, to see the world, to meet new people – but it was more about leaving than going somewhere new. It was about leaving Britain, London, my parents, my friends and of course my ghosts. It was about leaving the career world, and my husband hunt and starting afresh. I had gained some sort of clarity, now I wanted more. I was leaving and I might never come back. Really. Deep down I was sure I would, I might find the thing I was looking for along the way. I might also come to terms with how things were and find that what I'd left was not so bad after all. I wasn't just running away, although I know that's what you probably think. It just wasn't that. I was running to something, not away from it I wanted to embrace life, corny but true. I saw a future, opportunity. Ruth Butler was going to do something with her life.

I told my parents first. The main reason was that I was hoping to borrow some money and, also, they were easier to tell. My father thought it was a great idea; he kept calling me his 'explorer princess' and asked how long I'd be gone. I had thought this one out carefully and I told him about a year. I thought if I started talking about never coming back, it might cause problems.

My mother thought it was a little dangerous, but she was happy that Katie was going. I reassured them that going was the first step in finding out what career I wanted when I came back. I used phrases like 'breathing space' and 'clear thinking'. My parents were happy and relieved. Before I could mention the word 'money', my mother offered it and my father agreed, straight away. Not 'we should discuss this alone,' but 'yes, of course, we can help'. This help amounted to my feeling like a spoilt brat, and loving it. I told them they'd never have to buy me another birthday or Christmas present, but they just laughed.

Everything was starting to become real. My parents thought I was planning a trip and they were hoping that I'd come back all grown-up and career-minded. Maybe I would, if I got hit on the head by a sharp object on the way. Maybe I'd go somewhere and just know that it was the place for me and I'd stay there for ever. Or, as I said earlier, perhaps what I was looking for was already here. I just needed to leave, think more clearly, then the answers would appear. I needed to get away, because at the moment I associated London with the place I was most unhappy, and although I shouldn't blame London for my unhappiness, I needed to get far away before I could even think about exonerating it. I was leaving for good reasons, not bad ones. There was one thing I had and that was promise. This time promised to be a great, good and fulfilling time.

Out of my friends, I told Jess first. I don't know why,

perhaps because she had been my first friend at university. I told her when we were doing the washing-up. She just looked at me and said, 'At last you're moving on.' She hugged me and she cried. 'Ru, I'm proud of you, I know it hasn't been easy and I probably didn't always help, but this is what I wanted you to do, just something.' She hugged me again and then looked at me very seriously. 'You may never come back. You're not going to book a return ticket, are you?'

I shook my head and started crying. 'It's not that I'll never come back but, Jess, I'm such a headcase, how do I know where the hell my future is? I know it's not here at the moment. Maybe it's with some primitive housewife tribe in Africa, or something like that.'

'Ru, do you realise we haven't been apart in four years? I love you, but I understand you need this and maybe you will come back. I'm sure you'll come back and I'll miss you, you old-fashioned pain in the arse.'

'But I'm not going for ages,' I cried, and we hugged again. It was a weird emotional scene and I have to admit this was the first time I had felt sad since making the decision.

'Of course, if you do decide to stay out of England, I hope to God you pick somewhere nice. I don't want to have to visit you in some jungle or forest or desert. Perhaps you could bear that in mind.' The old Jess was back.

I laughed. 'You can visit me wherever I am. I'll miss you, Jess.'

She came with me to tell Sophie and Sarah. There was much of the same, tears, hugs, slaps on the back (Sarah nearly sent me flying), but the general opinion was that this was a celebration and we should, of course, get drunk. We did, and we talked about how we were when we first met. Jess the confident, Sarah the organised, Sophie the timid, and me a sort of Dorothy, always trying to find my way home. Later I called Thomas and he just said, 'Nice one, Ru,' which was enough.

I realised a lot of things then. I was over Ben and not trying to replace him. I knew I had a future that didn't look bleak and that one day I would find what I was looking for. Oh and hopefully I was no longer a monotonous bore.

I had grasped that I could be on my own and happy, that a relationship would be an added bonus but was not a necessary part of me. It had taken a year but I had finally got there. That's one hell of a long time. When I'd leave I felt like I'd be a different person. Oh, I'd still be me and I'd still never want to be a career woman and I'd never think it's great to be single, but I hoped I'd think it's OK. Maybe leaving my three closest friends and Thomas would make a difference. Perhaps I depended on them too much. I was looking for them to let me wallow, or solve my problems for me. Now, although I'd miss them, I felt that I would become a better friend. I hoped so.

I put my head through the wall I had started to build a year ago. Ben was its foundation, then I added all the men I had met and all the bad jobs I'd had. My feelings were stronger than any bricks or mortar. It had taken a year to break through it. A year of banging my head against it. When I saw through it, I started to look back on the year and I felt silly. All the fuss I had made about Ben and my embarkation on a mission to self-destruct. There is nothing wrong in looking for love. Love is central to human happiness. My aim was still the same, but my methods would change. A year of being silly had some good consequences. So you see, I really did put my head through the brick wall. And the other side looked scary and a little big, but I thought I can do it. No, I knew I could.

Chapter Twenty

I was facing the biggest dragon I'd ever seen. This was a mean mother. He breathed fire at me, he singed my beautiful hair and I knew he just wanted to eat me all up. I cried, I screamed. I looked for my knight in shining armour, the one who was supposed to kill the dragon and rescue me. He was nowhere to be seen. The dragon was getting angry. He was getting closer. Still no sign of my hero. I stopped screaming and realised that in the twenty-first century the damsel in distress cuts no ice. I picked up my semi-automatic gun and showered the dragon with bullets. He fell down, defeated. I wiped the sweat off my brow and felt triumphant. Just then, up popped the handsome hero, who said, 'Hey, cool chick, fancy a drink?' I accepted. After all, things were different now.

Everything was settled, or almost. I had bought guides on practically every country that wasn't England and I had planned and planned and planned. I was so excited. This was my new year, the one I had promised myself on Millennium Eve. Life was good.

I'd scarcely seen Sarah for a while and guessed her social life had picked up because she was never in and, in a way, I missed her. I noticed one Saturday morning that she hadn't come home

– her bed was unslept in – and I was intrigued. Had she broken her vow of celibacy? I told Jess, who told me that as usual I was letting my imagination run away with me. Of course Sarah was not having sex. But when she arrived home, smiling, in the afternoon, I just had to be sure.

'Where have you been?' I asked.

Sarah turned pink. 'Out. Why?' she answered, looking like I'd never seen her.

'All night?'

'Yes, I'm old enough. Are you my mother all of a sudden?' With that she swept into the bathroom. Now I knew that Sarah had definitely had sex. I rounded up Jess and Sophie and we summoned a post-bath Sarah to the sitting room. I told the others to be quiet while I sorted things out. I decided on the subtle approach. Jess, Sophie and I sat on one sofa. Sarah sat awkwardly on the other.

'Sarah, have you had sex?' Oh, well, subtlety had never been my strong point.

Sophie took over. 'Sarah, what we mean is, well, have you been seeing someone?'

'Yes.' Sarah blushed.

'Oh, my God.' Jess jumped up. I was too shocked to move. Sophie smiled.

'Who, Sarah, who?' Sophie asked.

Sarah glowed even more, if that was possible. She was playing with her hair, avoiding our eyes.

'Who?' Jess repeated, as she sat down next to her. We all looked at her expectantly.

'I guess you were going to find out soon enough. It's Johnny.'

We were dumbstruck. After what seemed like ages, Sophie spoke again. 'How?' she managed.

'It started after dinner. He called for a chat and I suggested a drink.'

'You asked him out?' Jess was excited.

'Yes, I did.' She giggled. Little-girl giggle not a Sarah snort. 'I guess he didn't think it was a date at first, but I told him that I really liked him and he said that was good and then it happened.'

'What. What happened?' Jess was practically jumping out of her seat again.

'He kissed me.'

'My God, I've heard everything now,' I said, and I thought perhaps I had. But my head was back and things started to make sense.

'How long have you liked him?' I asked.

Sarah stood up. She did a full circuit of the room with three pairs of eyes following her. She stopped behind me. 'Ever since I first met him,' she whispered, and went red again.

What a bloody surprise.

'So the celibacy, all this time, the career, the I'm-going-to-fall-in-love-when-I'm-good-and-ready was bullshit?' Jess said.

'No, no, it wasn't. I meant all that and I never thought Johnny would happen. I just hoped, dreamed. It was a hopeless crush, but not any more. No man measured up to him, that's why I didn't want one.'

'Like me and Ben,' I said, and I knew it was true.

'No,' she protested, 'no. I mean, we've never really been together.' She went redder.

'What do you mean, "never really"?' Sophie asked.

Sarah sat down again.

'OK. I slept with him once.'

'Holy shit,' I said.

'When?' we chorused.

'Graduation.' Here was something Sarah had kept from us for a whole year. None of us had had a clue.

'But he went to the ball with Sophie.' I was confused.

'He didn't leave with me, though,' Sophie pointed out.

'Oh, God, I knew you weren't together. It's just, you know, after the Ben stuff, well, I was worried and I asked him what he knew and then I slept with him.' There was silence again. Sarah looked at us, pleading with us to understand. I broke up with Ben, Sarah slept with Johnny and while I spent a year getting over Ben, she spent a year in love with Johnny. The difference was that it might have been worth it for her.

So I laughed and Sarah did, then the others did. 'Sarah, you're a dark whore,' I said, and we laughed even more.

After we had calmed down Jess spoke; 'So we can hold a ritual burning of your vibrators now?' Sarah hit her and we collapsed in laughter again.

I was distracted by Sarah's love life only for that evening. I had to keep planning my trip. The next morning, I settled at my desk, looking forward to seeing Katie. She hadn't heard the latest part of my plan and I had to tell her. I felt like I might burst. But she was late. Not Katie-late but late-late. I glanced at the clock and decided to give her another half-hour. I looked at the door expecting her to bound in swearing about the tubes like she had when I first met her. The door remained closed. I called her at home and got her answerphone. I left a message. I wanted to go round but I couldn't leave the office without arousing Jenny's suspicion. I told her Katie was ill and that was that. But I was worried.

At five on the dot I rushed round to her flat. There was no answer and I wanted to break the door down but wasn't sure how legal that was. I went home and told Jess. Jess told me that if Katie was in trouble I would know. I called a thousand times without any answer. I finally went to bed at midnight, exhausted from trying to figure out what had happened.

The doorbell woke me. I looked at the clock. It was three in the morning. I jumped out of bed and opened the front door. Katie was standing on the step.

'Hi', she said.

'Hi,' I said. Remember with Ben how I knew that it was an end-of-the-world moment? Well, this was the same. She was glowing, and I realised that again my life was about to change.

'Come in.' I found my voice.

'Ru, let's go for a walk. It's a fabulous evening.' God, now I knew something was wrong. It was cold, it was three a.m. But, for some reason, I didn't want to argue. Katie followed me into the house and I went to get dressed. We didn't speak.

We left, me huddled in Jess's coat, Katie wearing very little, considering, but she didn't look cold. I remembered walking with her when we had first become friends and I wondered if this was the last time. I don't know why, but it felt final.

'You weren't at work today.'

'No.'

'I was worried.'

'Sorry.' We carried on in silence until we got to a children's play area. We both sat on the swings and I felt my heartstrings pull. How I would like to have known Katie when we could have played on the swings together. I felt like I had, in a way, as if I'd known her for ever.

'Have you heard from Ben?'

'No. Sam the Hatstand called me to say thanks for dinner, but that's it.'

'How do you feel?'

'About him?'

Katie nodded.

'Well, I don't feel very much any more. Empty that's how it feels when I think of him, empty. I'm still jealous of her, but that's about me. I figured out that those are my feelings and they don't belong to either Ben or Sam.'

'So he wasn't the great love of your life, after all?'

I scuffed the toes of my trainers on the ground. 'I hope not, because if that was it, well, it's disappointing.'

'But all the mourning, was it worth it?'

'Of course not. And I wasn't mourning him. It was more about my inability to move forward. I just used Ben as a barrier to progress.' I giggled. 'He was an effective barrier.' Silence again.

'Ruth, if Ben had come home and declared his love for you, what would you have done?'

'I don't know. God, maybe I would have gone back to him and then I would've found out later that we weren't right. Maybe I would have told him to piss off, I really don't know. But I don't think he's right for me and I do believe that at some point I would have realised that, whether I was with him or not.'

'So you still believe in fate and love?'

'Of course. God, yes, that's my foundation, my religion. When I fall in love I'll know. I guess Ben was more like my dress rehearsal.'

'If you fell in love now would you still go away?'

'God, I'm not going to fall in love now. I mean, I don't even know any men.' I laughed then I stopped. Thud. It hit me. This wasn't about me. This conversation wasn't mine. I had neither masterminded it nor invited it. I was just here. It was Katie's conversation.

'He's back?' I said, amazed that the words came out from my lips and unsure how the knowledge got into my head, but now I knew and it all made sense.

'Yes.'

'When? How?'

'This weekend.'

'So when you said on Friday you wanted a weekend alone, you didn't mean it?'

'Yes, I did.'

'*No*, and you couldn't tell me that the real reason was because you wanted to shag some man who abandoned you years ago.' I was upset by this, but I didn't understand.

'No – God, Ruth. He came back. Can't you see how that would make me feel? He tracked me down, though God knows how, and he came to the flat. He said that he'd met someone who knew of me and they knew someone and so on. He came round and I was ignoring the door so he left a note with his number on. That was Thursday night. I didn't see him then and I didn't know what to do and I really did need a weekend alone to work out what was happening to me. I went haywire.'

'I'm sorry. What did the note say?'

'It said that I'd be shocked to know he was here and that he'd found me and he was shocked himself. Then he said he hoped I was well and he asked me to call him. He left his number. That was it, nothing huge or dramatic. I read it a thousand times. Can you imagine? God, I didn't know what to think – I couldn't think. All I wanted to do was to feel normal again but I couldn't. I cried, Ru, really cried all night. I couldn't sleep or anything, I couldn't make sense of it. He was there for me and then he broke my heart. Then, just as I get my life back together, he's back and none of it made sense.'

'I can see that. It must have been a shock.'

'It was, God, it was. I was just glad I hadn't opened the door. I don't know what I would have done. I thought about it on Friday night, then on Saturday, and Saturday night I decided to do it. I called him. I mean, I wasn't sure if I should or not, but then I had to because I couldn't sleep and I knew that one day I would need to sleep again and if I didn't call him I never would.'

'I would have called him,' I whispered.

'But, you know, I wasn't prepared for my feelings. They were still all there, right here. As soon as I saw the note, when I was thinking, I knew I still loved him, really loved him. I wasn't over him. That was scary. Not like with you. I mean, it was horrible for you but you were really over him. I wasn't and I'd thought I was and now so many things make sense, like why I never wanted to have another relationship. That was because I couldn't because I was in love with him. Can you see that?'

I swung gently backwards and forwards. It was like a gentle rocking. I thought about it and I could see it. I could see her finding the note, I could see her lighting a cigarette, standing, sitting, standing, walking from room to room, another cigarette, a bottle of beer, all the time the note in her hand. This had gone on all night. The next day she had come to work and she was Katie again, not lovesick Katie but my Katie.

Then she had done the same thing that night; she had resumed the pacing, the thinking, the fuddled head, the tears. I could see her crying. I could see her fear, but I knew she would call just as I would, and just as the panic and the fear subsided she would be pleased with her feeling of love.

I didn't want to know what came next, but at the same time I did. I wasn't being selfish, I understood how she felt, but I just wanted it to go back to how it was before, me and Katie, and now I knew that nothing would be the same again.

'I called at half past four on Saturday morning. Can you imagine? No concept of time. He answered the phone. He sounded sleepy but just as he always had, and when I said it was me, well, he just said, "I feel so much just hearing your voice," and I felt the same. We spoke for hours just hearing each other's voices. Then he asked if he could come over and I said that it was too soon so he should phone me tomorrow. I was rushing. It was so powerful. I couldn't think or see straight and again I just wanted to be alone with my feelings. Then I cried again but I wasn't sure what the tears were for. I think they were happy because I was happy.'

'So the next day?'

'Yes, he called me and I just had to see him. I felt that if I didn't, I'd find out he wasn't real, and I really wanted him to be real. I opened the door to him and I burst into tears. Floods of them. Matty stood there and he cried too. We both stood on the doorstep looking like babbling idiots and I knew.' This was so weird.

'Knew what?'

'That he was back for real.' Katie's story wasn't unfamiliar: it was just like the love story I had built in my head over the past year. The look, the tears, the love: it was the story I knew back to front. My fantasy love story.

'He apologised for leaving me. He said he had been young and selfish and searching for a dream. He said he had spent the years chasing stars, when the one thing he wanted was here all the time – me. It was weird, I was angry and ecstatic at the same time. I was angry with him for going away but so glad to have him back. He gave up the band, it wasn't working and he had stopped enjoying it. He came back a year ago and went to teaching college. I nearly fell over. He was becoming respectable. We kept a distance at first but, well, that didn't last – it couldn't. He's grown up, Ru, and so have I.'

'Sounds like it.' I was unsure of what to say. I should have recognised her look when I first saw her. The look Jess had had when she told us about Jerry, the look Sarah had had when we found out about Johnny, the look Katie had had when I answered the door.

'I still love him.'

'I can see that.'

'We're going to give it a go, properly.'

'Of course.'

'I'm moving in with him.'

'Of course you are.' For some reason I was full of tears.

'Please say something.'

'Katie, you're still in love with him and he loves you. What can I say? What should I say? I don't fucking know. I mean, it's the middle of the night and I just heard the best love story since Romeo and fucking Juliet and I just don't know what to say?'

'I know. Ruth, you're my best friend, my only friend, and it's only because of you that I can do this. You're the best thing that's ever happened to me. I started to trust again, then Matty came back. It's because of you.' I obviously hadn't ever done anything this good in my entire life. And it made me feel, well, I'm not sure how it made me feel.

'Are you sure?' I hated myself for asking, but I did.

'Yes.' She sounded so certain.

'Then I'm happy for you.' I hugged her.

'Me too. I'm so fucking happy! Christ, I'm happy and I never thought I could be.' Katie shrieked with laughter. 'Are you OK?' she asked me.

I thought about it and I decided that I was. 'A bit cold. Come on. I'll make you some hot chocolate.'

'With marshmallows?'

'If we've got some.' We linked arms and walked home. I was cold, but Katie didn't seem cold. I glanced at her and decided that I would remember her looking like this for always: she was beautiful. I made hot chocolate but there were no marshmallows – chocolate cookies substituted. Not the same, but good enough.

'I can't believe he still looks the same.'

'Well, I guess you always expect people to have changed and they don't necessarily.'

'You don't mind?'

'Why would I?'

'Travelling ...'

'I won't go, it's not the end of the world.' I was trying not to think about this in relation to me for once.

'You bloody well go. Christ, Ru, you made this decision and you don't need me. God, look at your plans. Please don't make me think I've ruined everything.'

I drank my drink. I guess I could go on my own. After all, I'd planned it with as much precision as a military campaign, hadn't I? I had people to call on in Australia, in the States and even in India. Why not? I could do it. It was about me, after all. In a way, maybe, I needed to do it on my own. The missing piece of the jigsaw had been found.

'OK.'

'Promise?'

'Katie lovesick Parry, I am going and you can stick it up your arse.'

'Good.'

'So, tell me about Matty.'

'Well, he's lovely, talented, but not as wound up now. God, I love him.'

'And he loves you?'

'I think he does . . .' We slept on the sofa, or dozed when we finally stopped talking. We had our arms linked when Jess found us in the morning.

'I'm going on my own.' The more I said it, even if it was to the mirror, the stronger I felt. You see, Katie had reaffirmed my belief in happy endings and I just knew that my happy ending was out there somewhere. Telling everyone was another matter.

Sarah was thrilled: she felt that in needing to find myself I needed to do it on my own. And she furnished me with more contacts. Jess said I was brave and she was proud; she told me of areas to avoid. Sophie just urged me to be careful, and Thomas and Johnny provided me with tips and advice. I was all set.

My mother wasn't as happy, but my father talked her round and gave me emergency money and a zillion phone cards, and after I had promised to call them all the time, they gave me their blessing. I was a privileged traveller. I just knew I would be all right.

As I prepared myself for my trip in the following months, things were good, rosy, different. I was good, rosy, different, and we were all happy. Well, happy-ish.

Jess was still in love, but still finding it hard. Jerry the journalist was dedicated to his job in a way Jess couldn't match, so she still had to put up with broken dates. She was beginning to incorporate this into her life, as any resourceful person would, and to understand the word compromise. Jerry was wonderful and Jess was living proof that you can almost have it all.

Sophie was enjoying her new-found status of single and almost tough. She was empowered and concentrating on her career. The TV period drama was soon to be screened – they'd just finished filming and Sophie had lots of offers to consider. I took comfort from the fact that I would have one famous friend, and if I ever came back, I would work for her as her constant companion. A suitable job for an unmarried lady.

Sarah was happy with Johnny. She looked as if she had been born to be part of a couple. She was also doing well in her new job and I expected that next time I saw her she'd have her own company, or a string of them.

Thomas had a job – he had passed his exams. We were looking forward to having a lawyer in the family. He was dating an Australian friend of Sam's, but assured me it was only because she was good in the sack. I still hoped to see him end up with Sophie but, then, that was my romantic world, not theirs.

Katie was so happy. I met Matty and he was perfect, but that was what I expected. They were so good together, and I knew that when I came back, if I came back, I would still have the best friend in the world.

Ben, well, he was still in London, living with Sam. No, I hadn't seen them since the dinner party, and I didn't want to. We'd all received invitations, but my friends had refused them, and so had I. They said that none of us needed Ben in our lives, which was nice and loyal of them. I still loved my friends.

I decided that I never wanted to see Ben again. Not out of anger, or misery, or still loving him, but because I couldn't think of anything I would gain from it. I had shut the door on that part of my life. I expect it to remain shut.

I had tickets and money. More importantly, I had determination. I was going first of all to South America then to the USA. I had a contact in New York, who said she'd help me get a job if I wanted. I would take it from there. I was excited, more excited than I ever thought possible.

Before leaving, I had a dinner. Another one. Jess, Sarah, Sophie,

RUBBER GLOVES OR JIMMY CHOOS?

Katie, Johnny and Thomas were coming to my last supper. They were my friends and although we had all changed a bit and gained more, we were still as close as ever. I had had a number of panics about leaving them. I had come to expect them always to be there. Leaving them was the only reservation I had about going. When I was planning the dinner party I asked Katie to invite Matty, but she refused. She said that he was too new a part of my life, and tonight I should be with the people who really knew and loved me. I was touched at that.

Before Thomas, Johnny and Katie arrived, I had one last thing to do; to ensure that I realised I was leaving and meant it. My parents were storing my precious belongings, but things I had acquired I was giving away.

'Jess, I'm giving you my electronic organiser.'

'Why?'

'I don't need it, actually I never did. You'll look after it well.'

'Thank you.'

'Sarah, I want you to have my briefcase.'

'No, really? I mean, it's a lovely briefcase.'

'I know, and I want you to have it. Sophie, I want you to have all my CDs and all my make-up. I seem to have loads that I've never used.'

'Thanks.' I felt like Father Christmas. All that was left were some clothes, which I gave away to a charity shop, and a couple of pictures of Ben. I didn't know what to do with them, so in the end I threw them away. It didn't make me feel satisfied, it made me feel sad. I was letting go, finally and properly. Sophie burst into tears.

'Soph, what's wrong?'

'It's like you're dying, giving away all your things. I feel like I'll never see you again.'

'Of course you will, silly. You guys are my best friends.'

'I know what she means. It's like a will – it feels so final,' Sarah said.

'Yeah, but I'm glad I got the personal organiser,' Jess said.

The dinner was ready, the wine flowed and everyone was happy. I thought fleetingly of the dinner party I had thrown for Ben, but shut it out as I had learned to do quite effectively now.

'I'm really going to miss you,' Jess said.

I welled up.

'Yeah, who can we moan at, laugh at and hear disaster stories from?' Thomas laughed but squeezed my arm affectionately.

'I bet we'll get regular postcards with one disaster or another on them. Ru won't let us down,' Sophie said.

'It will not be like that. I've changed,' I defended myself.

'No offence, but I can't believe that you, totally free in various different countries, are not going to make waves or, more probably, headline news,' Sarah said.

'Oh, you won't have to send postcards, Ru, we'll just watch the news every day.'

'I'm very sorry to disappoint you, but I shall be taking things seriously from now on. I'm not going to get into scrapes, with anything, man or beast. I shall not shag loads of men, get bitten by snakes, or set off volcanoes. Everything will go smoothly.'

They all looked at me. 'I don't think so,' they chorused.

I decided to ignore them.

As the banter continued I looked around the table at my friends. Through the mist in my eyes that threatened tears, I took a long, hard, last look. Every story has a moral, but mine, mine had a number. In honour of my best friends: if you had ambition, this was a great place to live. In honour of Sophie: independence can be emancipating. In honour of Jess, Sarah and Katie: love is the most wonderful thing in the world. In honour of Thomas and Johnny: do not encourage men to spend too much time with their feminine sides. In honour of Katie again: parties are for Christmas not for life.

'Let's drink to it, our unusual year, and the fact I survived it.'

'The fact we all survived it,' Thomas said. We drank to that.

We talked about the old days, me trailing Ben, all the freshers that trailed Sophie, Sarah going out with a socialist until her love for Margaret Thatcher got the better of her, Jess dating nearly the whole hockey team to keep me company, the balls we went to, the men we snogged for real and for dares, the house we lived in, the fun we had. I still loved those days with all my heart. Then we went quiet. I can't speak for everyone else, but it really hit me that it was over. University was now a memory, a nice memory, but it would never come back. A year had gone and more would pass and that was the way life was. I would see my friends soon enough. I looked at them and knew I'd never lose them. Even I wasn't that careless.

Ben was over, London was over and so was the best and worst year of my life.

Chapter Twenty-one

I was sitting in my cave, watching television and having a cup of tea, when I heard the voice again.

'Come out, come out of the cave,' it beckoned.

'Bloody hell,' I said. 'I've had enough of this. All right, you win, I'm coming. Just give me a minute to get my shoes.' I grabbed them, looked back at the cave that kept me warm.

'Goodbye and thank you,' I whispered, as I prepared to go into the unknown.